DALE E. BASYE

ILLUSTRATIONS BY BOB DOB

RANDOM HOUSE 🏠 NEW YORK

SNiVEL
THE FIFTH CiRCLE OF
~ HECK ~

Text copyright © 2012 by Dale E. Basye

Jacket art and interior illustrations copyright © 2012 by Bob Dob

All rights reserved. Published in the United States by Random House Children's Books,
a division of Random House, Inc., New York.

Random House and the colophon are registered trademarks of Random House, Inc.

Visit us on the Web! randomhouse.com/kids

Educators and librarians, for a variety of teaching tools, visit us at
randomhouse.com/teachers

wherethebadkidsgo.com

Library of Congress Cataloging-in-Publication Data
Basye, Dale E.
Snivel : the fifth circle of Heck / by Dale E. Basye ; illustrations by Bob Dob. — 1st ed.
p. cm.
Summary: Eleven-year-old Milton and his older sister Marlo are led by the
Grin Reaper to Camp Snivel, the level of Heck for whiners, but manage to escape,
only to be caught and taken to the court of Judge Judas to testify at Satan's trial.
ISBN 978-0-375-86834-4 (trade) — ISBN 978-0-375-96834-1 (lib. bdg.) —
ISBN 978-0-375-89884-6 (ebook)
[1. Future life—Fiction. 2. Brothers and sisters—Fiction. 3. Camps—Fiction.
4. Trials—Fiction. 5. Humorous stories.] I. Dob, Bob, ill. II. Title.
PZ7.B2938Sni 2012   [Fic]—dc23   2011013610

Printed in the United States of America

10 9 8 7 6 5 4 3 2 1

First Edition

Random House Children's Books supports
the First Amendment and celebrates the right to read.

THIS BOOK IS DEDICATED TO ME.
NO MATTER HOW MANY OBSTACLES I FACED
WHEN WRITING THIS BOOK, THERE I WAS,
EVERY STEP OF THE WAY, TIRELESSLY SUPPORTING
MY OWN EFFORTS, AS IF ENGAGED IN SOME
EERIE PSYCHIC DANCE WITH MYSELF,
AT TIMES EVEN FINISHING MY OWN SENTENCES.

★ CONTENTS ★

FOREWORD

As many believe, there is a place above and a place below. But there are also places in between. Some not quite awfully perfect and others not quite perfectly awful.

One of these places is as dreary, damp, and despairing as spending your birthday at school taking a standardized algebra test in soggy swim trunks using a number 2 pencil: made of real *number 2.*

It's a place filled with more blubbering than a pod of whimpering whales; as cheerless as a cheerleader with laryngitis; and as listless as, well, someone who lost their list of favorite things (you know, raindrops on neuroses, blisters on kittens, etc.).

There is a tired old expression usually uttered by people wearing tired old expressions: "Misery loves company." The meaning? No, it doesn't necessarily suggest that working for a company will make you miserable (good guess, though). What it really means is that misery likes to throw one heck of a pity party: an invitation-only affair where the downhearted rub slumped shoulders with one another until their gloom is spread as evenly as Feelin' Blueberry jam on wet toast that invariably falls facedown on the floor. Think of it as a disconsolate disco, with all those feet stomping on gripes until they make a truly fine whine.

And in this place—the fifth of Heck's dispiriting circles—the miserable have nothing if not each other: a camp of complaint that is going down, down, down. . . .

The mysterious Powers That Be (and any of its associated or subsidiary enterprises, including—but not limited to—the Powers That Be Evil) have stitched this and countless other subjective realities together into a sprawling quilt of space and time.

Some of these quantum patches may not even seem like places. But they are all around you and go by many names. Some feel like eternity. And some of them actually are eternity, at least for a little while.

So please return your postures to their fully downright positions and extinguish all hope. We're in for a bumpy landing. . . .

1 · A TRAM-ATiZiNG EXPERiENCE

MILTON FAUSTER—ELEVEN years old at the time of his untimely death—looked outside past the marble balcony jutting over the crater, stunned as he took in the dreary spectacle of Snivel. The sky was a deep, impenetrable gray. Hanging from the cloud cover was a gargantuan, pendulous glass enclosure that, Milton rightly assumed, was Camp Snivel. It was like a big teardrop, he thought, crying from the sky.

Through the camp's glass shell, at the teardrop's widest point, Milton could make out what looked like a capsized lake hanging, somehow, upside down. Above the upturned lake—or below, depending—where the camp was suspended from the clouds, Snivel narrowed to a stem.

"Must be an optical delusion," said Marlo, Milton's impulse-control-challenged older sister, as she blew a wayward strand of blue hair from her face. "Like how people dressed in the eighties."

More children—a slack-jawed boy, a long-faced girl, and a skinny Emo boy with a scraggly bob hairstyle—joined Milton and Marlo on the balcony of the Moanastery: a crumbling cloister where the Brothers of the Unconsolably Morose, Miserable, and Exceedingly Rueful (also known as BUMMER) practiced their peculiar penitence.

"Speaking of optical delusions," Marlo said as a pair of twins—an Asian girl and her sleeping brother physically joined at the shoulder and hip—stepped onto the roughly hewn balcony.

"They're Siamese twins," Milton clarified. "Not *delusions*."

"Actually, we prefer *conjoined*," the girl said with a look of mock reproach before revealing a mouthful of perfect teeth. The two siblings couldn't seem more different, Milton thought. The girl was fresh-faced and alert while the thick-featured boy frowned and grumbled in his sleep.

"Sorry, I didn't . . . ," Milton replied, a little dazed by the girl's smile. "I mean . . . you're pretty. Um . . . *unique*. Pretty unique."

Below the Moanastery was a massive crater piled high with millions of tons of reeking garbage, fed into the yawning basin through widemouthed discharge pipes. Waves of stench rippled in the fetid air as the decomposing mound exhaled its exceedingly foul breath.

"*What is that smell?!*" whined a pouting, scowling girl with freckles spattered across her cheeks. "It's like a family of skunks that choked to death on stinkbugs!"

"Down below you is the Dumps," Abbot Costello, a ruddy-faced monk wearing a steel-wool robe, explained wearily as he sulked out onto the balcony. "Are any of you familiar with the River Styx?"

Milton and Marlo shuddered in unison, recalling their own vivid memories of traversing the great tunnel of dung—the River Styx, the final, fecal resting place of all the world's sewage.

"Well, much like how the River Styx shuttles all that . . . *stuff* from the Surface down to h-e-double-hockey-sticks," the abbot continued while casually flagellating himself with a small leather lash, "the Dumps is where the world's detritus goes to decompose and demoralize. . . ."

Wails of anguish reverberated throughout the crater. Milton and Marlo clapped their hands over their ears at the tormented din and turned. Inside the Moanastery, a group of monks moaned into coiled brass funnels trained outward into the abyss beyond.

"*AH!*" Abbot Costello shouted over the roar of amplified sobs and rushing wind echoing throughout the crater. "OUR FREQUENT FRIAR MILES RETURNS TO FERRY YOU ACROSS THE SEA OF SIGHS TO

SNIVEL: THE CIRCLE OF HECK FOR WHINY, MOPEY CRYBABIES LIKE YOURSELVES!"

The wind had upturned layers of fresh, rotting garbage. Through the swirls of trash, Milton could see a rusty tram approaching, wobbling on a pair of cables suspended from the distended midsection of Snivel to the Moanastery.

"Snivel is . . . *upside down?*" said a gangly boy with an elfish face, flaming red ears, and a runny nose as he arrived onto the balcony. "But how—"

"You will have the opportunity to see for yourself!" the abbot yelled as the caged gondola arrived at the balcony. Out hopped a monk with sunken blue eyes, a ginger beard, and a broken nose.

"All aboard the ThighTram!" Friar Miles called out, gesturing to the children.

"The ThighTram?" Marlo mumbled as she and the other children were herded into the cramped, swaying cage. "This *better* not have anything to do with exercising. . . ."

"No, not ThighTram . . . *Thigh*Tram," the friar lisped as he tossed a roll of duct tape to the sniffling red-eared boy. "You'd better tape yourthelves in, my children. The Thea of Thighs is ethpecially thtormy today."

Friar Miles sat in the front of the tram behind a controller handle, air pressure gauge, and hand-brake wheel. *"Oh bother, that art tho heavy, woeful be thy name,"* he murmured softly to himself before turning the handle. The

SighTram lurched forward up the cable, reeling and rocking like a middle-aged mom with her iPod up too loud. The conjoined twin boy stirred awake on his sister's shoulder.

"What's going on, Sara?" he asked with a groggy, accusatory whine as he took in his surroundings. "Why are we—" he shrieked, his dark, almond eyes bugging out when he saw the Dumps beneath the rusty cage floor, before passing out.

"Narcolepsy," the girl explained to Milton as she clutched the tram's flimsy mesh-wire side. "Brought on by strong emotions—"

"Like the terror of realizing you're in a cage dangling above a rubbish heap," interjected Milton, gripping the conversation tight, like a life preserver, as he tried to tamp down his mushrooming fear.

The girl smiled her disarmingly warm grin.

"Yeah," she replied. "Like that. Unfortunately, I'm an insomniac and it's hard for me to sleep through anything."

The SighTram lurched forward, straining against the gale-force Sea of Sighs as it squealed painfully slowly toward the gargantuan glass teardrop ahead.

"Are we there yet?" whined the young Emo boy as he fussed with his designer glasses.

The tram was buffeted about as if it were a ball of yarn and the powerful gusts were a playful cat, batting the cage back and forth between its paws.

The slack-jawed boy with the curly hair gaped out the tram's side.

"I know that, like, some religious people can be born again, right?" the boy asked no one in particular. "But we can't, like . . . die *again* . . . right?"

"Maybe life and death are like a video game," the elfin boy speculated as he wiped his nose, staring down at the Dumps. "Different levels. Different ways to live and die . . ."

Milton leaned over, scooped up his backpack, and unzipped the top. Out poked the fuzzy white head of his pet ferret, Lucky. Milton gave Lucky a quick, reassuring pat.

"It's okay, little guy," Milton whispered out of the side of his mouth. "Just stay cool."

Milton caught Sara, the conjoined twin, looking over at him, smiling slyly. She held her finger up to her mouth, the international signal for "your secret is safe with me."

The rickety cage was halfway across the swaying span of cable connecting the Moanastery to Camp Snivel.

Marlo, duct-taped next to Milton on the bench, grabbed the back of Friar Miles's swiveling chair.

"Can't this thing go any faster?!" she shouted as the monk puzzled over his controls. Marlo stared down between her fidgeting feet at the grille floor, with the Dumps—3,000 feet below—all too visible. "Toxic waste is bad for my complexion!"

Friar Miles slammed his hand against the controller

handle, and the SighTram thrust forward. The air pressure gauge hissed, its needle tapping impatiently against the dangerous red end of the dial. The motor's high-pitched whine cleaved the dull roar of the Sea of Sighs in two.

Friar Miles struggled with the controller.

"It'th thtuck," the pinched-faced monk relayed.

Friar Miles gave the brake wheel a turn. It twisted off in his hand.

"Is that bad?" Milton asked, knowing the answer deep down in his roiling gut.

"Only if we want to thtop," the monk replied. "There mutht be garbage blocking the brake padth."

Friar Miles climbed out of the rocking tram and clambered onto its roof.

"Uh-oh," Marlo muttered as she tore herself free from her duct-taped seat belt and took the friar's seat at the front of the tram. "Look."

Up ahead, through a flurry of plastic bottles and disposable diapers, Milton saw the Gates of Snivel fixed behind a landing platform set at the midsection of the massive glass teardrop. And it was rushing toward them at breakneck speed.

"Now what am I supposed to do?!" Marlo shouted up to the friar, holding the hand brake.

"Wait until I thay *pull*."

"Thay *what*?!"

"PULL!"

Marlo reflexively yanked the hand brake. The

SighTram screamed to a stop a few yards from the landing platform and swung violently forward.

Friar Miles was pitched into the air and slammed into the Gates of Snivel. Milton—his duct tape giving way—soared out of the flying tram and into the friar.

"Oooompthh!" the monk yelled as Milton struck him, sending them both rolling into the rusty metal entrance with a clang. The remaining children screamed inside of the tram as the cage swung like a pendulum.

Milton rubbed his throbbing head as he rose to his feet. The Gates of Snivel swung open and closed with a grating *eeee-orrrr* creak.

"Jump when it swings close to the platform!" Milton yelled as the SighTram pitched forward.

Marlo clutched the sides of the bench. "No way!" she yelled. "We'll just stay put until it's safe!"

One of the cables fastened above the platform was yanked out of its mooring. The SighTram listed suddenly to the left, now rocking both side to side and to and fro.

Marlo swallowed.

"Now's good, too," she muttered as she made her way to the back of the tram, turned, and—as the SighTram swung close to the platform—sped down the aisle and leapt out the driver's window. She landed hard on her shoulder and rolled across the smooth marble platform next to Milton. He trotted to the edge of the platform.

"The rest of you have got to hurry!" Milton shouted through cupped hands.

One by one, the children ripped off their duct tape and jumped from the SighTram. Friar Miles padded across the balcony and studied the cable with his sunken blue eyes.

"Ath dangerouth ath my trip back will undoubtedly be," he lisped, "the Moanathtery ithn't anywhere *near* ath awful ath Thnivel."

He sprang to the cable, gripped it tightly, and, swinging hand over hand, worked his way to the SighTram. Friar Miles waved as he backed away across the Sea of Sighs, swallowed up by swirls of upturned foam packing peanuts and spent printing cartridges.

Milton and Marlo turned to face the Gates of Snivel. The corroded bars featured cast-iron tragedy/tragedy masks and tiny violins welded up and down the rods. When the wind brushed against the violins, their little metal bows scraped against the wire strings, creating a disconcerting concert of jeering screeches. Twined up along the bars were vines flaunting withered, heart-shaped flowers that coiled in a sad clot at the gates' twin handles: lumpy lead "fists" wiping away a string of opal tears leaking from a pair of eyes wrought in drooping loops. Beyond the gate was a thick curtain of shadows.

Tired of being pelted with bits of reeking, stinging garbage, Milton tugged open the heavy gate.

A skeletal hand reached out from the shadows. Bony,

knotted fingers gripped Milton's hand, seizing it tight with what felt like a clench of electric icicles. A devitalizing ache blossomed from the base of Milton's palm and spread through his body, filling him with a soft, sickening gloom. Milton was paralyzed, his mind like an old television tuned to a dead channel.

"Let go, Creepshow!" Marlo shrieked from behind her brother, yanking him free of the incapacitating grasp. Milton, suddenly able to move again, collapsed to the ground, the taste of blood forming in his mouth.

2 · GRINNING FROM FEAR TO FEAR

A WILLOWY FIGURE stepped into the weak gray light. The creature was just under seven feet tall, wearing a charcoal hoodie cinched tight around its neck with a half-frowny, half-smiley face screen-printed in olive drab on the front. As the sense of tingling dread relaxed its grip on the inside of Milton's chest, he noticed a flash of metal from something strapped to the creature's palm.

"A joy buzzer?" Milton mumbled from the balcony floor, rubbing his aching hand.

"Joyless buzzer," the creature replied in a way that made Milton unsure if he was actually hearing him or just *thinking* him. *"I forgot I had on when greeting you."*

The figure offered its hand to Milton in the half-darkness.

Fool me once, shame on you, Milton thought as he struggled to his feet. *Fool me twice . . . seriously . . . cut it out, not funny.*

The skeletal creature, Milton noticed, had what appeared to be a rubber chicken strapped to its side and a gag arrow piercing its hooded head. Marlo glowered at the figure with a fixed from-under stare that brought to mind a Goth bull about to charge.

"What *are* you?" she spat. "A party clown who's here because some kid's birthday wish was that you'd drop *dead?*"

The creature stared at Milton and Marlo with its doleful eyes, like two dull marbles filled with rainwater.

"*I'm Grin Reaper,*" the creature croaked.

"Reaper?" Milton replied, stepping back. "As in—"

"*Knock knock,*" the Grin Reaper interrupted, staring expectantly at Milton.

"Um, who's there?" Milton replied, unable to leave a knock-knock joke unanswered.

"*Is doorbell repairman.*"

"The doorbell repairman *who?*"

"*Ding-dong . . . all done!*"

"What?"

"*Is joke,*" the Grin Reaper explained in his halting hiss. "*Make laugh.*"

Milton, struck by the absurdity of the situation, let out an explosive snort.

The Grin Reaper swiftly yanked a green net with a

wooden handle from the pouch on his back. He studied the air around Milton's head with his gray wet eyes, as if something were fluttering before him. Suddenly, the cadaverous creature deftly swished his net, nearly swatting Milton across the mouth.

"What are you—?!" Milton gasped, pushing his new pair of broken glasses—two different lenses taped together at the bridge with duct tape—up his nose.

"*Shhh . . . you scare,*" the Grin Reaper whispered as something unseen struggled softly inside the pale-green netting. He carefully reached behind his back and snatched up two tarnished metal rings, one perched atop the other on his bony palm. With a twist of the wrist, he pulled the rings apart, activating a humming electric jar. The Grin Reaper tipped the jar's rim toward the net. Inside flitted what looked like a butterfly.

It was about five inches across, striated with pink and blue, with iridescent splotches on its hind wings that shimmered with a spectrum of rainbow colors, like an oily film on deep-blue water.

Watching the insect flutter filled Milton with a peculiar bittersweet feeling, as if something he loved very much were very far away . . . a feeling not uncommon in the afterlife but particularly keen now.

"*Is boy's laugh,*" the Grin Reaper said as he dropped a saturated cotton ball to the bottom of the jar. "*Chuckle, actually. Is different. One of five types.*" Milton's winged "chuckle" fluttered about for a few moments before sinking to the bottom of the jar and expiring. Milton felt like a jack-o'-lantern whose candle was abruptly snuffed out: hollow and chilly with the memory of lost warmth.

"You're joking," Marlo said with a sneer as she watched the Grin Reaper seal the lid on Milton's last laugh. "I mean . . . you collect *laughter*?"

"*I never joke about laughter*," the Grin Reaper rasped. "*I collect, yes. Keep in barrel. I cannot laugh. So I snatch from rich chaos of human nature. Temporarily brighten my luster-lack world.*"

The Grin Reaper pitched the jar back over his shoulder and into his pouch. The creature turned toward Snivel, his rainwater eyes glittering with unfathomable sadness.

A tunnel stretched out beyond the gates, with a moving sidewalk that gradually corkscrewed until, at the tunnel's end, the walkway was on the ceiling.

"But that's impossible," Milton muttered as the Grin Reaper brushed past him and onto the sidewalk.

Marlo shrugged and stepped onto the sidewalk behind him. Milton sighed, forcing himself to participate in something that openly mocked the laws of physics. He looked behind him to see the landing platform tilted subtly to the side, or so it seemed, as he was moved along onto the tunnel's wall, feet still firmly planted to the walkway.

"Artificial gravity," Sara offered with a smile. "Either centrifugal or superconductive diamagnetism. It *has* to be something like that."

Nearly upside down, Milton couldn't tell if his head-over-heels feeling was burbling infatuation or simply the play of gravity. Still, something tickled the inside of his chest and made him feel a little bit nauseous— but in a strangely good way.

"Yeah . . . some simulated gravity machine, probably," Milton replied, his face hot and his fingers tingling with nervous electricity. "Milton, by the way."

"M.I.L.T.O.N.?" the girl pondered with a crinkle of her sparkling dark eyes. "Is that an acronym for some theoretical microgravity device?"

"Um, no," he said, looking past her shoulder as the landing platform clicked near the twelve o'clock position. "*My name.* Milton. Milton Fauster."

"Oh . . . right," she replied with her easy smile. "I'm Sara Bardo. And this is Sam," she added with a tip of her head toward her snoring brother. "Most people just call us . . . well, a lot of terrible things, usually."

The corkscrewing sidewalk was now on the ceiling, which was now the floor. The Grin Reaper stepped off the moving walkway and toward a gently swaying wall of grimy vinyl plastic strips.

"*We're here,*" he wheezed, parting the dingy gray curtain and holding it out wide with his long, bony arms. "*Camp Snivel,*" he continued as a carpet of dark fog spilled onto the platform. "*Your last resort . . .*"

Behind Milton, the red-eared boy sneezed.

"Ugh." The boy sniffled. "Airborne mold spores.

Looks like you *can* take it with you . . . at least in terms of allergies."

Marlo swept past the Grin Reaper and entered the Circle of Heck for the inconsolably sad, sulky, and sensitive.

"Ugh . . . this is even worse than I thought," she muttered as she scanned the relentlessly grim surroundings. "It really *is* like summer camp!"

"*A* bummer *camp,*" the Grin Reaper clarified.

How bad can a bad camp be? Milton thought.

Milton joined his sister, hitting his head on a low-hanging wooden sign that Marlo had dodged. He could tell by the faded letters that it had once read:

WELCOME TO CAMP SNIVEL: YOUR LUCKY WHOLESOME FUN CENTER!

But now, thanks to an eternity of weather damage, it read:

W—O-E TO A—L—L WHO-ENTER

Milton also noticed, as he rubbed his throbbing noggin, that, somehow, his legs were cold and wet.

He looked down at his soggy sneakers. The blanket of stormy fog clung to the ground like sodden moss. Drops of rain splattered the underside of Milton's chin, rolling up his neck and into his ears. He couldn't believe it. It was actually raining *up.*

"But how?" Milton asked as a thuggish gang of storm mist clustered below, spitting up cold, slushy rain so that he was thoroughly soaked from toe to head.

The Grin Reaper walked toward a group of devastated weeping willows, stooped by the weight of some secret sorrow.

"*Special bioengineered rain fog,*" he explained. "*Made from He2O: two helium atoms for every oxygen atom. Make rain up. Dampens even highest spirit,*" the Grin Reaper continued as he looked up through the broken boughs. "*But there is something worse. . . .*"

Above was a sight that took Milton's breath away. The sky was filled with . . . *garbage.*

"The Dumps," muttered Sara as her brother Sam snorted himself awake, the raindrops tickling his nose. "It's our sky now. It's . . . *terrible,*" she wept, hiding her face in her brother's neck.

"Rain? In the underworld?" Sam complained, caught between the undertow of sleep and the cold drizzle stinging his face from below.

A hot gush of tears mingled with the helium water dripping up Milton's face.

The sky had always represented a sense of hope for Milton. And now it was a bottomless, festering heap of medical waste, plastic bottles, paint cans, rotting food, soiled clothing, and milk cartons.

Not landfill . . . but *sky*fill. The boundless vista of trash pressing down from above made Milton feel small and powerless, as if all hope had been left on the curb, waiting to be disposed of forever.

"*Helps keep child's outlook always down,*" the Grin

Reaper added as a fresh bank of storm mist colluded underfoot, birthing another torrent of lancing rain. *"Is one reason Camp Snivel wrong-side up."*

"It's eleven-fifteen and we all might as well give up," a voice sobbed in the distance to the clang of a bell. "I mean . . . *really*. What's the point?"

The Grin Reaper motioned the children through the trees.

"Town Cryer," he mumbled. *"Major downer but punctual. Come."*

Marlo stomped through the murky pea-soup mist, her shoulder brushing against a flyer tacked to the trunk of a weeping willow.

HAVE YOU SEEN ME?

The flyer had a picture of a round-faced Latin American boy with wet brown eyes and snot running down from his nose. Next to the flyer was another one, stuck fast to the tree with milky sap. This one featured a girl with dirty-blond hair sloppily cinched into pigtails with mismatched ties. Marlo counted twelve such flyers in this cluster of trees alone. Suddenly, out of the corner of her eye, she saw a shaggy dark blob streak through the gnarled underbrush.

Marlo swung around, startled.

"Who's there?!" she called out, but the only thing she heard was her own breathing. She quickly tore down one of the flyers and rejoined the group as they neared the edge of Camp Snivel's tree-lined border. With each step, Marlo felt as if she were getting heavier and heavier.

"Hey, Lesser Fauster," Marlo said to her younger brother. "Get this: a whole bunch of missing kids . . . and I thought I saw something back . . ."

The group cleared the fringe of trees. Before them was an enormous, deep green-gray lake—like the color of spoiled luncheon meat—with a humongous, screeching, forty-foot-tall stone wheel churning at the center. The wheel shook and tottered uneasily on its axis as, with its eight stone ladles, it whipped the center of the lake into a misty, agitated froth.

"Are we there—?" the Emo boy started before he was silenced by a slug in the shoulder from the pouting, puffer-fish-faced girl.

Surrounding the lake were three broken pairs of rotting docks, strewn about like the aftermath of a giant toddler's tantrum. Dozens of children sat along the edges of the broken piers, crying over pools of milky water.

"*Lake Rymose,*" the Grin Reaper rasped, skeletal arms akimbo as he stood on the uneven ridge of raised, knuckle-shaped mounds overlooking the lugubrious lagoon. "*Filled with tears of every Unhappy Camper sent to Snivel.*"

Milton felt drawn to the wobbly wheel—literally, as he found himself having to tilt backward somewhat to counteract its effects.

"Dukkha," Sara murmured softly. "Of course. *That's* what gives this place its dreadful gravity."

"Dookie?" Marlo interjected. "Like *poo?*"

"A *Dukkha* Wheel, you troll-haired hockey puck," Sam spat. "You know . . . *Buddhism?*"

Marlo drew in her breath, as if Sam were a birthday candle that she was about to blow out. "Would you like to meditate on *this*, Two-for-One?" she hissed, brandishing her fist.

Milton wedged himself between them.

"Enlighten us," Milton said. "What's a Dukkha Wheel?"

After giving her brother a sharp, nervous glance, Sara stepped to the edge of a bleak outlook facing Lake Rymose.

"The cycle of misery, unhappiness, and pain," she replied. "It turns like a squeaky, broken wheel about to fall off its axle, causing suffering and unrest . . . and, in Snivel's case, *gravity.*"

"So *that's* why I feel so heavy here," Marlo replied. "I knew it couldn't be the headcheese Stroganoff we scarfed before we came here. I lost most of it out the side of the SighTram, anyway, if you know what I—"

"It's a peculiar kind of gravity, too," Milton added. "I feel kind of drained and lethargic, in addition to really heavy."

Milton noticed the flyer crumpled in Marlo's hand.

"What's that?"

"Oh yeah," Marlo said as she flattened the flyer out on the back of Sam/Sara's shared shoulder. "A mess of kids gone missing. Plus I saw something back there in the trees."

"What did you see?"

"I don't know . . . I didn't see it," Marlo replied as she looked intently around her, swatting at a mosquito nibbling her neck. "But I spy with my kleptomaniac's eye something *else*."

"What's that?"

"A whole lot of nothing, at least in terms of demon guards."

Milton looked out past the sludgy gray-green waters of Lake Rymose and to a sad compound of waterlogged cabins: sagging structures that seemed to be commiserating with one another as the rain pelted up beneath them. Milton could only make out a handful of listless demon sloths sulking about the barracks, their knuckles dragging along behind them in the mud, and what looked like a gigantic leather snail crawling outside a tent. Both Limbo and Blimpo had been teeming with a malevolent menagerie of pitchspork-wielding demon guards, Milton recalled. And, according to Marlo, Rapacia and Fibble had no shortage of sadistic lawless-keepers patrolling their hallways.

"You're right," Milton replied. "There are hardly any guards. And the guards they *do* have don't seem particularly threatening."

"We need no sentries in this place," an eerily calm, hypnotic voice declared from behind them. "Camp Snivel guards itself. From the inside . . ."

The children turned.

There stood a cadaverous man—short of stature, thick and compactly set—whose head looked like it had been carved from a tombstone.

"The inside of *you*," the man concluded. "Debilitating sentinels stationed within the bosom of each and every Unhappy Camper."

The Grin Reaper drifted with haunting ninja stealth to the man's side. *"Children, meet Mr. Poe,"* the hooded creature wheezed. *"Your new vice principal."*

Milton swallowed, gripped by sudden dread.

"It's eleven-thirty and things keep getting worse and worse," the Town Cryer wailed, followed by a mournful clang of his bell.

3 · CAMPING THEIR STYLE

EDGAR ALLAN POE, Milton mused with a full-body shiver. The author's bleak, unnerving classics, such as "The Raven," "The Pit and the Pendulum," and "The Tell-Tale Heart" had given Milton countless nightmares. And here he was, in the pale flesh, poised to give Milton *day*mares as well.

Milton and the other children were led through blinding sheets of rain so merciless that 90 percent of Milton's body had officially gone from "damp and clammy" to "wicked pruney."

The children approached a cabin with cracked, mismatched windows on either side of a red door that hung off its hinges. To Milton, the structure's facade resembled the face of a maniac.

I wonder what twisted act of depravity he has in store for us, Milton thought as he stepped onto the stoop with a creepy creak.

The vice principal, after brushing back his dark, weblike hair, pushed open the door of the cabin. "I presumed you children would enjoy some light sustenance in the Mess Hall whilst enduring a brief Disorientation. *Good day.*"

The man curled his thin, liver-colored lips into a smile, then—with a swivel that made his pleated cape flap like a raven's wings—disappeared, swallowed up by the deluge.

The Grin Reaper urged the children inside, where they stood, drip-drying, in the doorway. They were in some kind of dining hall—filled with rows of ill-assorted tables. There was a serving counter at the far end. The scent of mass-produced food filled the hall.

"When I get depressed, I get hungry," Marlo said. She walked across the hall, parting the sea of sluggish children like a drenched Goth Moses, and stepped up to the serving counter, grabbing a tray.

A squat, turnip-shaped demon wearing a full-body hairnet held court over a tub of unappetizing muck, holding her filthy spatula as if it were a scepter.

"What are the not-so-specials?" Marlo asked.

"Woe-is-meatballs," the she-demon replied. "And leftover blubber casserole. It's where all of the week's scraps reunite for one final encore . . . though sometimes there is a repeat performance in the Unrest Rooms."

Marlo grimaced as she eyed a patch of mold coating the surface of the casserole, which was so old that the mold *itself* was starting to grow mold.

"Woe-is-meatballs, *por* no-*favor*," she sighed, blowing wet strands of blue hair from her face.

Milton joined her at the counter, grabbing a pitcher of water. Depression had the opposite effect on Milton. It made him nauseous. But, while soaked to the bone, he was somehow thirsty inside. He poured himself some water, but the glass would only fill halfway. He took a sip and spat it back out.

"Yuck . . . salty!" he choked. "Like tears."

A grubby girl in denim overalls-shorts shambled by, weeping. Milton noticed she had rags and sponges lashed to her shoes.

Marlo, cradling her tray of terrible food, nudged Milton with her elbow. "She must be *moping* the floors," she said with a wink. "Get it?"

The turnip-shaped lunch lady trundled out from behind the serving counter and, after killing the lights with two swift claps, walked over to an ancient film projector at the back of the Mess Hall.

The Fausters walked across the room and joined the other new recruits, having achieved a sense of solidarity due to their shared SighTram trauma. The Emo boy scowled at his food, pushed it away, and then pretended to check his cell phone, which he had drawn on his palm with a pen.

The lunch lady flipped the switch on the projector and the machine rattled to life. On a filthy white sheet hung on the far wall flickered an insignia of two leaky canoes crossed like swords, dissolving to GOOD GRIEF! THE NO-FUNDAMENTALS OF CAMP SNIVEL written in wood-carved letters.

A scratchy image of a girl sleeping in her bed filled the screen. She started up with a cry, spat out her mouth guard, and saw a boy hovering in her window. He was a twitchy, nervous-looking creature, clad in protective green padding and a safety helmet.

> "I'm Whingey," the girl shouted. "Who are you?!"
>
> "My name is P-Peter P-Panic Disorder," the boy replied between chattering teeth. "I'm one of the Lost Cause Boys."
>
> "Who are they?"
>
> "They're sickly, grumbling children who have just given up. They're sent far away to Never-Ever Land . . . to Camp Snivel."
>
> "Oooh!" Whingey cried out as she wrapped her arms around her nightgown. "Do we fly there?"
>
> "Nah . . . you sort of slide down the wind's back until it shrugs you off. . . ."

"This is lame," Marlo moaned.

"Not to mention copyright infringement," Milton added.

"So, any ideas, Brainiac?" Marlo asked as she nibbled a woe-is-meatball. She grimaced and spat it back out onto her plate.

"What do you mean?"

"E-S-C-A-P-E," Marlo replied, as if her eternal darnation were some kind of spelling bee.

"But where?" the long-faced girl sitting across from them whined.

"And how?" Milton added. "The SighTram is the only way out, and that thing almost got us killed—*again*."

"Well, what's *your* plan?" Marlo said, disgusted by both her meal and her tablemates. "To study real hard until they give us straight As and send us to Heaven or wherever? *Get real*, Honor Roll."

"Well, who knows? Maybe that's how it works here." Marlo snorted.

"*Right*," she chuckled mirthlessly. That's *never* gonna—"

A butterfly net swished over Marlo's blue-haired head. The Fausters turned to see the Grin Reaper gently cradling something caught in the net's pale-green mesh. He coaxed the invisible creature into his sputtering electric jar.

"*Sarcastic laugh*," the Grin Reaper wheezed sadly as he stared through the indigo energy field at the shriveled mothlike creature within. "*Not worth keep*," he muttered as he sulked away.

Marlo pulled out the crumpled HAVE YOU SEEN ME? flyer.

"Well, this kid—and a whole bunch of others— escaped," she said. "So it must be possible."

"Something terrible probably happened to them," the pouty girl offered, crossing her arms defiantly.

"Didn't you say you saw something in the forest?" Milton asked.

Marlo bit her lower lip nervously, catching it with her fang. "I *think* so. Something dark, woolly, and creepy-fast . . . out of the corner of my eye."

> "Here we are," Peter Panic Disorder murmured on the screen as he and the girl alighted on a cartoon campground alive with sparkling waterfalls and ponies tossing back rainbow-hued manes. "Camp Snivel. The supercool Never-Ever Land for kids like us. Here you can learn vital outdoor skills like stick-rubbing, tying and untying knots, and keeping to yourself, or you can engage in serene leisure activities such as a fun kayuck jaunt out on beautiful Lake Rymose."
>
> A pair of apple-cheeked children in a long yellow canoe sliced happily through the vivid blue waters of the animated lake.
>
> "But be careful of the Dukkha Wheel . . ."

"Told you," Sam said to Marlo before falling back asleep against his sister's cheek.

> "It's what gives Snivel its . . . um, awesome upside-downiness," Peter Panic Disorder relayed nervously, eyeing the sky above warily while biting his fingernails.

A pair of redheaded twins in pigtails pointed at each other's eyes.

"What are those?" they whined in unison. Their eyelids were crisscrossed with so many veins that it looked as if they had tiny purple volleyball nets suspended from their eyebrows.

"Those?" Peter Panic Disorder panted, riding a wave of anxiety. "A, uh, side effect of camping upside down in Snivel . . ."

"Look, I know that Heck is probably some elaborate, horrible game rigged so that all of us kids lose," Milton whispered to his sister over the film. "But we have to learn the rules before we can break them."

"I say we break *first*, learn later," Marlo interjected as she vainly tucked a wayward strand of hair behind her ear.

"And look where *that's* got you."

"Well, Mr. No-Duh Prize Winner, apparently that's gotten me exactly a foot away from *you*," Marlo replied with a sneer. "It's like we're joined together with invisible handcuffs for all eternity. So neither of us is really acing this whole 'beat the system' thing."

Milton had to admit that his sister had a point: a typically *blunt* point, but a point nonetheless. Neither of them had made much progress in the Escape from Eternal Darnation Department. Milton *had* managed to break out of Limbo—using the buoyant power of stolen Lost Souls—and make his way to the Surface, but in a barely functional "energetically challenged" state that had his body and soul maddeningly out of phase with one another. And what did Milton get for his trouble? A second death: poppin' the bucket in a crate of popcorn kernels shoved in a funeral home furnace.

Something nagged at Milton, though. And it wasn't just the fresh memory of having switched souls with Marlo just before Milton became Satan's production assistant and Marlo was sent to Fibble by Principal Bubb—an experience so thoroughly awkward that it hung in the air, heavy and unspoken, between the two Fausters. It was something that bothered him even *more* than the humiliation of literally walking in his big sister's shoes. Milton felt like he and Marlo were at the center of something *big*. His escape from Limbo, for instance, was apparently unprecedented in the near-infinite history of Heck. Then Marlo and Milton had unwittingly thwarted the rhyming, mechanical bunny that oversaw Rapacia—the Grabbit—and its plot to destroy the underworld by creating a black hole. Next, Milton had helped his best friend Virgil destabilize the power-hungry kingdom of Blimpo before reuniting with his sister to catch Fibble in an apocalyptic doozy of a lie that would have sent all of humanity halfway across the universe.

But, still, here he and his sister were, side by side, in another dismal destination—perhaps the *most* dismal—no closer to waking from this unliving nightmare than they had been when they had first passed through the grim Gates of Heck.

A greenish brown speck of light darted across the screen. The children in the film grimaced and waved the air in front of their noses.

"Ugh . . . what's that horrible reek?!" they choked in unison.

Peter Panic Disorder laughed tremulously.

"It's Stinkerbell, and she's here to read the rules of Camp Snivel: and these rules rule!" he said unconvincingly as the grubby fairy, leaving a malodorous vapor trail behind her, unfurled a roll of toilet paper with words printed on the sheets.

"Rule one," Stinkerbell squeaked. "No pranks will be perpetrated upon your fellow campers unless they have been officially sanctioned by a Camp Snivel staff member . . . or are particularly cruel and unusual in nature. Rule two . . ."

Marlo pushed away from the table in disgust. She walked over to the window and peered out through the blur of raindrops to Lake Rymose. Marlo watched several children hanging off the edge of a pier, crying over a chute of spilling milk.

Milton joined his sister.

"What are you thinking about?" he asked.

"I don't think," she replied, biting the tip of her thumb and definitely *not* sucking it. "*I am.* It's weird, but I just don't see myself here. Long-term. It's like when our files got mixed up at that weird gifted summer school back in Kansas. That math concentration camp."

"*Calculation* camp."

"*Whatever.* The point is that I knew *instantly* that I didn't belong there. And that I wouldn't be there for very long."

Outside the window, Marlo saw, out of the corner of her eye, a dark blob dart from behind one weeping willow to another. She craned her neck to see it head-on, but by then it was gone. *Again.* She sighed, fogging up the window with her breath.

"And I have the same feeling here," Marlo said as she drew a stick figure of herself on the cloudy pane. "Like I won't be an Unhappy Camper for very long."

She slashed a line across her drawing before it slowly evaporated into nothing.

4 · HOMICIDAL CHITCHAT

VICE PRINCIPAL POE sat slumped on a Victorian fainting couch in his cold, darkened office with a pad of paper and a quill on his lap.

"Well, Principal Bubb, that just about does it," he said, his voice both heavy and nebulous like fog clinging to a graveyard as he cradled the old-fashioned phone between his head and shoulder. "I appreciate your time in this matter. There are only two more names I'd like to sort out for my extracurricular . . . *activity*."

"And what is this 'activity' again?" Bea "Elsa" Bubb distractedly replied from her Not-So-Secret Lair in Limbo. Her bulk cinched tight in a Komodo dragon–skin kimono, the principal sat behind her mahogany desk, doodling on the back of an old *Bland's End* catalog the same picture over and over: herself seated upon a grand throne surrounded by lapping flames and cowering demons.

"A simulation, my good principal," Mr. Poe replied. "Er . . . just *principal*. I take the most sensitive of our overly sensitive student body and lead them through an exercise meant to re-create what and *who* they left behind on the Surface. An experimental therapy, of sorts . . . though I'm afraid some of the more delicate children may find the experience next to unbearable."

"Fine, fine . . . sounds in line with Heck's traditional kid-detested-mother-removed curriculum."

The principal's pus-yellow goat eyes settled on her clock radioactive: 13:13 blinked the blaring green readout.

"But let's wrap this up. It's getting late. Or early. Actually, exactly the same considering it's Limbo. All I know is that I'm in desperate need of my beauty unrest."

"Indeed you are," the vice principal replied. "We're almost through, so you can go to bed before it gets any more exactly the same. Now we're left with . . . Milton Fauster and his sister."

A bitter coppery taste formed in the back of Bea "Elsa" Bubb's cavernous throat, like an old penny dredged from a decommissioned wishing well.

"Mr. Fauster seems like an excellent candidate: anxious, introverted, prone to uncertainty . . . though not a textbook Unhappy Camper—he doesn't so much snivel as *stew*. His delicate constitution would seem a good match for potentially dangerous therapy."

"Yes," the principal replied with a grin, "he'd be perfect—"

A thought darted across the dark alley of the principal's mind.

"—ly wrong."

"Wrong?"

"Yes, *wrong.*"

Recent unbelievable events had clouded Principal Bubb's thinking like a squirt of squid ink in the ocean.

First and foremost, Satan had been removed from his post pending an investigation by Infernal Affairs as to his involvement in the most ambitious surreal estate scam ever conceived: selling Earth to an extraterrestrial race, evicting all humanity from its temperate blue marble of a planet to some dreadful beige rock halfway across the galaxy in the Sirius Lelayme system. And to think the principal herself unwittingly prevented the unauthorized sale of Earth, thanks to a bit of real estate law she had picked up from a Psychomanthium conversation with a once-living-yet-now-not-so-much lawyer named Algernon Cole. This legal loophole—deeming mankind as sovereign "squatters"—allowed humanity to wriggle out of the contract.

Secondly—assuming that the Baron of Brimstone would most likely be found guilty—that meant that someone, or some*thing,* would need to take over his position: a fact that the archangel Gabriel had brought up himself when Fibble, the Circle of Heck once reserved for lying little brats, became deluged with, of all things, pure liquid truth.

And, lastly, during Fibble's moment of brutal truth, the principal—after apprehending Milton and Marlo Fauster—had Annubis the dog god switch their unruly souls for added awkwardness and confusion. So now, in the principal's cesspit of a mind, Milton was Marlo. And vice versa. Little did she know, she had actually ordered Annubis to switch them *back*.

"*Principal?*" Mr. Poe inquired from the other end of the phone.

"It's just that, due to my unfortunate experience with these children, I've learned that Marlo Fauster's felonious bluster masks a fragile, insecure mess of a girl," Bea "Elsa" Bubb lied. "She'd be a much better candidate for your hopefully—I mean *possibly*—hurtful extra-credit experiment. Her brother, Milton, is actually the shrewder of the two."

"Really?" Mr. Poe said with a curl of his liver-colored lips. "*Fascinating*. He might be useful for another extra-curricular . . . *activity* I have planned."

Mr. Poe rose abruptly from the sofa.

"Thank you for your time, Principal," he said hurriedly. "And might I congratulate you on your impending promotion."

"Promotion?" Bea "Elsa" Bubb replied, cinching her kimono so tight that she nearly had a waist. "Whatever do you mean?"

"Well, it doesn't take a genius to see who the Powers That Be would appoint to replace the Big Guy

Downstairs," the vice principal said as he passed his dreary drawing room. "It's all the talk down here in the lesser realms. In any case, Principal, you can count on our support. In fact, I have a friend who may be able to help you seal the deal."

The vice principal hung up the phone.

"A secret friend hidden right beneath your hideous snout," he whispered to himself in the dark. "One who will help us—the miserable, tormented geniuses of the underworld—to unleash that misery and torment upon those above who squander their time in the light . . ."

5 · CROSS MY ART TEACHER AND HOPE TO DIE

SEVERAL EMOTIONS FOUGHT for control of Marlo's face as she stared at herself in the It's Only Fitting Room mirror: None of them were positive. She turned this way and that in her shabby denim overalls-shorts.

"*Overalls-shorts?* Don't make me laugh," she said to her reflection. "*Seriously.* It'll just add to the Grin Reaper's creepy collection. Maybe this T-shirt will help."

Marlo pulled on a grubby gray T-shirt with UNHAPPY CAMPER spelled out in slimy yellow letters.

"And that would be a *no*," she muttered as she buttoned the bib of her overalls. The "U" in "Unhappy" began to wriggle and ooze as Marlo cinched the straps.

"*Please* don't tell me these letters are hot-glued banana slugs," she said with a scowl of disgust.

Milton fastened the straps on his bib overalls-shorts and picked at the glistening yellow "y" stuck to his shirt.

"I think these letters are hot-glued banana—" Milton replied before Marlo leveled a coal-black gaze at him so withering that, had Milton been a flower, his petals would have instantly fluttered to the floor.

Marlo picked at her blotchy cheek.

"And what are these weird gray splotches on my face?"

The pouty, freckled girl next to Marlo in the leaking dressing room knelt down to tie the laces on her workboots.

"Ugh! These are, like, *three million* sizes too small," the girl said, exaggerating by about 2,999,997 sizes.

Milton tugged the neck of his rough gray T-shirt. Inside was a tag:

ONE SIGH FITS ALL

"And who *knows* who wore these before," the pouty girl continued. "They were probably at a Goodwill."

Marlo glared at the girl. "Don't be dissing Goodwill," she said. "It's like my off-site closet."

The blond, allergy-prone boy sneezed.

"Dusty," he complained. He screwed a tweed flat cap onto his head and glanced about over the broken dressing screens. "Probably mites and animal dander, too. Hey," he added, wiping his runny nose, "why are we all together here? Girls and boys, I mean? In Limbo, we were separated."

"Same in Rapacia," Marlo interjected as she knelt down to tie her boots.

"Apparently Snivel is a 'co-dead' facility," the long-faced girl said. "At least that's what one of the kids said back in the Mess Hall. It's supposed to make us feel even more awkward and miserable."

Milton looked over at Sam and Sara as they wrestled with a pair of extra-wide overalls-shorts. There was something about Sara that had left fingerprints all over Milton's imagination (apart from the whole Siamese, er, *conjoined* twins thing). She was a girl, yes, but approachable: exotic and faraway yet familiar and close, like a fallen meteorite. Sara caught Milton looking at her in the mirror.

"Yes?" she asked as she buckled the strap over her shoulder.

"Um . . . I . . . was wondering," Milton stammered, "well, why are you here?"

"How we died?"

"No, not that, really, but why you're in Snivel. You seem so . . . I don't know. *Sunny.*"

Sara smiled, proving Milton's point.

"Sam was yelling at a waiter so hard—complaining about the hot-and-sour soup being too hot and sour— that he burst a blood vessel that we, unfortunately, shared."

"I'm right here, you know," Sam grumbled as he

struggled to fit his head through the overtaxed neck of the Unhappy Camper shirt.

Sara rolled her eyes.

"So, I guess our souls must be conjoined, too, in some way. And since no one can grumble and moan like my brother here, that must have eclipsed my apparent *sunniness*."

She shrugged.

"But it's no biggie. At least we've got each other. That might seem weird, but having a sibling is . . . well, *complicated*."

Milton looked over at Marlo, the instrument of his own demise—his first one, when he was dispatched via exploding marshmallow sculpture, not popped to death in a carton of popcorn in a mortuary furnace.

"Believe me," he muttered. "I can relate."

The Grin Reaper appeared at Milton's side, looking down upon him with his weird, wet eyes.

"Is time leave," he hissed sadly, like a punctured, inflatable coffin. *"But first, must write letter to loved ones."*

The Grin Reaper pulled a wad of papers from the rubber chicken strapped to his belt and handed them out to the children. Marlo puzzled over the form letter: kind of like Mad Libs for the clinically depressed, trading verbs and adjectives for gripes and tragedy.

"Um . . . *why* should we even do this?" she asked, trying her best to look intimidating in overalls-shorts.

"Vice Principal has way of sending letter," the Grin

Reaper gurgled. *"Only chance for you make contact with dear ones."*

Milton, intrigued yet skeptical, took the pencil the creature offered and filled out his letter.

Dear _____

(Mom and Dad)
Mom and New Dad
Dad and New Mom
Legal Guardian, Institution, and/or Corporation

How are you?
[Space for intensely brief personal message]

I'd like to tell you that Marlo and I are in a better place now, but that would be lying. And after our experiences in Fibble (the Circle of Heck for kids who fib) and the barely thwarted plot to sell the Earth, the last thing I want to do is fill the world with any more lies. At least Marlo and I are together. That should count for something . . .

We just arrived at Camp Snivel. It's _____

Terrible
(Depressing)
Even worse than visiting Grandma's assisted-living facility

Well, I've got to be going. No rest for the wicked—
of which I am an official member, judging from my
eternally-darned-or-until-I-turn-eighteen-whichever-
comes-first status. Though Camp Snivel is fraught with
peril, the Grin Reaper—our awesome guide—says that
most of the kids make it. Most of them.

Hope you are
(Well)
Swell
Swelling in a well

Signed,
Your _____
(Son)
Daughter
More-intelligent-than-average pet

The Grin Reaper collected the children's letters, stuffed
them into the gaping beak of his rubber chicken, and
crossed the cramped labyrinth of rickety dressing screens
and piles of dirty clothes. The children followed, leaving
the tin dressing shed and trotting across the compound
through the stinging, soaking upside-down rain, arriving at
a circular yurt-style tent. Despite the rain, the children were
assailed by swarms of mosquitoes. The Unhappy Campers
huddled together, drenched, at the door of the yurt. The
Grin Reaper spread open the tent's beaded curtain.

"First-class service. Get it? Your first . . . never mind."
The creature sighed, noting the children's stone-faced
mirthlessness. "I go now. Must meet with Vice Principal."

Milton and Marlo entered the spacious yurt. Inside
was a circle of a half-dozen children stationed at easels,
each directly behind the other as if in a conga line. Joining them was a lanky, twitchy man with a scraggly red
beard and gauze wrapped tightly around the side of his
head. It was peculiar, Milton thought as he drew near.
He wasn't sure if it was the dim light in the room—
provided by suspended lanterns radiating soft blossoms
of weak illumination—or his broken, borrowed glasses,
but it looked to Milton as if the man—the teacher, he
assumed—was a little gauzy himself, as if he were rendered with strokes of hastily daubed paint.

"No . . . explore your own personal style by emulat-
ing *mine*," the man shrieked with a faint Dutch accent as
he nibbled on his paintbrush. "Paint me painting you as
I would paint *myself* painting you painting me!"

On the teacher's canvas was a painting of what the
boy in front of him was painting, which was a painting of
what the girl in front of the boy was painting: a portrait of
the next child's painting. It made Milton a little dizzy, this
loop of smeary infinity captured in thick, goopy brush-
strokes. He looked away, glancing at the chalkboard.

Arts and Crafts Therapy: Mr. van Gogh the chalkboard
read, the letters spattered on in streaks of gold and
blue paint.

Mr. van Gogh turned suddenly.

"Oh," he said, scratching his bandage. "I didn't hear you come in."

Right, Milton thought. Vincent van Gogh—perhaps the textbook example of "temperamental artist" (accent on "mental")—had once cut off his ear and given it to a lady he was smitten with. Milton could only imagine what anniversaries would have been like had they married: *"Honey, it's lovely, but I already have two—ears, that is. How about some long-stemmed roses next time?"*

"Where do we sit?" Milton asked.

"What?!" the teacher roared as he outstretched his open palm. "Talk to the hand!"

Attached to Mr. van Gogh's palm was an ear. Milton and Marlo gulped as one.

"Um . . . *WHERE DO WE SIT?*" Milton repeated, leaning into the teacher's hand as if he were ordering at a drive-through.

The teacher nodded and pointed to the far end of the tent.

"Grab a canvas and join the circle," he replied, carefully picking wax out of his palm with the tip of his brush.

The children grabbed easels from a pile and dragged them across the wooden floor. Water seeped through the moldy canvas of the tent, dripping up along the walls. Milton set his easel next to Sam and Sara. Marlo smirked at her brother, making a kissy face before setting her easel on the other side.

Mr. van Gogh fetched a number of rusty pails from the floor, each loaded with a random collection of art supplies.

"We'll return to my self-portrait later," Mr. van Gogh said as he kicked the buckets across the floor to each student. "But now, a little art therapy: the fast lane to self-expression."

Milton sifted through his bucket, which contained a tangle of stiff, paint-encrusted brushes, bits of macaroni, yarn, glue, torn *HAVE YOU SEEN ME?* flyers, pots of glitter, and—

Milton touched something both stiff and squishy.

"*A finger!*" he yelped. "A severed *finger!*"

Mr. van Gogh scratched his beard as he watched something flit about in the stale air inside the tent. "For finger painting, you silly boy," he replied.

Marlo scowled as she emptied her bucket onto the floor.

"How are we supposed to express ourselves with this junk?" she complained. "I mean, there isn't even any paint."

The deranged Dutchman staggered toward Marlo with a sly, lopsided smudge of a grin, like someone had rubbed away the lower part of his face to reveal a secret painting of a smile beneath.

"Knock, knock," he said, standing in front of Marlo.

She sighed. "Isn't there enough misery in this place without another lame joke?"

"Knock knock."

Marlo rolled her eyes. Sometimes a joke was like an invasive medical procedure. You just had to grit your teeth and let it happen.

"Who's there?"

"That was totally uncalled for."

"That was totally uncalled for—"

Mr. van Gogh slapped Marlo across the face.

Marlo's hand rushed up to her stinging cheek. "What was that all about, you psychotic one-eared freak?!" she shouted.

The teacher looked down at his ear-hand and shoved it underneath Marlo's nose. Smeared across his palm was a multicolored splotch with a dead mosquito in the middle of it.

The teacher separated the rainbow-hued sludge in his hand until he had a small palette of primary colors.

"The monochrosquitos," he continued, his breath reeking of turpentine. "They swarm about Snivel, sucking the color from every living thing: trees, grass, demons . . . and little dead girls. That's why everything is so gray, including your face."

Milton noticed a gray patch, about the size of a half-dollar, on Marlo's cheek, where the mosquito—or *monochrosquito*, rather—had bitten her.

"But they also make exceptional paint," Mr. van Gogh continued as he walked over to a collection of small copper pots by his easel. "The colors are so . . . *lifelike.*"

After wiping the colorful muck from his palm and distributing it among the pots, Mr. van Gogh handed each student a small bowl.

"With art therapy, the focus is on your inner experience: your feelings, perceptions, and imagination. It's about turning what's inside *out*—exposing your secret world—so that it can be harshly criticized, which is much better than being totally ignored, as *my* art was while I was alive," the teacher seethed.

Milton mushed up his bowl of bloody paint, separated the colors, held his freaky severed finger in his hands, and stared hopelessly at his canvas. He felt so many things that he didn't know *what* he felt.

He sighed, feeling suddenly unmotivated, hardly able to muster enough enthusiasm to hold up his severed finger. Milton had left Fibble with a fire in his belly for shutting Heck down for good, yet the mercilessly miserable atmosphere of Snivel had rained on his crusade. *At least,* he thought with a flicker of a smile, *Marlo and I are together.* Milton rummaged through the copper pot and pulled out a red HAVE YOU SEEN ME? flyer, featuring a girl with fire-orange hair. He glued it to his canvas.

He looked over at Sara, who was squinting at the hovering lanterns overhead.

"What are you doing?" Milton asked.

She smiled softly.

"I'm making the lights all blurry so I can see the halos around them," she replied. "So I can paint them like how van Gogh paints them—all those swirls and spirals. I thought that way I'd get a good grade. Shameless but—"

"Totally smart," Milton said with a grin.

"Hey," Sam snarled. "Give me the finger."

"Don't tempt me," Sara said between gritted teeth.

Sam bit his sister on the ear.

"Oww!"

"What's going on?!" shouted Mr. van Gogh from behind them. Sam's dark eyes rolled into his head as he lurched forward, startled into a narcoleptic sleep, and knocked over his painting. Pop went the easel as it collapsed to the ground.

The teacher examined the toppled painting.

"Nicely done," he said, nodding, while giving his beard a contemplative stroke. "Especially how you captured the lanterns."

Sara winked at Milton, which immediately sent Milton's complexion from "nerd white" to "flaming crimson."

Mr. van Gogh stalked behind Milton, glaring at his canvas.

"This one wouldn't be too bad if you kept the color inside the lines, you picked a new perspective, and asked someone with talent to paint it for you," the teacher said with a violent twitch.

Mr. van Gogh strutted over to Marlo's easel with his hands clasped behind his back. Marlo was staring blankly at her blank canvas, as inspiration was coming to her as slow as a constipated tortoise.

"I don't even know what we're supposed to be doing," Marlo complained as she scowled at her unpainted painting.

"You're supposed to paint what you *feel*," Mr. van Gogh replied.

Marlo's look of frustration turned into a triumphant smile.

"There!" she chirped as she folded her arms.

"There *what*?"

"I didn't feel like painting!"

Mr. van Gogh clenched his fists so hard his ear rang.

As the teacher reached out to strangle Marlo, the beaded curtains parted, sending in a blast of rain. In sulked the Grin Reaper.

"*I've come for Mr. Nurlington . . .*"

The Emo boy chewed the chipped black nail polish from his fingers.

"*Miss Thomas . . .*"

The pouty girl crossed her arms. "Figures," she fumed.

"*And Miss Fauster,*" the Grin Reaper concluded as he glided toward the children, skeletal arms extended as if in flight.

He scooped up Mr. Nurlington and Miss Thomas.

"Why us?" the Emo boy whined, his urge to resist suddenly sapped at the Grin Reaper's joyless-buzzered touch.

"*It nothing personal,*" the creature wheezed as his gray

marble eyes settled on Marlo. *"Just mandatory extra-credit Feel Trip for special campers."*

The Grin Reaper took Marlo's hand, his joyless buzzer bumbling like a woebegone bee in her palm.

"Marlo?!" Milton called out helplessly as the Grin Reaper dragged the three children toward the door.

Marlo, fighting the surge of dread spreading outward from her hand like a slow, debilitating poison swimming through her veins, gave her brother a weak smile.

"Don't worry, bro . . . you'll get worry warts," she replied softly. "I told you I wouldn't be here long. . . . Anyway, they can't hurt us—we Fausters are like superheroes."

With that, the Grin Reaper, Marlo, and the two other children were swallowed up by the thick, gray drizzle outside.

"Yeah, just like superheroes," Milton murmured. "Only our superpower is the ability to get into serious *trouble.*"

He stared at the HAVE YOU SEEN ME? flyer glued to his canvas, wondering if he would ever see his sister again.

6 · BAPTISM BY CAMPFIRE

THE SLOTH DEMON shoved a lantern beneath its hideous, decomposing face. Its tatty fur was matted with dried mud and slobber, its sunken, bloodshot eyes were rimmed with sores, and sharp yellow teeth grew out of its speckled gums like candy corn scattered across a slab of spoiled meat. It leaned into the fire.

"Mary, Lucia, and Beatrice were camping at the edge of the dark wood," the demon guard hissed. "The night was chilly and dark, with a barometric reading of 30.28 inches, indicating—"

A snailish demon sitting by the fire slugged the sloth in the shoulder with its distended eyestalk.

"Skip a bit," the demon said in its grinding voice, like two dull knives scraping against each other.

The sloth demon nodded as the children surrounding

the fire roasted their rotten eggplant and Brussels sprout skewers.

"Just trying to create an atmosphere. Anyway, as night fell, the girls started a roaring campfire. But the area outside the fire's rosy glow was pitch-black. Just like it is . . . *out there.*"

The sloth demon pointed out to the rim of the forest with one of its long, curved claws. Milton and the other children shivered as they cast wary glances out at the darkened woods surrounding Camp Snivel. Milton was still freaked out by his sister's sudden "extra-credit" abduction, making him especially susceptible to ghost stories. His gaze lingered on the sinister silhouettes of weeping willows and pines.

"It was from this blackness that the sounds of snapping twigs and the rustling of leaves came. For a long moment, there was nothing but the crackling of the fire. . . ."

For a long moment, there was nothing but the crackling of the fire. The sloth demon handed the lantern to its demonic comrade-in-arms, who—not having arms—hung the lantern off one of its tentacle eyes.

"Suddenly, a ghastly, bloodcurdling sound erupted from the deepest part of the forest," the snail demon rasped. "Terrified, the girls darted away, tripping through the underbrush. Unfortunately, their blind panic sent them running right into the gaping jaws of the . . ."

Both demons scanned the bulging eyes of the children expectantly.

"*. . . fuzzy kitten,*" the demons oozed together, cradling the words dangerously on their tongues as if they were verbal grenades.

Milton and the other Unhappy Campers traded dumbfounded glances.

"Meow!" added the sloth demon, claws raised like a frisky cat, thinking that the confounded children simply hadn't fully grasped the story's horrific ending.

"Was there something—*achoo!*—really scary *behind* the fuzzy kitten?" the allergy-prone red-eared boy asked.

"Was it dismembered?" Sara interjected.

"Or strangled by yarn?" posed the slack-jawed boy.

The sloth and snail demons eyed each other with dismay.

"This was an *exceptionally* fuzzy kitten, I assure you," the snail demon rasped through its tiny gash of a mouth.

The sloth demon scratched its throat. "I'd tell you a frightening tale about a prancing pony, but I'm afraid I'm a little hoarse," the mangy creature coughed.

"So let's have a little sing-along instead," the snail demon interjected, prompting a chorus of groans, mainly from the children who had been at Snivel before Milton and the other new Unhappy Campers had arrived. "Participation isn't mandatory, though all those *not* singing will enjoy some quality time with Vice Principal Poe."

The children went suddenly pale and silent.

"*Bummertime is here again,*" the snail demon sang, "*and you know what that means . . .*"

"*It's time for rashes, colds, and flu: no access to vaccines,*" the children sang in shaky unison.

> "*Cry our eyes out by the lake until our faces*
> *are so long*
> *that horses whinny while we whine the lyrics*
> *to this song.*
> *Spirits sunk so low now that it's like we've*
> *got the bends.*
> *Oh, Camp Snivel, how we loathe you: this*
> *bummer never ends!*"

Milton, Sam/Sara, and the other newbies arched their eyebrows at one another.

"I should get some more firewood," Milton said, standing.

"I'll help," Sara said as her brother grumbled, half-asleep.

"Us too," the three other new Unhappy Campers said, rising.

The demon guards glared at them suspiciously.

"We wouldn't want the fire to go out," Milton said as Lucky wriggled in his backpack. "You know . . . *kittens.*"

The demon guards swallowed.

"Don't be long," the sloth demon said with a shudder.

The children marched along the edge of the forest,

the sky beyond Snivel's glass dome a dim canopy of garbage. From the raised mound overlooking Lake Rymose, the Unhappy Campers could see the wobbling Dukkha Wheel churning the grim lagoon.

"Sorry about your sister," Sara said, giving Milton a faint smile.

"Yeah," the slack-jawed boy added. "She seemed really nice."

The six children stared at each other, before bursting out laughing.

"I know Marlo isn't exactly Miss Congeniality," Milton said with a sad smirk. "But it was nice to have her here. It made me feel like I was back home somehow. . . ."

"She was a mouthy punk," Sam said, his voice slurred with sleep, "but she had spunk."

"*Has* spunk," Milton corrected, uneasy with referring to his sister in the past tense.

Sara put her hand on Milton's shoulder. "I'm sure she'll be fine—she seemed like the kind of girl who can look after herself."

After a moment of shared silence, the weepy girl spoke.

"If there's one thing I know about camp," she whined, "it's that they're going to give us nicknames. *Terrible* nicknames. Unless we come up with our own."

"Yeah," the blond, elfish boy said with a sniff. "We could, like, give them to each other first."

Milton nodded. "That's a great idea. It's like a pre-emptive strike against humiliation."

"Well, like I told Milton here," Sara said, "my brother and I are used to being called all sorts of terrible things, so most anything would be an improvement."

"How about something cool like 'Gemini'?" the long-faced girl offered. "You know, the twins in astrology?"

"Yeah!" the boy with the runny nose exclaimed. "Way *über!*"

"I like it," Sara replied. "But it's like . . . hard being conjoined . . . with everyone thinking you're one person, not two. You know?"

Milton nodded. "That makes sense. How about just 'Sam/Sara'? It's quick but still acknowledges your individuality."

Sara smiled brightly as her brother began to grumble.

"Samsara is the Buddhist cycle of death and rebirth," she said with her hand clapped over her brother's mouth. "It's perfect! And, who knows, maybe one day we'll be reborn!"

Milton turned to the boy with the perpetually open mouth.

"What about you?"

"My name is Mortimer Franzenburg," the slack-jawed boy said. "But everyone back home called me Mouth-breather, because—"

"I think we know why," the red-eared boy with the runny nose interjected. "How about something fierce, like . . . I don't know . . . *Howler Monkey?* You know . . . turning your mouth thing into a—*achoo!*—sort of calling card."

Mortimer wiped the drool from his lower lip and smiled. "Yeah . . . sounds like a supervillain name!" he said. "What about you?"

"Tyler Skaggs," the elfin boy said. "My dad used to call me the Sunshine Sneezer. That's actually how I got here. I fell asleep in a tanning bed to help clear up my eczema, and the machine went crazy. I woke up and it was flashing so bright that I sneezed harder than I ever had . . . than I ever would again."

"Actually, I kind of *like* the Sunshine Sneezer as a name," Milton replied. "Reminds me of the Sundance Kid: Butch Cassidy's sidekick. Plus it's a way for you to be close to your dad."

Tyler wiped his eye. "Yeah . . . that's cool," he said with a sniff. "It's a keeper, then."

The children turned to the weepy, horsey-looking girl.

"Jaslin Chunder," the girl offered. "The kids at my school weren't particularly creative in the abusive nickname department. They just called me Crybaby."

"What about Waterworks?" Sam replied with a sneer. "Like, 'Hey, turn off the waterworks, Crybaby.'"

"That's not much better," Milton said. "How about something cool like Caterwaul?"

"Caterwaul?" Jaslin asked.

"It means to wail or howl," Sara said. "But in kind of an intense way."

Jaslin smirked. *"Caterwaul,"* she said with a nod, trying the name on for size in her mind. "I like it. A nickname with *claws.*"

Sam turned to Milton. "What about *you?*" he asked, glowering at Milton with his coal-black eyes.

Milton stroked his nonexistent chin hair.

"Well, there was 'Dweeb,' 'Brainiac,' 'Short Bus,' and dozens of other names my sister seems to come up with so effortlessly. There was another one," Milton added, swallowing. "'Milquetoast.'"

Sam snickered. Sara nudged herself in the side.

"The biggest, baddest bully *ever* used to call me that," Milton continued. "I hated that name. Almost as much as I hated *him.*"

After a moment's consideration, the Sunshine Sneezer chirped, "How about the *'Dork* Knight'?" The boy snickered. "Because you're kind of a leader but nerdy."

"I don't know," Milton murmured.

"I like it," Sara replied with a smile that instantly changed Milton's mind. "You *are* a leader—"

"Thanks."

"But not in the conventional 'handsome and heroic' way," Caterwaul added.

"Thanks."

Lucky squirmed inside Milton's backpack. Milton

unhooked the straps, set it on the ground, and scooped out his restless pet.

"When Lucky's awake—which is seldom—he is *AWAKE*. In all-caps."

Howler Monkey smiled, leaning down to pet the ferret as it stretched and shook. Lucky assessed the boy's hand and, grudgingly, deemed it worthy of touching him.

The campfire sing-along stopped abruptly.

"We'd better get back," Sara said.

Milton nodded.

"You guys go. I'll be there in a sec. I've got to let Lucky run around for a bit or else he'll wriggle, dook, and whine, and get found out."

"*Dook?*" Sara asked with a crook of her thin black eyebrow.

"It's kind of like a clucking noise. Like an irritated chicken."

"Cute." Sara smiled.

"Yeah," Milton replied, staring back at Sara's sparkling black eyes. *"Cute."*

The Unhappy Campers turned toward the campsite.

"We'll cover for you . . . *Dork* Knight," the Sunshine Sneezer called out with a grin as the group left Milton and Lucky alone at the edge of the forest. Lucky shivered, coiled around a dead shrub poking out of the sodden ground, pooped, then frisked around for a bit. Suddenly, the ferret stopped and stood stock-still, sniffing the air. Lucky hissed, his bristly white back arching into a harrowed hoop.

"Lucky?" Milton said as he came closer. "What's—"

Lucky bolted across the slick mud, parting the rain-fog that clung to the ground in wispy patches, and shot straight into the heart of the forest.

"Lucky!" Milton called out as he ran after the ferret, now nothing but a fuzzy, flickering streak at the back of Milton's retinas.

I lost Marlo today, Milton thought as he ran blindly into the clammy gloom. *I'm not going to lose Lucky, too.*

Milton leaned against a weeping willow, winded and lost. The dark wood was a chaotic, monotonous tangle, with the only light coming from the faint twinkle of metallic garbage fixed like shabby stars up above—or down below—Snivel's glass dome in the Dumps.

A branch snapped, followed by a scraping rustle. Milton spun around, but the arrangement of trees made the sounds impossible to locate with certainty. They seemed to come from all around, as close as a whisper.

"Lucky?" Milton gasped. The only reply was his own breath panting back at him. Yet as Milton quieted his breathing, he could still hear something puffing like a bellows. A dark, disheveled shape, blacker than the blackness of the forest, darted past in the corner of Milton's eye. He turned, spinning on the ball of his foot, as another shape dashed between the trees, again only noticeable out of the corner of his eye.

Something crinkled beneath Milton's foot. A damp, smeary picture of an Indian boy, with the words HAVE YOU SEEN ME? scrawled atop his miserable face, lay in the mud. *Is this what happened to Marlo?* Milton thought.

The chill of despondency seized him by the midsection. It was as if these mysterious, nearly imperceptible creatures—like shaggy wolves with heads hung low—radiated cold and despair as they stalked the forest in silence.

A splintering noise sounded, rousing Milton from his melancholy with a jolt of fear. Milton ran through the forest, eyes blind with tears, conscious only of his helplessness. He dodged trees and patches of slick mud as icy breaths beat down his back. Banking away from a clutch of withered pine trees, Milton tripped on a knotted clump of roots. He sprawled forward, stumbled, and fell down the raised mound separating the forest from Lake Rymose.

Milton landed with a thump against a saltwater-rotted beam jutting out from one of the lake's six docks. He heard a splash. A figure—someone or something—jogged away from the far shore of the lake back toward the camp. His stomach sick with motion and adrenaline, Milton rolled onto his side and stared out across the lake's murky waters. Something small, like a bottle, sped toward the Dukkha Wheel, disappearing in the foam.

That sinking heaviness returned, having briefly disappeared when Milton was freaking out in the forest. The water rippled and flickered faintly, glowing a sickly dark green, as if reflecting light. But, aside from the drab twinkle of garbage above, Snivel was as dark as a raven's wing.

The light must be coming from the bottom of the lake, Milton thought as he got onto his scraped knees, wincing with pain. *But how?*

The Dukkha Wheel shuddered as it turned, threatening to shake itself loose from its axis. Beneath the roar of the wheel was a wash of muffled beeps, chirps, and twitters. Milton crawled to the edge of the dock to try to make sense of the sounds. There, below the rim of the lake, was something else bobbing in the water. Milton leaned over the dock, straining to reach it, and finally snatched it up by the neck. It was an old, green-tinted glass bottle with a brass plug on top. Milton rolled the bottle in his hands, examining it by the weak light drifting from the lake. He unstoppered the bottle and found, coiled up inside, a note.

Dedicated. Focused.
Shrewd. Nimble. Tenacious. Twitchy.

Do you have what it takes to become a member
of the one and only OFFICIAL
Arcadia Gr8 G4m3rz Club?
If selected, would you vow to:

- Adhere to the rules and bylaws of the Arcadia Gr8 G4m3rz Club?
- Remain vigilant in the Sense-o-Rama, no matter how realistic your virtual opponents seem?
- Compete mercilessly against your peers?
- Abduct new recruits so that they can have awesome fun, too?
- Disclose the secret location of the Sense-o-Rama, like, never?
- Ingeniously master all five levels?
- Acquire valuable badges to advance in the Arcadia Gr8 G4m3rz Club ranks?

If so, then you MAY have what it takes to be one of our Gr8 G4m3rz!* Sit tight and await further instructions as to how YOU can join! Not just anyone is allowed into Arcadia: only the best!

* In fact, we're almost certain.

Milton rubbed his thumb pads against the paper. It was strangely smooth and . . . *tingly.*

"A video-game club?" Milton wondered aloud. "It can't be here in Snivel. The kids here seem too depressed even for *Super Mario.* Arcadia? Maybe this is one of the Grin Reaper's lame jokes—"

Something scraped behind Milton on the dock:

something with claws. Milton turned slowly. There, shivering in the dim light, was a small, fuzzy creature.

"Lucky!" Milton gasped as he rose to scoop up his ferret. Lucky backed away, spooked.

"What's the matter, little guy?" Milton whispered gently. "What did you see that made you like this?" Lucky's white fur was raised all over in quill-like bristles, and one of his pink eyes bulged bigger and wider than the other.

A piercing whistle rent the gloom.

Milton grabbed Lucky and tucked him and the note into his backpack.

"Ferret-frisking time is officially *over*," Milton mumbled as he trotted off the dock and toward the camp compound. "Hopefully we can make it back before lights-out . . . though the lights don't ever really come *on* in this sucky place."

Milton pushed open the door to the Totally Bunks. His fellow Unhappy Campers were already snoring away— especially Howler Monkey—in the leaky, moldy cabin. They twitched in their sleep as small, slender serpents coiled around their wrists and ankles, securing them to their beds.

"Guys?" Milton whispered as he tread across the squeaky floorboards, down the aisle of broken bunk beds.

Sam/Sara stirred in his/her bunk.

"Milton?" Sara murmured, her voice craggy with sleep. "Good . . . you made it back. We tried to stay awake . . . but this place . . . It makes us all so sleepy. And heavy. Our bedtime story—a dramatic reading of the Boring, Oregon, phone book—didn't help."

Sam grunted in his sleep, his face a scowling mask of "don't bother me."

Milton pulled the note from his backpack.

"I was chased by some creatures I couldn't see. And then I found this. . . ."

He unfurled the note and showed it to Sara, who rose to her elbows as best she could considering the serpent restraints. She squinted at the paper, then at Milton, confused.

"A piece of paper?"

"What do you mean?" Milton asked as he looked at the scroll.

It was blank.

"It was an invitation to this cool video-game club," he murmured, feeling baffled and somehow betrayed. "To a place called Arcadia."

Sam gnashed his teeth together with a grimace as he tried to turn himself and his sister over onto his side to face the damp, mildewy wall.

"I'd better go back to sleep," Sara whispered as she slowly lost the tug-of-war with her own body. "Sam gets grumpy if he doesn't get his twenty hours of rest."

Sam/Sara turned away, leaving Milton to ponder the clean sheet of stiff, tingly paper in his hands.

Disappearing ink? he thought as he found an empty bunk beneath an especially prodigious leak in the rusty tin roof. *Or did I just imagine it?*

He crawled into the lower bunk as Caterwaul whimpered in her sleep above.

Milton sighed as he laid his head on the lumpy, burlap sack of a pillow, staring up at a patch of black mold that resembled a grinning skull.

"It's ten forty-five and all is, if not lost, then forever misplaced," the Town Cryer wailed outside with a clang of his bell.

Maybe it's my mind playing tricks on me since Marlo isn't here to do that, Milton thought as he succumbed to the sluggish pull of Snivel. *I'll figure things out . . . maybe confront Vice Principal Poe. In the meantime . . . I'll just try to . . .* Serpents slithered from the sides of his bunk, coiling together into knots, binding Milton tightly to the bed.

Relax.

7 · A SHADOW OF HER FORMER SELF

MARLO AND THE two other Unhappy Campers were heaved out into the thick, drenching downpour. Marlo struggled against the devitalizing effects of the Grin Reaper's joyless buzzer, pressed firmly into the small of her back. Night was falling, sharp and sudden like a guillotine, and it was hard to make out anything through the grim sheets of rain pelting the children from below.

The weeping willows beside Marlo suddenly trembled, as if something large had brushed against them. She turned and, just like before, could only see something vague, black, and shaggy at the edge of sight before it vanished completely.

"And I told him he could *stuff* it," the mangy sloth demon told its fellow guard, a walking snailish creature that left a trail of glittering slime behind him. "But the taxidermist said that Twinkles had been dead for too long—"

"Are we *there* yet?" the gangly Emo boy grumbled behind his long, side-swept bangs as he pretended to listen to the music not-playing on his hand.

Marlo shot the boy a double-barreled glare and vented in one, breathless gush: "First, your iPod's on the Surface—get over it—and, anyway, it's loaded with music that wasn't really cool even when it *was* cool. It's like listening to someone barf up their feelings all over your shoes. Secondly, no, we aren't 'there' yet, and 'there' is obviously someplace even *worse* than this blowsome pit of lameishness, so what's your hurry, Tickle Me Emo?"

The boy, his angular face mottled with gray monochrosquito bites, swayed like a sail after a sudden squall.

"It's Ferd," the boy mumbled after a beat. "Ferd Nurlington. But the kids used to call me AWTY. You know, for 'Are We There Yet?'" He gave Marlo a shaky, smitten smile.

Marlo sighed. She was all too familiar with that dweeby grin. "I absolutely *forbid* you from having a crush on me," she replied. "I'm putting a restraining order surrounding all thoughts of me. Got it, AWTY?"

The boy nodded meekly and pretended to shove his imaginary earbuds deeper into his ears.

The freckled, put-upon girl stopped short in a puddle of mud.

"Ugh!" she complained as her left foot emerged from the oozing muck *sans* shoe. "Figures. Stupid extra-sticky mud!"

"Where we go, you no need the shoe," the Grin Reaper rasped as he urged the girl onward.

"Where we go?" Marlo asked, swatting away a swarm of monochrosquitos feasting on her pigment.

"There *we go*," he said, nodding to what looked like an out-of-order outhouse up ahead at the crest of a hillock. They slogged through the mud and stormy sheets of rain-fog to the small shack nestled in stinging nettle.

"I take them in," the Grin Reaper said to the demon guards. *"Area restricted. Go lead other children in optional-yet-obligatory campfire sing-along."*

The demon creatures nodded as they slunk away, swallowed up by the rain and fog. The Grin Reaper slid open a keypad panel to the side of the shack's door. His skeletal fingers punched out the sequence so fast Marlo couldn't make out the code. The door unbolted from inside with three mechanical pops. The Grin Reaper pressed the children through the cramped portal before entering the shack. The door whooshed shut behind them.

Marlo scanned the bleak, dilapidated shack, illuminated by a bare bulb dangling from the ceiling.

It's like something out of a horror movie, she thought with a shiver. *Right before the stuck-up cheerleader takes a shower.* Damp seeped up the claw-scratched walls from the stained concrete floor. Suddenly, a white, feathery shape swooped through the shack.

"Boo *who* . . . boo *who*," the creature screeched before flying *through* the wall.

The children, bug-eyed with terror, stared at the Grin Reaper for some kind of explanation.

"Owl ghost," he replied casually as he knelt down in the corner in front of what looked like a shabby doll. He tugged on the porcelain toy's arm.

"Mama," the doll bleated, its blank black eyes rolling back in its head as the floor fell, lightning fast, sending Marlo and the other children down, down, down, screaming.

Marlo shook her dizzy head, which was hanging limp below her shoulders as her knuckles and knees pressed hard against the concrete floor. The shack had plummeted so fast that it felt as if she had left her internal organs behind like lost baggage.

The sour-faced girl writhed beside her. Marlo struggled to her feet, then held out her hand.

"Here, um . . . ," Marlo offered.

"Petula," the girl grunted as she took Marlo's hand. "Petula Crabbe. But everyone calls me—"

"Let me guess," Marlo replied, eyeing the large, lead door with its polarized glass window in front of them. "Crabby."

The Grin Reaper swished past them, flicked open

another keypad with his long, bony finger, and punched in six numbers—again too quick for Marlo to track.

The lead door slid open with a pneumatic whoosh. Glaring ultraviolet light spilled into the chamber. *It's like an atomic tanning bed,* Marlo thought as the Grin Reaper urged them forward with a snakelike curl of his finger.

"Come," he gurgled. *"Before elevator shoot back up. Maybe it smoosh you on ceiling. Maybe it not."*

The children followed the hooded creature into the chamber. The door behind them sealed shut with a hiss of expelled air. Marlo's eyes adjusted to the light.

Twining up the middle of the humongous cube-shaped room like a shoot of metallic ivy was a long contraption coiling to the ceiling. Sprouting from its dull stalk of braided cables were dozens of tripronged satellite dishes clicking and twitching restlessly as they trained brilliant golden light on . . .

Marlo gasped.

Children.

Ten kids, Marlo now saw, were trapped inside small, rectangular tanks stacked on three levels of shelving, each level connected by a rickety staircase. Stuck like flies in amber, they struggled softly in the tanks, their shadows cast against white panels mounted behind them on the walls. With a lump in her throat, Marlo noticed that there were three empty tanks perched atop the highest shelf.

"Bonswa! Welcome to the Shadow Box, petites," a

slender figure in a white top hat and tuxedo purred as it approached Marlo, Ferd, Petula, and the Grin Reaper. The man had a weird Caribbean French accent that felt like hot buttered rum poured into Marlo's ear. "This be the 'eadquarters for the Decease Corps," he added with a rumbling cackle.

"The *what* corpse?" Petula asked, folding her arms defiantly.

Marlo noticed that the girl's thick, freckled arms were shivering.

The man—his face an ebony canvas painted chalky white like a skull—had a mouthful of dazzling teeth and cotton plugs stuffed into his wide nostrils.

"The Decease Corps is a volunteer program for petites . . . *children* . . . eef you be stretchin' the definition of 'volunteer' to include 'shanghaied and recruited by force'!" the man boomed in reply. "You will be ambassadors for the underworld, sent abroad on an ill-will mission."

"Why us?" Marlo asked. "And who *are* you? You're like something someone would hang on their door for Halloween."

The man's head pitched back, his gaping mouth issuing a resonant bray of a laugh.

"*N'ap boule!* Why you, indeed!" he managed after regaining composure. "You were han'picked by your vice principal."

The man's wide, red-rimmed eyes darted to a silhouette lurking at the back of the Shadow Box before quickly returning to bore into Marlo.

"*Troublemakers,*" he continued in a hush. "Grating, defensive children better *elsewhere.*"

"Who are you calling *defensive?*" Marlo replied. "*You're* defensive."

"*Rete!*" the man shouted, holding his palm up to Marlo's face. He straightened, now as tall as a college basketball player.

"I am Baron Samedi," he said with a quick tip of his top hat. "In-specter general on loan from Dead Letter Office. Now, *prese prese!* Wastrel Projectors are now online and I must train new operator. . . ."

His bulging eyes settled on the Grin Reaper, who fidgeted from foot to foot, with either sudden excitement, discomfort, or incontinence, Marlo couldn't be sure.

She turned to the golden, almost tragically beautiful light cascading up the coiling spindle piercing the center of the Shadow Box.

"Is *that* a Wastrel Projector?" Marlo asked as she eyed the ripples of resplendent light pulsing up the fiber-optic coils of the metallic vine. It flowed almost like luminous honey more than light. "What does it do?"

The silhouette across the room coughed. Baron Samedi gave a slight nod before grabbing Marlo and Petula roughly by the shoulders.

"No more *labba labba,*" Baron Samedi said as he shoved

the children toward the stairs leading to the top shelf. "It time to mek haste and see the light . . . to *be* the light . . ."

Marlo, transfixed, followed the brilliant gleam as it streamed up the stalk and through the first satellite dish. Light gushed out like a supernova in a blinding, radiant discharge, bathing a boy trapped in one of the rectangular tanks in its shimmering brilliance. The boy's shadow, cast on the white panel behind his tank, jerked and swayed like a puppet. Marlo watched as the shadow seemed to drip down, like wet black ink, into a dark purple duct. The pulsating, veinlike pipe sucked the shadow down the side of the wall, joining a network of other throbbing pipes, ultimately coiling and disappearing at the base of what Marlo assumed was the Wastrel Projector.

Baron Samedi shoved Marlo to the first step of the stairwell. . . . The Grin Reaper's joyless buzzer vibrated at the base of Marlo's back, filling her head and heart with dull, debilitating sludge. She longed to struggle, to break free, to run somewhere—*anywhere*—but her inner fire was scarcely stronger than a damp aromatherapy candle at this point.

"*They transmit child's weak energetic shadow up to Surface,*" the Grin Reaper whispered into Marlo's ear as he urged her up the second flight of stairs.

"*The Surface?!*" Marlo yelped with muffled excitement. Baron Samedi stopped short and glared at the Grin Reaper. The hooded creature gazed back with its twinkling, steel-gray eyes.

Baron Samedi glanced furtively down the coiling stalk of the Wastrel Projector at the man lurking in the shadows below.

"Through Wastrel Projection, your 'absence' is transmitted up to Surface, *mon*," Baron Samedi whispered between his thick, white-painted lips, his voice still deep and reverberating despite the hush. "As long as there are three people with strong, sad memories of the deceased. This is how machine can triangulate the projection."

Marlo glanced at the satellite dish nearest her as it blasted light at a little girl with pigtails, trapped, squirming, in her tank. The dish had three prongs, each sending shimmering threads of light that fed the main beam flowing from the center. All of the satellite dishes twitched nervously, like the eyeballs of someone asleep, dreaming.

"On edge of this high-powered absence and tragic recollection, this *mizé*." Baron Samedi continued, the inside of his mouth as red and wet as the inside of a pomegranate, "The dead petite—*you*—can weakly manipulate the real world as a shade."

"F-for how long?" stammered Ferd.

"Six day, six hour, and six minute," the lanky in-specter general replied as he fingered his bone necklace. "If flow of light is unbroken, if you perform your tasks, and if nothing . . . *interferes*."

"Interferes?!" Marlo replied. "What do you—"

"What tasks?" Petula interrupted with a scowl, her

indignation at being asked to do something blundering past all concern for her well-being.

Baron Samedi scratched underneath his top hat.

"Spreading the malaise—"

"Spreading *mayonnaise?*" Ferd interrupted.

"*Malaise* . . . discontent. The incurable sadness. You must keep three people—as you petites say—*supremely bummed out* so projection stay strong. Then herd as many children as you can to seek out false happiness."

Baron Samedi shot the Grin Reaper a quick, meaningful look. The Grin Reaper nodded his hooded head and squeezed his rubber chicken until it vomited out wads of letters through its gaping latex mouth. One of the letters floated lazily down to the floor. It landed near a large shaft at the base of the Wastrel Projector. Through the flares of pulsing light, Marlo could see a mirror set inside the shaft at the tube's elbow where it turned away sharply, reflecting the light like a periscope.

Where is that weird light coming from? Marlo pondered as the Grin Reaper handed the letters to Baron Samedi.

"By wheespering letters from the dead to the living," Baron Samedi said as he shoved the crumpled letters into the hands of the children, "you fuel inconsolable grief." He pulled out three envelopes from the inside pocket of his tuxedo coat.

Marlo studied the small white envelope that, creepily, had her name written on it in ornate cursive lettering.

"Who is making you do this?" she asked.

Baron Samedi laughed as he shoved each child successively up to the top shelf, where the three empty tanks awaited.

"*Bourik swe pou chwal dekore ak dentel,*" he grunted.

"*What?*" Marlo replied nervously as the towering man neared.

"The donkey sweats so the horse can be decorated with lace—old Haitian proverb," the baron said as he reached Marlo.

The tanks were tilted slightly back, their glass doors open in sinister invitation.

"Now do the Decease Corps proud and spread the bad word upstairs," the baron said as he shoved Marlo, hard, into the tank. "You no wanna romp wit me."

He slammed the glass door shut—the tank burping like Tupperware—then stalked toward Ferd.

"Um . . . ," the boy said, quailing, as he backed away from the imposing tuxedoed man. "Are we there yet?"

Marlo rolled onto her side, feeling like a bug under a microscope. Suddenly, her tank began filling with translucent, jellylike foam.

"What's going on?!" she screamed as the foam shot through nozzles from all four sides of the thin, cramped tank.

"*Is bad memory foam,*" the Grin Reaper said before walking to the wooden railing of the shelf. "*To help you interact with world of living. Like shadow puppet.*"

Marlo tried to block the foam spraying out of the

nozzles, but the pressure was too strong. The bad memory foam was now up to her neck. She could feel it congealing like unflavored Jell-O around her legs . . . her waist . . . her stomach. Across the Shadow Box, through glass fogged by her gasping breath, Marlo could see another tank set on a middle shelf flicker, then go dark.

"Baron Samedi," the silhouette shouted from below. "We seem to have lost yet another to the merciless talons of the Litsowo." A flash of light from the Wastrel Projector briefly illuminated the man's face. It was Vice Principal Poe.

"*I stop machine,*" the Grin Reaper said as he descended the staircase. "*Maybe can retrieve boy.*"

"Do so and you shall render our agreement null and void," the vice principal replied, his delicate white hands at his hips. "And your ribs will never tickle with the rich, boundless laughter I have promised you."

The bad memory foam choked Marlo's tank and was now congealing on her face, becoming dense and stiff— like the egg-white-and-Pepsi facial masks Marlo used to make back home on sleepovers with her friend Aubrey Fitzmallow. Before the foam hardened into thick rubber in her ears, Marlo heard Poe's voice one last time.

"The boundaries that divide life from death are at best shadowy and vague," the vice principal proposed. "Who shall say where the one ends and where the other begins? I leave these matters to spiritual crossing guards such as the baron. Now I can focus on how the other, less-willful children can best fulfill my wishes . . . my *destiny*."

Suddenly, an explosion of blazing honey light filled Marlo's chamber. She tried to scream, but the instant she did, the memory foam seeped into her mouth and stifled the howl before it even left her throat. Marlo could feel the light coursing through her, streaming in between every molecule, every atom, every thought, radiating outward until Marlo's consciousness bubbled over like a shaken can of warm soda.

The Wastrel Projector's light throbbed relentlessly. Marlo felt like a piece of chewed gum, pulled apart into a long, glistening strand that threatened to break at the slightest provocation. Everything went white.

Dizzy, her brain hot with fever, Marlo opened her eyes. There before her, in shimmering waves of visual heat, was the corner of Wooster Way and Arbuckle Avenue.

Generica, Kansas.

"I don't believe it," she said, her voice a flat, hollow vibration, like when your ears are plugged up from a cold. "I must be here because of my parents . . . my shade held here by their sad memories. But that's only two. Baron Samedi said it took the anguished memories of *three* people who couldn't let me go. Who else would love me enough to keep me here with their pain?"

8 · HEADED STRAIGHT
FOR THE POE HOUSE

THE SNAIL DEMON, with its waggling eyestalk, gestured toward a drab tent at the edge of camp.

"Vice Principal Poe's tent," the creature said in its irritating scrape of a voice. "His door is always open. . . ."

Milton nodded as he screwed his cap tight to his head and began trudging toward the tent.

"But children, once they pass through that door," the demon guard rasped against the roar of stinging rain, "have a hard time finding their way out."

Milton slogged through the mud toward the shabby tent. The door, strangely, was massive. It looked like it was made of iron. It was also ajar.

Milton heaved the door with his shoulder until he made a gap wide enough to pass through. The door's weight caused a sharp grating sound as it moved upon its hinges.

"Hello?" Milton called out tremulously into the dim, mournful vault. "Vice Principal P-Poe?"

A single dim ray, like the thread of a spider, shot out from a bell jar across the small, dusty room. The gleam of light looked like an unblinking eye staring back at Milton. His heart tried to pound free of its rib-cage jail. In fact, Milton's pulse throbbed so loudly that it nearly sounded as if it were booming back at him from the other side of the room.

From the outside, the large circular tent seemed scarcely different from the others dotting the solemn, sodden campgrounds of Snivel, Milton thought. Yet, as seen from the inside, Vice Principal Poe's office, from its dark draperies to its marble lining, was indistinguishable from a mausoleum.

Maybe I shouldn't have come here, Milton fretted, feeling as if he had trespassed upon someone's tomb. *But perhaps Poe knows something about Arcadia and whether that's where Marlo and the other children are. And if he does know something but denies it, maybe I can find some clue here in his creepy lair.*

Milton's eyes soon grew accustomed to the dark. Books and furniture lay scattered about—all of them comfortless, antique, and tattered—at the rim of the round, reinforced tent. He breathed in the chamber's dust and desolation, feeling the atmosphere of sorrow sit heavy in his lungs. An air of stern, deep, and irredeemable gloom hung over and pervaded all.

Be gone, be gone, be gone, Milton's heart seemed to be telling him as it throbbed in his chest, though, again, its cautionary pulse sounded as if it were coming from across the room.

"Lenore?" a groggy voice exclaimed.

Vice Principal Poe arose from the sofa that he had, apparently, been lying on the whole time, as silent as a corpse.

"Who wanders weak and weary in my drawing room dreary?" he asked as he wiped the sleep from his eyes.

Milton's throat swelled closed with fear, as if his lower body were trying to forcibly block all passage of distressing input from his head. His heart banged like a drum in his ears.

"My name is M-Milton Fauster," Milton faltered, his mouth as dry as a mummy's bath towel, "and I was wandering—*wondering*—if I could have a word with you."

Vice Principal Poe rested his darkly luminous gaze upon Milton, instantly chilling the marrow in his young bones.

"A word is a very dangerous thing, as it often leads to sentences," the vice principal replied in his stumbling, unsettling manner. "Regardless, you have roused me from my reverie. What word is it, exactly, that you wish to have with me?"

"I was walking by Lake Rymose last night and found a message by the shore."

The vice principal's thin lips curled subtly, his mustache straightening into a sort of sly salute.

"A message?" he replied with thinly veiled amusement. "My, how intriguing. Whatever did this message say?"

Milton dug for the rolled-up paper in his pocket and held it out to the vice principal, yet stopped short just as the man moved to seize it.

"First, I need to know where my sister is . . . Marlo," Milton said, his teeth gritted with determination. "Where have you taken her?"

Vice Principal Poe's sour face curdled until it resembled a waxy lump of feta cheese.

"O! How brazen we are . . . such bluster!" he mocked.

"You're not answering my question," Milton said.

The vice principal tightened his crimson cravat. "Perhaps we should retire to a more . . . *relaxing* venue for discussion."

The bell jar on the chamber's far shelf quaked and quailed.

Be gone! Be gone! Be gone! the jar seemed to chant in a deep, resonant thrum. Milton caught sight of the hideous contents of the jar: *a beating heart.*

Vice Principal Poe strode across the tent, pulled a hand-knit cozy out of a writing desk, and thrust it snugly over the pounding jar. Stitched across the gray and pink woolen cover were the words HOME IS WHERE THE HEART IS.

"Now, now, don't have a *you* attack, my tattle-tell-taling friend," the vice principal said as the muted heart palpitated beneath the cozy. "Save your bleeding heart tirades for someone who cares."

The man turned to Milton, who stood, paralyzed with shock, as the stifled heart pounded in protest.

"Shall we retire to my Conversation Pit and air out our issues?" Vice Principal Poe asked in a stern voice that turned his question into an order.

Milton found it difficult to respond as the pulse in his head and the one thumping across from him fell into sync. The vice principal sidled up to a stone bust of a woman set atop the shelf. He tilted back the woman's head to reveal a red button.

"I'll take your silence as consent," Vice Principal Poe said as he pressed the button. "Now stand back."

Milton backed away as the metal floor directly in front of him seemed to break apart with a groaning chorus of gnashing squeals, coiling itself downward until it became a spiral staircase corkscrewing to a secret chamber below the tent. The vice principal urged Milton downward with his deathly cold hand.

"A vast, perhaps larger portion of the truth arises from the phantasms of the mind," Vice Principal Poe said, the heels of his dull black shoes striking the iron stairs so that they tolled like funeral bells.

"Phantasms?"

"Figments of our imaginations. Perhaps your so-called message in a bottle is similarly phantasmagorical."

Milton stopped suddenly on the last step and turned to the vice principal.

"I didn't say anything about a bottle," he replied suspiciously.

Vice Principal Poe stiffened, his face a cadaverous slab of inscrutability.

"I assumed, rightly it seems, that the message was contained within some watertight vessel, or otherwise it would have been rendered illegible. But, please, make yourself comfortable—or else you might find yourself *un*comfortable."

The man made a quick, nervous gesture with his hand toward a pit in the middle of the dim, dungeonlike room. Nestled inside was a round, lushly upholstered, red velvet cushion. Above the pit was a broken wooden sign that had been split down the middle. Sliced, by the looks of it. Lit by a patch of flickering candlelight cast from a collection of candles burning on a stone mantel were the words CONVERSATION PIT—.

A mixture of curiosity and fear helped to clear Milton's mind of Snivel's will-sapping gloom. Vice Principal Poe's slip about the bottle betrayed a secret knowledge. Of what, Milton could not be sure. He shrugged, walked over to the pit, and—after a cursory inspection of the plush cushion—hopped inside and lay down, instantly lulled into a peculiar, almost silky-cool sense of relaxation.

"So let us clear up any misconceptions through a forthright chat," the vice principal said while gazing at a portrait hanging on the stone wall of a hauntingly beautiful woman with raven-black hair and large, gazelle-like eyes.

"Okay, then, where is my sister?" Milton asked.

"Your sister is involved with a secret extracurricular program of mine," the vice principal replied dryly. "That shall remain as such—*secret*—until I decide to reveal its aims and ambitions to a greater audience. Principal Bubb was quite adamant that your sister be involved, due to her exceptional sensitivity."

Sensitivity? Milton thought. *Marlo is about as sensitive as a concrete Brillo Pad.*

"I assure you that before the week is through, she and the others will probably return, more than likely as sound as they were prior to their engagement."

"Probably?! More than likely?!" Milton replied with exasperation. "Thanks for putting my mind at ease. . . ."

Vice Principal Poe's lip and mustache again curled into a sly smile.

"Then perhaps this will provide some distraction," he said as he pressed an embedded button at the base of the portrait's gilded frame.

Suddenly, a sort of foam gushed out of nozzles set

inside the rim of the pit. Instantly it conformed to Milton's body, hardening all around his sides until he could barely move. As he struggled, Milton could see the other piece of the broken sign from his new, unfortunate vantage point: —AND PENDULUM.

As if on cue, a massive, antique pendulum emerged from a crevice in the stone ceiling and swept across the chamber in a deadly arc six feet or so above Milton's chest.

Of course, Milton thought as he struggled anew, his head hot with fear: *"The Pit and the Pendulum": Poe's story of a prisoner being tortured, both physically and psychologically, in a nightmarish dungeon. Poe has brought his twisted story to life . . . in death.*

9 · A LAKE AND A PROMISE

"IS THIS WHAT happened to all the missing children?" Milton cried as the sweep of the pendulum came closer, descending downward while whistling through the stale, lifeless air.

"Of course not," the vice principal retorted with a sniff. "Those children, I fear, are merely victims of the loathsome phantasms restlessly stalking the forest."

So it's true! Milton thought as he struggled vainly in the hardened restraining foam. *There is something terrible lurking in the woods, and maybe that something is what's preying on the Unhappy Campers.*

The blade above was a crescent of glittering steel as keen as a razor. It was appended to a weighty rod of brass. The deadly device hissed as it swung through the air, dropping closer.

"I'm severely vexed, Mr. Fauster. I don't mind telling

you," Vice Principal Poe continued as the whoosh of the pendulum snuffed out the candles on the shelf. "You burst into my office, hot with accusation, disturbing the quietude of my chamber . . . my innermost thoughts. You question my motives, my character, and rave of nocturnal lakeside imaginings. I will not stand for it," he added as he sat down on a stool next to an oddly glowing phone inset in the wall.

"You're insane," Milton spat as the pendulum swept so closely over him that it fanned him with its metallic breath.

"Perhaps you're right," the man muttered as he stared longingly at the portrait on the wall. "Losing a soul mate can do that to a man. But let me make this point clear: There will be no more mention of Arcadia. And don't even *think* of trying to escape there."

Milton panicked and struggled to force himself upward against the sweep of the fearful scythe. Down, steadily down it crept, until it threatened to fray the front of Milton's threadbare overalls.

Arcadia? Milton thought, the word bobbing to the surface of his rushing fear. *Did I mention Arcadia to Poe?*

"To help keep you mindful of my rules, I will leave you with a little reminder slashed across your chest—"

The glowing phone on the wall rang. Vice Principal Poe sighed and pressed the button in the picture frame with his thumb. The pendulum's deadly, arcing sweep slowed.

"Hello?" the vice principal said as his bony fingers

scratched beneath his vest. Milton noticed that the man's hand seemed to reach inside his chest, his shirt and vest puckering into a small, fist-sized cavity. "Yes. Hello. I know it's you. You're the only one who's ever on the other end of this line. . . . Please, take a breath and slow down, Nikola. . . ."

The phone, Milton now realized, was upside down, with a pulsating cord of golden light running up from the floor into the base behind its cradle.

"I trust you've concocted a way of distracting Bubb?"

Vice Principal Poe covered the receiver with his gaunt hand.

"You may leave now, Mr. Fauster," the vice principal said as the foam imprisoning Milton liquefied into a chunky, melting stew. "And mark well my words."

Milton clambered out of the pit and ducked his head to avoid the pendulum as it drew itself back into the ceiling. After rushing up the spiral staircase, Milton hung in the doorway of Vice Principal Poe's office to eavesdrop.

"Yes, another recruit who I'm nearly positive you should be expecting momentarily," Poe whispered into the phone. "A perfect balance of feisty and fearful. I believe this recruit will not arrive alone, as he has the faint whiff of 'leader' about him, as well as a lingering blend of roasted s'mores and burnt popcorn. He should be an excellent addition to your little 'club.' "

Be gone! Be gone! Be gone! the tattling heart in the jar beat from beneath its knit cozy.

"And nosy, by the sound of it. Excuse me . . ."

Milton squeezed his way through the iron door and out into the drenching rain.

I don't get it, Milton thought as he trotted across the soggy campground. *Poe doesn't want me talking about Arcadia, which means it probably has something to do with Marlo or the other missing kids, but he was talking to someone on the weird glowing phone about me being a recruit—for what? For Arcadia? And what was all that about distracting Principal Bubb?*

He saw a light on in the Mess Hall.

I need to talk this through with somebody, Milton thought as he creaked across the stoop and stepped inside the cabin.

Inside, Sam/Sara, Caterwaul, Howler Monkey, and the Sunshine Sneezer sat miserably at a table sipping from glasses as a timeworn copy of *Old Yeller* was projected on the wall.

"Milton!" Sara chirped as Milton wrung out his sopping wet cap in the doorway.

"You mean the *Dork Knight,*" Sam mumbled sleepily before yawning so widely that his face seemed at risk of splitting in two.

Milton pulled up alongside his friends. All of their faces were gray from monochrosquito bites, and their droopy eyelids were crisscrossed with purple veins.

Mine probably are, too, he thought.

"What's going on?" Milton asked.

His friends slurped a collection of beverages with broken paper umbrellas bobbing at the top.

"Unhappy hour," Caterwaul replied with a catch in her throat. "We were all forced here at spork-point to watch movies—you just missed *The Yearling*—and drink these terrible sodas."

The bubbles in Caterwaul's soft drink floated down to the bottom of her glass, where they collected in a sad, grumbling throng. Milton glanced over at the soda-fountain dispenser, which featured a number of cheerless offerings, including 7-Down, Mountain Don't, Phanta, Spite, Barf's Root-of-All-Evil Beer, and Tab.

"I just came back from Vice Principal Poe's torture chamber, otherwise known as his Conversation Pit and Pendulum," Milton said. "I went there to confront him about the note I found—"

"You mean . . . *achoo,*" the Sunshine Sneezer said/sneezed, "the note you *think* you found."

"No, he really did, like . . . find a note," Howler Monkey added between breaths as his mouth multitasked as both an airway and a language center, "but the note had nothing written on it."

"But it did!" Milton exclaimed. "And I have proof . . . kind of."

Just then, Mr. van Gogh walked in, looking at the children with his eyebrow suspiciously arched just below his dirty gauze head dressing. He curved his left palm outward, training his severed ear on their conversation. Milton leaned in to his friends.

"Something is fishy with Poe," Milton whispered. "But we can't talk here."

Lucky wriggled restlessly in Milton's backpack like a load of laundry with a sneaker in it. He poked his twitching nose out from under the flap, sniffing in Mr. van Gogh's direction.

"Your—*achoo*—ferret," the Sunshine Sneezer said as he scratched his red, protruding ears. "His dander is making me sneeze."

"What *doesn't* make you sneeze?" Sam snorted with a scowl.

"Lucky has an ear thing," Milton replied as he cinched his backpack tight until it was escape-proof. "He likes to nibble on them like chew toys. Anyway, we need to talk about this, but Poe has spies everywhere."

"What if we had a code?" Caterwaul asked as she slurped down the last of her soft drink.

"Like Morse code?" the Sunshine Sneezer replied. "That's too easy to break."

"How about *Remorse* code?" Sara said with a smile so contagious that instantly Milton was grinning from ear to ear.

"Yeah," he replied, scooching his chair in as close as he could. "Where, instead of dots and dashes, we could use . . . sniffs and sobs."

"Perfect!" Caterwaul said, her face actually not looking as if it were on the verge of collapsing into a state of blubbering despair.

Mr. van Gogh and two sloth demons sat at a nearby table, pretending to cry as Travis, up on the screen, got his rifle. The teacher surreptitiously dangled his palm underneath the table and aimed straight at the children. Milton cleared his throat.

"*Snort-sob-snort-snort, snort, sob, snort-snort-snort. Sob-sob-snort, sob-sob-sob.*"

The other children traded quick glances with one another before nodding in understanding. Howler Monkey lingered, confused.

"Let's go," Sara whispered to him as they pushed away their chairs and made their way to the door.

The up-pour outside had let up until it was simply a thick, sulking fog.

"*It's seven forty-seven, and it's time to uncork the whine,*" the Town Cryer moaned after tolling his bell. "*And let it breathe . . . its last breath.*"

The children stepped off the creaky wooden stoop of the Mess Hall cabin and headed toward Lake Rymose. Mr. van Gogh and his sloth demon henchmen were close behind, working too hard at appearing nonchalant. Milton coughed.

"*Sob, sob-sob-sob. Sob, snort-snort-snort-snort, snort. Snort-*

sob-snort-snort, snort-sob, sob-snort-sob, snort." (To the lake.)

Sara looked quickly back over her shoulder at Mr. van Gogh.

"They follow," she warned in sobs and snorts.

The Sunshine Sneezer cleared his throat. "Diversion," he suggested in Remorse code.

Caterwaul tucked a sopping wet strand of mousy-brown hair behind her ear and nodded toward Milton and Sam/Sara.

"You two go," she sniffed and blubbered.

"*Three,*" Sara snort-sobbed with a hint of irritation.

"Sorry. Three."

The Sunshine Sneezer sneezed, then coughed. "We run," he advised. "Now!"

Suddenly, the Sunshine Sneezer, Caterwaul, and—lagging behind—Howler Monkey bolted across the muddy campground to the Totally Bunks.

"Hey!" shouted Mr. van Gogh. "After them!"

The teacher, with the demon guards trotting sluggishly in his soggy steps, took off past the Unrest Rooms and into a swollen tuft of drifting fog.

"Hurry!" Sara said, taking Milton's hand as they ran to the sickly shores of Lake Rymose. They walked tentatively across the rotten planks and out to the end of the pier.

"Look!" Sara yelped as she pointed to the foamy rim of the lake. "A bottle!"

Milton fell onto his stomach and strained to clutch the neck of the bobbing bottle.

"There!" he said as he grabbed the bottle and fished out another rolled-up piece of paper.

Sara knelt down beside him as her brother, passed out from the excitement, snored fitfully against her neck.

Enclosed is your FREE ARCADIA CLUB ENTRY EXAM!

Earn badges! Gain points! Play the latest games until your fingers (and possibly other extremities) fall off! Carry your OFFICIAL MEMBERSHIP CARD! Wear your OFFICIAL Arcadia beret and sash! And don't forget your secret handshake—or your secret hand! JOIN the OFFICIAL Arcadia Gr8 G4m3rz Club TODAY! NOW! DO IT! C'MON!

Rush me my Arcadia Gr8 G4m3rz Club Entry Exam! I understand that, if accepted, I will be required to exhibit exceptional gamesmanship: 24/7! After successfully filling out my OFFICIAL FAN CLUB ENTRY EXAM, I will not attempt to make contact with Arcadia, as traditional means of communication are not to be trusted. Instead, I will wait for further instructions.

Check here if you are:
- Prone to seizures
- Acousticophobic (unable to tolerate extremely fun sounds)

- Photoaugliaphobic (unable to tolerate superawesome strobing lights)
- Olfactophobic (unable to tolerate hecka-bold, all-that-and-a-bag-of-sniffs odors)
- Geumaphobic (unable to tolerate a full range of intensely radical flavors)
- Haphephobic (unable to feel ridiculously kickin'—sometimes scratchin' and bitin'— sensations)
- Phobophobic (possess an irrational fear of irrational fears)
- Related to any employee of Heck and its subsidiaries
- Inclined to check things

Do not bungle, botch, or otherwise fail to take advantage of this most exciting opportunity! Just imagine: you, a small person with a big responsibility, an honored part of the most exclusive club currently in existence! FUN, ADVENTURE, SECRETS, CAMARADERIE, and the ADMIRATION OF ALL await! JOIN the OFFICIAL Arcadia Gr8 G4m3rz Club TODAY!

Question 1—Are you Milton Fauster?

Then—just as with Milton's last nighttime excursion— a piercing whistle tore through the stillness of Snivel.

The weeping willows fringing the patch of forest

nearest Lake Rymose rippled as unseen creatures charged past them. Sara grabbed Milton by the shoulder.

"C'mon," she said with trepidation as she turned back toward the camp. "We'd better bolt."

Milton nodded as he ran alongside Sam/Sara through the patchy mist and drizzle.

"At least you know you're not crazy!" Sara chuckled, an exhausted grin smeared across her face.

Yes, Milton was apparently uncrazy—at least in terms of bottles bearing mysterious messages. And though he was no closer to solving his sister's disappearance or locating Arcadia, his feeling of vindication—and running alongside Sara—was enough to beat back the creeping hopelessness of Snivel.

At least for now.

10 · MAiDEN THE SHADE

MARLO'S ETHERIC BODY and soul were stretched so thin that she felt as if the blazing sunlight of Generica, Kansas, could shine straight through her, giving her once-beating heart a case of serious sunburn. She viewed her hometown as if through the wrong end of a pair of binoculars duct-taped to her head. Everything around her seemed both far away and so close. Marlo was *here* . . . but she wasn't. Not quite. Not enough to matter.

She moved her legs and arms slowly and sluggishly as if she were walking across the bottom of a swimming pool. Marlo winced at the glaring light that washed out Wooster Way and Arbuckle Avenue. Like a vampire working the day shift, Marlo sought out the comfort of shadows, finding a soothing clot of darkness beneath a WHOOPING COFFEE shop awning and a mailbox.

Weird, Marlo thought as the coolness of the shade

wrapped around her, as snug and comfortable as your favorite coat. *I feel more . . .* me *here in the shadow. More together. But . . . why? Is it because, like Baron Samedi said, I'm some kind of freaky spiritual shade and I'm, I don't know, more comfortable hanging with my own kind?*

A man in a brown business suit walked by, talking on his cell phone.

"Excuse me," Marlo said, her voice strangely hollow in her own ears. "Hey . . . business guy!"

The man stopped a few feet away from Marlo, by the mailbox, scowling quizzically at his phone.

"Hello? Mr. Bourret? Are you still—" The man sighed.

"Guess I lost *that* deal," he grumbled as he stormed down the street, working out his frustration by playing a game on his phone.

A mother and her son walked out of the coffee shop.

"Hey, lady," Marlo called out. Her voice seemed to die just as it left her lips.

"Yum!" the pudgy boy cooed as he lapped the abundant, structurally unsound pile of whipped cream teetering precariously atop his drink. "I love skinny, extra-whipped loco-mocha-luscious frappa—"

The boy's drink fell and exploded like a caffeine-and-sugar grenade on the sidewalk. His mother, clutching a handful of letters as she leaned over the mailbox, turned to console him and accidentally deposited her wallet in the slot.

"It's okay, dear. Mommy will just buy you . . . Uh-oh."

A teenage girl strutted by in a plaid minidress, purple ankle socks, and white oxfords, rocking out to her iPod. Marlo stepped in front of the girl and waved her arms.

"Hey!"

"Oh come back, baby, my heart you fed," the girl warbled tunelessly. *"But now I'm starving, boy, I feel like I'm—"*

Startled, she looked down at her iPod, her eyes bugged out with alarm as she stopped *in* Marlo.

"Dead?" the girl gasped. "All of my songs . . . like . . . totally wiped! And I spent *forever* illegally downloading those!"

The teenage girl sulked away, leaving Marlo alone beneath the coffee shop awning.

She passed right through *me,* Marlo thought with a shiver. *Am I a ghost? Should I start charging a toll?* She turned and got a glimpse of herself in the window's reflection. Rather, she got a glimpse of where she *should* have been but wasn't. Not exactly. *I'm not here. Then how . . . Wait.*

At the fringe of the awning's shadow, Marlo noticed a vague smudge of shade, almost like something stuck in your eye. It was a silhouette of her head.

I'm a shadow. A real shade. *But I'm not even really here to cast myself. I'm down in Snivel in that Shadow Box . . .*

A homeless woman drove a shopping cart through Marlo, temporarily derailing her train of thought.

That machine, the Wastrel Projector. I'm down in Snivel and that machine's freaky, powerful light is casting my shadow all the way up here, to Generica. But I'm not just a shadow. I'm me. Sort of. But no one can see or hear me. I might as well be a substitute teacher. So why am I—

A plump, middle-aged woman in a jogging suit that obviously had never been worn for jogging stepped out of the coffee shop and onto the sidewalk.

"What a beautiful day!" she chirped, sipping her iced double-Dutch chocolate fudge mocha with bacon bits and low-fat whip. As the woman brushed past Marlo's shadow, her bright smile disappeared, as if it had been Etch A Sketched across her face, then shaken away. "But it will probably rain," the woman grumbled as she dragged herself across the street, heedless of the cars honking at her. "It always does. . . ."

I'm here to funk people out! Marlo realized. *No one knows I'm here, but they can feel my shady presence—my absence— and it gets them seriously bummed! That must be why—*

Marlo remembered the letters and envelopes Baron Samedi gave to her, Ferd, and Petula before they were shoved into their tanks. She pulled out one of the crumpled letters. Marlo recognized her brother's writing, though there was some creepy scrawl at the top.

WHISPER TO SURVIVING KIN...

I'd like to tell you that Marlo and I are in a better place now, but that would be lying. And— after our experiences in Fibble (the Circle of

Heck for kids who fib) and the barely thwarted plot to sell the Earth—the last thing I want to do is fill the world with any more lies. At least Marlo and I are together. That should count for something. . . .

Marlo wadded the letter back into her pocket and pulled out the envelope. Of course, it was only a shadow—like the letter, sort of like burnt paper—but she could still handle it, feeling it faintly in her fingers. She ripped it open. Inside was Marlo's itinerary for her six days, six hours, and six minutes up on the Surface.

1. 33 Paradiso Crescent

That's my *address*, Marlo thought as she held the smudgy-dark paper shadow in her hands. *Or at least it was, back in the day.*

2. Fragopolis, 646 Spawn Boulevard

Some lame arcade where socially awkward, pasty-faced, monosyllabic, joystick jockeys swarm like flies on . . .
A girl got out of a red Hyundai across the street. She was pale and full figured, with pink cotton-candy hair and wire-rimmed glasses.
Aubrey? Marlo mumbled to herself. *Aubrey Fitzmallow?*
The girl leaned into the open passenger window.

"I'll be done in about two hours, *Lenore*," she said with a sneer. "You can pick me up right here after your weird Jamaican yoga thing."

A thin, salt-and-pepper-haired woman with large dark eyes, hoop earrings, and a peculiar air of haunted beauty stretched her long neck from the driver's seat.

"Look, Aubrey, I'm not asking you to call me 'Mom' or anything, but the least you could do is not say my name like it's some sort of embarrassing disease. And it's not Jamaican yoga. It's Pilates of the Caribbean. And since when does it take two hours to cut hair?"

Aubrey rolled her muddy green eyes.

"And a dye job . . . not that you'd know anything about that."

The woman tossed back her black-and-gray mane as she put the car in drive.

"I *like* my hair. It's natural. In a witchy way. So see you here in two," Lenore said, shooting Aubrey one last confirming look before driving away.

"Aubrey!" Marlo screamed, though her voice didn't have enough force to even make it past her mouth.

Aubrey had been Marlo's best friend since second grade. They had hit it off instantly, trading Bubblicious back and forth as if it were currency. She was a fellow Goth, though she took it in that theatrical "cabaret" direction, whereas Marlo's style was more "classic" Goth.

Aubrey and her sketch pad were inseparable: She could almost always be found under a tree sketching her weird comic books (sorry, *graphic novels,* as she called them) about lost little girls encountering trickster spirits. Basically seeing how many ways she could reinvent the movie *Labyrinth.* She'd even tried to get Marlo interested in tarot cards, but Marlo had never liked the notion of her future all laid out in spades. Or pentacles. Whatever.

Aubrey, decked out in a dingy white thrift-store wedding dress and black lace arm warmers, was headed down the street toward the Curl Up & Dye salon. Marlo stepped out of the shadows to follow her, but the intense light made it almost impossible for her to move. It was as if her whole body were numb and asleep, like how her mouth felt at the dentist's. She struggled across the street, fluttering laboriously like a lead butterfly.

Fluttering will get me nowhere, Marlo thought as she eyed the noonday sun overhead. *Noon. The sun is at its highest, meaning hardly any shadows.* A bus turned the corner. The T-Dious line, heading out to Dious Avenue and Paradiso Crescent. Marlo was sucked into the bus's slender shadow as it whizzed by. Her insides felt cool and smooth, sort of tickly as the street combed through Marlo's shadow body. The bus stopped at the corner, outside of the salon. Marlo crawled out of the bus's shadow and onto the sidewalk, using the dappled shadows of a red maple tree like monkey bars to "swing" her way to the Curl Up & Dye window.

Inside, she saw Aubrey sitting in the swivel chair, showing the trendy hairdresser a picture.

"That's me!" Marlo yelped silently as the hairdresser took Marlo's obituary photograph—her last yearbook picture—and set it on her workstation, right by a bottle of Blue Your Mind hair dye.

Aubrey crossed her thick, stripy-stockinged legs and stared at herself in the mirror. A devious smile spread across her face—like a cat stretching in the sun before pouncing on an unsuspecting mouse—as the hairdresser clipped off the ends of Aubrey's hair until it was *exactly* the same length as Marlo's.

What is Aubrey doing? Marlo asked herself. The sun broke through the canopy of leaves overhead, making Marlo's mind go hot and fuzzy. The bus closed its doors as it prepared to leave the curb. Marlo panicked. There were only a couple of shadow clusters on the sidewalk now that the sun blazed full force above.

What'll happen to me if I'm caught here without any shade? I'm just a shadow in the harsh light of day. Will I just scatter like, like . . . ashes?

Not wanting to find out the hard way, Marlo leapt from shadow patch to shadow patch until she reached the curb, then hurled her energetic absence to the slim band of shadow skirting the bus, clinging tight as it drove away.

★　★　★

The late-afternoon sun stretched the shadows long across the driveway of a black-and-white two-story house, with THE FAUSTERS looped in wrought-iron cursive outside the cracked stucco fence.

Marlo swung from shadow to shadow, finally nestling in a dark pool cast by a ceramic gargoyle her mom had made after quitting smoking for the third time.

The garage door was open. Marlo smirked. The bottom of it was still scuffed from when Marlo had taken her father's station wagon out for a late-night spin and miscalculated the delicate garage-door-opening-to-car-speed ratio.

Inside was a labyrinth of old cardboard boxes, each overflowing with a jumbled collection of clothes, books, records, and assorted memorabilia. Beside a totem of boxes was Marlo's father, Blake Fauster. The middle-aged man took off his glasses and wiped his eyes with the back of his hand as he stared into a seemingly bottomless box of personal effects.

"Dad?!" Marlo shrieked as she traveled along a long shadow cast from a chimney across the street into the garage, walking it carefully, her arms held out at her sides as if it were a plank poised above shark-infested waters. "It's me! Marlo!"

Blake Fauster shivered, despite the heat of the afternoon sun, and scratched his graying goatee.

"Haunted," he mumbled as he stared at a picture of Marlo perched at the top of a mound of photographs, the only surviving photograph of her in her Brownie uniform, "by the ghosts of memory. Eating away at me from the inside . . ."

"Dad . . . *it's me*," Marlo wept as she strained to touch the sleeve of his tweed jacket. "*Marlo*. I'm here . . . sort of."

Tears streaked down Blake Fauster's face, their salty trails banding along his cheeks like prison bars.

"What's the use of love when it turns to pain?" the broken man murmured as he set the picture down and closed the flaps of the box, securing them with duct tape. "Leaving behind pictures I can't bear to look at and names I can't bear to say out loud."

The door to the house creaked opened. Marlo's mom, Rosemary Fauster, poked her head out into the garage, her normally smiling eyes dull and red-rimmed.

"Oh, I . . . didn't know you were still here," she lied. "Do . . . do you need any help?"

Blake Fauster smiled, but it was a smile without warmth or authenticity.

"I do need help . . . *I do*," he replied. "It feels so odd to say those words—*I do*—considering the circumstances."

"Blake, don't," Marlo's mother said, crying without tears, her tear ducts spent and dry. "Don't make this worse than it already is."

Marlo watched the scene, helpless, somehow sharing this awkwardly painful moment while simultaneously aware of her motionless, disembodied self trapped in memory foam back in her Shadow Box Chamber.

"Mom," Marlo whimpered, unsettled by her once obnoxiously cheerful mother's cold look of despair. "What's going—"

"I don't see how I could," Blake Fauster replied as he hefted a box to the nearly stuffed trunk of his white Rambler station wagon. He slammed the door shut. "Make this worse than it already is. But I suppose, once you hit bottom, you can always dig deeper."

Rosemary Fauster clapped her hands over her ears, grabbing her dark brown, gray-streaked hair with her fists.

"That sounds like something . . . *she'd* say," the woman wailed. "I can't do this, Blake. It's just too . . . *I can't.*"

Marlo's mom slammed the door as her father, shoulders slumped, head barely held up, walked alongside his battered car—a car that actually *looked* like him—and slid behind the wheel.

"You can trash the rest!" he shouted as the station wagon lurched into the street.

The sun sank below the roof of a neighboring house. Marlo felt as if she were a bucket of black ink poured into a black lagoon. Her thoughts seemed to spread and spill over each other.

My parents are breaking up. Getting a divorce. Because of me. Because of my memory . . . and Milton's. They've been through so much. Too much. I can't let it happen . . . I can't, Marlo thought, before losing the ability to think altogether.

11 · LEND ME YOUR EAR

MILTON AWOKE TO a sight that he had never seen before and hoped to never see again: a severed ear dangling in front of his nose.

"Euuugh!!" Milton yelped as Lucky held Mr. van Gogh's ear tight in his little ferret jaws, his hot sardine breath panting in Milton's face with a mixture of pride and excitement. Milton squirmed out of his serpent restraints and out of the lower bunk.

"Lucky . . . why?" Milton whispered. "Now Vice Principal Poe and the staff will be on our case, and we can't just return it because then, you know, they'll find your little teeth marks on it and—"

Lucky gazed back at Milton. His pink eyes shone with incomprehension. All Lucky wanted was the unhinged joy of sinking his needle teeth into his latest acquisition. Milton sighed.

"We'll figure it out," Milton said softly as he scritched Lucky underneath his jaw, the ferret leaning into Milton's touch. "You can't help who you are," he added, quickly snatching the ear from Lucky's unsuspecting jaws before shoving his angry, wriggling ferret into his backpack.

"Is that our art teacher's ear?" Sara said groggily from her bunk.

Milton nodded, staring at the detached auditory organ in his palm.

"Yeah," he said. "Lucky must've ferreted it out somehow. He sure can smell."

"You're telling me," Sam said with a bleary sneer.

"I mean his *sense* of smell," Milton clarified, despite the fact that Sam had already fallen back asleep. "It's like his nose has a mind of its own."

Sara giggled while the Sunshine Sneezer blew his nose in the bunk above her.

Milton picked out a strange brass disk from the canal of van Gogh's ear and stuck it into his own ear.

"Maybe it's a hearing aid or—"

Footsteps pounded on the soggy stoop outside. Without thinking, Milton plopped the ear into his mouth. Instantly, he could hear a disgusting, smacking assortment of wet noises and gurgles: the sounds *inside* his own mouth. Mr. van Gogh and two demon sloth guards filled the doorway.

"Have you seen my ear?!" Mr. van Gogh shrieked.

"No, but, like, have you heard my eyes?" Howler Monkey said as he rubbed his eyes so vigorously they squeaked.

The flying-off-the-handle Dutchman examined the Totally Bunks with dubious sweeps, the teacher's bulging eyes settling on Milton.

"And what do *you* have to say for yourself, Mr. Fauster?"

Outside, the Town Cryer's bell tolled.

"*It's six fifty-nine and time to face another pointless day,*" the voice wailed pitiably.

Mr. van Gogh sighed.

"*Fine.* Off to class with the lot of you . . . and *haast je!*" he said, adding a wave of his paint-smeared finger. "But don't think you've heard the last of my ear!"

Just as the teacher and guards turned to leave, Milton rolled away and spat the ear into his hand.

"Yuck," he mumbled as the Unhappy Campers hopped to the cold, wet floor. "I don't think Mr. van Gogh has ever swabbed this thing. Lucky's fish spit doesn't help."

Sara sat beside Milton and patted him on the back. Milton dug the brass disk out of his ear canal and stuck it back inside van Gogh's spit-soaked ear.

"Well, no matter how many disgusting, dignity-robbing things they put us through down here, one thing is for certain."

"What's that?" Milton asked, staring back into her kind, sparkling eyes.

"We'll always have *class*," she giggled. "C'mon."

Milton fluttered his eyelids. It looked like he was behind bars in some deep-purple prison. The blood vessels on his eyelids were darker and more pronounced than they had been just yesterday.

After a quick inventory of his fellow classmates, Milton realized he wasn't the only one. It made him feel trapped. Hopeless. He knew that if he were to escape to Arcadia at all, it would have to be soon, while he and the other Unhappy Campers still had some fight left in them.

Question 1—Are you Milton Fauster?

That was the first, last, and only question on Milton's Arcadia Club Entry Exam—at least as far as he had been able to tell before the exam's weird, disappearing ink faded. How did they know about him? And who, exactly, were *they*? And why did Vice Principal Poe seem both intent on prohibiting and simultaneously *pushing* him there? All Milton knew for sure was that the answer lay coiled somewhere within Lake Rymose, like a mysterious Loch Ness monster just begging to be un-Loched.

"Where's the—*achoo!*—teacher?" the Sunshine Sneezer said as he and the other children sat in a circle in the round leaky tent. Through the curtain of beads sulked a pale, dark-haired man wearing laurels in his hair and, unfortunately, little else, save for a diaphanous white tunic draped across his hips. The man seemed both young and impossibly old, like an ancient statue of a young man brought to life. The girls in class—including Sara, to Milton's strange, sudden displeasure—seemed to perk up slightly at the mopey man's entrance. He listlessly picked up a piece of chalk, sighed deeply, then scratched across the chalkboard "Mr. Orpheus, Music Depreciation."

The piece of chalk fell to the ground and shattered. The teacher's dark eyes welled with tears.

"Taken down before your time . . . just like my beloved Eurydice," he muttered with profound sadness.

Caterwaul rested her chin on a fist, a moony expression cast across her long face.

"What a *dreamboat*," she cooed softly to herself.

Milton and the Sunshine Sneezer shared a commiserating smirk.

"Commencing eye-roll sequence," Milton muttered.

Sara's dark eyes darted over to Milton, crinkling into a smile that allayed Milton's budding jealousy.

"My name is Mr. Orpheus," the teacher said in a low wheeze, like a gust of cold wind whistling through a cemetery. "Some of you may know me as the leader of the band The Minor Keys."

"I just *knew* he was in a band," Caterwaul whispered. "He has that tortured poet thing going for him."

"No?" Mr. Orpheus said, surveying the uncomprehending expressions on the students' faces. "The pioneers of Glum Rock? Consistently making *Rolling Tombstone's*

Most Depressing Bands list, due—primarily—to my scorching lyre solos?"

Mr. Orpheus sighed. He picked up a long, black drum and smacked its sagging skin. It let loose a muffled boom that instantly filled Milton with a muffled gloom, smothering his spirits as if with a soggy pillow.

"'Tis no matter," Mr. Orpheus said, setting down his drum. "Music, as many of you know, has the ability to transport the soul. It makes the people come together, the bourgeoisie and the rebel. It hath the power to expel disease. It is a sovereign remedy against despair and melancholy and can reportedly drive away the devil himself. Especially polkas. It can make lovers more enamored and a religious man more devout. This, in music, we appreciate. . . ."

Mr. Orpheus picked up a lyre leaning against the moldy canvas walls of the tent. A long tangled black cord connected it to a small amplifier. He slung the instrument over his shoulder by its strap.

"But this, I'm afraid, is Music *De*preciation. Where we deconstruct music to such a ludicrous degree that it is stripped of all transportive magic, rendered merely a collection of auditory vibrations. Its beauty becomes but a delusional figment conjured somewhere between our eardrums and the brain."

Mr. Orpheus sighed, the defeated exhalation of someone whose heart once pumped wine and now only spewed vinegar.

"Music has let me down . . . *and it will pay.* I could

once enchant wild beasts with the beauty of my music. But it wasn't there for me when I needed it the most. When I lost my dear wife, Eurydice."

That's *how I know him*, Milton thought. *Orpheus. The ancient Greek poet and musician who, when his wife, Eurydice, died, went to the underworld to rescue her. He wasn't supposed to turn around and look at her until they made it back to the land of the living. But he did . . . and she didn't. Make it back, that is.*

"Music Depreciation examines the painful, disharmonic psychoacoustic potential of music and its effect on the brain and spirit," Mr. Orpheus continued. He went over to a warped wooden cabinet containing a number of black drums. He grabbed an armful and handed them to the students.

"These are doldrums," he explained in his sad, distracted voice. "Their heads are made from the stretched hides of clinically depressed goats fed nothing but existential poetry. They produce the most doleful sounds imaginable. And that effect is magnified when multiple doldrums are struck concurrently. You, young man," Mr. Orpheus said, pointing at Milton. "To the center of the circle for a *demonstration*."

Milton reluctantly obeyed as Mr. Orpheus claimed Milton's seat.

"On the count of three, class, I want you to smack your doldrums," the teacher instructed. "One . . . two . . . *three*."

Milton's bones rattled as the dispiriting, whooshing throb of the drums drained him of any lingering trace of happiness Snivel had yet to pilfer. Head hung low, Milton stood slumped and shaking.

"As you can see," Mr. Orpheus said, rising, "our unfortunate young scholar hath been adversely affected by the doleful tones of the doldrums."

"Is he okay?" Sara asked with concern.

Mr. Orpheus smiled coldly.

"Yes, the effect is temporary. We can boost his spirits, however, if you like."

Mr. Orpheus plucked a note from his electric lyre.

"Now, miss, sing this tone."

Sara obliged, singing a clear, pure note.

"Now you, dear," the teacher said, nodding to Caterwaul, who nearly swooned after being referred to as "dear." "Sing *this* note."

The teacher plucked another string. Caterwaul, though a little croaky from a lifetime of sobbing, hit the note with eagerness, hoping to impress the ancient Greek poet.

Mr. Orpheus sang in a clear, beautiful tenor, providing the last note in a cheerful three-part harmony. Milton instantly felt better.

"Excellent," Mr. Orpheus commented. "Now take a deep breath and try that again."

Sara and Caterwaul sang their notes again, with the teacher joining in again, only this time a halftone lower. A faint whisper of sadness spread throughout Milton.

"See?" Mr. Orpheus explained, crossing his bare legs. "We went from a major key to a minor, causing vague melancholy. Any number of emotional states can be achieved in this way. A major seventh chord can approximate the wistfulness of unrequited love, as I will demonstrate on the lyre."

The teacher strummed his instrument, filling the tent with nostalgic yearning. The sound of autumn leaves falling to the ground.

"And finally, by moving the fifth note of a minor chord down a half step, we create the most dispiriting chord of all. *The diminished.*"

Mr. Orpheus swept his thumb across his electric lyre. The trembling notes gnashed against one another like gnarled teeth, squeaking with tension and distress. Milton felt himself collapse inside, crushed and crumpled, like a busted piñata bled of candy, left out in the rain to rot.

"Young man," the teacher said as he trudged sluggishly back to the front of the class with weary sandal flops, "you may sit down."

Nauseous with despair, Milton stumbled to his chair, gripping it tight, craving something solid to hold on to, since inside he felt sick and slushy. He felt Sara's hand on his shoulder.

"Are you okay, Milton?" she asked.

"Of course he isn't okay," Sam added with a contemptuous smile. "He's an incurable dweeb."

Milton wiped the sweat off his upper lip.

"Yeah, I'm fine," he replied shakily. "I'm starting to feel more . . . more *myself.*"

"Too bad for you," Sam muttered as he and his sister returned to their seat.

Mr. Orpheus swung his arm like a windmill, striking his electric lyre and summoning a power chord bristling with clangorous force. The students clapped their hands over their ears until the clamor dulled to a crackling drone.

"Each of you will have the opportunity to experience disharmonic, microtonal therapy firsthand," the teacher said as he tuned his lyre with excruciating fastidiousness. "Or first-*ear,* anyway. After multiple sessions, I can guarantee that each of you will realize full musical depreciation, where that once transitory state of melancholy—or light sorrow—will take permanent residence within your souls. Fixed in your disposition, a dullness and vexation of vitality impossible to remove."

At this point, even Caterwaul seemed to have lost the bloom of infatuation with her handsome, sonically sadistic teacher.

"Before our class comes to a close, I'd like to subject you all to my latest decomposition:

"You breathe in the air
And fall with despair . . ."

As Mr. Orpheus tortured the class with his latest disheartening ditty, Milton nudged his desk closer to his fellow students and cleared his throat.

"Meet at lake," Milton said in Remorse code.

Sara leaned toward him.

"When?" she sob-snorted.

"Tonight."

Howler Monkey scratched at his monochrosquito bites, his face almost completely drained of color.

"Why?" he blubbered and sniffed.

Milton shot a quick, hateful glance at Mr. Orpheus, twanging away with narcissistic abandon.

"For you know where
You are:
Nowhere . . ."

Milton cleared his throat and faced the other Unhappy Campers, his eyes burning with determination.

"We're getting out of here."

12 · DROWNiNG THEiR SORROWS

KNEELING AT THE edge of the dock, Milton scribbled onto the bottom of the scroll of now-blank paper.

Yes, I am Milton Fauster.

He rolled up the paper and stuffed it into the bottle. Milton gripped it tightly by the neck and tossed it as hard as he could toward the whirlpool beneath the churning Dukkha Wheel. The bottle was instantly tugged toward the swirling funnel and, after a few agitated bobs, was swallowed up by the gloomy green waters of Lake Rymose.

He stood up and swiped clean his hands.

"Well," he said to his fellow Unhappy Campers

standing beside him on the rotting dock, "I guess all we can do now is—"

"Wait!" Sara squealed, pointing to the wheel. "There's a bottle!"

"It probably just floated back up," Sam said in his deep, cynical rumble of a voice. "This is a complete waste of time."

"No, this one is different," Sara replied. "It's bright gold."

Milton wiped the rain off his glasses and peered into the riot of mist pouring from the Dukkha Wheel. Sara was right: A golden bottle was speeding *away* from the whirlpool toward the shore. Milton fell onto his belly and, outstretched at the edge of the pier, grabbed the bottle that had somehow sped straight to him. He sat on the dock and spanked the bottom of the bottle. Out popped another roll of thick, plasticky paper.

Congratulations, Milton Fauster!! After extensively reviewing your application, we have decided to allow you into the OFFICIAL Arcadia Gr8 G4m3rz Club: the most EXCLUSIVE CLUB in the AFTERLIFE! You are hereby requested to appear—with any uniquely intrepid gamers seeking election that you see fit to sponsor—IMMEDIATELY, if not sooner. Simply follow the arrow included, at no extra charge, at the bottom of this letter. Again—wow—CONGRATULATIONS! You must be quite justifiably envious of yourself!!

The Unhappy Campers crowded around Milton as the note slowly faded, leaving only a red arrow—winking and teasing like a Cheshire cat's grin—pointing straight to the seething whirlpool at the center of Lake Rymose.

"Where do we, like, go?" asked Howler Monkey, breathing loudly through his mouth and into Milton's ear. Milton moved the paper from side to side. The blinking arrow moved in kind, always pointing straight at the Dukkha Wheel.

"The whirlpool it is," Milton said as he rose to his feet.

Caterwaul gaped at the water with distress. "But we'll drown for sure if we try to swim in . . . *that*," she said tremulously, wringing her hands.

Milton scanned the lake. Something bumped against one of the dock's barely-support beams. Jouncing in the water against the decrepit pier were three slimy yellow boats.

"Canoes," he muttered.

Sam/Sara peered over the pier.

"More like can*olds*," Sam replied as he glared in disgust at the mucky, smelly-like-someone-had-vomited-in-a-moldy-sneaker boats.

Milton shrugged as he carefully stepped into one of the canoes. It was unsettlingly squishy, like a hollowed-out mutant banana slug. In fact, the slugs hot-glued to Milton's shirt wriggled as if saying hello to their monstrous new friend.

"There's room for two of us in each," Milton said.

Sam/Sara stepped into a nearby canoe with a gross, wet squish. Caterwaul and the Sunshine Sneezer climbed aboard a boat and pushed off the dock, with Milton and Howler Monkey close behind.

Milton dipped his paddle into the deep-jade waters of Lake Rymose, an eerie glow radiating from its unfathomable depths.

"Are you sure about this?" Sara shouted over the churning groan of the Dukkha Wheel as it wobbled on its wooden axis.

If uncertainty were a city, Milton would surely be its mayor. But somehow, rowing toward a seething vortex with a screeching stone wheel at its center seemed like the right thing to do.

"You saw the note," Milton said. "Before it disappeared, that is. *Arcadia is real.* It's probably where Marlo and all of the other kids are. And this whirlpool is some kind of gateway."

Three shaggy black creatures emerged from the forest. Their paws snapped the willow branches like brittle bones beneath their bulk as they padded to the shore. Milton wiped the thick spray off his glasses but still couldn't clearly make out the dark panting beasts. They were like large, woolly dogs, exhaling a freezing cold despair that chilled his bones. The Sunshine Sneezer looked back quickly over his shoulder at the edge of the lake before attacking the water with his paddle.

"Well, it looks like *that's* settled," he said with a wet snuffle.

The roar of the forty-foot-tall Dukkha Wheel was deafening as each of its eight giant ladles hungrily scooped up the lake's murky, deep-green water. Poking through the rhythmic splashing and sloshing was a gurgling cacophony of blips and bleeps.

Milton's canoe was caught in the outer ring of the foaming whirlpool revolving around the Dukkha Wheel in diminishing orbits. *We'd have to clear the massive ladles to make it to the funnel,* Milton thought. One of the stone dippers snatched up a load of water, rocking the canoe, before revolving away.

"Paddle!" Milton screamed above the noise as he and Howler Monkey rowed furiously toward the center of the whirlpool. The water around them swelled into a black, mountainous ridge. The whoosh of water and spray screamed as the three canoes, now all clear of the ladles, careened round and round toward the middle of the surge.

As his canoe bobbed up into the air, Milton could briefly see the shore. A man tromped out to join the three bushy creatures panting at the edge of the dock.

Vice Principal Poe.

After a wild lurch to starboard, Milton and Howler Monkey, his howls lost over the din, rushed headlong into the abyss, sucked down into the maw of the swirling funnel. Milton's stomach fell victim to the sick-ening sweep of descent.

The sense of falling stopped. Milton slowly wrenched open his eyes. He and his friends seemed to be hanging, as if by magic, midway down the smooth, spinning fun-nel, its sides gleaming and radiant, like a bouquet of green-tinted sunbeams. From below streamed a flood of golden light. Milton turned to look back over his shoul-der. He could see the great wooden axis of the rotating Dukkha Wheel and, beyond, a sky full of twinkling gar-bage. Suddenly, the opening of the tunnel closed with a surge of agitated froth. Round and round, skimming down across the walls of the funnel, Milton and his friends were swept, held tight in the embrace of the whirlpool, swallowed up by the chaos of light and foam.

13 · WHATEVER FLOATS YOUR VOTE

BEA "ELSA" BUBB, the Principal of Darkness, shrieked as she awoke from her nightmare. Her pus-yellow eyes darted frantically about her Not-So-Secret Lair.

The readout of her clock blinked 13:13.

She sighed with relief, her fetid breath dragging her three-headed Hound of Heck, Cerberus, out of his three-fathoms-deep slumber. He licked the air with sleepy laps, hoping to savor the rotting fish-skunk-socks he sensed with his six nostrils.

"School dreams," the principal mumbled. "You never graduate from them." Bea "Elsa" Bubb looked down upon Cerberus and smiled, or at least exhumed her burial site of decaying teeth in an expression approximating pleasure. She scritched Cerberus with her talons just beneath his left jaw, right on the crusted-over sore that never seemed to heal properly.

"Yes, my Prince Harming," she cooed like a pigeon on life support, "maybe we just need a wee whittle snackity-whack in our tummity-tums before we go sleepy-bye." Principal Bubb swooped him up in her arms, kicked on her new Lop Bunny slippers—*still warm*, she thought—and padded out into the darkened hallways of Limbo.

"Hello, Principal Bubb," a simpering demon guard—a cross between a troll doll and an upholstered leather peanut—called out from its post beyond the Teacher's Lounge. "A word about my promotion . . . you know, if you get the job?"

Job? the principal thought. *There it is again. . . .*

The principal held out her arms and fluttered her beady eyes.

"Sleepwalking," she mumbled, inflating an armada of spit bubbles with her sour breath. "Never wake up a sleepwalker."

The demon guard nodded, shaking its greasy rainbow hair.

"Right . . . right. Wait," the guard replied quizzically. "If you're asleep, how come you answered me?"

The Principal of Darkness shuffled away, calling over her jiggly lump of a shoulder, "A coincidence. Am dreaming dream of talking with irritating guard I'm considering transferring to latrine duty: emphasis on *dooty*."

"Oh," the guard mumbled dully as Bea "Elsa" Bubb entered an unmarked room by a burning torch mounted on the wall. Inside was a tastefully decorated den, with a plush couch and decaffeinated coffee table strewn with children's magazines—*Deranger Rick, Lowlights, Rickets,* and a disconnect-the-dots book. The principal set down her displaced lapdog, currently having no lap to call its own, and rubbed her claws together with anticipation.

"Haggis," Principal Bubb murmured as drool dripped down her chin, punctuating her request with a dry, leathery clap of her claws.

Suddenly, the small room was packed tight with the traditional Scottish dish of sheep's guts boiled inside the once-bleating animal's stomach. The principal tucked in with abandon.

Me . . . filling Satan's vacant throne, Bea "Elsa" Bubb chewed over while chewing offal. *Leaving this* Hearsery School *to claim the underworld's ultimate seat of absolute, ripe-for-abusing power . . .*

Having eaten a path from the door to the couch, Principal Bubb's belly ached, her stomach full of stomachs. She lay on the creaking sofa, crossed her hooves, and gazed languidly at the sea of glistening sheep entrails.

But what chance would I have in an honest-to-badness election?

"Principal Bubb?" the simpering demon guard said, his troll peanut head poking through the door. "Are you still asleep? You have a Fretful Distress delivery." He tentatively entered the chamber and set a padded envelope down on the table.

Wiping bits of boiled sheep from her hairy chin, she studied the tiny package, her name written in a tight, exacting script on the front, the return address reading only "A Friend." The paper smelled of ozone, of electricity.

She slit the package open with her index talon and plucked out a small, brass earwig with a metal hook attached on top.

An earring?

Just as Principal Bubb was about to fling the envelope at her guard, out fell a small, gleaming heart-shaped pillow of platinum with a girl's picture inset in the middle.

Principal Bubb cradled the charm in her claws. The principal's goopy, yellow goat eyes fixed on the tiny picture.

"You've *got* to be kidding me," she croaked as the frog in her throat vainly tried to hop out of her mouth. *"Marlo Fauster?"*

The blue-haired girl with the turned-up nose and mischievous Cleopatra eyes smirked back at the principal from the charm.

The principal shrugged and jabbed the hook of the earring into her scabby earlobe. Immediately, the brass earwig began to buzz.

"Principal Bubb," a reedy voice with a vaguely

Eastern European accent spoke from the bug dangling from her ear. *"Hello. I am a charms dealer who has taken an interest in your, shall we say, situation."*

The principal waved her demon guard away.

"Think of me as an invisible puppet master, one who could turn even you into a serious candidate for zhe lowest office in zhe underworld."

Principal Bubb's eyebrows rose like a drawbridge, allowing her steely glare to pass beneath like a warship.

"I can turn something zhat zhe cat refused to drag in into something zhat makes voters sit up and go 'meow,'" the mesmerizing recording continued.

Bubbles of joy tickled the back of Bea "Elsa" Bubb's throat like champagne reflux.

"I won't lie to you. Zhe competition will be as stiff as a boardroom of cadavers. Especially now zhat, according to my sources, Lilith Couture, zhe former devil's advocate, has expressed interest in zhe position."

The principal's insides bungee jumped several thousand feet.

Lilith Couture, the haughty, hawkish companion to Satan, whose gleaming shark-toothed smile had never known unsightly tartar buildup. Even though she had been demoted to mere "teacher" in Rapacia by Chairman Mammon for letting the Hopeless Diamonds be stolen—which had nearly allowed Rapacia's former vice principal, the Grabbit, to create a surely calamitous black hole—the thought of Lilith Couture crawling out of her career crypt with those French-manicured fingers to meddle with Bea "Elsa" Bubb's shot at the big time made every molecule in the principal's loathsome body well up with disgust.

"*But not to worry, Bea,*" the mysterious voice droned soothingly. "*While Ms. Couture has beauty, charm, poise, eloquence, experience, connections, and a keen intellect, you have something even better.*"

"And what's that?" Principal Bubb asked softly.

"*And you may well ask what zhat is,*" the recorded voice continued. "*It's your mediocrity! Here's zhe thing about zhe electorate: You can tax them up to their eyeballs, saddle them with billions in debt, and none of it matters as long as you— just before Election Day—serve them up some idealized carica- ture of themselves. If you do, John 'Corpse' Public will vote you into whatever office you like simply because your homespun, plainspoken villainy reminds him of . . . him. Zhat's what zhe broken, maddening masses want, after all: something they don't have to aspire to. Something they already are.*"

Principal Bubb, her eye slits sparkling with kindled ambition, scratched just under the place her lips should have been.

"Who *are* you?" she murmured to herself.

"*Think of me as a friend,*" the voice buzzed. "*A little bug in your ear zhat's obsessed with zhe mess zhat is you. You'll need a makeover, of course. A make-all-over.*"

The principal self-consciously patted her scraggly clumps of kelplike hair.

"There's a little salon I know zhat gives zhe best Marie Antoinette treatments—total head removal. But I don't think we have to go zhat far. Presenting you as an appealing 'friend of zhe dead' won't be easy. Far from it. But I love a good challenging lump of clay to work with. And you are zhe lumpiest lump I have ever encountered. I'll be in touch with more motivational messages."

The earwig earring gave one last rattling remark.

"You won't forget me when you're zhe next Big Guy—excuse me, Gal Downstairs, will you?" The recording cut out to the hum of static.

A grin spread across Bea "Elsa" Bubb's face like an incurable rash. She hadn't felt this good since before Milton Fauster's baffling arrival in Heck. She sighed and gave one of Cerberus's sleeping heads a distracted pat. But, with Milton and his unruly sister secure in Snivel, the Principal of Darkness wouldn't be unduly distracted by a pair of infuriating Fausters. Instead, she could throw her full weight, of which there was plenty, to the task at hand: becoming the power-drunk ruler of h-e-double-hockey-sticks.

14 · CLUBBED INTO SUBMISSION

THE FIRST THING Milton felt as he regained consciousness was an incredible, tingling warmth prickling his face and arms. And even though his eyes were closed, he awoke to a brilliant orange light streaming through his eyelids, like a pair of glowing tiger's eyes staring back at him through fading purple bars. Next, as each of his senses came back online, a tidal wave of electronic chirps, bleeps, gloinks, warbles, and static blasts washed over him.

It sounds like I'm at R2-D2's family reunion, Milton thought sluggishly. He stirred, wet sand squishing between his fingers, and heaved himself up onto his elbows.

He opened his eyes to daggers of golden light piercing his retinas. His pupils cinched closed like the fists of a greedy baby.

"Oww!" he groaned, vainly trying to shield his eyes from the intense honey light that seemed to ooze from everywhere. Milton could make out beside him the shimmering shapes of his friends as they slowly came to on the sands of some blazing bright shore. The Sunshine Sneezer sneezed himself awake.

"The light . . . the light," he mumbled.

"Are you all okay?" Milton asked, his head growing strangely dizzy with each breath.

A strange, muffled voice boomed above him.

"Concern for his team," the hollow voice rattled. "He'll be perfect for the collaboration-based multi-players."

Milton looked up. Bathed in a rippling apocalyptic radiance, as if lit by a perpetual nuclear explosion from above, were eleven fidgety figures, all wearing khaki shorts, berets, sashes festooned with colorful badges, and silver gas masks. The tall figure at the front took off its mask. She was a large girl with dark, gleaming hair. The gas mask dangled by a corrugated tube hooked to a wheezing bellows clipped onto the girl's belt.

"Well, well, look what the tide brought in," the girl said, glowering with wide, crazy-dark eyes as her comrades crossed their arms defiantly.

"Invasion *FAIL*," a spry, red-haired boy said.

"*Invasion?*" Milton said, his voice slurred. "We're not—"

One by one, the figures took off their masks until,

crowding around the dazed and damp Unhappy Campers, there was a row of stern boys and girls, their faces spasming with more nervous ticks than an overcaffeinated grandfather clock. The children suddenly erupted with laughter.

"*Epic!*" the red-haired boy laughed, his voice braying, unhinged, like a preteen hyena.

The large girl offered her hand to Milton and tugged him swiftly to his feet.

"Welcome to Arcadia, Nanowatt Plebe," she said in a husky voice. "I'm Numero Uno. Number One. Also known as Tasha. Leader of the Zetawatts."

The red-haired boy moved to shake Milton's hand but instead stopped short and gave him a sort of fist bump with a wiggling thumb.

"I'm Zetawatt Number Two: I know—gross!—don't flush me!" the boy cackled breathlessly. "You can call me Wyatt!"

An Italian girl helped Sam/Sara to their feet.

"Whoa! Two for the price of one!" she giggled, her left eye twitching up a storm. "Libby. Zetawatt, Level Three."

As Milton's eyes adjusted to the brightness, he began to recognize some of the children from the HAVE YOU SEEN ME? posters back in Camp Snivel. Seeing their faces was like meeting Facebook friends in the real world: strangely familiar but mostly just strange. It's like he shared some imaginary bond with them.

"You're the missing kids from Camp Snivel," he said. "Did you all get here like we did? Through the whirlpool in Lake Rymose? Is Marlo here? My sister?"

Tasha, Wyatt, and Libby smirked as they were joined by a skinny, serious-looking girl with long dark hair clipped neatly with a barrette.

"Hazelle . . . Gigawatt, Level One," the girl said, giving Milton that weird fist bump/thumb-wrestling move while never taking her intense blue eyes off his. "Only Provost Marshal Tesla is authorized to answer these types of questions, according to the *Arcadia Handbook*, chapter twelve, paragraph nine."

"Gigawatts," muttered Libby under her breath to Milton. "Always memorizing the tutorial before they play . . . terminally spunk-deprived. Zero Zetawatt potential."

Milton was now fully awake. In fact, he seemed kind of energized somehow, his head clear and sharp.

"I need to see my sister," he said, feeling as if he was on the verge of hyperventilating. His head started to throb. "What's with the light?" He looked up at the sky.

"Don't look up!" the Arcadians yelled, with Tasha grabbing Milton's head and covering his eyes. "If you want to see First Fire, you've got to use the smoked mirror."

Hazelle grabbed a dark compact from her utility belt and flipped it open.

"Here," she said crisply as Tasha uncovered Milton's face. "Look down."

Reflected in the smoked mirror was a sizzling ball of glorious fire.

"First Fire?" Milton murmured. "What's—"

Milton stumbled, his hands and feet tingling. A big, round-faced boy with a dark brown crew cut caught him under the arms before he fell.

"We need to get him a mask," the boy said to Tasha. "He's getting too much oxygen."

"Oxygen?" Milton replied, rubbing his temples.

"It feeds the First Fire," Wyatt added before he was hushed by Hazelle's scolding look.

"Hazelle's right—we need to take them to Provost Marshal Tesla," Libby said, her freckled cheeks flushed.

Hazelle crossed her arms as she glared at her comrades, her deep-blue eyes framed by blinking LED lights.

"They can't enter the compound until they take the Gr8 G4m3rz Pledge," she said sternly. "You all know that. It clearly says as much in the manual, chapter four, paragraph three—"

"Yeah, yeah," Tasha said as she took a long gold joystick from her utility belt. "Got it. And can you just say 'Great Gamers' instead of spelling out all that 'Gr8— G4m' stuff? This is taking up too much of our fragtime as it is."

"Agreed," Wyatt added shakily, biting his twitching lower lip. "I was racking up a *serious* body count in *Denizen Turpitude*."

Tasha held out the golden joystick.

"If you Nanowatt Plebes would grasp the Controller of Lightning-Quick Response . . ."

The Unhappy Campers glanced at one another before shrugging and coiling their hands—fist over fist—around the joystick.

"Repeat after me," Tasha ordered, with the disoriented Milton, Sam/Sara, Caterwaul, Howler Monkey, and the Sunshine Sneezer following obediently.

"On my honor, I will fulfill my duty to the Great Game. To play with the utmost aim, purpose, cunning, and resolve, no matter what gaming platform, what level earned, what character selected, or what armament provided. I believe the Arcadia Great Gamers Club to be the ultimate cheat code to mastering my own powers and targeting the ultimate use for my talents. I humbly offer my rank and influence to the Great Game, in my communities—both virtual and real—and in my contact with others, regardless of avatar attributes, quality of powers, and quantity of lives. To this, I pledge my sacred honor."

Tasha holstered her joystick.

"By repeating this pledge before your fellow Arcadians," the tall, wild-eyed girl said solemnly, "you have thusly *become* an Arcadian, sealing your eternal loyalty to the source code of the Arcadia Great Gamers Club."

The eleven veteran Arcadians donned their gas masks and leveled their fingers, pointed like guns, at the new recruits.

"Welcome, Nanowatt Noobs," they chanted as they emptied their finger guns into the skulls of the freshly initiated. "*BOOM!* Headshot!!"

The sun above flared, then grew temporarily dim. After a few seconds, it returned to its normal sizzle.

Tasha bit her upper lip as she stared at the blazing globe through her smoked mirror.

"It's almost game time. And this ain't no beta."

Milton looked back over his shoulder as the group marched up the steep knoll of ludicrously green grass. Each blade was perfectly uniform, swaying in a meticulous choreography, like the waves of a flawless green sea.

He and the other Unhappy Campers had taken an after-death-defying dive to the bottom of Lake Rymose only to emerge, somehow, on the shores of another lake. While Lake Rymose had been murky, stagnant, and cold, this *new* lake was a warm, boisterous, clear blue lagoon that was positively Jacuzzi-like. *Probably due to Arcadia's miniature sun,* Milton thought. *First Fire, they call it.*

He watched the sun's reflection, broken apart into gleaming orange diamonds by the surface of the turbulent lake. It had a discomforting energizing effect, like one of those seasonal affective disorder lamps set on "kill." This lake also had no Dukkha Wheel. *That would explain why we're all marching practically straight uphill and none of us are even winded. It's like walking on the moon. Every step is kind of . . . bouncy.*

"Dude, do you need to borrow my gas mask?" Wyatt asked as he tromped beside him.

"No, I'm good," Milton replied. "The extra oxygen is kind of invigorating—"

"Yeah, until it fuzzes you out inside," Wyatt said. "But you get used to it . . . though you still have to be careful. That's why we have the masks. You start to feel too epic, like your head is going to float off your body."

"Still, it feels great after Snivel. The air there was so stale and dead . . . like breathing a moldy bagel."

"That's 'cuz Arcadia siphons out lots of the oxygen from there, to help feed the First Fire."

"Seriously?!" Milton replied, aghast. "That's unbeliev—"

They cleared the top of the grassy knoll, revealing a dazzling compound comprised of massive, vividly colored buildings. The noise sucker punched Milton in the head. A steady IV gush of video-game sounds surged into Milton's ears as his brain struggled to define the vibrant hues rushing like a frenzied mob through his eyes.

"—able."

The nearest building was fifty feet tall, bright yellow and the spitting image of Pac-Man. It was connected to a row of red, turquoise, lavender, and golden ghost-monster structures by a tunnel broken up by blinking yellow "pac-dot" rooms. Beyond those was a cluster of red-and-white-spotted mushroom towers with smaller space-invader-shaped formations radiating an eerie green glow at their stems. Along the rim of the knoll across the lake was a long, bright-red centipede building surrounded by a colony of other familiarly shaped structures, such as a neon-blue hedgehog, several dark-green frogs, what simply *had* to be a golden Q*bert building, and—barely visible from the glare—a pair of Italian plumbers at the feet of a gargantuan gorilla skyscraper, with the ape, a red tie cinched around its neck, holding up a coliseum-sized dome. Milton noticed that many of the buildings had similar domes, connected with snaking tubeways and frosted with rows of sparkling solar panels.

Weird, Milton thought. *The underworld is the* last *place I'd expect to run on solar energy.*

The downy hair on Milton's forearms began to rise. Wyatt's red hair reached up to the sky around his Arcadia beret, like a fuzzy flower opening to the sun. In fact, *everyone's* hair began to stick up. Just then, bolts of white-purple chain lightning streaked across the sky from a tower in the distance, looming over the Pac-Man building like a brooding, electromagnetic bully.

"What's that?" Milton asked, pointing his spiky arm at the structure: a rounded, copper-colored high-rise with a silver, saucer-shaped top. It hummed and crackled like a humongous hive of burning bees.

Wyatt smirked impishly.

"The Coil," he replied. "Otherwise known as the place you're headed to."

Hazelle sidled up to the boys, straightening her badge-bedecked sash and beret.

"Its *official* name is Provost Marshal Tesla's Mainframe."

Her blue eyes, glittering with the blinking lights of Arcadia, gazed at the tower with a mixture of awe and fear.

"And, judging from the fireworks, he's all juiced up for your arrival."

15 · iNSANiTY iS THE FATHER OF iNVENTiON

MILTON'S MIND REELED as the glass elevator shot up the side of the tower. Arcadia unfolded before him, all streaking colors, glitter, noise, and possibility. It was all too bright, too exciting, too loud, too . . . *everything.*

"The First Fire," Milton murmured to himself, sent alone to see Provost Marshal Tesla. He glanced up at the elevator's smoked-glass roof, the great ball of flame sputtering above. "It must be what makes this place so *overstimulating.*"

His thoughts tumbled like mismatched socks in the dryer. Just when Milton latched on to one, it was consumed by the chaotic swirl of his buzzing brain.

The elevator stopped abruptly, pitching Milton's stomach somewhere out past the top of his head. The doors opened, overwhelming the elevator with the peppery-wet smell of ozone.

"Provost Marshal Tesla," Milton mumbled, his head burning like a hibachi. "*Tesla* . . . of course." It helped Milton to verbalize his jumbled thoughts. "Electrical engineer and . . . inventor . . . nineteenth century . . . I think I did . . . a report on him. . . ."

Milton stepped out of the elevator and into a large, rounded penthouse. Arcs of surging blue-white electricity pulsated back and forth from tall copper posts like a game of high-voltage hot potato. Needlelike shocks pricked Milton's face, neck, and arms.

"Hello?" Milton called out as he walked tentatively across a singed Victorian throw rug toward a massive metal object, blurred by the blinding flashes of light. "Provost Marshal? You wanted to see me? Alone? To meet, face to . . . ?"

Head. The object was a huge bronze head resting on its side.

Milton stared at the enormous bronze sculpture and, through its hollowed-out eyes, saw a slim figure inside.

Milton walked around to the head's open neck. With the sculpture's metal beard, prominent nose, and stern expression of torment, it seemed Greek (though most every sculpture looked Greek to Milton). A man's mumbling voice reverberated from inside the bronze head.

Milton rapped his knuckles against the sculpture's neck, his tap amplified by the hollow head until it pealed like a church bell. Milton could see the man now, reclining back in a gauzy web of electrical tendrils, with a throbbing purple neon tube hanging down the front of his shirt like a tie. The man, Provost Marshal Tesla, flicked open his dark, sparkling eyes. Milton gasped. His face was like a crazy person's math homework, his features subtly mismatched and crooked, yet arranged with a cryptic precision. The lines etched around his eyes and mouth made them seem somehow parenthetically contained like the factors of an algebraic equation puzzled out in flesh.

"Um, sorry, I . . ." Milton quavered as the static electricity coursing through the head made his hair stand on end. "There wasn't a door."

Provost Marshal Tesla reached for a dial beneath two glowing vacuum tubes. The web of electricity sputtered before dying out to nothing but a weak mist of tingling ozone.

"A door?" Provost Marshal Tesla replied, his mustache fanning out beneath his nose like a sleek, black moth. "I need a door in this thing like I need a hole in zhe head." Tesla stepped out of the bronze head, extending his hand in greeting. Milton shook it, then jumped back in shock. "Milton Fauster," he said. "I've been waiting for you. I am Provost Marshal Tesla."

He quickly straightened his purple neon tie-tube.

"You and I are soldered to zhe same circuit board," Tesla continued in a clipped, mile-a-minute Serbian accent. *"Exceptionally sensitive.* I could hear zhe ticking of a watch from three rooms away, and a fly alighting on a table caused a dull thud in my ears. And you—such initiative! Zhe first child to ever escape from Heck—"

"What is this place?" Milton interrupted, his eyes traveling quickly around the circular penthouse. Its curved windows afforded breathtaking views of Arcadia's dazzling landscape.

Tesla smirked. "This is my Rumination Nook where, due to optimal voltage, I do my best, most lucid thinking. Zhe scientists of today think deeply instead of clearly. One must be sane to think clearly, but one can think deeply and be quite insane—"

"No," Milton broke in. "Not this specific place but—"

"It's fashioned after zhe head of Prometheus, who stole fire from zhe hearth of Zeus and gave it to mortals," Tesla continued, patting down his bat-wing hair that seemed poised to flap away at the slightest provocation. "This fire gave man dominion over beasts. They no longer shivered in zhe cold of night. Animals dared not attack. It was zhe ultimate game changer. Though its flames have been passed along for centuries, nothing can match zhe burning intensity and blazing clarity of zhat first fire."

"First Fire," Milton murmured. "That ball of blinding flame above that seems to power this place."

"Yes! You are understanding!" Tesla exclaimed. "Zhe name Prometheus means zhe 'foresight.' Zhe predicting of what will be needed in zhe future. After teaching humanity how to use zhe fire—there were a lot of singed monkey paws—Prometheus invented mathematics, architecture, metalworking, writing . . . *progress*. Zhe spread of civilization may be likened to zhe fire. First, there is a feeble spark, next, a flickering flame—insights to solutions in want of problems—then mighty blaze, ever increasing in speed and power."

Milton breathed deeply to calm his jittery nerves. His attention span could scarcely bridge one thought to the next.

"But Arcadia—"

"For this, Zeus punished Prometheus, chaining him to a rock where an eagle picked painfully at his liver every day, only to have it grow back again each night. Like mankind needs another reason not to like zhe liver."

"WHY AM I HERE?!" Milton shouted, unable to endure being talked over, his head full of thrashing thoughts.

"Zhe ultimate question!" Provost Marshal Tesla cried out as he rocked back and forth in his seat with an almost unbearable excitement. "You are here, Milton Fauster, because you are vital to zhe success of Arcadia!"

"Me?" Milton replied. Lucky wriggled in his backpack before settling back to sleep. "Why?"

"In my lifetime above on zhe Surface, I held zhe patents for over three hundred innovations zhat defined zhe twentieth century and set zhe stage for zhe next," Tesla replied as he rubbed his eyes, which seemed both frighteningly awake and impossibly tired. "But nothing could hold a candle—or Edison's feeble lightbulb—to Arcadia."

Milton scratched at the electric prickles nagging his arms.

"The Great Gamers Club," he interjected, exasperated and agitated. "I found an invitation in Camp Snivel, then an entry exam where the only question was my name. If you wanted me here, why go through all the trouble?"

Provost Marshal Tesla stood, extending his imposing six-foot-four-inch frame with a stretch.

"So zhat *you* would go through zhe trouble." Tesla smirked slyly. "You see, escaping from Snivel to Arcadia *was zhe entry exam*. It proved your worth. Your fortitude, ingenuity, and ability to inspire others."

"But I'm a loner," Milton replied with a dispirited shrug. "I've never inspired anything but wedgies and merciless teasing."

"Do you like being part of a team?" Provost Marshal interjected.

Milton thought back upon his miserable time at Camp Snivel and how the companionship of his fellow Unhappy Campers had made the experience somewhat bearable.

"Sure."

"Well, do you know what they call a loner who likes being part of a team?"

"No."

"*A leader,*" the strikingly thin man answered. "Gifted with zhe ability to galvanize individuals yet still, somehow, always standing apart. Alone. Perfect for tactical shooters or role-playing games. You know what happens if you're always thinking about Number One?"

"No, what?"

"You find yourself deep in Number Two . . ."

"But what about Marlo?" Milton replied, scratching his neck. "My sister . . . ?"

Tesla climbed out of his Rumination Nook.

"She—and others like her—are not Arcadia material," he said dismissively as Milton followed behind him, the man strutting about with hungry steps. "Undisciplined rogues and spineless whiners do *not* make for great gamers. You and your friends, however, are determined and resourceful. You acknowledge zhe rules even as you break them. And every game needs rules."

Provost Marshal Tesla stood before the expansive polarized window of his penthouse and took in the sweeping vista of Arcadia.

"A game without rules has no purpose. Is no fun," he said, the electric crackle leaving his voice, the pace of his words relaxing to merely hectic. "A game without rules is . . . *life.* At least as it is now. Before everything changes . . ."

Tesla turned swiftly on his heels. His dark, glittering eyes were bracketed by deep creases, his gaze boring into Milton. Milton trembled with uncomfortable energy.

"We have an understanding, no?" he said. "I have given you and your friends extra points, but you have many levels to best. Report to HQ-Bert so zhat your clothes and personal effects can be disposed of. You'll then be fitted for your uniform."

Milton swallowed. He could feel Lucky's warmth burning into his back.

"D-disposed of?" he croaked. "My backpack has lots of . . . medicine. For my allergies."

Provost Marshal Tesla smiled. The ebony wings of his mustache fluttered briefly above his lips.

"There are no allergies here. Have you felt anything less than robust since your arrival?"

Milton, although a hive of uneasy energy, *did* feel healthier, more awake, than he had ever before.

"No . . . I guess not. But my backpack is important to me. It has . . . *lucky things in it*. Things that help me win games. I know it's superstitious, but it works. I rack up some serious points just knowing that—"

"All right, all right," Tesla said with a twinge of fatigue, rippling his long, articulated fingers toward Milton like bony white tarantulas. "I will keep it here, though. Zhe games are meticulously calibrated. I don't want artifacts from zhe outside confusing zhe advanced technologies therein."

Milton nodded. Out of the corner of his eye, he saw a pulsating cord of glowing light leading to a phone installed at the back of the penthouse.

Just like in Vice Principal Poe's Conversation Pit and Pendulum.

As Tesla returned to his Rumination Nook, Milton unhooked his backpack and laid it on the floor outside the bronze head. Inside, Lucky lay sleeping, his slack jaws wrapped around Mr. van Gogh's severed ear. Milton saw the small brass disk inside the ear's canal. He dug it out with his finger.

Milton had an idea.

He cinched his backpack closed and set it by Prometheus's nose. Milton put the brass disk inside his left ear and grabbed his former art teacher's amputated auditory organ.

"Marlo always said if something sounds too good to be true, it probably is," Milton mumbled as he jumped up alongside the bronze head and slapped the ear just below the sculpted lobe of Prometheus, where it stuck like a suction cup. "This way I can keep my eyes on the game and my ears—*all three of them*—on Tesla."

16 · A LEVELED PLAYiNG FiELD

FROM THE INSIDE, Arcadia didn't just *look* like a dazzling, droning den of intensely focused video gamesmanship, Milton thought as he was led through the first gaming level at the mezzanine of the Donkey Koncourse. It looked as if he was actually *inside* a video game. Right down to the strewn rubble, abandoned cars, and grated metal catwalks that encircled the smoked-glass atrium.

"Level One," Hazelle said, marching in perfect step to a disciplined drumbeat inside her head before allowing her stern face a peeved smirk. "Mostly vector-based, eight-bit twitch games . . . not that you'll spend much time here, considering all of the points Provost Marshal Tesla gave you—"

"We *earned* them," Milton clarified testily. "As part

of our escape, according to Tesla. And where are my friends?"

"*Provost Marshal* Tesla," Hazelle replied tartly. "In any case, we all got here the same way you did, just not all together. As a team. So . . . *brazenly.*"

Wyatt, with his nervous, elfin demeanor, appeared at Milton's side.

"W00t, huh?!" he laughed, his bloodshot eyes rimmed dark from lack of sleep. He leaned in close to Milton. "Don't mind her . . . and some of the other kids. Okay, all of them. I think it's EPIC that you guys shot up your wattage in just a twinge. It gives us all something to shoot for—something that won't shoot back, that is!"

Milton took a sip from the canteen hooked onto his thick belt. The drink tasted like an intensely sweet, over-carbonated blend of Staminade, Iced AnxieTea, and Beverageous! power drinks. He wiped the neon-purple dribble from his quivering lips.

The last thing I need is more nervous energy. But I feel like a hummingbird, my metabolism cranked into fifth gear, craving sugar water for fuel. I'm nearly jumping out of my skin.

"It's made from Hypool-Active Overstimu Lake water," Wyatt interjected as he took a greedy swig from his canteen. "You know . . . the lake we all came through. First Fire gives it a seriously supremium kick! Provost Marshal Tesla says it has something to do with the blue-green algae, mixed with hecka sug 'n' caff."

Hazelle shot the prattling Wyatt her patented TMI

look. To her, information was a form of currency that had to be earned through hard work, not doled out like free samples at a supermarket.

All of the Arcadians, Milton noticed, were wound tighter than a midget's banjo. And they looked like they hadn't slept in weeks but were somehow keen and hyperalert, though tense and a little smeary around the edges.

"You didn't tell me where my friends are," Milton said, staring into Hazelle's blue eyes.

She sighed, her cold shoulders melting one or two degrees Fahrenheit. "Your friends are—"

"Here!" Sara called out.

Milton turned.

There, in their tailored Arcadia uniforms, were Sam/Sara, Howler Monkey, the Sunshine Sneezer, and Caterwaul. Milton tugged self-consciously at his shorts. Everything about his Arcadia uniform, from his fitted ankle socks to his snug beret, was so contoured to not interfere with gaming that it almost felt like he wasn't wearing anything.

"H-E-Y," Milton said in Remorse code, smiling through the sobs and snorts.

Sara dragged her smiling eyes from the distracting rows of video games and gave Milton a friendly wink. Sam was semiawake on her shoulder, surfing the crest of another narcoleptic episode.

They all looked different. Shiny and edgy, like a set of serrated knives. Not saggy, soggy, and defeated like back in Snivel.

Caterwaul's cheeks were dry and Howler Monkey's mouth, while still slack, was now at least in sync with the jaw-dropping sights around him.

"Sunshine Sneezer," Milton said. "Your eyes aren't red and your nose isn't running."

"Yeah," the boy replied with a grin. "My allergies cleared up the second we got here."

"If I were your nose," Sam said, slurring his words, "I'd keeping running until I was as far from your face as possible."

Sara rolled her eyes.

"So how was it with Tesla?" she asked. "Isn't it awesome that we got all those points just for showing up—"

"It's *Provost Marshal* Tesla," Hazelle interrupted, "and it's time to show you Level Two." She led the group up the dimpled metal stairs connecting the mountainous domed gaming hive. "Mostly sims: life sims, vehicle sims, construction and management sims, even *sim* sims."

The level was lined with dozens of large, blocky metal capsules thrashing about on noisy hydraulic platforms. The sound of gunshots and yelling pierced the mechanical veil of whooshing pneumatics and whirring accelerators. Milton scratched the side of his neck, his skin still prickling from the heightened electromagnetic atmosphere, as he and his former Unhappy Campers followed Hazelle to the next level of games.

"Tesla was just kind of welcoming me, I guess," Milton said, leaning in to Sara. "And he told me all about First Fire."

Milton's voice couldn't compete with the lion's din of computerized mayhem they were entering. It was like World War 2.0.

"And this, Level Three," Hazelle said with a dismissive sniff, "is reserved for FPS games." She paused to clarify, even though—with all the rifles and merry mayhem—this level's purpose was perfectly clear. "First-person shooters."

In terms of gaming preference, Milton was not necessarily the pixel-packin' gunslinger type. He could hold his own with a virtual weapon, but the chaos of close-quarters combat and frantic firefights made Milton go numb, his killer instinct running AWOL. He was a decent sniper, though. There was something almost murderously Zen about lurking on the edge of the action and just cherry-picking. It was like taking fatal free throws.

A line of Gr8 G4m3rz lined the level, their straight backs to Milton and the other Unhappy Campers, each occupying a gaming station with monklike intensity (save for intermittent, bloodcurdling whoops of delight). Their silhouettes were haloed with dancing oranges and reds from frag grenades and Molotov cocktails.

Hazelle turned to the Unhappy Campers, arms outstretched at her sides like a stewardess demonstrating how hugging your seat will somehow protect you from a plane crash.

"Level Four: strategy games and RPGs—role-playing games," Hazelle said as she climbed the stairs, her shiny patent-leather shoes tapping the metal in measured steps. "That's where you'll be spending the bulk of your game time, as per Provost Marshal Tesla's instructions."

The tour settled on the upper catwalk, surrounded by gaming quads with clusters of wide, wraparound high-definition screens. With cinematic sweep and remarkable texture, the displays depicted lush vistas with startling clarity. One of the games, *Holy Temple Raider,* featured a stately religious sanctuary glittering in red sunlight, resplendent with hundreds of turrets and minarets. It looked magical, like the handiwork of countless fairies and gnomes working conjointly. They walked past game after game: *Catho-strophic Combat, Presby-terror Assault, Episcopalooza!, Pentecostal Fantasy IV* . . .

"Why are all the games religious?" Milton asked.

"Provost Marshal Tesla feels that gamers play harder if a game is aligned with their personal belief systems," Hazelle explained. "They tend to play *for keeps.*"

"What if you don't *have* a belief system?"

"Then *that's* the game for you," Wyatt interjected, attached to Milton like Velcro to a poodle.

He pointed to a nearby quad of black screens, the darkest black Milton had ever seen.

"*Game Over: The Atheist Game,*" Wyatt said quickly. "It's the hardest game in Arcadia."

"Why?"

"If you lose even once, that's it: The screen goes, like, the pitchest black ever, and you're locked out. Forever."

Milton noticed a group of Indian boys playing a game called *Hindu or Die.* "What's that game all about?"

"It's EPIC," Wyatt interjected. "The colors are the *awesomest* with all sorts of cool realms, like Kali-Fornia and Shiva Las Vegas. Best of all, if you die, you just come back as something else. One game I came back as a dung beetle because of the morally questionable things I did in my previous game as a human."

Ahead was a quad of games unique in that all of the four gaming consoles had, instead of chairs, little prayer rugs, and they all faced the same direction.

"*Mega Mecca Mania,*" Hazelle announced.

"How come—" Milton began before Wyatt, lacking the patience to allow a question to be fully posed, chimed in.

"Muslim game. EPIC. All the consoles face the Muslim holy city of Mecca, for flawless gaming unity."

"Can you just play, you know, any game you want?" Howler Monkey asked.

"Yes—" Wyatt replied before Hazelle interjected.

"And no. Only the games Provost Marshal Tesla authorizes will accrue points."

"And what's the point of playing a game without points?" Wyatt laughed.

Four jittery boys puzzled over a quad of games labeled *Mormonster Attack!*

"Mormon game," Hazelle said out of the side of her mouth as she led the tour crisply down the aisle, on some secret schedule dictated by her hyperefficient metabolism. "Don't ask me what it's about. You find a book, and if you lose, you're forgiven, sometimes, and if you win, you get your own planet or universe or one of three heavenly kingdoms or something. No one can quite figure it out, but the players are really, really polite."

Next along the catwalk that wound inside the dome-shaped building was a quad of games crowded with celebrity avatars.

"*ScientoloG-Force,*" Hazelle said. "Another hard game to explain, much less play. It's sort of a sci-fi strategy game with 'point-and-clique' elements. Lots of aliens, volcanoes, and celebrities. The key is to know the right people . . . which should be second nature for you newbies."

Milton rolled his eyes at Hazelle's innuendo that he and his friends were the recipients of some sort of favoritism. Milton didn't care about scores or status or pleasing Provost Marshal Tesla. He was just happy— *almost giddy*—to be out of Snivel.

He turned away from the fray and looked off past the steel railing down into the dimly lit Donkey Koncourse.

Three levels were tiered below, with splotches of brilliant light radiating like a captive aurora borealis. Dramatic swells of pulse-pounding music and flocks of synthesized bleeps and blasts spilled out into the arena. Milton looked above. The building was capped with a black metal ceiling. He traced the path of the stairs upward, ending abruptly at a hatch embedded in the roof.

But this is only Level Four, Milton thought. *The note I found in Lake Rymose said there were five levels of Arcadia. Where is the rest of the arcade?*

Hazelle appeared at Milton's side. "No deviating from the tour," she scolded.

"Where is Level Five?" Milton asked. Hazelle glared over her shoulder with eyes the color of the sky just before it becomes space. Milton sighed and raised his hand.

"Where is Level Five?"

Hazelle glanced up at the ceiling with a near-religious reverence.

"*Up there,*" she replied, pointing across the expanse with her nose to the hatch. "The highest status level of them all. The top of the accumulated-score-and-social-position pyramid."

"But what's it like?" Milton asked with a curiosity that burned so hot inside his chest that he broke out in a sweat.

"SPOILER ALERT," Provost Marshal Tesla said from behind them, his voice like a fresh peal of thunder. Hazelle, Wyatt, and the other Arcadians stood at attention, giving their leader a fist-bump-with-wiggling-thumb salute.

"Let us just say it is zhe Valhalla of gaming," Tesla continued. Tasha—arms crossed, face as unreadable as homework after it goes through the wash—appeared by his side. "A game so intense zhat, once played, *you may never play another.*"

Tesla's mustache fell to one side like an unevenly stacked bookshelf. His expression seemed to flow with alternating currents, one charismatic and forthcoming and the other darkly guarded. Tesla rubbed his spindle-fingered hands together.

"But, alas, zhe Sense-o-Rama—Level Five—is only for Zetawatts," he said, his purple neon tie glowing with what Milton assumed was pride. "And is currently awaiting its first team for its inaugural game."

Tasha, Wyatt, Libby, and two other Zetawatts exchanged glances packed tight with trepidation and excitement.

"But I have a feeling—right about zhe base of my spine—zhat you lot are next in line," Provost Marshal

Tesla added, nodding toward Milton and his friends. "Zhe next team of truly 'great gamers,' led by zhe only boy to ever escape from Heck . . ."

Tesla sighed, a static-filled sound that made the hairs on the back of Milton's neck rise.

"Like a flash of lightning, an instant of truth, zhe technology to create zhe ultimate gaming environment was revealed to me. And, with similar rapidity, I set about its construction. *Edison* would have probably tested his creation while opportunity whizzed past like confetti in a windstorm. But why waste precious time testing when zhe *players* can find zhe bugs for you?"

I should sneak back to Tesla's penthouse to rescue Lucky, Milton thought as the tall, gaunt inventor—gesticulating wildly like a marionette beset with termites—went off on his tangential tirade.

But maybe I could just play a few *games first,* Milton considered, biting his lower lip, his hands balled up into fists with tense, nervous energy. *I'm sure Lucky's just asleep, anyway. There's plenty of time for me to get him back . . . plenty of time . . .*

"Sense-o-Rama?" Sara interjected when Provost Marshal Tesla had taken a rare breath.

The man's eyes glittered with secret knowledge. "Ahh . . . my bad, as you say. I don't want to leak too much and affect your . . . *experience.* I will just say zhat gameplay is driven by *sensation* rather than story line.

An all-consuming, nonverbal poem zhat you both experience and engender. Zhe Sense-o-Rama allows players to lose themselves to zhe game like never before."

As if a switch had gone off in his brain, Provost Marshal Tesla turned suddenly to leave.

"But I have taken away enough of your game time," he said from the stairs, giving the ceiling a fleeting, adoring look one might give someone they were deeply, shamelessly, in love with. "You will need all of your senses sharp if you are to survive the Sense-o-Rama."

He stopped short on the stairway.

"Zhe game, I mean . . . of course."

Tesla turned to the five Zetawatts.

"It's time."

The Arcadians nodded with grave anticipation, following Provost Marshal Tesla up the stairs to the ceiling. With a swish of his card key, the hatch fell open. The children stepped inside. As soon as they passed through, Tesla sealed the hatch behind them.

"Play well," he murmured as he descended the staircase, walking past Level Four, lost in his thoughts. Hazelle followed, swept away in Tesla's wake, leaving Milton and the Unhappy Campers to themselves.

"I guess the tour's over," Caterwaul said with a shrug.

Milton found that his fingers were, inexplicably, twitching. So were the restless digits of his friends.

"We might as well, you know . . . ," the Sunshine

Sneezer said, his eyes reflecting a nearby game called *Tarnished Halo Storm*. "Play."

"Yeah." Milton nodded as he spied an open quad. "How about *that* one?"

Milton, Sam/Sara, Caterwaul, and the Sunshine Sneezer sat down at the gaming quad.

"That's okay." Howler Monkey nodded, hovering over the Sunshine Sneezer's shoulder. "I'll watch and switch out with one of you later."

Milton wrapped his hands around the controls. They felt . . . right. Like they were made for him.

Welcome, Milton Fauster, the screen blinked back at him. *Would you like to play?*

Milton nodded reflexively. The game somehow acknowledged this by switching into play mode.

The Unhappy Campers were a grubby group of heavily armored angels parting a valley of varicolored grass, many peculiar shades of which Milton had trouble assigning names to.

The model fidelity and motion control were flawless. No "jankiness" at all. And the more Milton played, the more connected with the characters and the world they inhabited he became. The action was intense and fiercely competitive, with Milton fighting alongside his friends in Team Play mode. Together, they were unstoppable: their movements, their thoughts, their reflexes in total sync.

It was the best game Milton had ever played. A little

run-and-gun with clever stealth elements. As Milton moved through the game's world—an apocalyptic wasteland hazy with expertly rendered smoke—a vibrating elation spread from his lungs to his extremities. The ceaseless chatter of his brain eased up.

Milton, his pupils dilated, stole a quick glance at Sara after she delivered a swift, fatal judgment to a nonbeliever with her atomic bugle.

"Nice," Milton replied, feeling happier than he had ever felt before. Really happy. Uncomfortably happy.

Almost . . . *too happy.*

17 · THE 'RENTS MUST BE PAID (A VISIT)

MARLO FELT LIKE a stranger in her own life. Only it wasn't her life anymore. It wasn't *anyone's* life, by the looks of it. Her room was like a seriously underfunded museum. Or a *mausoleum,* only with band posters—Funeral Petz, Supernovocaine & Abel, and the You Wouldn't Understand—tacked up on the walls. It was so freaky-strange to be here, haunting her old room, a Marlo-shaped shadow cast by a beam of sunlight streaming through the window. *Mom finally won the Battle of the Tin-Foil-Reinforced Black Velvet Curtains,* Marlo thought with a smirk.

When night had fallen, Marlo's shade-self had been absorbed by the darkness, like a piece of broken seashell on the shore reclaimed by the tide. Her consciousness had gone all liquidy, getting weaker and weaker until she couldn't hold together a thought to save her afterlife. It was like sleeping, only . . . *wider*.

Marlo could see circles of melted red candle wax stuck to her floor, chipped partially away by her mother's fingernails, alongside her match-burned throw rug.

From my last tarot card reading with Aubrey, Marlo thought. She never really bought the whole tarot thing—her relationship with it was more like window-shopping—but Aubrey was spooky into it. She was always saying that "she read tarot cards like scars" or something, but that sounded more like a regurgitated Incurable Necromantix lyric than an actual philosophy. All those wands, cups, and swords . . . there was something para-*ab*normal about it.

Marlo saw a card poking out from beneath the rug: a card with a skeleton riding a horse across a grim field strewn with lifeless bodies.

The Death card.

Okay, Marlo thought as her shadow-throat swallowed a lump of cold darkness, *maybe there is something to tarot cards. The occult is like everything else: all fun and games up until it's not.*

Marlo's patch of sunlight had shifted, now a brilliant shaft leading to the door. She drifted to the hallway past a series of family photographs hanging on the wall. Most of the pictures were various groupings of Mom, Dad, and Milton, as Marlo had adopted a strict "you take my picture, I take your life" policy early on. In fact, the only photograph of herself she saw hanging had been taken shortly after she was born.

ROSEMARY'S BABY, Dad had written—judging from the tidy handwriting—at the bottom of the photograph, which showed Marlo as an infant swaddled in a pink blanket in her mother's arms. Marlo's mother had a peculiar expression on her face. She was so young, probably just twice Marlo's age when she died, and her deep-brown eyes shone with a mixture of pride, elation, fear, and fatigue. Her smile was wide, but almost tacked on. Like she was putting on a brave face, even though inside she was a bowl of quivering jelly.

Marlo's cheek prickled with tears.

I'm probably crying back in my Shadow Box Chamber. She sniffed. *Crying like a baby over a baby picture.* She wasn't sure why it got to her so much. Maybe it was because her mother seemed terrified of her future *as* a mother, while Marlo—just a shadow cast across her own memory—was fresh *out* of future. She knew that the world had gone skipping along without her. But it was another thing entirely to have it rubbed in her face.

Another patch of sunlight, thrown from the living room window, left a cool, straight shadow leading out to the garage. Marlo edged her way along the hall and underneath the door. Mom's used Porsche—an anniversary gift that Dad couldn't afford but somehow *could*— was gone, though the garage was still warm from it.

Through the garage door's three dingy windows, Marlo could see her dad's leftover boxes were now at the curb.

Mom must've dragged them there before she left for work, Marlo thought as she slid beneath the garage door.

The driveway shaded from the morning sun, Marlo made her way to the curb. She stooped to peek at what her dad had left behind. Several notes—again, in her dad's meticulous, slanted handwriting—had fallen out of a leftover box. The corner of one, written on nice stationery, was currently absorbing carburetor grease.

Dearest Rosemary,

I think of you so much—only of you—that it borders upon the too-much. It seems to me that no woman was ever to a man what you are to me. And it's near tragic, that long wilderness I spent without my blossoming Rose, that unfilled capacity for happiness, like a gaping hole, before this electric surge. But now I bask in the wonder, as if standing in a dream, somehow unable to fully believe that I am awake, held absolutely—in your sweet sway. . . .

Yours,
Blake

Marlo could feel her face grow bright red, even as a shadow cast from one world to another.

Whoa . . . Dad's old love letters to Mom. Good thing I'm

not diabetic. The pure, treacly sweetness would send me into a coma. Jumpin' Jeebus, Marlo thought as she spied another yellowed letter. *There's more. This one's written on the back of a Ugandan Quinine Quencher label. Must've been when Dad was in the Harmony Helpers, that hippie group that went to dig wells in countries no one had ever heard of.*

> My Rosie,
>   Please only write to me once a week. I cannot endure daily reminders of your absence. Whenever I read one of your letters, I lie in my cot, paralyzed in sweltering agony, my heart pounding throughout my entire body. Sometimes I feel that I shall surely implode from chronic lack of you. Absence does not just make the heart grow fonder. It makes it melt. Absence makes the heart . . . fondue.
>
>   Yours, as always,
>   Blake

Marlo cringed so hard that she feared she'd suffer internal injuries back in her bad-memory-foamed chamber. She had always known that her parents, you know, loved each other, but it never really struck her that they had ever been *in* love. Much less *passionately* so. These letters peeled away their protective layer of "parentness" until they were raw, tender, and something that Marlo had never fully considered before. *Human.* But, like most realizations, this one had arrived too late to do anything about it. Her parents were breaking up the act and going solo. And here Marlo was to rub salt in the wound. The last note, torn from Dad's ever-present moleskin binder, was, though crumpled, obviously written recently.

R,

   If I were to draw a picture of my heart as it is now, it would be exactly as you left it: tastefully decorated, hung with your photographs, yet now miserably empty save for three unoccupied chairs. We began as fast friends; then came the days of love and innocence; next an unerring respect deepened by parenthood and an affection only heightened by time. I cannot tell you what pleasure knowing you has given me. Because of this I will always be overwhelmingly in your debt. Time passes swiftly and—as we have been burdened to know—so does life, even young life. Yet, even amidst the tragedy, the treasure we have gathered together remains undiminished. I still love you. And always will. We will always be together even if you cannot bear us being together.

                                                          B

Marlo's silhouette grew dark and focused in the patch of sunlight peeking out from behind the roof.

"He still loves her!" Marlo exclaimed in that flat, dull voice that never seemed to pass her lips. *And I'm sure Mom still loves him, too! She just needs reminding. These letters will fan the embers—I just know it. It's not too late! All I've got to do is—*

A grating, metal-scraping-metal noise erupted from down the street. A truck stopped in front of the house, idling noisily like a garbage disposal full of forks and knives.

The garbage! Marlo fretted as two men in filthy navy-blue overalls hopped from the truck. The men— one blond, spindly, and eating a banana, and the other burly and slouching—stomped out to the curb.

I've got to stop them! Mom needs to see these letters! They're the only way to keep them together!

Marlo threw her shadow between the garbagemen and the boxes. The lanky man passed through Marlo. His banana went instantly black.

"Figures," he muttered with disgust as he tossed the banana into one of Blake Fauster's boxes before tugging it to the back of the truck. The squat, sour-faced man scooped up the letters and threw them in the remaining box.

"Looks like rain," he complained as he heaved the box out into the driveway. Marlo hurled her shadow-self at the man, hoping to slow him down with a debilitating dose of depression. The drooping, dumpy man stopped to glare accusingly at the sky.

"Yep, definitely rain," he continued before hauling the box into the back of the dump truck. "It'd be a good day to just stay in and play some of those video games all the kids are playin' these days."

The two men climbed into the shuddering vehicle. Marlo scrambled up a patch of dappled shadows into the cab of the truck and threw herself onto the seat between them.

"I'm just a lone cowboy with a defaulted loan," blared a country singer from the CD player. Marlo cast a weak shadow onto the dashboard. *"Looking for a rich gal to pay the bill for my phone-phone-phone . . ."*

The CD skipped. The spindly, sandy-haired man frowned.

"That music was bumming me out, anyway," he said as he ejected the disk and tossed it out the window.

"Hey," the stout, sullen man said next to him. "That's littering—someone has to pick that up."

They glanced at each other for a moment, then burst into laughter. Their short-lived mirth was quickly consumed by the undertow of mutual melancholy. A deep-gray storm cloud passed in front of the sun. Marlo's hold on the truck weakened.

Can't . . . let . . .

A wave of shadow bore down upon her, blotting out the sky.

. . . go!

Marlo tumbled out of the truck, rolling across

broken shards of sunlight and ultimately resting in a crisp clump of shade provided by a trio of newspaper boxes. The dark, darting shape of a monstrous bird streaked across the asphalt. Marlo looked up but couldn't see anything in the sky above.

"Weirdness," she murmured with a note of distress as the shadow slurped down the sewer. She backed into the shade of the newspaper boxes.

Must be seeing things . . . but what else is new? she sighed to herself. *I've got to get those letters to Mom, but I'm less than useless as a roving, sad-making smudge.* Her eyes traveled to one of the newspaper boxes above.

THE FREE WEEKLY GENERICAN-DO SPIRIT SENTINEL X-PRESS TIMES

GENERICA GAME CENTER GETS GHOSTLY GIFTS

By Monk Ashland

A collection of overhauled Psychomanthiums—rare "mirror-gazing" and "apparition" chambers reputed by assorted nut jobs and fruitcakes to be conduits to the spirit realm—has just been delivered to Generica's hottest (and only-est) new game spot, Fragopolis. The artifacts have been scrupulously refurbished and donated by Las Vegas–based, religious-themed gaming company Virtual Prayground. One of these Psychomanthiums was purchased from Topeka's now-defunct supernatural sideshow, the Paranor Mall, to help owner Lester Lobe with his extensive legal costs. Two months ago, Lobe's establishment served as the grisly scene of nearly barred lawyer Algernon Cole's death at the hands—or illegal jellyfish beans—of cult leader/claims adjustor Ervil LeBaron, otherwise known as the Guiding Knight of the Subordinate Chapter of the Lower Midwestern Sect of the Knights of the Omniversalist Order Kinship (K.O.O.K.).

Lest you think that you can now feed quarters to a machine to help you facilitate reunions with deceased loved ones, think again: These chambers have been converted to stunning, state-of-the-art gaming booths.

Fragopolis, Marlo puzzled as she reached into her shadow-pocket to pull out Baron Samedi's list.

2. Fragopolis, 646 Spawn Boulevard

Hmm . . . maybe if I can figure out why I'm supposed to be haunting an arcade, I can figure out some way of getting back Dad's love letters and THEN get Mom and Dad back together.

After spending most of the day hopping sun splotches and stowing away on accommodating bus and car shadows, Marlo finally made it to Fragopolis: a bustling collage of glare and noise that strobed like a Grand Mal Christmas. The arcade's flickering dazzle made it hard for Marlo to navigate. She had to hopscotch from streaks of light to irregular shadows: The light gave her shadow-self purchase in this disorienting place, while the brief, skittish shadows gave her split-second pauses to collect her thoughts. It was exhausting, like competing in the Twister Olympics.

She felt like a peripheral ghost here, not even able to give any of the bleary-yet-twitchy gaming geeks a proper "boo."

I don't know what the big deal is about haunting people, Marlo thought as she skated along flashes of light thrown onto the floor by the eclectic assortment of video games. A kid playing *Grand Theft Otter* picked his nose next to her and, of course, wiped his booger off underneath the game. *You can't really scare anyone, and all you get for your trouble is to see how gross everybody is when they think no one is looking.*

Marlo soon grew bored. Then she noticed a group of kids—mostly boys—swarming around a half-dozen large gaming booths.

Marlo gasped as she saw the Gothic neon writing blinking on the side of the booths.

COMING SOON
HECK: WHERE THE BAD KIDS GO
THE GAME

18 · JOKER iN THE PACT

DALE E. BASYE was many things now: rich, famous, unfortunately tattooed. . . . But of the many things he was, there was one thing that he was very much *not*. And that was happy.

Soaking in his marble hot tub, his freshly spray-tanned back resting on the solid-gold question mark snaking up the side, he drained the last of his acai-berry-spirulina-caviar smoothie and brooded.

He had it all:

> *1. A McMansion in the most coveted gated community in Las Vegas—Avalawns at the United Estates of Nevada. It was a high-security neighborhood for the suddenly startlingly rich, fastidiously designed to keep out the kind of people who the residents had been only last week.*

2. A prosperous career on the cusp of becoming a bona fide brand.

3. A brand-new trophy wife—former Uzbek super-model Goldie Grrr, premodeling name Fatma Dijaka-meli. (Dale's former wife, through hurled words and plates, had expressed her considerable disinterest in wasting her life as some sort of human "prize" occupy-ing Dale's metaphoric mantelpiece.)

4. Two trophy children leased from local talent agency Tykes 'R' Us and even a trophy pet: a purebred shar-pei currently undergoing plastic surgery to have its tail shortened, its ears lengthened, and a full-body face-lift to tighten up its droopy, wrinkled skin.

With all of these trappings of wealth, why did he feel so hollow inside? Success was all that he had ever wanted, but now that he had it, he felt as if he had spent his life playing some kind of shell game, a sleight of hand where—thinking that utter contentedness was hidden under the halved walnut of fame—he found himself mystified, and somehow cheated, when he came up empty-handed.

He inhaled a deep abdominal breath just as his Tuesday-Thursday therapist, Dr. Crustes, had taught him. Dale thought that perhaps doing an inventory of the extraordinary events leading him to this hot tub of steaming ennui would help him find the "hole" in his life . . . like psychological plumbing to discover where his love of life had leaked out. He could simply hash out things with his Monday-Wednesday-Friday therapist, Dr. Virago, later that afternoon, but she was mainly for mother issues, and this nagging emptiness didn't seem to have that unique "mother-inflicted" quality to it.

Shortly after the "unpleasantness" at the Paranor Mall in Topeka, Kansas—where Dale had been lured by a pubescent psychopath named Damian Ruffino with an equally psychotic yet oddly inspired book idea about children sentenced to an otherworldly reform school and a flaky lawyer had been poisoned by some nut-job cult leader—Dale had seized an opportunity amidst the chaos. More to the point, he had seized a *manuscript* amidst the chaos. *Heck: Where the Bad Kids Go.* It was a travesty of a story relying far too much on puns and cleverness and not enough on a compelling plot and believable characterization. But it had possessed a certain irreverent charm about it, and Dale, his ability to generate fresh ideas long since stranded like a broken-down car in the middle of the Mojave desert, desperately needed something original to plagiarize until it was his own.

Guilt had briefly nibbled at Dale's conscience, lazily, before moving away, unnourished. But the boy *had* intended for Dale to ghostwrite the story, and he had indeed done so—only the "ghost" had decided to take full-on demonic possession. Besides, the boy, Damian, would have enough to worry about, what with his religious death cult disbanded and his odd, temporary home—an ex-hippie's paranoid delusions turned into a museum of modern artifice—shut down pending legal investigation.

Dale had then shopped the reworked manuscript around until Picatrix Publishers—known for their handling of the patently unpublishable (*"If It Shouldn't Be on Shelves, Then We Put It There"*)—snatched it up after a bidding war as bloodless as a pacifist thumb-wrestling match. *Heck: Where the Bad Kids Go* hadn't exactly set the bestseller lists ablaze, though a sizable percentage of its meager sales were attributed to easily offended church groups who purchased multiple copies specifically for public burnings.

Just when Dale's dreams of success seemed dashed against the rocks of reality, he had received a call from Virtual Prayground Technologies, makers of religious-themed video games designed to engage, entertain, and ultimately scare the vestments off gamers so that they'd lead more virtuous lives. The company had already enjoyed several colossal, break-out successes such as *Protestant Evil, Immortal Combat,* and *Seventh-Day Adventurists,* making them one of the most influential, and wildly profitable, gaming companies in the world. The company—in particular the intensely irritating VP of engineering, Phelps Better—was intent upon purchasing the exclusive rights to a video game version of *Heck: Where the Bad Kids Go* to inaugurate its upcoming chain of immersive arcades. Dale felt he had no choice but to entertain an offer. And, upon hearing (and instantly accepting) the ludicrously generous offer, he found himself entertained to the tune of 10 million dollars.

The rest had been a blur of failed relationships, failed investments, and failed private pilot's license exams. He hardly wrote at all anymore. He spent most of his time either inundating himself with needless luxury to fill the void inside or attending regular meetings with Virtual Prayground to review the latest game developments. Speaking of which . . .

Dale looked at the clock—a one-tenth-scale model of Big Ben in his McMansion's inner courtyard.

Almost time for my meeting with—sigh—Phelps Better, Dale grumbled inwardly. There was something about the man that aggravated Dale on an almost molecular level. Just being in his presence was like having his psychic fur rubbed the wrong way. But, as Goldie's hearty spending and Dale's recent passion for gambling— a hamster wheel of a pastime in that he gambled to relieve the stress of his money woes, which only created more money woes, therefore more stress to gamble away—took their toll on his bank account, he needed his Virtual Prayground "creative consultant" stipend more than ever. Dale toweled off, then shaved in front of the mirror, which was specially warped and tinted to make himself appear younger. He stared at his manipulated reflection, trying to connect with the person he used to be. It seemed that with every meeting, he strayed one step farther from where he felt comfortable, giving in to bizarre game modifications, artistic compromises, and ethical concerns that on their own didn't seem like such a big deal but when strung together made him feel as if he had lost his way in the dark wood of error. . . .

Typical, Dale thought as he waited outside the grim Virtual Prayground industrial office park just off the Las Vegas Strip, fuming at his Zapple EyeWatch. *Always forty-five minutes late. Somehow even when I'm forty-five minutes late on purpose . . .*

A flaming red Mazda Miata sports car roared into the parking lot, the grating din of talk radio pouring out of its stereo. The car raced past a teal AMC Hornet and into the handicapped parking space right in front of the entrance. A spry, insectlike man with a yellow power tie and pale-blue polo shirt tucked into khaki chinos hopped out of the sports car.

"*Better* luck next time, Mahaffy," the man chuckled at the other driver, whose windshield sported a handicapped sticker. "Get it? Because of my last name?"

The man, Phelps Better, stuck out his hand as he walked up to Dale.

"I'm *Better,*" he said with a disingenuous smile overcrowded with large teeth, like the bleached-white tombstones of an exclusive graveyard just for giants. "Get it? Because of my last name."

"Yes," Dale grumbled as he tried to free his hand from the man's viselike grip. "And I've gotten it every time you've made that joke."

The driver of the AMC Hornet hobbled by, scowling.

Phelps Better winked his beady black eye at Dale, as if they were coconspirators in some hilarious prank. He walked into the Virtual Prayground offices with Dale close behind.

"Sorry I'm late," Phelps Better said before winking at the pretty receptionist, who managed a forced, obligatory smile in return. "I've been securing the delivery of the tricked-out Psychomanthiums—the gaming environments—to all of our Fragopolis arcades. Some are already functional, while the others are just there to create intrigue."

Dale walked alongside Phelps, unable to shake his irritation at having been kept waiting.

"It's just that I have better things to do than—"

"But the reaction is phenomenal: presales admissions to an arcade game, no less. It's unheard of."

"I'm a busy man—"

"And if my calculations are correct, *Heck: Where the Bad Kids Go* will be the biggest video game of all time before the week is out."

Dale stopped abruptly in the hallway as Phelps continued his strut through the drab hive of cubicles like some kind of royalty.

Biggest video game of all time.

Dale really didn't know much, if anything, about video games. The closest he'd come to playing a video game was trying to get the aerial on his old television to actually get a signal. But he knew that the words "biggest" and "all time" would make him somehow historic.

Phelps slapped a series of backs, chortled loudly about nothing in particular, and essentially assaulted a gauntlet of dispirited, uneasy underlings through the intimidating bluster of his affronting personality. As he reached his corner, the office resumed its usual, reassuring hum of idle banter.

"Hey, Pops, I don't have all day," he called out to Dale. "I'm a busy man."

Dale emerged from his stupor.

"Right . . . sure," he said as he trotted toward Phelps's office.

Somehow, he did it again, Dale thought. *Flustered me with some vague yet irresistible promise of wealth and acclaim. Now I'm forced to endure his unendurable awfulness. As usual.*

"Close the door," Phelps said as he eased into his overpriced Herman Miller chair, requisitioned just after the last round of layoffs. Dale obliged, then sat down.

"Foosball?" Phelps said, pointing at the large foosball table crammed into his office. "I don't play much," he lied. Phelps played at least four hours a day so that he could best any employee unfortunate enough to agree to a game. "But if you want—"

"I don't play."

"I didn't think so," Phelps replied with a dismissive snort. "Now, about my—"

Phelps held his finger up as he typed on his laptop.

"I've got to launch a salvo of threatening e-mails, warning of further 'restructuring measures' if our overworked staff doesn't meet our next impending, highly unrealistic deadline," he snickered, his black eyes shining flat like buttons. "Textbook middle-management productivity technique."

At least Genghis Kahn had the guts to be overtly evil, Dale thought. *This guy just rots the lives of all around him gradually like fungus on a toenail.*

"Okay," Phelps said, his laptop snapping shut like the jaws of a crocodile. "The ad spots for the game—'Play the game that plays *you*'—have really caught on. Throngs of children—and I literally mean *throngs*—are lining up to play the first full-sensation arcade game. It's, dare I say it, a *sensation*." He smirked, no one quite tickling his funny bone as thoroughly as he. "And—this is brilliant even for me—I've set aside some of our advertising budget to secretly fund a group called AGHAST."

"AGHAST?"

"Adults Galled by Heck and Such Things," Phelps clarified. "A coalition of parent activists who want the game shut down."

"Shut down? But it hasn't even really debuted yet . . . not officially."

"*Exactly*. We've been feeding the parent groups that protested some of our other games certain *concerns* about *Heck: Where the Bad Kids Go* gleaned from our internal testing. Reports of mild, to use the medical term, *zombification*."

"What?!" Dale exclaimed.

"Lethargy, twitchiness, and an overwhelming urge to play the game as much as possible," Phelps continued. "Not a far cry from what happens to habitual gamers, only with *Heck: Where the Bad Kids Go,* the addiction is more acute . . . and almost immediate. We couldn't have asked for a better gaming side effect. But by helping to stoke the ire of these parent groups, pooling them together into one, then giving them money for high-profile campaigns, I've turned this supposed 'negative' into the ultimate 'positive.'"

Dale shook his head. "I don't follow."

"Of course you don't," Phelps laughed, again rubbing Dale's psychic fur the wrong way in a steady, disrespectful rhythm. "You're old. *You're a writer.* You're lucky to be along for the ride."

"But it's my—"

"See, with AGHAST's help—causing mass parental outcry—we've virtually assured the game's success with its intended demographic. We're practically *daring* kids to play this 'dangerous' game that their parents can't stand."

Dale wouldn't openly admit it, but this was a brilliant marketing move.

Phelps's face crinkled like a sinkhole, as if all his disagreeable features were about to be swallowed up by his prodigious nose. *If only.* He unholstered his smartphone and scanned its touch screen.

"I've got to respond to this," Phelps said as he pulled a sheaf of papers from the top of his desk drawer. "It's our new tech consultant for the game, Mr. Nikola. Some mysterious contractor from somewhere. He doesn't seem to sleep. I'll get these crazy messages at all hours."

"I'm not sure about all of—"

Phelps tossed Dale a Virtual Prayground pen/laser pointer.

"You need to sign these," he said, barely acknowledging Dale's presence as his thumbs tapped away on his phone. "Standard liability contract."

"Liability?"

"It's a word." Phelps smirked, shaking his feathered hair that might have been fashionable forty years ago. "It means that you accept responsibility for the ramifications of your concept. It also means you get a higher percentage. And do you know what it means if you don't sign it?"

"Let me guess . . ."

"No check," Phelps said, pushing a bank draft for a million dollars across his desk.

Dale stared at the check, with its six beautiful zeroes.

What do I know about gaming, anyway? he rationalized with a sigh as he grabbed his new contract. *I'm just helping to provide the ultimate gaming experience for kids. I'm sure it's harmless. The zombification or whatever is probably just because the game is so . . . fun. Just a teensy-weensy side effect, like those panic attacks I got with my antianxiety meds.*

Dale looked up to see Phelps still composing a message on his smartphone. He noticed that the man had what looked like two tiny little horn nubs poking out from his sandy-blond hair. Dale wiped the spray-tan residue from his eyes, but the horns were still there.

"What are those . . . things . . . on your head?" Dale asked.

Phelps quickly smoothed his hair to cover the nubs.

"Prosthetic horn nubs," he said, his black button eyes flashing quickly at Dale. "A trendy body mod in the gaming community. Everyone on the *Heck: Where the Bad Kids Go* development team is getting them," he lied. "Great for brand cohesion."

Dale snorted as he leaned over to sign his contract.

"It's funny," he said as Phelps went back to his smartphone, "but with the horns and the game and all, I feel like I'm signing a contract with the devil."

Little did Dale know, but he was half right.

19 · SO FAR, SO GIDDY

MILTON HAD NO idea how long he and his team had been playing. Fifteen minutes, fifteen hours, or even fifteen days, would have all seemed within the realm of possibility. Milton's lack of sleep, his canteen full of Hypool-Active Overstimu Lake water, and the dazzling free-flowing immersion of Arcadia's games had all conspired to erode Milton's sense of time and sense of who he was. He was inseparable from the control console that seemed to fit him, snug and effortless, like a prosthetic limb. Milton, Sam/Sara, Caterwaul, Howler Monkey, and the Sunshine Sneezer played their team-based role-playing strategy games as one creature endowed with multiple joysticks. It was as if they were dreaming a mutual dream full of glittering geometry, physics-defying heroes, breathtakingly improbable landscapes, formidable villains, and a liquid blur of action that they drank in with their bloodshot eyes.

"I think we just made Terawatt," the Sunshine Sneezer murmured, his eyes engaged in a tug-of-war with the screen.

"Awesome," Howler Monkey mumbled, releasing his death grip on the gaming console just long enough to wipe the drool from the corner of his mouth.

The arcade noise washed over Milton like a soothing shower of sound, massaging away all thoughts of why he came here in the first place. He surrendered to the games—*Anglican Avengers, Sufi-Sonic Cyborgs, Shalom Rangers, The Gospel Troop,* and now *Guardian Angel Strike* (about a group of winged spiritual guides abandoning their assigned earth dwellers in disgust and forming a labor union). Sara thought, as Hazelle had suggested, that the game themes were designed to instantly engage a variety of different children based upon their core beliefs (a topic of burning importance to most every dead child, trying to reconcile the afterlife with their expectations). However, Sam thought the themes simply made for great gaming, as the stakes—especially for the fundamentalist games—were extremely high: If you won, you won *big*. If you lost, well, it was a case of "good-bye, cruel world. Hello, infinitely *crueler* afterworld." Sam and Sara had argued their points, leading to one of the most interesting shoving matches Milton had ever seen.

As a team, the newly ranked Terawatts were unstoppable. Each brought their unique skills to the arena:

MILTON FAUSTER, AKA THE DORK KNIGHT
Rating: S for "shrewd"
Status: Happy with a side of edgy
Strengths: Strategic, diplomatic, able to keep eyes on big picture

JASLIN CHUNDER, AKA CATERWAUL
Rating: E for "empathetic"
Status: Dry-eyed
Strengths: Intuitive, can feel way around corners

MORTIMER FRANZENBURG,
AKA HOWLER MONKEY
Rating: Z for "Zen"
Status: So close to winning he can almost taste it
Strengths: Dogged calm, clarity in chaotic situations

TYLER SKAGGS, AKA THE SUNSHINE SNEEZER
Rating: T for "twitchy"
Status: Nothing to sneeze at
Strengths: Lightning reflexes, allergic to failure

SAM AND SARA BARDO, AKA SAM/SARA
Rating: DT for "double trouble"
Status: Two heads are better than one
Strengths: Consistency; deadly, unwavering focus; can take shifts (Sam recharging with power nap while Sara takes charge and vice versa)

It's not that the games weren't challenging. Far from it. It's just that Milton and the Terawatts were locked completely in the flow of every game they played, their scores climbing to ludicrous heights, like the stock market during the Internet boom.

A guardian angel nearly assailed Howler Monkey with a halo blast before Sam/Sara "scabbed" the angel by shoving him out of the picket line. The angel dissolved into twinkling dust.

"Whoa! Thanks, Sam/Sara!" Howler Monkey exclaimed.

"You owe me, Noob," Sam chuckled. "Let's cut the jabber. Less QQ and more *Pew Pew* . . ."

Milton gave his fingerless wrestling gloves a quick, tightening tug before he clasped the console, preparing for another deadly airing of divine grievances. Just then, he heard a burst of static slice through the game chatter, followed by the sound of footsteps coming closer.

"Do you guys hear—" Milton said before remembering the receiver lodged in his ear.

Van Gogh's ear . . . it's online.

"Hello?" Milton heard someone say—Provost Marshal Tesla—through the earpiece. "*Ah, yes. Hello, Edgar. Sorry. I know, I was supposed to call you. . . . Could you please turn your heart down? Thank you. I was talking to my connection . . . up on the Surface.*"

Milton started. *The Surface?*

"*Guys!*" Milton called out to his friends. "I'm listening to Tesla!"

The Terawatts stared, unblinking, at their game screens.

"You'd better be paying attention, Dork Knight," Sam replied with a sleepy slur. "You're my wingman . . . and the fighting is getting heavy, which means . . . my eyelids are getting heavy, too. . . ."

"Van Gogh's ear," Milton replied. "I stuck it in Tesla's penthouse. I can hear what he's talking about. It sounds like he's on the phone with Vice Principal Poe."

"Poe?" exclaimed Howler Monkey. "Why would, like, Provost Marshal Tesla want to talk to a downer like Poe?"

"They're talking about the Surface."

"Whoa!" the Sunshine Sneezer said, wiping his dry nose out of habit, not out of necessity. "That's wild. But what about *Guardian Angel Strike?*"

"Set it on Contract Negotiation," Milton said. "That'll buy us some time. Come here!"

The Terawatts huddled around Milton's earpiece, which was lying on his outstretched palm.

"*You know zhe double-yolk egg?*" Tesla said, his voice frenetic and inconsistent, like an ungrounded electrical outlet. "*Souls are like eggs. Most are normal, and sometimes you get a double-yolk soul—your Gandhis, your Martin Luther Kings—but there are also zhe half-souls. Very rare. Born on this side. Really, I know, extremely rare to zhe point of almost* unheard of. *Born on this side, so they die and then spend eternity on zhe other side. Anyway, my connection on zhe other side is one. A half-soul. I'm arranging zhe last few details with him. Mainly connection issues from zhe Sense-o-Rama to zhe Surface. It's—"*

"The Sense-o-Rama?" Sara said, waking from her short catnap.

"—being worked on," Tesla continued. *"Between zhe Sense-o-Rama and zhe Shadow Box, it has been a considerable drain on zhe First Fire. But we'll soon collect all zhe fuel we need to feed its unquenchable blaze . . . and zhe power to achieve our ends.* Our new beginnings . . ."

"What is he talking about?" Caterwaul asked, her once-dry eyes again growing shiny with tears.

"I won't lie to you, Edgar. There have been some glitches. Zhe first team wasn't challenging enough."

"Challenging?" Sara whispered. "What does he mean? A *game* is challenging . . . players are *challenged.*"

"They played skillfully but not soulfully," Tesla continued. *"They were overwhelmed. Perhaps your Shadow Box efforts drove too many to zhe converted Psychomanthiums too soon . . ."*

"Psychomanthiums?!" Milton gasped. "Like at the Paranor Mall!"

"What's . . . *Psychomanthium?*" Howler Monkey asked.

"They're these supernatural mirror boxes that can connect the world of the living with the world of the dead . . . with *us.*"

"Zhe team has only now just gone offline," Tesla added. "Zhe game is on autoplay now: addicting but not immersive enough. But I have another team waiting in the wings zhat I believe will put up much more of a fight. Perhaps less technically proficient, but much more instinctual. Zhe perfect adversaries for full-sensory gaming . . . Wait. I hear something. A . . . rustling."

Uh-oh, Milton thought. Lucky must be awake.

Milton was guilt-stricken. His all-consuming marathon gaming had short-circuited his conscience, overriding all thoughts of what was truly important to him. Namely, Marlo and Lucky. And figuring out some way for them— for everyone—to escape from Heck, the dismal capital of underaged woe. But in Milton's haste to leave one prison, he seemed to have rushed into another, one that incarcerated with bars of dazzle and distraction.

"It's probably nothing," Tesla continued, his voice squawking from Milton's palm. "Perhaps just another solar flare. Like Thomas Edison's crude, flickering lightbulb." The mad inventor laughed bitterly.

A familiar, wet snuffling broke through Tesla's cackling.

"There it is again," the man faltered briefly. "My point, Edgar, is zhat Edison's brilliance was zhat he invented something tangible first. Zhe lightbulb. Without electricity, though, it is worthless. My current made it valuable. But, alas, no one values what they cannot see. I only powered Edison's legacy."

Milton could hear Lucky's faint squeaks of obsessive delight, followed by tiny tongue laps. Tesla's voice grew gradually fainter.

"I won't make zhe same mistake again, Edgar. My genius will be boldly evident to all. Ideas so powerful zhat they— unlike a lightbulb—will never grow dim. What? Speaking of dim? Oh, yes. Principal Bubb. I am keeping her in zhe dark about our activities, yes. Distracting her with her own ambition. And, in zhe event she does win, then Heck will be ripe for secession: each circle solely ruled by its own respective vice principal. And, to think, all it involves is zhe artful bending of her . . . ear!" Tesla yelped, causing feedback to squeal from Milton's palm. *"Holy govno!* What is zhat thing doing with zhat ear?!"*

Panting, puffing harder and faster, oozed out of the earpiece, followed by frantic scrabbling and the sound of a door whooshing open.

"Stop!!" Tesla yelled in the distance, his leather shoes scrambling across his floor. *"A spy in zhe house of Tesla!"*

The door slid closed. The steady thrum of Tesla's elevator rumbled in Milton's palm, causing the receiver to skitter across his hand before falling to the ground.

"Lucky's . . . *escaped,*" Milton whispered.

Sara set her hand on Milton's shoulder. "He'll be okay," she soothed. "You don't get much more self-reliant than a ferret."

"What are we going to do?" Caterwaul asked with a sniffle.

"About . . . what?" Sam grumbled, his face nearly stretching apart with a wide yawn before he fell asleep.

"All of this," Milton said. "It's some kind of . . . *revenge* for Tesla. And, by the sound of it, Vice Principal Poe, too. Snivel and Arcadia are connected—to each other and to the Surface."

"But, like, why?" Howler Monkey asked, trying to pull his gaze away from his high-definition wraparound gaming screen.

"I don't know," Milton answered.

It was so frustrating. As soon as Milton had achieved something close to an idea, his thoughts scattered to the sky like frightened birds.

"If we can . . . somehow . . . cause a disturbance," Milton managed. "Get the kids here mobilized . . . something to stall whatever Tesla has planned . . ."

"Maybe we could, like, you know," Howler Monkey interjected, "start a Dance Dance Revolution down in the music-and-rhythm-games zone and see if it catches on. . . ."

"I know what we should do, *Dork Knight*," Sara interrupted, her voice eerily calm like the eye of a storm.

"What?" Milton answered.

"Keep playing."

"Huh?" said Howler Monkey.

"It's like this," Sara continued, rubbing her weary eyes with her fist. "We keep racking up points like the crazy point rackers we are until we can enter the

Sense-o-Rama. *That's the key to this whole place.* So either we get in and have a blast playing the most intense game ever invented . . ."

"Or?" Caterwaul asked, her voice tinged with worry.

"We find out what Provost Marshal Tesla is up to," added Milton.

"And what happened to the Zetawatts," the Sunshine Sneezer said grimly. *"Firsthand."*

20 · UNFAIR GAME

MILTON KNELT DOWN and picked up the earpiece. He heard ferret claws scratching across metal and the roar of arcade games.

Lucky! He's here!

"Come back, you fuzzy white stowaway!" Tesla yelled in the distance.

"Tesla's coming!" Milton exclaimed as he shoved the earpiece into his tight brown Arcadia shorts.

Lucky billowed across the Donkey Koncourse floor as the Arcadians, oblivious, fed their attention like quarters into the blinking, blipping machines.

No green smells. No brown smells. No blue smells. Just gray man smells. Their stare boxes. Endless of them. But there's one smell—the boy—among the other people scent.

So familiar! Salty sweet and kind! Tangled knot of odors, faint but true. Up and up high. Atop broken clatter floors. The boy! The ear! Happy, teeth-feet peace feeling!

"What?!" gasped Caterwaul.

"Lucky's nose is second to none," Milton explained. "He can always sniff me out, even right out of the shower. He's coming, but, unfortunately, so is Tesla."

"What should we, like, do?" Howler Monkey asked.

Milton ran over to the guardrail and looked down. A tiny white blip of fuzz streaked up the staircase. Through the sliding smoked-glass doors of the main entrance between the gargantuan gorilla's feet ran Provost Marshal Tesla, spindly and freaky fast like a Serbian water-skipper.

Milton turned to his fellow Terawatts.

"Keep playing," he said, his eyes darting quickly back to Lucky, hoping to urge his pet up the stairs faster through sheer concentration.

Lucky raced past Level Three, stopping briefly, confused by the sounds of trigger-happy chaos and blood-chilling screams of the first-person shooters, before he spilled up to the last level. Milton edged along the stairs, hoping to avoid Tesla's gaze, and rushed toward Lucky.

"Lucky!" Milton said, scooping him into his arms. Provost Marshal Tesla's frantic footsteps pounded the metal spiral stairs. Thinking fast, Milton pulled off his Arcadia Gr8 G4m3rz's kerchief and folded it into a pouch, then tucked Lucky inside. He trotted back to his gaming quad just as Tesla careened onto Level Four, panting, his purple neon tie flickering with exertion.

"Have you . . . seen a . . . white rodent?" Provost Marshal Tesla wheezed in his crumbled Eastern European accent, a telephonic headset around his neck.

The Sunshine Sneezer shrugged.

"If it wasn't in my line of fire," he said, disgruntled angels reflected in his eyes, "then I didn't see it."

Tesla scanned Level Four dubiously. Lucky wriggled softly in Milton's kerchief pouch before his master's heat made him drowsy. The ferret tucked himself into a ball of sleeping fuzz. Provost Marshal Tesla marched toward the Terawatts' gaming quad and studied the screens. Milton's game was frozen on a picket line of indignant guardian angels on the cusp of civic unrest.

"This is a video game, not a safari," Tesla said with a scowl. "You have to actually *interact* with it, especially if you want to get to zhe final level and download zhe special Screen Savior."

He leaned into the quad and studied a string of numbers streaming past the bottom of the screen. His eyes widened with admiration.

"Well, whatever you are doing, it is working. Your accumulated scores have far surpassed my expectations."

After one last, frenetic sweep of the level with his

eyes, Provost Marshal Tesla straightened his purple neon tie.

"It is time," he said, his voice as dark, cold, and treacherous as black ice. "Congratulations: You have graduated from Level Four and earned entry into a game of infinite possibility. Come. Follow me. . . ."

The Terawatts rose to their feet. Milton's stomach gurgled in sickening waves like a digestive Lava lamp.

"Are you sure we're ready?" he asked as he and the other gamers reluctantly followed Tesla to the stairway. "It's just that . . . we want to be worthy of this honor," Milton added, carefully probing for information, as if he were searching for broken glass in an ice bucket. "Are you sure our skills are a good match for what's inside the Sense-o-Rama?"

Provost Marshal Tesla snorted, swishing the sides of his waistcoat with his long strides as he ascended the metal stairs.

"Zhat is for *you* to show *me*. You will see things no one else has seen. You will live a story in a way no one else has. I can only point you toward your destiny. It is for you to find it . . . to conquer it . . . to *master* it. . . ."

The stairway ended just below the black ceiling.

"Don't we get to pimp our avatars before we go in?" the Sunshine Sneezer asked, stalling, as the Terawatts huddled anxiously beneath the hatch. Provost Marshal Tesla's face shifted, his expression recalculating like a facial abacus with a twitch of his mustache.

"There is no need with zhe Sense-o-Rama to—as you say—'pimp' your avatars," he replied with a crackle of light sputtering behind his dark eyes. "I have conquered zhe Uncanny Valley Problem—where zhe more lifelike zhe nonliving are, zhe more unsettling they appear to zhe player—with a solution so obvious it has eluded game developers. A way to both be yourself while *losing* yourself. To actually *be* zhe game."

"But what about the other—" Sara interrupted before her question was waved away like a bad odor by Tesla's long, slender hand.

"Enough!"

He swiped his card key through the slot to the side of the hatch's iron wheel, then gave the wheel a twist. The heavy metal door fell open, slowly, on pneumatic hinges. The provost marshal urged the Terawatts through the portal. His electrified hands felt like cattle prods on Milton's back. The children were swallowed up by a vast dungeonlike rotunda, dark save for the sizzle of torches— hundreds of them—inset along the rounded chamber's damp stone walls. Faint glimmers of light danced on the floor. Milton looked up.

He gaped at the expansive domed ceiling. Hundreds of unblinking eyes twitched above, fixed in the domed ceiling like stars, the faces of their owners masked by an impenetrable darkness.

"The Surface," Milton mumbled in a semi-audible hush.

Glittering red specks drifted across the ceiling and clustered into letters.

Hᴇᴄᴋ: Wʜᴇʀᴇ ᴛʜᴇ Bᴀᴅ Kɪᴅs Gᴏ

Milton turned the letters around in his mind, as if they were written in the steam on a shower door and he was trying to decipher them in the bathroom mirror.

Hᴇᴄᴋ: Wʜᴇʀᴇ ᴛʜᴇ Bᴀᴅ Kɪᴅs Gᴏ

"Players like playing as people who resemble themselves," Tesla added as he backed out of the Sense-o-Rama. "And zhat is exactly how you will play. *As yourselves*. For as long as you possibly can. As if your afterlives depended on it."

The team of Terawatts had graduated to Level Five and gained entry into the hallowed gaming halls of the Sense-o-Rama. Yet, as Provost Marshal Tesla shoved the hatch closed, the honor, to Milton, seemed more like an after-death sentence.

The hatch sealed behind them with a hiss. In that moment, Milton knew with nauseating certainty that he and his friends would never pass through that hatch again.

MiDDLEWORD

There are a number of quaint terms humans use to rationalize the irritating things they do and feel. Take the inappropriate display of aggravation with "venting one's spleen." To vent one's spleen means to "unburden oneself." This is different from "spilling your guts," which means either "to divulge a secret" or "Help, get me to the doctor!"

The spleen is a nasty, purple, fist-sized organ located in the low-rent portion of the torso, just east of the stomach. In medieval times, the spleen was thought to produce a saddening black bile, one of four bodily "humors" (and medieval doctors had a real sense of humors). Later, eighteenth-century writers spent their time waiting for the invention of the typewriter by worrying of the spleen's supposed connection to dangerously high levels of imagination (sadly, the "overabundance of imagination" proved a condition all too easily cured through such modern marvels as reality television, blogs, and DVD extras).

Truth be told, most people would rather spend their lives venting spleen than risking the fickle, sloppy uncertainty of happiness.

Complaining is, in essence, how the overly sensitive protect themselves from life. They wrap themselves tight with an insulation of indignation, a buffer of bellyaching. And while sensitivity—a person's very soul coated with twitching cats' whiskers—can open up one's heart to the full spectrum of beauty around one, an overly sensitive soul can soon become a most burdensome possession (not to mention pure torment for anyone in the immediate vicinity).

When our skin is too thin, we capture every nagging nuance around us while exposing our vulnerable selves to the world. It's where sensitivity becomes enslavement: to our emotions, to others, to most everything but ourselves. Yet, while acute sensitivity can be a most malignant condition, it can also be our greatest gift. Hope—a substance that, while undetectable to the naked eye, is stronger than any tank and louder than any bomb—resides in the most sensitive part of the soul (right around your soul's scritchy spot) and only appears when most everything seems lost. But if you find yourself so foul-tempered that you can't even acknowledge hope when it avails itself—like some vampire groundhog that casts no shadow—then you may find yourself with some serious ex-spleening to do. . . .

21 · NEAR-LiFE EXPERiENCE

BE THE FIRST TO PLAY HECK: WHERE THE BAD KIDS GO. WE DARE
YOU! read a banner hung over the converted Psychoman-
thiums in Fragopolis. BEFORE YOUR LAME PARENTS SHUT IT
DOWN!™

The dazed kids flitted about the booths like drowsy
flies around drugged poop.

"Game . . . awesome," a boy with headgear mumbled. "Must play. Again."

"Was . . . intense . . . then stopped," a boy with a
clip-on eyebrow piercing gurgled. "But said . . . back up
soon. Not soon . . . enough."

Their unblinking eyes were as glazed as honey-baked
hams. Like one-way streets leading to abandoned ghost
towns.

Why a game? Marlo thought from a shard of bright
light spilled across the Fragopolis carpet, framed by a

curtain of shadow. *Isn't it bad enough that the souls of the darned must toil in Heck for all eternity, or until they turn eighteen—whichever comes first? Now kids up on the Surface have to endure Heck, too, feeding it attention like some leisure-time-eating virus? And the million-dollar-and-some-change question: What the heck am I doing here? Why do they need me to bum kids out when they have this dumb game here that can do it for them?*

The kids traded monosyllabic grunts like verbal Pokémon cards. They stared with hunger at the gaming booths, shaking with withdrawal, wanting more than anything to play again.

A pair of geeky boys walked through Marlo toward a *Wii the People* game, where kids could virtually manipulate the quills of America's founding fathers to help sign the Constitution before the colonies were besieged by British "rust-coat" robots armed with boiled-beef bazookas.

One of the boys—a pimple-studded pixie-stick of a boy in a striped ROSES ARE RED, VIOLETS ARE BLUE, ALL MY BASE ARE BELONG TO YOU sweatshirt—stopped short by Marlo's spot on the terminally '80s carpet.

"I don't know, Hans," he said, shoulders slumped. "I suddenly don't feel like playing that game . . . *any of the games.* They all seem so lame . . . except—"

Hans? Marlo thought.

"But, hey, what's *that* one?" the boy said, pointing toward a Psychomanthium. "For some reason, I want to play it more than anything!"

Man, even his finger has pimples on it, Marlo thought. *The other boy . . . Hans. He seems super familiar. He's got to be one of Milton's friends. Like fate sprayed him with loser cologne. There's some weird thing that's like . . . drawing me to him.*

Hans scratched his woolly red hair.

"Yeah, I know what you mean," the boy replied with a resigned squeak of his preadolescent voice box. "I haven't felt this bummed out since . . . well . . . *she . . .* you know . . . but that game *does* seem really—"

Marlo noticed the boy had a school binder clutched beneath his arm. Plastered across it were pictures of . . . *her.* Marlo. Dozens of them. The few gaps between the pictures were decorated with dozens of little black hearts.

That's it! Marlo thought. *Hans Jovonovic. Milton's friend with the bushy hair so fiery red that you could practically talk to God through it. The geeky matchstick boy always mooning around me—borderline stalking by the looks of it. Guess he had an Orange Crush on me. Who could blame him? He must be why I'm here! The third point in my triangle, sticking me to the Surface to bum people out! Maybe that's why I feel so weirdly . . .* focused *around him.*

"We might as well check out that new game," Hans said with a shrug. "There are a bunch of kids hanging around it, so maybe it's not as sucktastic as all the others."

The boys slunk away toward the *Heck: Where the Bad*

Kids Go game among the clamor of frenzied bleeps, static explosions, and cheesy music loops. Just then, a girl blocked Hans's way.

"Holy cats!" Marlo yelped, her voice ringing in her ears. "It's me!"

A girl with stylishly scraggly blue hair and layers of meticulously mismatched Victorian mourning dresses stood defiantly in front of Hans. Had there been any color in the boy's face, it surely would have drained away. The girl was spooning a jar of baby food into her mouth with a Twizzler: Marlo's trademark negative-attention-getting snack. It added another dimension to her freakdom. But who was this wannabe wolf in black sheep's clothing? It couldn't possibly be—

"Hey, Hans," the girl said coyly. "Smokey the Bear asked me to come and put out your hair."

Aubrey! Trick-or-taunting as me!

Hans stood there, stupefied, clutching his binder so tight that it made his white knuckles almost translucent. The boy's beanpole-of-a-friend stepped up.

"Hi, Aubrey," the boy said with a confident smirk belied by his quivering lower lip. "Um . . . you are, like, so sweet that I . . . um . . . get cavities just looking at you!"

Aubrey gave the boy a stare as spicy cold as frozen gazpacho.

"Humberto," Aubrey replied, slurping her Twizzler

spoon. "If you want to talk to me directly, you're going to have to fill out a *U-R-A: DWEEB* form and fax it to the home office in You Wishistan. Expect to be completely ignored within six to eight weeks."

Humberto's whole body crumpled. With his striped sweatshirt, he resembled a forlorn candy cane.

"I'll be in line for the new game," he mumbled to Hans as he joined the growing crowd of glassy-eyed kids milling about the *Heck: Where the Bad Kids Go* booth.

Hans swallowed.

"Hi, uh . . . Aubrey," he managed. "Sorry, it's just that you . . . well . . . you look so much like . . . you know . . ."

Aubrey smiled and smeared the last bit of her baby food with her finger.

"It's okay," she replied carefully, twisting her baby-girl voice into something lower and huskier. "You can say her name. *Marlo.*"

Hans winced at the mention of Marlo's name, as if its mere utterance were an invisible dagger twisting in his heart.

"She's gone, Hans. Sometimes life is like a game of *poker* and you just have to *deal*," Aubrey said, punctuating the word "poker" by poking *him*.

Aubrey glanced down at the boy's Marlo-covered binder, her black-lipsticked lip curling at the sight of it, as if it were a rival.

"But I'm here . . . *alive*," she said, her eyes sweeping across Fragopolis with disdain. "And seriously bored. Buy me something. Or, better yet, *steal* me something."

Hans cast a nervous, desperate glance toward Humberto across the bustling arcade, as if his friend were a life preserver floating just out of reach in a stormy crazy-girl sea.

"Well, I was going to play that new game. . . ."

Aubrey rolled her heavily eyelinered eyes.

"*C'mon* . . . there's trouble to make—with a capital 'T' that rhymes with 'me.'"

What is Aubrey's damage? Marlo thought, following the unlikely couple—Aubrey practically dragging Hans out of the arcade by his sweaty hand—using the broken shards of light streaming down onto the carpet from the arcade's track lighting as a sort of pathway. *It's like she's got split ends all the way down to her brain. What is this Marlosquerade all about, anyway? And what's so hot about Hans, other than his raging-campfire haircut?*

A twinge of lovesickness spasmed in Marlo's chest like a dove wounded by rose thorns.

Zane, she thought wistfully as her mind and heart filled with images of the sullen-sweet British boy she had first crushed on in Rapacia and who then later—in Fibble— she had gotten to really know and fall for . . . so hard she had practically skinned her knees. But in Fibble, she had been in her brother Milton's body, so their relationship hadn't really had a chance to even *be* a relationship. She sighed as she watched Hans's and Aubrey's silhouettes hanging in the doorway of Fragopolis.

Marlo studied Aubrey, creeping closer in a band of sunlight-sharpened shadow just outside the arcade to get a better look.

Her nose is bigger than mine. Her eyes are smaller, spaced a bit farther apart and almost blue. And she's got calves so large they're practically cows. But still, with the makeup and outfit—she's really rocking that mourning dress—she is, if not me, an amazing simulation.

"Hey, let's go to the park and play ball!" a little boy called out to his friend just before passing through Marlo's shadow. The boy stopped, the winds of outdoor frolic taken out of his sails.

"But we'd probably just get hurt and sunburned," he mumbled, turning toward Fragopolis. "Not like if we spent the day playing video games," he said with a dispirited shrug as he pushed open the door with his shoulder. "That's, like, fun designed by *professionals*. Way better than what we kids could come up with on our own— like that new game about dead kids."

"Whoa," Marlo exclaimed. *That's why I'm supposed to be here, hanging around the arcade. I'm like somebody dressed as a hot-dog monster outside of a Franks 'n' Steins, luring them in with bite-sized chili puppies. Only instead of food samples, I'm doling out the doldrums. Free funk. Get it while it's not. Making people depressed so they seek out the consolation of a gaming console.*

Marlo watched as Aubrey convinced Hans to leave his Fortress of Geekitude for some misdemeanor pseudo-date. Marlo sighed with the envy of the dead.

"You're a mess," Aubrey said, licking her palm to pat down a rogue tuft of Hans's unruly orange hair. "But you could be a *Euro* mess with a little help."

Hans blushed and, suddenly, Marlo's shadow winked out and she saw the Shadow Box—all gauzy and faint like a half-remembered dream—from inside her chamber. To her side, as if through a veil of steam, she could see Baron Samedi fretting in front of the chamber belonging to Ferd, aka AWTY—the irritating Emo boy back in Snivel.

"I theenk we lost thees shade to the Litsowo," rumbled the dark man with the grinning skull painted across his face. "Trouble no set like rain." He shrugged, bunching up his tuxedo coat with his shoulders. "That bird wraith has big wanga-gut for stray, wanderin' souls, stretched thin and *pyaa-pyaa* by the Wastrel Projector . . ."

Marlo's consciousness winked on and off, returning to the outside of Fragopolis. Hans took Aubrey's hand away from his flaming red hair. Marlo's shadow gradually sharpened in a stain of sunlight.

My grip on the Surface, Marlo pondered, her thoughts as worn and fuzzy as an animal at a cheap petting zoo, *it's dependent on three people's grief. Sort of a triangle of torment. And one of those points is—of all people—Hans Jovonovic. But if Aubrey sinks her mitts into him, this Gothlet is gone. A shade no more. I'll be replaced by a psychotic tub of I Can't Believe It's Not Marlo!*

A large, birdlike smudge streaked across the bank facing the arcade. But just as Marlo caught a glimpse of it, it was gone. She swallowed, praying that she wasn't the prey of some weird bird wraith, or whatever Baron Samedi was *labba labba*ing about back in the Shadow Box.

And I have to hang around long enough to bring Mom and Dad back together. Which means getting Aubrey and Hans untogether. And somehow getting Hans to help me. But how?

A businessman texting a client stumbled through Marlo's shadow. He stopped abruptly and puzzled over his handheld.

"Which means getting Aubrey and Hans untogether? And somehow getting Hans to help me? But how?" the man mumbled before shaking his head. "Wacko client . . . must've forwarded me a text from his kid or something . . ."

The businessman crossed the street, leaving Marlo puzzling on the sidewalk.

That's it—I think, therefore IM! I not only mess up cell phone signals, but I can, somehow, manipulate text messages. Sweet!

Aubrey coyly tapped her china flats against the sidewalk.

"Don't you like me?" she asked with a practiced pout, looking like a preteen cemetery angel. Hans, flustered, stared down at his shiny black belt buckle.

"No . . . I mean, *yes*. I do like you. It's . . . it's just that I'm not sure if . . . you know . . ."

Marlo noticed that Hans had one of those InfoSwank Wi-Fi touch-screen belt buckles. She crawled across a braided checkerboard of light and dark, stopping at Hans's smudged white Converse sneakers before scaling a streetlight shadow slashed across his corduroys.

Marlo concentrated. This had been challenging enough for her in her three-dimensional form, but doubly so as a weak, Marlo-shaped energetic absence.

Hans. Meet me at the dump. Marlo "The True Blue" Fauster

"If I'm ready to . . . ," Hans said before making that startled face everyone makes when their phone is set to vibrate, like they're about to fart fireflies. He craned his neck low to scan the upside-down readout of his belt buckle:

Hans. Meet me at the dump. Marlo "The True Blue" Fauster

Hans gave a shiver so fierce that he nearly shook off his freckles.

"Hans?" Aubrey said, her spooky self twitching beneath her cool facade. "You look like you've just seen a ghost."

The ghostess with the mostest, you cheap knockoff!

Hans's InfoSwank belt buckle went off again, Marlo having accidentally texted her wrath. Hans swallowed and gave a nervous look up and down the street.

"Well?" Aubrey asked, her face growing red at the edges around her corpse-white foundation. "Who's calling you, Red? Your mommy?"

"Aubrey?!" a slender, middle-aged woman with flowing black-and-gray hair called out from across the street. "Is that you?"

Aubrey cringed. Marlo could sense a supremely irritated tremble, as if life itself were rolling its eyes. Aubrey took her time turning to address the woman.

"Yes, *Lenore*," she said, stretching out the woman's name. "It is indeed me, Aubrey Fitzmallow, your stepdaughter-whatever. Apparently the glaucoma has not advanced to such a degree that you failed to recognize your own not-of-flesh-nor-blood legal burden."

Lenore gave Aubrey a decent eye roll of her own, accentuated by the woman's wide, expressive eyes. The woman had a sort of doomed Gothic beauty about her, Marlo thought, as if she were a heroine in one of Vice Principal Poe's creepy books.

"The hair, the clothes, are . . . interesting," Lenore said with a faint smile. "The attitude not so much." She sighed. "C'mon. I'm double-parked outside Curl Up and Dye: *where you said you'd be.*"

Aubrey abruptly turned to Hans. She took off her silver snake ring, grabbed the boy's clammy hand, and slid it onto his ring finger.

"Meet me here tomorrow: same bat time, same bat

channel," she said, crossing the street before locking eyes with Hans over her shoulder. "Or there will be consequences."

Hans scratched his head and walked over to a mint-green Camaro parked on the street, staring at Aubrey while fumbling for his keys.

Sweet ride, Marlo thought, hugging Hans's shadow.

As soon as Aubrey and her stepmother turned the corner, Hans put his keys back into his pocket and walked over to the bike rack.

Marlo snickered, accidentally. setting off Hans's vibe-ringing cell phone buckle. He looked down in front of his bicycle at a girl's silhouette that spilled out onto the sidewalk like a chalk drawing. Marlo fluttered her fingers like a friendly black spider just before the boy with the flaming red hair fainted.

22 · PRESSED TO PLAY

THE TERAWATTS WERE crowded together—back-to-back—at the center of the coliseum.

Milton's eyes, nose, mouth, ears, and fingers prickled painfully. The colors—vivid reds, oranges, and indigos—slashed at his retinas. The sounds of sizzling torches and labored panting pounded his ears like fists. The scent of sulfur was overpowering. And Milton nearly gagged at the taste of his own fear.

He couldn't bring himself to make eye contact with the arched ceiling, a firmament of unflinching stares peering down from the Surface. And the flickering film of light separating "up there" from "down here" was branded *Heck: Where the Bad Kids Go*. Eternal darnation had been turned into an arcade game, where the misery and toil of dead children were now the diversion and amusement of the living. It reminded Milton of gym class, only writ supernaturally large.

"M-maybe this will, um . . . be fun," Howler Monkey stammered as he gaped at the dank, dripping walls of the expansive stone arena.

"I don't get a strong fun vibe from this place," Milton said, squinting at a thick red liquid oozing from the roughly hewn flint blocks. "And I have a feeling that's not Cherry Kool-Aid leaking out of the walls."

"Look, over there," Sara said, pointing to a patch of floor a dozen yards to her right. "There's a big trapdoor or something."

On the stone ground was a circular outline with a red number 1 stenciled on it.

"I wonder if—" the Sunshine Sneezer said just before he was interrupted by the scrape of stone. Two garbage-can-sized openings appeared on the wall nearest the hatch entrance.

"What's going on?" murmured Sam, waking from his fear-induced nap.

Schwoop!

Suddenly, two canvas sacks shot out of the openings, landing on the floor—one with a thud, the other with a clatter. The gunnysack bundles fell open at the feet of the Terawatts, revealing a heap of weapons and a pile of what looked like armor. Fiery red letters blazed above.

WEAPON: FIRE MAGE
PROTECTION: UNITY-TARD ARMOR
WHIRLY-BLADE

A siren split the silence like a butcher's knife through a slab of beef.

Scrench!

Another gateway slid open with the squeal of stone against stone. This opening was much bigger than the hatchway that the six Terawatts had passed through. Milton had a sickening feeling that the portal was intended to accommodate the passage of something really large.

"Twenty . . . nineteen . . . eighteen . . . ," a demonic voice boomed from above, while a bloodred digital readout blinked above their heads, counting down.

Caterwaul began to snuffle back tears. The Sunshine Sneezer, after a quick sniffle himself, comforted her with a pat on the back.

Milton felt responsible for the suffering of his new friends. After all, he had been the one to lead them here. And, whether this was a killer game or a game intent on killing *them,* Milton knew it was up to him to somehow lead them out of harm's way. Out of the Sense-o-Rama. Out of Arcadia.

"Provost Marshal Tesla!" Milton shouted to the Sense-o-Rama walls. "Can you hear me?!"

"Sixteen . . . fifteen . . . fourteen . . ."

"You told me that every game needs rules and that even rule breakers must study the rules they break. So how do you expect us to play a game where we don't even know the rules?"

Tesla sighed through speakers set into the stone walls.

"Fine," he said, his voice reverberating throughout the arena. "I suppose you deserve to know what you're in for, especially with zhe unlikelihood of you fighting your way out."

"Twelve . . . eleven . . . ten . . ."

The Terawatts picked through the piles. Milton examined the armor: a weird sort of "muscle suit" studded with tiny brass nodes.

"Your Unity-Tard," Tesla said, his voice spilling out into the arena. "It connects your movements to zhe players—"

"On the Surface?" Milton interjected as he slipped on his armor, looking like some steroid-abusing preteen weight lifter.

Tesla chuckled.

"Yes, to zhe Surface. Your movements are controlled by zhe players, while you simultaneously influence zhe decisions of zhe players. Player and avatar fused into one."

"Eight . . . seven . . . six . . ."

"How does it work?" Milton asked as he examined the weapons: a wand with a long chain at the end, ending in a tiny metal cup, and a leather arm strap with a machete-like blade set atop a motor.

The Terawatts cinched each other's ridiculously muscled armor. They looked like the Spartan High Glee Club.

"Zhe Sense-o-Rama stimulates a gamer's five senses—sight, hearing, touch, taste, and smell—to create a fully immersive gaming environment zhat is more than virtual reality. It's *augmented* reality: more exciting, more intense, more all-consuming for both player and played."

"*Four . . . three . . . two . . .*"

"But why?" Milton exclaimed, his upper lip beaded with sweat as he lashed his Whirly-Blade to his forearm.

Provost Marshal Tesla snickered, his voice exploding like an overtaxed transformer. "How about this, Mr. Fauster: For every level you survive, I will answer a question . . ."

More fiery words sizzled from above.

"*Begin Oblivia: Preliminary Sense-o-Round Warm-up.*"

"Now play . . . as if your afterlives depended on it."

A spotlight trained upon the opening of the tall gateway.

"*In a world where injustice, torment, and cruelty flow like tap water,*" the demonic voice hissed in a sinister baritone, "*where being a kid means being a fugitive from all that is kind and good, one group of children stood alone. . . . You are about to enter a place—a terrible place—where the souls of the darned toil for all eternity, or until they turn eighteen, whichever comes first."*

Clop! Clop!

Hoof-falls echoed, slow and deliberate, from beyond the gateway.

"Meet your Principal of Darkness—the Great and Terrible Bea 'Elsa' Bubb!"

Milton swallowed. Her name alone had launched a thousand lunches.

Then, stepping into the light from the gateway was a woman. But instead of the hideous demonic lump held together with sores and spite, *this* Principal of Darkness was a shapely stunner, clad in bruise-purple leather from head to toe, with brilliant red hair that spilled out across her porcelain face, revealing one gleaming green eye peering from beneath. Her wings—wasplike pinions marked with skulls and crossbones—fluttered faintly with simmering malice.

"Unwelcome to Heck," the woman purred. "Population . . . *you.*"

Florch!

A great plume of fire and smoke erupted in front of her. As the dense black smog cleared, an ornate iron gate appeared, decorated with spikes, skulls, and barbed wire.

"This cozy little place is for despicable little brats

such as yourselves to be rehabilitated and punished: *mostly punished*," the faux Bubb said as she strutted through the gates, swishing her long, pointy tail. "So that when your souls reach maturity, they can be judged and sentenced to the full extent of the law." She snickered, revealing a mouth full of gleaming white fangs. "That is, if you ever *reach* maturity!" She threw back her head and laughed, disappearing in the shadow surrounding the spotlight as a bell tolled. The ground shook beneath the Terawatts' feet as a small army made its way through the large gateway across the arena.

Roarg!!

Suddenly, bursting into the spotlight were six hulking, snorting, eight-foot-tall demons brandishing deadly pitchforks, their keen tines glinting in the glare.

The creatures' backs were hunched, their skin deep green and reptilian with coarse red fur thatched from below their chests down to their three-toed talons. Pointy ears protruded from their bald, roundish heads, a single horn sprouting from their crowns. They gaped at the Terawatts, jaws dripping with saliva, and their blank, pale-yellow eyes squinted like creatures of the night unaccustomed to the brash antagonism of light.

Milton felt his Unity-Tard twitching, forcing him forward. His friends soon followed, awkward and stiff as they fought against their player-controlled armor. The demon creatures fanned out, circling the Terawatts.

Grunt! Snarl!

Milton desperately studied his Fire Mace. On the chain wand was only one control: Ignite. Milton thumbed the switch and a small ball of fire blazed in the metal cup at the end of the dangling chain.

"How does a Fire Mace work, anyway?" Sara said as she squared off against a demon that had singled out her and her brother.

"Like this," the Sunshine Sneezer said with an elfin grin.

He spun his sizzling fireball over his head and hurled it at the nearest demon.

Zort!

The fire exploded across the creature's chest. Though it yowled in pain, the demon quickly recovered. It sprang at the Sunshine Sneezer with its pitchfork, scratching the boy's upper arm.

"Oww!" he yelped as he staggered back. "What good is this dumb armor, anyway?"

Howler Monkey twitched and scooted forward.

"Some idiot up there keeps, like, forcing me straight into those demons!"

Milton could feel it, too. The gamers above wanted to send their avatars into a battle that the Terawatts didn't want to fight. Milton toggled a switch on his arm from Off to Slow to Fast. The Whirly-Blade attached to his forearm began spinning.

"A shield!" he said. "The blade moves so fast that it's nearly solid!"

Milton surrendered to the will of his player and lurched forward. A demon reared back, straightening its ridged hump, then jabbed its pitchfork into Milton's whirring shield.

Skutch!

The pitchfork glanced against it with a shower of sparks, throwing Milton back into his friends.

The flash of sparks seared Milton's eyeballs. The smell of sweat . . . the sound of grunts . . . the electric prickle of his Unity-Tard . . . all of Milton's senses were heightened. His feverish mind fought to keep up.

Yowl!

Caterwaul screamed in agony. Milton whipped around to see her lying on the ground at the other end of the Sense-o-Rama, rubbing her bleeding thigh. He fought the electrical shocks goading him into combat, and instead rushed to Caterwaul's side.

"It . . . it jabbed me away from the rest of you," she said as Milton helped her to her feet. "Then my suit got scared or something. I started running and I couldn't stop myself."

Milton looked back at his group of friends as they were prodded apart by the snarling demons. The beasts panted with excitement.

"They're trying to separate us!" Milton shouted as he pulled Caterwaul back to the group. "We need to work as one."

The Terawatts huddled together, back-to-back, as

the demon beasts took turns tirelessly butting their massive pitchforks against the children's spinning-blade shields.

"This isn't a . . . *strategy,*" Sam said as he drifted in and out of consciousness.

Unfortunately, Sam's right, thought Milton as a shower of sparks pelted his forehead. He looked down at the controls of his spinning blade, set to Fast. An idea popped into his head. Milton flicked his switch to Slow and heaved himself forward. His demon opponent was taken aback, but after sizing Milton up with its soulless yellow eyes, it roared and charged.

The demon thrust its pitchfork at Milton's chest.

Whoosh!

Milton caught the creature's weapon between the slow-moving blade of his shield and his forearm. Milton jerked himself back, grimacing in pain as he grabbed the pitchfork with his other arm, disarming the demon.

The other Terawatts grinned, reset their shields, and charged.

"Aaaaarrrrggghhhhh!!" they yelled, throwing themselves upon the demon horde. The confused beasts retaliated with a frenzied pitchfork assault that soon left them empty-clawed.

"*Epic,* as Wyatt would have said," Sara said triumphantly, beaming at Milton with her sweat-shiny face. "Now what?"

The demon beasts stalked closer, their ridged backs arched, cloven hooves stomping the floor. One of the creatures swiped the air with its talons, claws so sharp that the air whistled back in a howl.

"I think the only w-way that we'd totally disarm them," Caterwaul said shakily, "is if we ripped off th-their actual arms."

The counterfeit Bea "Elsa" Bubb sashayed out through the gates.

"Tsk-tsk," she said with a shake of her brilliant red hair. "And I've told my whittle demon babies not to play with their food."

The wanna-Bea rose to her hooves and, with a crack of her whiplike tail, she swept toward the large gateway, cackling.

The assault of sensations was giving Milton a full-body migraine. He felt as if he were on the verge of shorting out, like all five of his senses were appliances plugged into the same overloaded power strip.

That gateway must lead somewhere. If we can just distract the demons long enough to make a break for it . . .

Milton examined his Fire Mace. He leaned in close to Caterwaul. "On the count of three, we throw fireballs above their heads, right above the tall one in the middle, then run for the gateway. Pass it on."

Caterwaul nodded and whispered to Howler Monkey next to her. Milton flicked on his Fire Mace. As

Sam/Sara got the message to Milton's right, Milton drew in a deep, sulfurous breath.

"One, two . . . *three!*"

Flizzle!

The six Terawatts slung their fireballs above. Streaking the air with sooty contrails, the fireballs exploded in a blinding hot blaze.

Splorch!

The beasts grabbed their stinging eyes and yowled in pain.

"Now!" Milton yelled.

The Terawatts dashed to the gateway. As they crossed the circular outline on the floor, it opened beneath their feet. They screamed as they tumbled down a corrugated metal shaft. The shaft coiled and twisted for a few hundred feet until ending at another hatchway.

The Terawatts fell through the hatch and rolled onto a smooth, bile-green floor in another arena, its walls pulsing in sickly green throbs.

"*Ten . . . nine . . . eight . . . ,*" the demon emcee hissed.

Milton looked up. Again, they were scrutinized by a star field of glazed eyeballs.

"Where are we?" Caterwaul murmured, rising from the floor.

A flickering film of light appeared above. Twinkling red lights formed letters.

"Three, two, one. Begin Oculux: Sense-o-Round One . . ."
Two bells tolled, and as their clang reverberated to
one last shallow echo, the chamber filled with the bogus
Bubb's wicked laughter.

23 · A SIGHT FOR SOARING EYES

IT WAS AS if the universe were holding its breath. This new arena—Oculux—was eerily still and silent save for a barely audible, subsonic thrum.

Whoo-whoo-whoo . . .

Milton noticed a figure across the bile-green coliseum. A person, curled up in a fetal position.

"Look," he said to his teammates, pointing across the dim room. "Do you see that?"

"Yeah," Sara answered, though her stare was fixed at the rim of the ceiling. "But there's something *else*. It looks like a bunch of big eyeballs."

"You mean the players on the Surface?" Milton replied.

"No, you chowderhead," Sam spat back. "This is something new. Something *worse*."

Milton looked above but his vision was blurred, as if he had been crying.

"Keep your eyes on the Vizzigorths," the sultry game version of Principal Bubb warned with mock concern, "because they've certainly got their eyes on *you.*"

Milton could make out trembling clusters of large, faintly luminous bubbles—hundreds of them, twitching along the rim of the ceiling.

Glizzle!

Suddenly, the arena was filled with a molten surge of sparkles. Each glittering speck of light hovered around the children, equidistant like a sky full of orderly stars not wanting to encroach on one another's personal space. "It's like we've been submerged in some sort of disco hair gel," the Sunshine Sneezer said.

"They're kind of pretty," Sara said as she reached her hand toward the nearest sparkle, "almost like fairies that—"

Zap!

"OWWW!!" Sara yelped. She massaged her smoldering hand.

"Fairies that *bite,*" Sam whimpered, sharing the same nervous system as his sister.

Milton studied the floating motes of light.

"If we're careful," he said, stepping forward, "maybe we can squeeze past them and—"

Zapple!

"OWWW!!!" Milton was pitched back onto the arena

floor. His chest felt like a nursery of freshly hatched electric eels.

"They've got some force field around them. We'll have to figure out—"

Whoosh!

Something swooped above Milton's head. Caterwaul screamed. Milton strangled his own shriek.

The "bubbles" that Milton had made out earlier were actually large, flying eyeballs: slimy piranha-like creatures about the size of beach balls. They dove at the high-voltage twinkles. There was a blinding, strobing flash as the creatures snatched them up with eyelids lined with jagged teeth.

"Those must, like, be Vizzigorths," Howler Monkey gasped.

"And it's their feeding time," Caterwaul added with a sniffle.

Whenever a Vizzigorth swallowed one of the electric sparkles, there was another horrible flash. Milton shielded his eyes, which seemed to be getting weaker and weaker. He strained to see a round, whitish outline on the floor across the arena by the figure he'd seen earlier. It had a number 2 etched on its middle.

"The way to Sense-o-Round Two is on the other side," Milton said, rubbing his eyes. "At least, I think . . . I'm having problems seeing."

"Me too," Caterwaul, Howler Monkey, and the Sunshine Sneezer chimed in.

Sam/Sara shook their heads.

"Not me," Sam said, taking off his glasses. "In fact, I don't think I even need these anymore."

Suddenly, Howler Monkey lunged at a clump of twinkles with his blade shield.

"I'm . . . being . . . *played!*" he grunted as he vainly swatted at the sizzling motes. "And my shield . . . *won't spin.* . . ."

Milton toggled the switch on his arm. Nothing. He tried his fireball mace as well, whipping it toward one of the swooping Vizzigorths, but he couldn't summon a spark. The creature dove at the lashing chain, seized it with its razor-toothed eyelids, and yanked it out of Milton's hand. Howler Monkey fought against the pull of his armor and stumbled back to the Terawatts.

"Useless," he panted as he unstrapped the charred shield and let it fall to the floor with a sad clatter. "Weapons from other levels must not, like, work in—"

Schwaa!

A small portal slid open on the wall twenty feet away from the Terawatts. Out shot five long wands with nooses of looped metal at the ends. Flaming words sizzled above.

WEAPON: ROTO-REEL

The devices skittered at their feet. Milton crouched down and picked one up. It was like a cross between a fishing rod and an eggbeater.

Swoop!

A Vizzigorth darted down from the ceiling and nipped at Howler Monkey's shoulder. He cried out in pain.

Brushing the hair from his eyes, the Sunshine Sneezer squinted at a Vizzigorth that fluttered in a tight circle several yards away, as if caught in an invisible eddy of energy. He flicked the switch on his weapon. The noose of metal ribbon began spinning. The Sunshine Sneezer cast it like a fishing reel, then snapped the wand back, seizing the squealing Vizzigorth around the midsection.

Snatch!

"I got it!" the Sunshine Sneezer yelled triumphantly. The Vizzigorth screeched—a shrill, wet gurgle of rage—before pulling the boy into the web of floating sparkles. "Or it's got"—he screamed in agony as each electrified sparkle ricocheted off his body—"me!"

The Sunshine Sneezer let go and the Vizzigorth flitted away—its wings like gauzy fins sprouting out from its sides—with the weapon dangling from its body. The boy staggered back, hitting one more swirling clot of jolting glitter light as he rejoined his friends.

"What good are these, then?!" the Sunshine Sneezer said as he tossed his weapon to the ground.

Clatter!

Milton watched, as if through gauze, the Vizzigorths roosting on the ceiling. The glistening creatures bore their terrible gaze into the children, hungry for eye candy. Milton could see Howler Monkey's blood staining one of the Vizzigorth's teeth.

Milton squinted his eyes at the energy sparkles. They fuzzed out into pom-poms of light, like the stars in Mr. van Gogh's paintings. Milton flicked the switch of his fishing reel weapon on and off, watching its metal noose spin.

"Maybe we can use these things another way," he said, screwing up his eyes at the nearest twinkle. Milton cast out his Roto-Reel, the noose flying out on a length of metal ribbon. He cinched it tight around the sparkle's fuzzy halo. Milton opened his eyes wide. The noose seemed to be levitating in the air around the sparkle.

Crackle!

"The force field is actually *part* of its body," he said. "We just can't see it."

Milton tugged the flickering energy sphere inch by grudging inch.

"If we can just . . . budge them . . . ," he said between gritted teeth, "maybe we can make . . . *a path.*" With a heave, Milton accidentally flicked the switch. The electrified sparkle spun in a spiral of mesmerizing light. A flock of Vizzigorths shriek-gurgled overhead.

"Uh-oh," Sam muttered with distress before nodding off, using his padded shoulder as a pillow.

Five Vizzigorths plunged from their perch toward the Terawatts, blinking their rows of jagged white teeth.

★ ★ ★

Figures, Marlo thought sadly amidst the acres of moldering garbage mounds, their hot, spoiled-milk stench rippling off the heaps in sickly waves. *My first date, and it's with Hans Jovonovic at a garbage dump, and I'm a gloom-inducing shadow cast from the underworld.*

Hans swatted away a seagull as he stooped over yet another broken cardboard box. Soiled papers were spewed out everywhere, like corn dog and elephant ear bits on the side of a roller coaster. The late-afternoon sun struck Hans's red hair, igniting it into a brilliant blaze.

He's being a trooper, Marlo thought as she traveled along a shaft of waning sunlight. She spread her long shadow at Hans's sneakered feet like a dare. The boy sighed. His shoulders slumped into a kind of resigned submission. He crossed Marlo's shadow just like she had taught him.

Any luck, Heat Miser Hair? Marlo thought-texted to Hans's touch-screen belt-buckle phone. He looked down at his waist.

"No," he replied vaguely, still not completely convinced that he wasn't talking to himself. "It seems like everyone in Shawnee County decided to heave boxes full of old papers into the dump on the same day."

As Marlo stared at the mounds of trash—the castaway remnants of people's lives—she thought about how her parents' marriage of twenty years was now just that: a worthless rubbish heap of memories. *All because of me . . .*

Hans puzzled over Marlo's sobbing, trembling shadow, her head hung in her shady hands. Awkwardly, Hans put his hand around Marlo's heaving shadow back, patting the air softly around her absence.

"There, there," he said, glancing over his shoulder nervously for any school bullies who happened to be trolling the garbage heap, looking to expand their tetanus collections. "It must be hard being, you know . . ."

A Pisces?

"Um, no, I meant . . ."

I know what you meant. You can say the D-word. Dead. If anyone knows I'm dead, it's me.

Hans and Marlo shared a stretch of silence, like Lady and the Tramp sharing a strand of spaghetti.

You're still not completely sure I'm me, are you?

Hans jumped as his belt buckle vibrated.

"This will sure make my parents' monthly phone bill more interesting," he muttered as he read Marlo's texted thoughts. "It's not that I don't think you're *you*, exactly. It's just, well, far more likely that I've lost my mind, thinking my dead soul mate is haunting my belt buckle."

Soul mate?

Hans stopped short, as if he had been going for his morning jog and suddenly found himself in a minefield.

"I . . . well . . . it's just that . . . ," Hans faltered, his face now roughly the same color as his hair.

What do you like so much about me, anyway? Marlo thought-texted as Hans stepped into her ever-lengthening shadow.

Hans scratched his temple. The sun began to set over a mound of garbage. His hair was now a controlled burn of redwood twigs.

"Most girls either ignore me, laugh at me, or act like my social awkwardness is a communicable disease. Not you. You would make fun of me, sure, but never in a mean way like the other girls. You were actually funny. And every day it was something different. Like you were making an effort to connect with me somehow. And, of course, the whole 'being beautiful' thing . . ."

Beautiful? Marlo thought reflexively, not intending to text. She wasn't sure what to do with all of these new revelations. Her mom would have arranged them neatly in a scrapbook. Her father would have jotted them down in his sloppy handwriting, then stored them away in a—

Box! That's it! Over there, by the oozing medical supplies!

"Which one?" Hans asked, supremely relieved at the change in subject.

The one with the little dials and buttons drawn on the side in Sharpie.

Marlo recognized the box as the "time machine" Milton had made when he was little. He'd climb inside and Marlo would tell him that the box would send him forty-five minutes into the future. She'd then drag the box down the stairs to the basement and lock the door for nearly an hour.

Marlo's mind grew smooth, cool, and fuzzy around

the edges. She looked over at the horizon of rubbish. One lone ray of orange light shone over the heap.

Oh no. In a couple of seconds, I'll be lost to the shadows.

Hans crouched over the box, shuffling through the papers on top.

"This is it!" he called out. "Now what am I supposed to do with—"

The sun fell below the mountains of garbage, and Marlo's consciousness was pulled apart by blackness.

Wump! Wump! Wump!

Flapping leather wings stirred Milton's hair with hot wind. He willed his eyes open. There, hovering around the swirling sparkles, were the Vizzigorths, staring at the corkscrewing whorl, utterly hypnotized.

Sara squinted her eyes at the baffling scene.

"It's like van Gogh's *Starry Night*," she said with a nervous smile as she watched the deceptively playful swirls and "stars" ablaze with their own drunken luminescence.

The Sunshine Sneezer cast his fishing noose at the nearest sparkle.

Floong!

"More like *Scary Night*," he said as he captured one of the twinkles. "And we're going to lose more than an ear if we don't follow Milton's lead."

He flicked the wand and dragged the spiraling light

off toward the side of the Sense-o-Rama. Almost immediately, another flock of Vizzigorths swooped down to be mesmerized.

Whumpada-whumpa-whumpa!

The dazed players above soon caught on to the Terawatts' strategy, assuming it to be *their* strategy, and the movements of Milton and his friends became easier and more fluid. Soon, the Terawatts had lassoed dozens of electrified sparkles and sent them spinning, subduing scattered flocks of flapping eyeballs while carving away a narrow path leading to the next level.

Milton edged along sideways like a crab, followed by the other Terawatts, with Sam/Sara—due to their size— at the rear.

A figure clad in muscle-padded armor lay on the ground by the Sense-o-Rama wall.

"It's one of the Zetawatts!" Milton yell-whispered as he neared the Sense-o-Round Two entrance. "At least I think it is. Everything's still so fuzzy to me."

Flumpa-whoosh!

Without warning, a rush of leathery wing flaps erupted from the rafters rimming the ceiling. A Vizzigorth darted down, its eye-mouth blinking away its trance. It gobbled up one of the whirling sparkles with a ravenous wink of teeth.

Skree!!

A small flock of dazed Vizzigorths shrieked in anger as their mesmerizing twinkle was devoured. They attacked the invading Vizzigorth from all sides and ripped it apart with their savage batting eyelashes. Covered in freshly shed gore, the Vizzigorths' eye-mouths were dilated with bloodlust as they flitted about the Sense-o-Rama in erratic jerks.

"Uh-oh," the game version of Principal Bubb giggled wickedly. "It looks like we're shifting from 'eye see you' to 'I.C.U.' as in, intensive care: *STAT!*"

Milton made it to the edge of the Level Two portal. He crawled on his hands and knees to the prone body just beyond, careful to avoid a crackling, low-lying sparkle. He rolled the figure over. It was a Zetawatt named Ariel.

"Ariel? Are you okay? What happened?"

Her freckled skin was blanched, her normally dark, mischievous eyes now blank and lost.

"C-can't see ... held them ... back ... ," she murmured dully before fainting dead away.

Scromp!

Sara screamed as a Vizzigorth tore into her arm. Caterwaul beat the creature back with her rotating fishing wand before another Vizzigorth ripped it out of her hand.

"We've got to, like, get out of here!" Howler Monkey yelped as he cleared the sea of sparkles. Caterwaul squealed as a Vizzigorth dive-bombed her head.

"Help me with Ariel," Milton said to the Sunshine Sneezer.

"But, dude, she's going to slow us down."

Milton grabbed Ariel by the hands and heaved her across the floor.

"No child left behind," he grunted before backing into a painful sparkle jolt. The Sunshine Sneezer sighed and grabbed Ariel's leg, helping to drag her to the circle etched on the floor.

Flumpatta-whoosh!

The Sense-o-Rama strobed with sparkle death flashes as a school of Vizzigorths—their irises flaring like embers among gnashing teeth—winged their way toward the Terawatts.

"Now!" Milton screamed to Sam/Sara. The conjoined twins plowed toward a trio of bobbing sparkles, howling in painful glitter shock, and joined their friends.

The floor beneath them opened up, like the aperture of a camera. The Terawatts fell into the next level as the Vizzigorths tore into one another, furious at their prey's sudden escape.

24 · A CASE OF
TRiAL AND TERROR

THE BALD, POINTY-BEARDED Russian man and his bushy-browed American counterpart sang fervently across from Principal Bubb in her Not-So-Secret Lair/Campaign Headquarters.

> *"Demon sleaze, vote for me.*
> *Let me be your law.*
> *And, demons, please, say to me.*
> *You'll let me hold your claw!*
> *Now let me hold your claw . . .*
> *I wanna hold your claw . . ."*

The principal gave a dismissive wave.
"Hmm . . . it's catchy, but then again, so is scabies.

But it's just too . . . I don't know . . . *needy*. I hired you—the infamous and unlikely songwriting duo of Russian revolutionary Vladimir Lenin and anti-Communist zealot Joseph McCarthy—to create the definitive campaign jingle. And so far I have yet to hear that toe-tapping Lenin-McCarthy magic."

"Vee have another!" Mr. Lenin exclaimed. "Is anthem. We save best for last." He nodded to Mr. McCarthy, who strummed a jaunty tune on his acoustic guitar.

> *"There's nothing you can do, so give it up.*
> *Nowhere to run, ill-fated schmuck.*
> *Nothing you can say but just a vote can*
>   *change the game.*
> *It's easy.*
> *All you need is Bubb.*
> *All you need is Bubb.*
> *All you need is Bubb, Bubb.*
> *Bubb is all you need."*

A claw rapped against the principal's chamber door.

"*Yes?*" she called out with a blast of anchovy-gym-sock breath.

"'Scuse me, Principal, ma'am." A beaked, feathered demon leaned into the room. "Your campaign advertisement is on."

Principal Bubb rose to her hooves.

"Mr. Lenin, Mr. McCarthy, if you'll excuse me," she said as she clacked to her desk. "I'll be in touch."

The two singers stood and bowed.

"I'd like to zay thank you on behalf of the group and ourselves, and I hope vee passed the audition," Mr. Lenin said before the two men scooted out of the principal's lair.

Bea "Elsa" Bubb flicked on her radio.

"Benito Mussolini . . . His name sounds like a terrible Italian dish," said the radio announcer's deep, cool, sarcastic voice. *"But here's the 'dish' about this one-time leader of the Italian Fascist Party: He was once arrested for vagrancy. Do you really want a former hobo to be in charge of h-e-double-you-know? Don't let him make a 'Mess-o-lini' of things. Pass the buck to Bubb."*

The principal's gruesome features contorted into a wicked gash of a smile.

"Pretty strong meat there from candidate Bea 'Elsa' Bubb," another newscaster noted. *"Rancid meat, judging from the tone of her negative campaign ads. But Bubb needs whatever nasty edge she can muster, judging from the latest Gallows Poll that has the principal of Heck and rival Lilith Couture virtually neck and . . . well, whatever Principal Bubb has that connects her head to her shoulders. Speaking of Ms. Couture, here is her latest campaign ad."*

The put-upon expression carved deep into the principal's barklike face deepened.

"You've all heard of Lilith Couture," a lilting voice cooed. *"Her exquisite face plastered on the cover of the underworld's most elegant magazines, her lithe form seen draped on the arm or tentacle of the rich and powerful. And, after serving as devil's advocate for time immemorial, she's got more chops than a pig with a black belt in karate—"*

"'Scuse me, again, Principal, ma'am," the feathered demon interrupted as it fluttered into the room. "I have something for you."

"What is it?" Bea "Elsa" Bubb barked as she switched off the radio. The twitchy creature goose-stepped to the principal's desk, holding out a rolled parchment. Principal Bubb snatched it out of his webbed hands.

"A summons, ma'am," the demon clucked nervously.

Principal Bubb's eyes shot burning-hot skewers of rage into the poultry excuse for a demon. "If you call me ma'am again, I'll *maim* you," she muttered under her breath as she unfurled the parchment.

ATTENTION PRINCIPAL BLOB:
You have been summoned as a witness in the Trial of the Millennium: the State vs. Satan. You are hereby required to attend the Provincial Court of Res Judicata—a place with literally no appeal— within twenty-four hours of receiving this document. If you are currently in Limbo, then simply count to 86,400, then leave.

"They're really going through with it," the principal muttered as she leaned against her massive mahogany desk. "An actual trial."

She stroked the thicket of bristles sprouting from one of her chins.

"I'm sure there are plenty of eager witnesses," she murmured to herself as the feathered demon backed his way out of her lair. "But what lawyer would *possibly* represent the epitome of all evil? I mean, most every attorney throughout history has struck an unfortunate deal with Satan at one time or another."

Principal Bubb etched another scowl into her permanently scowled face.

"Whoever he is, he's a complete fool. He's just inherited a case no one could win."

Algernon Cole squinted at the bare lightbulb dangling before him. He tittered nervously as he gazed into the moat of complete darkness beyond.

"Sure, why not?!" he laughed. His ponytail—thinning hair corralled into a scraggly graying braid of feigned youth—bobbed behind. "This is all some kind of joke, anyway. Are you guys with a community theater group of some kind? I used to dabble in my day. Had an addiction to grease paint and limelight. Knew my way around a show tune. We did this groovy, nondenominational version of *Godspell* one summer solstice. . . ."

A large, leathery fist smashed the top of the claw-marked table.

"Enough!" the beastly voice bellowed like a garbage disposal full of gravel.

The creature heaved a bulging folder across the desk. Algernon Cole pushed his wire-rimmed glasses up the bridge of his long nose.

"Do you think he has a shank to stand on?" the creature roared.

The newly deceased lawyer winced and patted his aching stomach.

"Ugh, those jelly beans are certainly having one heck of a disagreement with my tummy . . . *whoa.* Anyway, the defendant has a record longer than a box set of Grateful Dead bootlegs, but I'm always up for a challenge. Even in this weird dream."

"For the millionth time," the beast roared, "you are dead."

Algernon Cole shook his long, narrow head and laughed.

"Right. I've got long legs, Mister Boogeyman. You're going to have to work harder to pull them."

"It's Boogey*person*," the creature clarified.

"This is one crazy, crazy dream," the spry lawyer mumbled. "No more off-brand colas and Funyuns for me. They aren't even particularly 'fun' . . . or 'onions' for that matter."

"So you don't have any conflict of interest," the creature thundered from the darkness, "considering who—*or what*—the defendant is?"

Algernon Cole shrugged and pulled up his mismatched socks: one beige, the other light brown.

"Hey, I'm a lawyer. If my fee can earn me some interest, then there's no conflict," he chuckled. "Seriously, who am I to judge? I leave my scruples outside the courthouse . . . along with my watch, belt, and class ring. Those metal detectors are touchier than a blind masseuse! I'll be honest with you, Mister Dream Monster. I'm looking to make a name for myself, so I'll represent anyone who'll have me. Besides, every felon deserves his day in court. Even this"—Algernon Cole squinted at the top sheet of the folder—"*Louie Cipher* fellow . . ."

Damian Ruffino stared at the television in his older sister's moldy basement. Sunflower-seed husks stuck to his lower lip, and he picked at a small white feather sprouting from his pimply chin.

"I don't believe it," he murmured. His dark, cruel eyes—accustomed to dispassionately viewing the world as a petting zoo of chumps to be fleeced and / or bullied—were glittering with the realization that *he* was now the chump.

An unnaturally tanned woman, so orange that she

should have a Sunkist sticker stuck to her blank, chemically smoothed forehead, peered out of the television from behind her news desk.

"Local gamesters are flocking to Fragopolis—Generica's new video-game hot-spot—to go to Heck," the woman said with a smirk.

"Heck?" her male newscasting counterpart interjected beside her. "You mean like—"

"Yes," she replied as the game's Gothic logo appeared on a screen behind her. "H-e-double-hockey-sticks for kids. Bad kids. It's the latest gaming sensation, drawing crowds not seen since last summer's tragic all-toddler tractor pull. In the game, players are sent to a special place—a terrible place—in the underworld reserved just for naughty children."

"Dumbian!" shrieked a bloodcurdling voice—as sharp and furious as a tornado in a knife factory—from upstairs. "Your girlfriend is here."

Damian blanched. The only thing in this world and the next that *truly* terrified him was his horrible, horrible sister Harrida. But, considering that their mom and stepdad vanished after the accident at the Paranor Mall, fearing any legal repercussions their troublesome, once-dead-now-living son may have incurred, Damian had nowhere else to go. Damian's adopted-then-soon-commandeered cult—the Knights of the Omniversalist

Order Kinship (KOOKs)—had disbanded after the Guiding Knight had attempted to poison Damian with illegal Japanese jellyfish beans. Luckily, for Damian anyway, his barely-lawyer Algernon Cole was the one who kicked the proverbial bucket after scarfing a handful of killer candy.

"Is our show on?" said Necia Alverado, a spooky, rat-like girl from his former cult, as she stepped onto the crusty orange shag rug. For some reason, she still felt that Damian was, in the words of the KOOKs, "the Bridge between this world and the next"—some kind of super savior. While Damian didn't buy the whole "Bridge" thing, he had put it on layaway, never knowing when he'd need to exploit Necia's creepy devotion for his own gain.

Damian gave a soft cluck before clearing his throat.

"Nah . . . I'm watching something else," he replied from his nest of junk-food bags and straw in front of the television. Damian leaned in close as a familiar face appeared on the screen.

" . . . Dale E. Basye, creator of the *Heck: Where the Bad Kids Go* game, along with Virtual Prayground Industries, is the focus of parental backlash," the anchorwoman continued. "A group called AGHAST—Adults Galled by Heck and Such Things—is waging a nationwide publicity campaign against Basye's ghoulish gold mine of a game, claiming it leaves its players numb and oddly soulless . . ."

Necia scooted next to Damian and handed him a small plastic bag full of worms.

"This is all the bait shop had," she said with a tight twitch of a smile. "They were out of your night crawlers, so I got you a wad of the dark-red ones."

Damian tilted his head back and swallowed a wriggling pinch of worms.

"Thanks," he forced himself to reply, expressions of gratitude as foreign to his tongue as Latin. "Did you get me a bag of that other stuff, too?"

"Your Choco-full of Oinkrageous Flavor-Brand Fudge-Dipped Pork Rinds?"

"Yeah," Damian replied, wiping drool from his pimply chin.

"Hmm, let me see . . ."

Necia's perplexed expression quickly gave way to one of mischief.

"Of course I did, silly! I know they're your favorite," she said as she pulled a large brown-and-pink bag from her tote. Damian quickly snatched the bag from her hands, bit the corner off with all the intensity of a soldier pulling a pin from a grenade, then emptied the contents into his mouth. The precision blend of chocolate, pork, fat, grease, and MSG sure hit the spot. In fact, apart from the sunflower seeds and worms, Choco-full of Oinkrageous Flavor-Brand Fudge-Dipped Pork Rinds were pretty much all he ate lately.

Necia examined Damian's face.

"That stuff is making you break out. I saw something on TV that can help cover your zits up at least."

Damian wiped chocolate pork dust off his snubbed nose, which now seemed oddly rigid and cast with a yellowish tinge. He didn't mind the weird "chickeny" stuff he was going through since his return from the dead, but his etheric energy—the energy gluing his physical and spiritual selves together—was all wonky. Damian had lost his etheric energy when he died, yet he'd regained it, somewhat, when the KOOKs had sacrificed a flock of chickens to bring him back from the dead. He had found himself growing increasingly out of phase with himself— his body and spirit unaligned, in need of some kind of supernatural chiropractic adjustment—making it challenging for Damian to live up to his notorious bullydom.

"Isn't *Kickin' with the Kult* on?" Necia asked, referring to the hot new sitcom inspired by the Knights of the Omniversalist Order Kinship tragedy that she and Damian watched, if not religiously, at least with a fervent zeal. "Hey, who's the old guy on TV? He looks familiar."

"Dale E. Basye," Damian replied, fuming. "The jerk who stole the idea I stole. The idea that was going to send the KOOKs straight to the top of the death-cult heap."

" . . . Dale E. Basye has been unavailable for comment regarding the harmful effects of his supposedly dangerous video game," the anchorwoman continued with a flip of her lacquered hair. "But the mobilized mob of outraged parents that make up AGHAST are determined to draw Basye out his self-imposed seclusion in his Las Vegas home with a massive protest. . . ."

"Should we go to Fragopolis and play his game?" Necia asked hopefully as she tightened her already tight mousy brown hair with her twitchy rat fingers.

"I'd sooner eat sushi off a boys' room floor," Damian grumbled. "I'd like to give that middle-aged goon a piece of my mind, though—and by 'mind' I mean merciless fists, and by 'piece' I mean blow-after-crushing-blow."

" . . . AGHAST are looking for children who have suffered from playing Basye's wildly popular game to join them at their Las Vegas protest," the anchorwoman said. "Those interested should contact the organization at the number below."

The male newscaster shook his head dismissively before releasing the full power of his bleached-white smile.

"I don't know what all the fuss is, Storm," he chuckled as he straightened a stack of blank papers on his desk. "Let the kids play their Pong or whatever . . ."

The downy white feathers on the back of Damian's neck ruffled as he hatched a rotten egg of an idea. He turned to Necia and gave her his most messianic smile.

"How would you like to go to Vegas with me? To see that guy?"

Necia blushed and hugged her bony, stockinged legs. "I thought you said he was a complete jerk."

"Yeah, he's a complete jerk," Damian said with taut malevolence, "but he won't be *complete* for long . . . not if I have anything to do with it. Of course, we'll need money. You can help out with that, right, Necia? My one true believer?"

If Damian was anything—besides unrepentantly despicable—he was determined: determined to leave his smudgy mark on this world (and the next), and determined to exact his considerable revenge upon Dale E. Basye.

"Sure," Necia said demurely. "As KOOK treasurer, I still have some of our membership dues. It should be more than enough."

Damian stared at a cigarette burn in the rug, practicing looking completely empty. He'd have to appear as vacant as a roach motel on the moon if he were to join forces with AGHAST as their game-damaged poster boy. If he played his marked cards right, he could mobilize a new group of reactionaries to do his bidding, draw Dale E. Basye out of exile, and take what was wrongfully his: *everything*.

25 · THE TRAGIC TOUCH

THE TERAWATTS TUMBLED roughly into the next level. Milton was sore all over, as if he had played a game of slug bug at a Volkswagen factory. He rubbed his eyes. A grim, aquatic light rippled around him.

"I think I'm going blind," he said. "I can barely make out anything. It's like we're submerged in the Black Sea after an oil spill."

Sam/Sara groaned in a weary, two-part harmony and rose to their feet.

"I think this place is feeding on our senses," Sara said as her brother scanned the arena. "The last round seemed to affect your vision. But there's not much to see here. It's pretty dark. Plus, it's weird."

"I can barely feel my arms and legs," Sam finished in his slurry, sleepy voice. "It's like I've gone kind of numb."

Milton realized that, in the last few moments, his

aches and pains had been replaced by a strange, faraway tingle.

"Yeah, me too."

The other Terawatts nodded, save for Caterwaul.

"Not me," she said, her wide, wet eyes glittering. "I'm actually the opposite. I can even feel your guys' breath on me. It's kind of creepy . . . *and* crawly. I can feel every stitch of this stupid armor suit."

"*Ten . . . nine . . . eight,*" the demon emcee bellowed from above as the ceiling blinked with a hundred eyes.

Flickering red lights spilled out above, forming words.

ЅƎИɿ⅃-O-ᴚUOИᗡ Two: ᴚOTA⅃ᗑA⊿

"Perpetor?" Milton murmured, screwing up his eyes toward the ceiling.

"*Palpator*, dimwit," Sam grumbled as he tried to stare down the glazed multitude of eyes staring down at him.

Ariel, still senseless on the ground, stirred as if fighting to emerge from a bad dream. Just then, two figures shot out of the darkness and ran across the coliseum's vast muddy plain: a small bespectacled boy and a blue-haired girl.

"It's . . . you and your sister," Sara gasped.

Snapping at the heels of the two children was a horde of brawny demons brandishing pitchforks. The figures disappeared into the murk beyond.

"Three . . . two . . . one. *Begin Palpator: Sense-o-Round Two . . . ,*" the announcer roared.

Fiery red letters and numbers appeared above.

GRAVITY: −4
RESISTANCE: +7

The children's armor rippled and twitched. Milton fought for control of his Unity-Tard suit. Inside, tiny cattle prods zapped his muscles, forcing him out toward the center of the arena. His friends, limbs spasming with shock, were forced there with him.

Twizzle-zip!

The sultry form of Principal Bubb's severely altered alter ego swished into view, clad in a clingy chain-mail evening dress.

"You know me, you worthless guttersnipes," she said, her harsh words flowing like poisoned honey. "I'm not the touchy-feely type. But for your sakes, you'd better get in touch with your feelings: *while you can still feel them . . .*"

Her throaty cackle echoed throughout the Sense-o-Rama as she was enveloped in shadow. A wave of putrid stench, like the smell of thousands of decaying fish carcasses, spilled out from the far end of the arena. A mountain of writhing spikes slid into view amidst the churning murk.

"Behold the mighty Tactagon!" Bea "Elsa" Bubb roared. "A creature whose bear hugs no one can *bear*!"

Glorm!

The creature rumbled forward, briefly illuminated by a wobbling band of simulated underwater moonlight. Even though Milton's vision was faltering, there was no mistaking the monstrous threat before him. The Tactagon was the size of a small hill, carpeted with countless barbed tentacles. And it was coming closer.

Snorfle!

The Sunshine Sneezer lurched forward.

"Am . . . being . . . played," he grunted. He leapt into the air, hovering—almost swimming—before returning to the ground. "The physics of this round," he muttered as he fought for control of his armor. "They're different. Like floating in water."

A portal slid open to the left of the Terawatts.

Schwaa!

Out shot a half-dozen weapons, clanging at their feet. Words blazed above.

WEAPON: SHRIEK-SPEAR

Milton stooped down and felt around the slick floor with his numb hands. He grabbed a weapon and held it up close to his face. It was like a trident, with tiny windmill blades covering its tines.

Milton sprang into the air, soaring above the heads of

his friends before gently floating back to the ground. The monster lumbered forward in a patch of billowing, pale-green light. Milton's fuzzy vision could make out a shaggy form, mottled in splashes of blue and pink, swaying its sawtooth limbs like a sea anemone. Milton turned to his friends.

"I say we slash our way to the next level, then rush back for Ariel. Maybe, for once, we just surrender to the game and let the kids above fight."

Sara shrugged.

"It couldn't hurt. . . . Well, it might, but it's worth a try."

The Terawatts trained their tridents ahead in the leaden gloom.

"Now!" Milton yelled.

The children were tugged into the air by the players above, like marionettes on rubber bands wielded by invisible giants. Milton waved his Shriek-Spear in the air.

Wheeeesh!

Its windmill blades screamed. Instantly, the Tactagon flung its gigantic, jagged tentacles wildly in every direction, slicing open the armor on Howler Monkey's chest.

Wargle-lash!

Howler Monkey screamed as he was tossed against the Sense-o-Rama's sloping wall. Another tentacle lashed at the Sunshine Sneezer's back, sending him spinning in the air.

Skeech!

The boy slammed into Sam/Sara, with the three Terawatts sent sprawling onto the muddy floor.

Milton swung his trident in whistling arcs above his head.

Wheesh! Wheesh!

The Tactagon bowed what must have been its head— a hideous, mewling orifice surrounded by twisted, translucent horns—and vented a piercing, keening shriek.

Squeeeerp!

Milton sliced at the air in front of him.

Wheesh! Squeeeerp!

The creature screamed.

Hans had gone overboard without a life vest. Every square inch of his school locker real estate had been devoted to a picture or news clipping of Marlo. Hans's obsessive dedication to her bordered on serial killer, though Marlo had little to worry about, being dead and all. He even had a calendar of crucial Marlo-centric days: her birthday, her unbirthday (Marlo assumed Hans couldn't quite bring himself to celebrate her death), and various supposedly Marlo-specific days of mysterious import only to Hans.

"I can tell you're here," Hans muttered, not wanting the other kids to think that he was any weirder than they already thought he was.

How? Marlo thought-texted as her shadow grazed his InfoSwank multimedia belt-buckle phone.

"Because when you're here, I miss you," he whispered. "It's weird. It's like eating a sandwich and getting hungrier."

He sighed miserably as he pulled out his textbooks and slammed the door of his locker.

"Though I could just be down because, instead of studying for my precalculus exam yesterday, I was digging through a garbage heap on some sentimental archaeological dig."

Did you bring them? The letters?

Hans nodded as he glanced down at the stained papers poking out of his Pee Chee folder.

"Yeah, I—"

A jock splashed water on Hans's head from his water bottle.

"Sorry, man." The square-jawed boy smirked, his sincerity as fake as a three-dollar bill. "I thought your hair was on fire!"

The boy joined his braying friends as they traded shoulder punches.

Hans mechanically pulled out a handkerchief from his jeans pocket and patted down his hair. Marlo had a feeling that the handkerchief was used expressly for the purpose of cleaning up after jock-related acts of humiliation.

"Brought them," he continued, undeterred.

Marlo felt a strange sense of protectiveness for Hans. A connection. It wasn't like they had fallen in love or anything, at least not from Marlo's perspective. It was more like they had fallen into a snug mutual weirdness. She skittered along the fluorescent-lit floor and threw herself in the jock's path. The glint of merry malice in the boy's blue eyes was instantly doused.

"I feel . . . lame about that," the boy murmured with a haunted sadness. "He's just a kid like me, trying to get through his day. Maybe *I'm* the loser."

Marlo skittered back to Hans across a shuddering band of fluorescent light.

Meet me after school at my house . . . 33 Paradiso Crescent.

"Yeah, I know where you live," Hans muttered. "I used to hang out there all the time . . . you know, with Milton. You probably don't remember."

Right. Of course. Sorry. I'm brain dead. Everything dead, actually. Get it?

Hans swallowed nervously.

"I, um, was supposed to meet . . . uh . . . someone at Fragopolis."

Yeah, yeah. Aubrey. Try to squeeze me in, you double-timing Romeo. Heck hath no fury like a dead woman scorned. I'm going to wander around town—leaving gloom in my wake, I guess—then head to the arcade, one of the spots I'm supposed to haunt.

The class bell rang like a nuclear migraine down the hall.

"Okay, I'll meet you then," he said as he looped the

strap of his backpack over his skinny shoulder and trotted down the hall. "Bye . . . um, Marlo."

Marlo relaxed beneath the shadow of an overflowing garbage can.

It's all so complicated, she thought from her patch of cool darkness. *Here I am, running around like the shadow of a chicken with its head cut off, and Milton's probably just kicking back in some lame class, trying to keep his geeky eyes open. . . .*

Milton fell to the ground, slowly, as if he were deep-sea diving. Beside him lay a wriggling tentacle. The Tactagon retreated back into the murk.

Milton crawled on his hands and knees toward his fallen friends.

"Are you guys okay?"

The Sunshine Sneezer nodded.

"If it wasn't for the simulated water environment breaking our fall," he replied, "we wouldn't be having this conversation."

Sam/Sara pushed themselves off the floor.

"The full-body numbness helps, too," Sara said, brushing the hair from her almond eyes. "Though I can feel the pain jabbing through."

Milton peered off into the murk. The Tactagon's massive silhouette rippled in the distance like a thorny undersea leviathan.

"Maybe we can hack off another tentacle," Milton said while the creature bleated unnervingly from the other side of the arena.

Sara pointed at the Tactagon. "Look!" she said.

Milton tried but could barely make out more than its bristling outline.

"It's growing back," Sara continued with horror. "Its tentacle. It looks like it's growing *two*."

"You're kidding," Milton replied, appalled.

"There's no way we can win," Sam said with weak certainty. "The more we hurt it, the stronger it'll get."

Milton drew in a deep breath of fetid fish air and stood, gripping his trident.

"Then we'll just have to hit it as fast and as furious as we can. Not all of us will make it, but maybe *some* of us will."

The Terawatts glanced at one another gravely. The Sunshine Sneezer sighed with resignation as he rose to his feet.

"Might as well get it over with," he said with a sniffle as he prepared for a ludicrously one-sided battle.

"Wait!" Caterwaul yelled. The other children turned. There, crouched on the muddy ground, was Caterwaul, her long face quavering and her right arm thrust up to her elbow inside the Tactagon's dismembered pink tentacle.

"She must be in shock," Sara whispered to Milton before turning to the girl. "That's a very nice arm you have there, Caterwaul," she added slowly and deliberately, as if talking to a crazy person. "Very pretty."

Caterwaul slid her arm out of the tentacle and wiped the slime off on her armor.

"No, you don't get it," she replied. "I can *feel* what the Tactagon feels, and it feels scared."

"What?" Milton asked, giving a sideways glance to the behemoth at the other end of the arena. "That massive spiky mountain of death, scared?"

Caterwaul rose. Her wide eyes were shiny, not with her usual gleam of fear and unease but with conviction.

"I used to see this counselor who was always telling me to 'get in touch with my feelings,'" she explained. "I'd always been afraid to do it, thinking it would hurt, even though she kept saying it would help me to get over my fears. So, here in this awful place, I just freaked out. Total panic attack. And that's when I put my hand in the tentacle—"

"Which begs the question *why*," Sam interjected.

"Because I . . . I don't know . . . *felt* like it," she replied. "Doing something—anything—was better than just being scared. And when I put the tentacle on, I could feel all of these weird sensations fresh and strong. A blend of fear and anger. It—the Tactagon—really can't stand the whistling sound the tridents make. Sends it into this furious, terrified rage. It just lashes out, because it doesn't know what else to do."

The Sunshine Sneezer brushed sweat-matted strands of hair from his eyes.

"The Shriek-Spears actually *cause* the fighting?"

Milton stared out across the dark ooze and muck. The Tactagon's mountainous barbed body blocked all passage to the next level.

"So what are we supposed to do?" Sam said with a bitter laugh. "Just wait here until the kids upstairs run out of quarters?"

"No," Caterwaul replied. "We pet it."

"Pet it?!" the other children gasped in unison.

"And maybe a tickle or two," Caterwaul continued. "See, I got the sense that it actually feeds on touch . . . and it is starving. If we pat and stroke it nicely, maybe it will get docile and let us pass."

A shiver of electricity shot up Milton's spine and out to his arms. He fought the urge to run at the Tactagon and lance it with his trident.

"The players are getting restless," he said. "They want some action."

"Brock, brock, brock," the fake Principal Bubb taunted from the shadows. "Chicken cleanup on aisle four . . ."

Milton set his trident down.

"Let's give that thing the scritch of its life."

Howler Monkey, the Sunshine Sneezer, Sara, and—lastly—her brother set down their weapons and made their way across the swampy floor of the coliseum, each taking turns dragging Ariel behind them.

Glorm-foddle!

The Tactagon reared back, extending its fore-tentacles like gigantic slimy sabers. The Terawatts twitched violently as the players above tried to pitch them into bloody battle. Milton stepped beneath what appeared to be the beast's head.

The Tactagon raised two of its tentacle spines above Milton. The creature's limbs tensed into points at the ends, curving into trembling hooks poised to pierce Milton clean through. Milton found bare areas between the Tactagon's barbed appendages and gently caressed the creature's spongy, vaguely electric flesh.

Squickle!

Caterwaul pressed her hands into the Tactagon's squishy skin.

"It's working!" she said with a wide toothy grin.

As the creature's spines relaxed, Milton could see a vague, circular outline in the mud, with a dark blob at the edge.

"It's another Zetawatt!" Sara said, her keen vision slicing through the shadowy murk. "Wyatt, I think."

"Take Ariel to the portal," Milton said to Sam/Sara as he scratched the Tactagon around the rim of a tentacle. "We'll keep petting this thing until you're there, then make a run for it."

Sara nodded. Sam just rolled his eyes, not liking to be ordered around, but he worked in tandem with his sister regardless.

"Excellent teamwork, Terawatts," Provost Marshal Tesla's voice boomed from the arena's hidden speakers.

"What is going on?!" Milton cried.

Tesla laughed, a sputtering, hyena giggle that hissed like static.

"That's right," he replied. "I promised you information for every Sense-o-Round you survive!"

He paused, his silence an audible hum filling the arena.

"Zhe players above are thoroughly immersed," he continued. "Brilliantly done. Zhe Zetawatts dropped out too soon, one by one, giving zhe game fewer variables."

"Why are we here?" Milton asked.

"Answer number one: Every trap needs bait," Tesla explained. "And you're it. All of you."

"Bait? For what?"

"Answer number two: You didn't think this—zhe most extraordinary gaming experience of all time—was created merely to bring joy to zhe world's joystick jockeys?" He twittered like a delirious European bird. "Why, Mr. Fauster, it is zhe crown jewel of an elaborate stratagem to snatch zhe souls of children straight from their living bodies . . . straight from zhe Surface!"

Milton swallowed, a hard, cold lump of dread that traveled down his throat, slow and painful, like a jagged, bitter pill.

"But how? *Why?*" Milton managed as Sam/Sara made it to the circular portal etched on the Sense-o-Rama floor.

"Zhat, my unwitting colleague, is an answer you have yet to earn—down in Sense-o-Round Three!"

26 · EAR-RATIONAL BEHAVIOR

"THREE...TWO...ONE. Begin Auralla: Sense-o-Round Three..."

The Terawatts were submerged in humid darkness. Milton's right ear had, almost immediately, become so sensitive that it throbbed with pain. He could hear his heart pounding in his chest, the blood surging volcanically through his veins, his breath a creaking bellows, and his stomach doing gastric somersaults. Even his footsteps tread like a tap-dancing elephant.

"Something is out there. I can feel it," Caterwaul whispered.

"Of course something's out there, crybaby," Sam grumbled. "This isn't solitaire."

"Could you guys stop fighting?" the Sunshine Sneezer pleaded. "It's hurting my ears. At least one of them."

"Mine too," Milton replied.

"My ears are all, like, plugged up," Howler Monkey said.

"What?" Sara asked. "I can't hear you because my ears are all—"

"Shhh!" Milton scolded, his voice tearing the air like an amplified paper shredder. "I hear something. . . ."

Eeeeeekakaeeeeeeee!

There was a steady, ceaseless trill hovering in the uppermost belfry of Milton's ability to hear. Like a field full of crickets, only with no pause in between the high-pitched chirps.

"I hear it, too," the Sunshine Sneezer whispered, trying not to hurt his own suddenly superpowered ear.

"And I feel this odd heat," Caterwaul murmured. "But as soon as I zero in on it, it seems to . . . hop away."

"Look, there's a three-headed blob!" Sara said, pointing ahead in the darkness. "Wait . . . it's gone."

Sproing!

After a moment of high-pressure silence, Caterwaul whispered in the dark. "Do you think this game is really stealing souls?" she asked sadly. "Like Tesla said? And that we're, by even being here, somehow helping him?"

"Maybe we should just, like, throw the game," Howler Monkey offered.

"And end up like those zombie Zetawatts Milton has us dragging around?" Sam replied. "Not me."

"Sam's right," Milton replied. He never thought that those particular words would pass his lips. "If we make it through all the levels, we might find a way to stop Tesla. If we give up, he'll just send in the next batch of Arcadia kids to replace us."

Schwaaa . . . clang!

A metallic clank, horrific at least to Milton's sensitive ear, reverberated several yards away.

"New weapons," Sara said. Milton could hear her and her brother's footsteps. "Some kind of hoop with—oww—spikes."

Fiery red letters blazed above.

WEAPON: BARBA-HOOP

Milton felt around on the floor until he found his weapon: two metal hoops bound together, one on top of the other, with spikes along the rim.

"They're like hula hoops," Sara said. "So maybe we just—"

A blinding shower of sparks stripped away the darkness. Sam/Sara's spiked hoop weapon swiveled on their hips, sending forth a gleaming cascade of light. The glow, unfortunately, illuminated what awaited beyond.

A twenty-foot-tall creature, like a nightmarish cross between a one-eared vampire bat and a furry orchid, loomed ahead. Its gargantuan ear—like a pointed cobra's hood, minus the cobra—faced outward, apparently serving as the creature's face, with a small hole at the center fringed with teeth.

Eeeeeekakaeeeeeeee!

Sprouting on either side of the creature's yellow-brown midsection were three tiny arms with silver claws at the ends that spun like deadly pinwheels. It didn't seem to have legs. Instead, it bobbed softly on a coiled, springlike tail. The monster lurched forward, hissing—as did the two other, identical creatures behind it.

Caterwaul screamed as Sam/Sara's Barba-Hoop fell to the ground. Everything went dark.

"Food, meet the Oscithrauds," the game version of Principal Bubb announced from the other end of the arena. "Oscithrauds, meet your food. I'm sure you have a lot to talk about . . . though, it's rude to talk with your mouth full."

Dale E. Basye walked out onto the dock overlooking his gated community's simulated bay—the corporately sponsored Gulf of Texaco. Light jazz music drifted across the lagoon as the Avalawns at the United Estates of Nevada hosted its nightly small-scale regatta. Dale lifted up the chain barring access to the dock's edge—carefully looking out for Mrs. Fitzgerald, head of the estate's Synthetic Recreational Waterways Safety Board—and sat down, legs dangling over the shamelessly blue water in brazen contradiction of estate policy.

Twilight slathered the Las Vegas sky in reckless oranges and decadent magentas as tiny sailboats skimmed across the miniature gulf course.

It would be beautiful if it wasn't so perfect, Dale thought as he redialed Phelps Better's number yet again on his iSlab.

"Hello?" the man's smug voice replied on the other end of the line.

"Yes, this is Dale. Look, I've been having second thoughts—"

"Ha! *Gotcha!* Leave a message after the beep and I'll get back to you if I don't have anything better to do. Get it? *Better.* Because of my last—"

Dale jabbed off his phone app and brooded, watching several children across the glitter-infused water glide on skate-shoes to an inflatable castle. He typed a note on his iSlab.

Irrational Fears #6,072 and #6,073:
kids on skate-shoes and large bouncy castles.

Dale wished his surroundings were more in line with his internal turmoil. Pouring rain would be more fitting for the sense of haunted melancholy, the emotional dusk he felt inside. All he wanted was what anyone wanted these days: to realize the American Dream. But in a city with a case of neon-agitated insomnia, who could even sleep, much less dream? And as he considered the supposed victims of the game that was to make both his name and fortune, even the pursuit of sudden, unearned riches and fleeting fame seemed somehow . . . *hollow.*

Still, it takes two to make an accident, Dale rationalized. *Heck: Where the Bad Kids Go* was only his idea—well, that kid Damian's, if you wanted to get technical. It was that creep Phelps Better and the engineers at Virtual Prayground who made it something potentially dangerous.

A mysterious green light, feathery and far away, rippled in the water at the end of the dock. It had a hopeful quality to it, pure and sincere, that was at odds with the vulgar, gaudy neon glow of the casinos framing it.

It was in that moment that Dale E. Basye—the "E" typically standing for "Easy Way Out"—knew what he had to do. Something difficult. Something awkward. Something potentially damaging, career-wise. He would call a press conference and nip the festering outrage his game had aroused among parents in the proverbial bud. Dale would appear before the angry mob of his detractors and turn their fury into opportunity: an opportunity for redemption, to clear his name and perhaps even embolden it in the process. And if the American Dream was about anything, it was about the opportunity for a second chance. Even in the arid soul desert of Las Vegas.

He smiled at the green light that, for an instant, seemed to understand him as he wanted to be understood, believe in him as he would like to believe in himself.

Dale caught the wizened, judgmental form of Mrs. Fitzgerald cutting across the obsessively manicured golf course—her act in itself worthy of report—toward the dock. He quickly ducked beneath the chain. *So this is what it feels like to do the right thing,* Dale thought while jogging toward the vulgar sanctuary of his McMansion.

The fake principal's throaty laugh filled the coliseum.

"They've seen us . . . the *Oscithrauds,*" Milton whispered to his friends. "We've got to spread out or we're toast . . . or whatever those gross things have for breakfast."

The Terawatts scattered. Milton could hear the creatures springing in the dark.

Auralla, Milton thought as he tried to calm the clamor of his terrified body. *Like aural . . . relating to hearing.*

Milton felt inside his armor. There, tucked in his Arcadia belt, was van Gogh's ear. He pulled it out and held it to his bad ear, the left one. Suddenly, he could hear in stereo again.

Eeeeeeekakaeeeeeeee!

The wavering chirp seemed to come from everywhere.

Bats use echolocation—sending out sound and reflecting it off their victims—so maybe that's what the Oscithrauds are trying to do. We've got to locate them first.

Milton had an idea.

"Sunshine Sneezer," he whispered. "Come here. Follow my voice."

The boy joined his side.

"What is it?" he muttered.

"Which ear is your good one?"

"My left."

"Mine is my right. I'm using van Gogh's ear. Press your head against mine. It should give us three-dimensional hearing. The ability to triangulate the Oscithrauds' positions."

"Brilliant," the Sunshine Sneezer said. "Let's try."

The two boys pressed their heads together. Instantly, the chirping formed a sort of picture in their heads, an aural sculpture, with Milton sensing the Oscithrauds' hideous shapes with crisp, sonic clarity.

Eeeeeeekakaeeeeeeee!

"Hostiles at one, five, and nine o'clock," the Sunshine Sneezer whispered. "They're circling us—and we thought we were circling *them*. What should we do?"

"I guess the only thing we can do is hurl these hoops at them. Let's try the closest one. The one at five o'clock."

"Okay, on the count of three. One . . . two . . . *three!*"

The two boys hurled their spiked hoops into the dark.

Whooshle-whoosh!

Milton's hoop grazed the Oscithraud's side, while the Sunshine Sneezer's weapon hit the creature squarely on the base of its spring tail. It screamed, an ultrasonic whistle that felt like barbed-wire floss through Milton's ears. The wounded Oscithraud hopped erratically around the coliseum squealing in pain.

Screaleach!!

The noise made Milton drop van Gogh's ear. Now the only thing Milton could hear was Sara's terrified shriek in the sticky hot blackness.

27 · SiNG FOR
YOUR STUPOR

MILTON'S ARMOR TWITCHED with the bloodlust of the gamers above on the Surface. He fought the reckless, electrical twitches spreading across his body.

Screech! Swipe!

"My leg!" Howler Monkey screamed. "Something sliced it open!"

The weapons aren't helping, Milton thought desperately in the dark, the chaotic sounds of fear and pain ricocheting all around him. *I've got to think of something before those things bounce us apart . . . something more defensive than offensive, like with the Tactagon.*

Ooohlalargh!

The Oscithraud's wail had an almost musical quality to it, a jagged warble of lament.

That's it, Milton thought as he grabbed the Sunshine Sneezer by the hand and pressed his head against his. "C'mon, we're going to use our voices to soothe those savage beasts."

"What?"

"Like in Mr. Orpheus's class," Milton explained as he followed the whimpers of his wounded friends using van Gogh's ear to triangulate their positions in the dark.

Milton collected Sam/Sara, Howler Monkey, and lastly, following her sobs, Caterwaul.

"Let's start with something simple and cheery," Milton said. "A major C chord. I'll start with the root, C. Sam, you sing E. Sara, you'll be the G on top. The rest of you double up, to thicken the sound. Okay?"

The team mumbled their unconvinced assent.

"It's like singing at our own funerals, but sure, whatever," Sam replied as he and his sister drew in a deep breath.

"We've got to get this right the first time," Milton said. "With all of us singing, we'll be pretty easy to track down, so here goes."

Milton sang his note, with Sam/Sara joining in. Howler Monkey doubled Milton's C, with the Sunshine Sneezer and Caterwaul filling out the upper registers of the chord. Milton, head pressed against the Sunshine Sneezer, held out van Gogh's ear into the darkness.

Eeeeeeekakaeeeeeeee!

He could hear-see the Oscithrauds, frighteningly

close around them. They stopped bouncing and swayed their great, pointed ear heads from side to side.

"I think it's working," the Sunshine Sneezer said in between breaths.

Sproing! Sproing! Sproing!

Suddenly, the three Oscithrauds resumed their springing with renewed vigor. As the massive creatures bounded across the coliseum, their bladelike claws spinning at their sides, Milton swallowed. It was even worse than watching his parents try to imitate the latest dance move.

"We need something less peppy," he suggested. "A minor chord. Sam and Sunshine Sneezer, slip down a half note to D-sharp."

The Terawatt singers drew in a deep breath as the Oscithrauds vaulted around them, violently happy, in the dark. The children's voices weaved together into a somber harmony, a ragged gray tapestry of sound. The Oscithrauds lost their dangerous spring and wilted like a monstrous flowerbed watered with tears.

"Caterwaul, make some sparks with your Barba-Hoop thing so we can find the portal to the next level," Milton called out. "Sam/Sara and Howler Monkey, help me with Wyatt and Ariel. And don't stop singing!"

The group slunk past the drooping creatures and to the outline of the next portal.

"More baggage," muttered Sam sourly as he spotted another figure sprawled out on the tarnished metal floor.

The girl's dark hair spilled out around her head like a fatal brunette head wound.

"Libby," Milton muttered as he leaned down by her side. "Can you hear me?"

The girl fluttered her eyelids. Glazed eye whites, like tiny hard-boiled eggs trembling in her sockets, shone through her lashes. A patch of blood oozed through the chest of her armor. Libby nodded weakly and managed to push herself up off the floor, as if she were trying to sleepwalk but was just too exhausted.

Eeeeeeekakaeeeeeeee!

The Oscithrauds lifted their cavernous ear-flap heads, training them on the Terawatts as the children's voices faltered. Milton looked up at the glimmering sky of dull eyeballs.

"Okay, Tesla!" Milton shouted. "We beat this round. Now we want some answers! You said you were snatching human souls from the Surface! But there's no way . . . I mean, how could anyone do that? Not to mention *why*—"

Sam/Sara dragged Wyatt to the rim of the portal as Tesla's voice crackled through the arena's embedded speakers.

"Though your victory is a touch premature," Tesla relayed in his manic Eastern European stumble of a voice, "I will reward your curiosity at my masterwork . . . zhe Sense-o-Rama. Mass entertainment began with one dimension—zhe novel; then two dimensions—movies and television; then three dimensions—zhe three-D movie; and now, with zhe Sense-o-Rama, four-dimensional entertainment: full-sensory engagement. And in zhe cradle of zhe senses like a diamond rests zhe human soul."

Skizzle!

The twin hoops around Caterwaul's hips—gyrating in opposing directions to create their shower of sparks—wobbled unsteadily. In the flickering light, Milton saw the Oscithrauds jouncing uneasily on their coiled spring tails. The children's singing voices roughened into a chorus of barely musical croaks.

"Zhe Sense-o-Rama—as you have learned from zhe inside out—engages each of zhe senses in a specific way with a specific intensity," Tesla continued. "As zhe game progresses through each of its five levels, zhe senses are systematically overloaded, loosening zhe grip that zhe human body has on zhe soul. Zhe body's hold grows slack—zhe corporeal lock housing zhe human soul can be picked from afar—and zhe soul is thusly drained."

"Drained?!" Milton said, horrified. "But why?"

Tesla chuckled.

"Short answer: *why not?* A brilliant invention is its own reason for being. Long answer . . . well, you must earn zhat now, mustn't you?"

Caterwaul, exhausted, let her hoop weapon clatter to her ankles.

The Sunshine Sneezer yanked Milton onto the portal. The Terawatts, unable to sing another note, huddled together in the circle. The Oscithrauds screamed, incensed, in Milton's overly sensitive ears.

"We've got to go!" the Sunshine Sneezer said as the aperture opening beneath them slowly unfolded. "Or those monsters are going to get an earful—*of us*!!"

Hans Jovonovic fidgeted on the Fausters' doorstep.

"No one must be home," he muttered nervously to Marlo's silhouette, splayed out beneath the SOLD sign out by the stoop. "I'll just leave the letters in the mailbox."

This isn't a game of doorbell ditch, Marlo thought-texted to the jittery redheaded boy's belt buckle. You've got to hand them to her. It will jolt her out of her woe-is-me daze and she'll actually pay attention. Did you text my dad? Tell him to be here nowish?

"Yeah, of course I did," Hans murmured. "I'd do anything for—"

Three progressively louder creaks sounded from the other side of the door, followed by the unlatching of the dead bolt. Rosemary Fauster's face pressed out from between the door and the jam. To Marlo, her mother looked like the haunted heroine of a silent film. Like someone who had been tied to train tracks by a dastardly man with an interesting mustache. Disheveled yet beautiful, even her face looked like it was black and white.

"Yes?" she asked with a shaky smile she couldn't quite commit to.

"I," Hans squeaked before clearing his throat. "I . . . Hello, Mrs. Fauster."

"Hal?"

"*Hans* . . . How are you?"

"Fine," she lied. "What can I do for you?"

Hans swallowed and pulled the letters from his Pee Chee folder.

"These are for you," he said in one breath, handing her the sheaf quickly, as if he were a sheriff serving someone papers to appear in court. "I . . . found them in . . . some stuff. Stuff Milton must have . . . *left* . . ."

Rosemary Fauster scanned the first letter, confused.

"But why would Milton—"

A white Rambler station wagon squealed to a stop outside the house.

"Rosemary?!" Blake Fauster called frantically as he hopped out of the car. "Are you all right?"

The woman's face scrunched with confusion.

"Blake? Yes . . . why *wouldn't* I be okay?"

The middle-aged man scratched at his salt-and-pepper goatee and glanced down at his cell phone.

"I got a message . . . a text," he replied, his urgency melting into puzzlement as he walked toward the house. "From one of Milton's friends. Saying that you needed help . . ."

Both adults stared at Hans and his unaccountable

presence, like a singing duo who had just been joined onstage by a vaguely familiar stranger.

"I've gotta go," Hans said as he fled to his bike leaning against the garage. He whispered from the corner of his mouth to Marlo's shadow, "See you later—at Fragopolis?"

Sure. I'm going to see how this goes down.

Hans gave a quick nod and hopped onto his bike, pedaling furiously.

"Hey, you!" Blake Fauster yelled in his deep, professorial tone. "Come back!"

Rosemary Fauster, her attention dragged deeper into the letters as if they were quicksand, seemed to crumple onto the porch. Her wet eyes quivered as they scanned the pages in darting sweeps before, unable to hold back the pressure any longer, they gushed with tears, like a levy weakened from lack of levity suddenly releasing a flood of water down into an unsuspecting valley.

"Oh, Blake," she sobbed. "What are we doing?"

Her husband set his hand awkwardly on her shoulder before taking it away, then, after a moment's reconsideration, set it back. Blake leaned in to his weeping wife and read the letters over her heaving shoulder.

"Where did you find . . . ?" he said shakily. Blake sat down beside Rosemary. "I thought I threw these away."

Rosemary held out Blake's latest, undelivered letter.

"How come you never gave me this?" she asked, her pale cheeks slick with tears. She read from the letter:

" 'We will always be together even if you cannot bear us being together.' "

Rosemary set the letter in her lap, the paper quivering in her shaky hands.

"I . . . I feel the same way," she said weakly, unable to prevent her suddenly heavy head from resting on his shoulder. "I can't bear the thought of being away from you, but it's just too painful . . . too painful to have you here, like nothing has happened, when the worst thing that can ever happen *has*. Being with you makes me feel like a frame without a picture. Empty. But without you, I feel somehow *less* than empty."

Blake squeezed her shoulder closer to him.

"It's odd, but somehow I know that Marlo and Milton are together," he murmured. "That should count for something."

Marlo's parents started to cry as one, their sobs synced together in mutual sympathy.

"Maybe we could get away for a bit," Rosemary suggested. "To that place in Maine, near where you did your residency."

Marlo could feel herself back in Snivel, crying. She didn't fight it. It actually felt good, like throwing up after eating bad seafood.

Parents are like time machines, she thought as they chattered on about old times, each memory releasing another. *They can send each other back to any point in their relationship.*

Marlo grew dizzy. Her shadow-self felt fuzzy and loose, as if it could be snatched away by the wind.

A swooping shadow streaked along the sidewalk toward Marlo: wings like great pointy triangles at its sides, a beak as sharp and determined as a knight's sword. Suddenly, the shadow overtook hers, and the two other-worldly smudges tangled in chaotic fury like flattened black alley cats fighting and scratching on the asphalt.

28 · SCENTS AND SENSE-ABiLiTY

THE FOURTH SENSE-O-RAMA level was like the inside of a giant red golf ball: a geodesic sphere tinted dark scarlet and covered with dozens of hexagonal panels. A wide steel ring wrapped around the sphere's equator, cinching the concave honeycomb of hexagons into two massive hemispheres.

"*Ten . . . nine . . . eight . . . ,*" the demon announcer barked.

Droooorn!

A hum, so thick that Milton could feel it vibrating against his seminumbed skin, filled the arena. He and his friends walked unsteadily away from the rim of the entrance portal as it slid closed behind them.

Foomp!

Milton stepped onto one of the glowing red panels, each about the size of a large, six-sided trampoline. The vacant eyes of the gamers from the Surface were spread throughout the sphere, not all bunched up at the ceiling.

"Six . . . five . . . four . . . "

A film of backward green letters covered the eye clusters like neon contact lenses. Milton could barely make out the words as his vision—and most every sense save for his hearing—was fading fast.

Ƨᴚᴉꓑꓤ-o-ꓤoᴜᴎꓷ ꓑoᴜꓤ: OᴌꓞᴀꓛTᴚIX

Above and beyond the group of Arcadians was an open iron gate, suspended upside down, surrounding the only green panel.

"Look!" Caterwaul said, pointing to a figure struggling on the gate.

It was one of the Zetawatts, a small, wiry boy named Joey. He hung from one of the gate's twisted spires, which had skewered his shredded armor.

"This shouldn't be, like, too hard," Howler Monkey said. "We just need to climb—"

" . . . One . . . Begin Olfactrix: Sense-o-Round Four," the announcer bellowed.

"Olfactrix," Milton repeated. "Like *olfactory*, relating to smell."

He sniffed the air around him but felt stuffed up, only without the congestion.

Milton turned to his team. "Can any of you smell?"

Howler Monkey sniffed his underarm.

"I'm sure I probably reek. But I can't smell a thing."

In fact, none of the Terawatts could discern any odor whatsoever.

"Oh dear," the game version of Principal Bubb said, fluttering above them on black feathered wings, clad in a bronze bikini that set off her smooth green skin. "If none of you can smell, then I have a feeling that this level is going to *stink*."

Schwaa!

Suddenly, two panels bracketing the gate slid open. From one fell five large, flat doughnut-shaped boards. Blazing red letters appeared in the air above the Terawatts.

WEAPON: SKIMMER RING
GRAVITY: 360°

Sam/Sara stooped down before the board closest to them.

"It's like a round skateboard," Sara said as she held the smooth, flattened ring in her hands. She examined it with her odd, heightened vision. "Only no wheels . . . but there's this weird porous grid on the bottom."

She set it down on the ground and stepped on it.

"And there's a sort of foot switch here—"

The board purred and, with a whoosh of air, hovered inches off the ground.

"Cool!" the Sunshine Sneezer said, an elfish grin crinkling his pointy face. "An air-hockey table you can ride!"

Milton hopped onto his board and switched it on.

This is almost fun, he thought as he skimmed along the floor. He kicked at the ground through the hooped board's center. *If we ace this level and the next, we can figure out how to pull the plug on Tesla's plot.*

Droooorn!!

The low-level buzz of the arena swelled.

Zoop!

Suddenly, a gush of supersized wasps flew out from the open panel above, about a dozen to Milton's faulty eyes. The insects were the size of small dogs, with three long, lacy wings sprouting from each of their yellow thoraxes; black pincers on what looked to be their heads; and big, flared openings at the tip of their butts from which streamed a shimmering trail of purplish vapor.

"The Azafooms are especially agitated today, by the smell of it," Principal Bubb noted above, sniffing the air with her dainty nose.

Zip! Zizzle!

The Terawatts crouched on the ground in fear. A riot of clashing odors pricked Milton's nose, but his sense of smell was so dull that he couldn't make any sense of them. Grass clippings, moldy cheese, cherry Jell-O, *very*-used kitty litter. As soon as one muffled odor elbowed its way to the front of the pack, it was over-taken and dragged back into the mob.

"But then again, they always get that way," the demoness continued, "around feeding time."

Whoomp!

A honeycomb panel slid open twenty feet away from Milton. Inside was a fat, snarling pustule with a gaping cave of gnashing teeth.

Snarp! Snarp!

Long, bladelike claws twitched along its sides, thrash-ing blindly at the air around it. The panel slid closed, just as another panel—revealing yet another hungry, boil-like creature—opened.

Whoomp! Whoomp!

The arena's red panels slid randomly open and closed. The ravenous beasts inside popped out with all the manic ferocity of an especially gruesome game of Whac-A-Mole.

"Awww, they're so cute when they're young," the fake principal said as she flitted through the gate above. "Now, one Azafoom will lead you to freedom with its ever-changing bouquet of sweet fragrances. The others will lead you to the hungry mouths of their young through their pungent, distracting reek," the shapely principal called out over her gleaming shoulder plate as she dove toward the exit.

Thoop!

The lights went out.

"Your noses know. Let's just pray they're up to snuff," she laughed. "Not that I would know anything about *praying* . . ."

Marlo's shade-self wrestled with the vicious bird shadow along the otherwise placid streets of Generica, Kansas. She could feel the creature's sharp, ice-cold beak jabbing at her, as if trying to peck away . . .

My soul! Marlo realized as she rolled along the gutters in a dark, feathery tumble. *This spirit is trying to fillet my soul! It's been hunting me ever since I got to the Surface, and I guess when Mom and Dad started to come to grips with me being dead and all, my grief connection got weak, and this thing swooped in for the kill!*

The bird spirit mercilessly poked holes through Marlo's shadow and kept dragging her to the darkness of the city's sewer grates. She fought to gain purchase on a sharp patch of sunlight in the street, a place where she could recoup some sense of definition and strength, but Marlo could feel her hold grow slack under the flapping shadow's unrelenting tug.

"*Baron Samedi,*" the Grin Reaper shouted from outside Marlo's chamber. "*We losing girl. To Litsowo.*"

The dark, slender man in his top hat and tails knelt down before the controls of the Wastrel Projector below.

"The vice principal won't be likin' this—turnin' up the light juice—but he won't be wantin' us to be losin' another *timoun* to de big shadow zwazo, neither."

Baron Samedi's bulging eyes examined a row of fluctuating meters and digital readouts. He sighed.

"Light like likid . . . like water," the man mumbled, watching the flow of light. "Is Haitian voodoo belief that the *nouvo* dead be slippin' into rivers and streams for a year and a day before they reborn."

Baron Samedi turned a dial.

"But mebbe some spirits too young and not be knowin' how to swim . . . get swallowed up by big mal fish."

The golden trickle of light coiling up the Wastrel Projector's network of fiber-optic vines flared with dangerous radiance. He patted his white-gloved hands with satisfaction.

"Yuh did see dat?" he said, grinning beneath the already grinning skull painted on his face. "A dun deal. Nothing to—"

A great blast of blinding honey light surged up the Wastrel Projector's stalk, engulfing the baron with a sickening sizzle. With his sad, wet-marble eyes, the Grin Reaper peered down from the railing above, considering the pile of hot ash that had, moments ago, answered to the name Baron Samedi. A yellow phone at the base of the machine rang. The Grin Reaper slunk down the stairs to the main level and plucked the oddly glowing phone from its cradle.

"Hello, you reach Shadow Box. This is . . . yes, Vice Principal. It was machine. The baron turn it up. We were losing another. You want talk to him?"

The Grin Reaper stared at the baron's smoldering cinders.

"He is on smoking break," the hooded creature replied as the Wastrel Projector shuddered and spasmed beside him. *"May I take message?"*

Marlo's shadow seared the sidewalk—sharp, dark, and strong, as if she had been spray-painted in black onto the asphalt with a *her*-shaped stencil. She kicked the bird spirit as hard as she could, flinging the menacing silhouette across the street under the awning of the All Washed Up Laundromat. Marlo hurled herself to the streaking shadow of a passing SUV.

I've got to get to Fragopolis, she thought as she sped down Wicked Wichita Way. *I need some of Hans's grief-stricken devotion to keep my connection strong, or else I'm birdseed.*

29 · WHIFF OR LOSE

SOMETHING WRIGGLED AGAINST Milton's side beneath his Unity-Tard.

Lucky, Milton thought as he reached inside a gash in his armor to free his squirming ferret.

The Sunshine Sneezer, groping around in the dark, latched on to Milton's arm.

"What are you doing?" the boy asked.

"Feeling Lucky," Milton replied as he held his flustered pet in his arms.

Sam snorted as he and the other children huddled around Milton.

"Blind optimism isn't going to get us out of this, *Dork Knight,*" he said.

"No, but my ferret might," Milton replied with a grin that no one but the Sunshine Sneezer could hear. "*Lucky.* He thinks with his nose."

Zoof! Zun!

The whoosh of darting Azafooms brushed past the Terawatts' heads. Lucky's tiny pink nostrils flared as they were assaulted by a blast of intensely pleasant odors: coconut suntan oil, Toll House cookies, pine trees, and Froot Loops. He stretched out his long, slender body and, straining toward the odor, struggled in Milton's grasp.

"You know seeing-eye dogs?" Milton said as he balanced on his Skimmer Ring. "Well, Lucky will be our *smelling-nose* ferret. His snout has got hold of something now, I can tell. Quick, let's form a train, everybody holding on to each other, and I'll use Lucky like an odor compass to lead us out of here. Grab the three Zetawatts, put them on your boards, and let's go."

Thum! Snarp! Snarp!

A hatch opened nearby. Milton could hear the monstrous baby Azafooms, slavering with mindless hunger, their jaws snatching at the air.

"Now. Before we're grub grub."

Zoop!

Milton felt the Sunshine Sneezer grab hold of his sides. A flying Azafoom whizzed past, its six tiny wings buzzing like dentists' drills, and nicked Caterwaul's ear. She cried out.

Milton kicked at the ground with one foot, propelling the Skimmer Ring forward like a skateboard. The train of Terawatts sped into the darkness.

Thoom!

Lucky strained forward, latching on to the sweet-smelling Azafoom. He stretched out, arching his fuzzy white body toward the smell so that Milton would know which direction to go through the confounding aromatic maze. Suddenly, another odor assailed the ferret's nose: something sharp and citric, like the smell of a veterinary hospital floor. Lucky shook off the smell as another crossed his path. Milton, feeling his wobbling ferret stiffen in one direction, kicked at the ground, pushing his Skimmer Ring faster.

Ziff!

The ferret struggled to regain hold of the coconut-cookie-pine-Froot-Loops smell. Lucky nipped Milton's hand.

"Faster!" Milton yelped. "Lucky's losing the trail!"

Caterwaul screamed from behind. "I almost fell into one of those nasty bug nurseries!"

"Keep close, everybody!" Milton yelled, kicking at the ground with his foot.

Thum! Snarp! Snarp!

A great blast of hot stench hit Milton's face, as if he had opened the door to an oven broiling Limburger lasagna. Though he could barely smell it, he found that he could taste it in the back of his throat. Milton leaned hard to his right and sped his friends away from the eager jaws of the baby Azafoom.

Zoosh!

A full-grown Azafoom dove from above, leaving behind the smell of freshly mown grass. Lucky twitched, confused as to which trail to take up, until an undercurrent of gasoline and sweat permeated the creature's wake. Lucky latched on to the original scent and stiffened to his left, with Milton adjusting his course in kind.

Suddenly, the gaming arena of Olfactrix was filled with light. Milton's stomach rolled over and played dead as he saw, with his failing eyes, that he and his friends had scooted halfway up the sloping side of the sphere and were—due to the Sense-o-Round's altered physics— nearing the ceiling, skimming the walls of the arena like a roller coaster in slow motion.

Honeycomb panels harboring ravenous baby Azafooms slid open and closed, randomly, around them. Milton could see, sixty or so feet ahead, the gates surrounding the exit portal. A jackal-headed man weighed souls just beyond the gate.

Annubis! Milton thought with a brief burst of joy. Then he realized that his friend the dog god was just another piece of Milton's afterlife repurposed into some game bent on draining children of their souls. Hope seemed distant, a dream viewed through a telescope. The lights went out.

Ziff! Ziff!

The arena was crisscrossed with puzzling trails of scent: wet cardboard, greasy chicken fingers, nail polish. Lucky drew in frantic lungfuls of smell. An Azafoom shot past Lucky, leaving an overwhelming odor that was keen, electric, and damp. It smelled like his master. The ferret squirmed. Suddenly, Lucky's nose tickled with the puzzlingly pleasing blend of suntan oil, cookies, pine, and Froot Loops. Lucky latched on to the odor—the smell of freedom—and held on to it with a ferret's unshakeable will.

Thum! Snarp! Snarp!

The air brushed Milton's matted hair as he kicked the ground beneath his Skimmer Ring. Mewling baby Azafooms snapped at his sides.

"Almost there . . . almost there . . . ," Milton said between gritted teeth as he tried to push his human train forward faster.

Lucky weaved through a tangle of rotten teeth, curdled milk, and soiled laundry odors. A hatch housing a snapping baby Azafoom opened up ahead.

Thum! Snarp! Snarp!

"Watch out!" Milton shouted as the chain of children banked hard. "We're hanging one heck of a Louie!"

The ferret wriggled, fighting to regain the aroma leading out of this insidious nest of hideous scents. A rich clot of odors commingled at the back of Lucky's throat—coconut, pine, Froot Loops—a fireworks display of victorious aromas.

Zoof!

Lucky was right on the Azafoom's tail as it closed in on the gates.

Howler Monkey, the middle car of the runaway train

of Terawatts, slammed his shoulder into a snarl of metal bars.

"*Oww!*" he yelled as the clang reverberated throughout the arena.

Milton stamped down on the tail of his Skimmer Ring. It skidded to a stop. He could hear the Zetawatt boy, Joey, struggling to free himself from the spire as his friends hurtled into the exit portal behind him.

"We've got to rescue—" Milton shouted.

"Yeah, yeah, Saint Milton," Sam grumbled. "The shishke boy. I can sort of see him. We'll climb up and grab him."

Milton scritched underneath Lucky's panting jaw.

"Nice work, fuzz ball," he cooed in his pet's tiny flap of an ear. "Thanks to you, we came out of this smelling like a rose."

Milton tucked Lucky back into his little kerchief pouch and yelled at the coliseum's ceiling.

"Tesla!" he roared, cupping his oversensitive ear. "We've beaten this level and we're ready for answers!"

Provost Marshal Tesla gazed out of the smoked-glass windows of his penthouse. Arcadia's vibrant skyline glittered and crackled with frenetic energy. The skinny, agitated man raised his eyebrows suspiciously at the orb of First Fire hanging in the sky. Its usual steady, perpetual blaze was now a mercurial conflagration of flare and sputter. Milton's voice crackled and squawked through his headset.

"We've beaten this level and we're ready for answers!"

Tesla sat stiffly inside the giant bronze head of his Rumination Nook. He was bathed in a faint blue-white web of electricity.

"I—like society—need children as fuel. If children are too much like zombies, then they can't contribute. If they are too awake, then they wouldn't buy into all of zhe unseemly consequences of fueling adult society. Of fueling my plans for zhe future, as opposed to their ridiculous unformed ambitions. Children need to be numbed *just so. Goldilocks* numb, so zhat they both fuel and feed and do so unquestioningly. Draining children of their souls, yet leaving them with their initial spark of life, does just that: creates an apathetic yet functioning workforce."

He leaned back as tendrils of energy caressed his twitching face.

"It also gives what me and my machines so desperately crave: *power.*"

"Power?" Milton said through a sudden flurry of static.

"First Fire is said to be inexhaustible. A ceaseless forge for hammering out man's ambition. But I have found, by stoking zhe fire beyond its intended specifications, I am able to push it from 'inexhaustible' to '*inconceivable.*' Piercing zhe Transdimensional Power Grid to transport matter from 'here' to 'there' using zhe ultimate fuel."

"What?"

"Zhe children's souls," Tesla said matter-of-factly. "Just skimming off zhe top is enough to cause First Fire to blaze like never before."

Milton felt sick to his stomach. A low-level hum vibrated in the dark around the Terawatts.

"Milton," Sara said. "I think—"

"But what good does all this do you?" Milton shouted above him.

Tesla's nervous laugh skittered around the arena.

"In essence, I've taken control of human progress—zhe future—away from humanity, who would just squander it. I vill enslave mankind by enslaving childrenkind, to bring my innovations to life."

"Milton," Sara repeated. "We've got to go. I can see something—"

"The present is for the dim—for same-old-same-olders and nodding-rule-sticker-toers like Edison," Tesla continued as the hum grew louder and more furious.

Zum. Zum.

"The Azafooms," Sara yelped just as the lights came on. "They're swarming."

"Zhe future," Tesla said, his voice a rushing river with gravel running along the bottom, *"is mine."*

Zip! Zoom! Zaggle!

The adult Azafooms buzzed in angry circles around the exit portal. Their pincer mouths gnashed at the gate as they passed, one creature yanking out a rusted bar and snapping it in two as it darted away. The air itself reeked with delirious rage: a sulfurous soup of jalapeño and kerosene. Sam/Sara tugged at Joey's torn suit, freeing the squirming Zetawatt from a wrought-iron spike. They tumbled onto the exit portal.

Zot! Zot! Zazzle-zot!

"Hit the deck!" Milton yelled. He and his friends covered their heads as the infuriated Azafooms stormed the gate, buzzing and biting, the gate as bent out of shape as the furious insects themselves.

30 · TOSSED iNTO THE NOSH PiT

MILTON AND HIS friends fell headlong into the fifth and final Sense-o-Round level. The damp stone floor slanted downward dramatically, so much so that Milton had to sprawl out on the ground to prevent himself from rolling into the shadowy abyss below. The dank, humid arena was like a massive, medieval seesaw, with something huge resting at the bottom in the darkness.

Clink! Clank! Clunk!

The Skimmer Rings from the last level clattered down the slope and into the murky gloom.

Zoof!

Above their heads buzzed an Azafoom. It darted into the shadow beyond, the insect's infuriated hum quickly silenced with a massive wet—

Chomp!

"*Ten . . . nine . . . eight . . . ,*" chanted the unseen demon announcer with his deep, throaty rumble.

The ceiling was spiked with hundreds of dripping stalactites surrounded by patches of glazed eyeballs from the Surface. Only now there were far fewer players, and their collective gaze was so vacuous that Milton felt like he was the judge in a mortuary staring contest. Milton's Unity-Tard now gave off only a low-level tingle. With each progressive level, the players seemed to exert less control over the Terawatts. They probably felt that they were still playing, rather than being played out.

"What's that?" Sara asked, pointing to the ground ahead, just before the edge of the wall of shadow.

Milton shrugged. "I don't know. You and Sam are the only ones who can still see clearly."

"*Seven . . . six . . . five . . .*"

"It's a mega-trail of rainbow slime," Sam replied. "Like the kind a slug leaves. *Wait,* there are a couple of adults stuck in it."

Milton squinted and could see two figures trapped in some kind of sparkly swirl. One looked like an old man in a suit, and the other looked like—

"Blackbeard the Pirate!" Sara yelped. "And Richard Nixon, the ex-American president!"

"*Four . . . three . . . two . . .*"

"Argh!" bellowed Blackbeard. "That great beluga's gonna slurp me down its gullet!"

Floom . . . Splork!

A big, slimy sack shot out of the darkness. It landed with a wet plop next to the struggling, screaming adults.

"*Begin Gustator: Sense-o-Round Five,*" the announcer ordered.

"I am not a snack!" shouted Mr. Nixon, writhing on the ground.

The sack opened up like a Venus flytrap before snatching up Richard Nixon, then Blackbeard the Pirate in two hungry bites.

Slorp!

The gooey pouch was yanked back into the darkness by its long pink umbilical cord.

"The Nyarlathorp is a creature wound tight with appetite, as tight as the elastic around your tighty-whities," the fake Principal Bubb purred as she emerged from the wall of shadows dressed in an armored tank top with a smoking turret protruding from her chest. "And though it has just had its noontime nosh, there's always room for dessert."

The principal twirled a pistol holstered to her cutoff jeans, then judged the Terawatts with a sour face.

"Though the Nyarlathorp may be a creature of taste, it exhibits very *little* when considering its next meal."

She laughed, a sharp explosion of one-sided mirth.

"*You.*"

★　★　★

"What do you think?" the *real* Bea "Elsa" Bubb nervously asked her demon stagecoach driver, a bucktoothed shrew with scales, from the back of her stagecoach. "Do you think I should lose the blouse?"

The demon turned and took in the principal's fuchsia-and-lime spattered top. The blouse looked like Hello Kitty's hairball hacked up after a seaweed binge.

"I think you should burn it," the demon said with a clack of its curved, gnashing teeth. "If you simply 'lost' it, then you'd run the risk of finding it again. Ma'am."

Principal Bubb scowled and pulled out a small bauble from her baby-sealskin attaché case. Her goat eyes—lined with thick blue eyeliner so that her peepers resembled runny yolks resting in a puddle of microwaved crayons—fixed on the tiny inset picture of Marlo Fauster.

"Don't forget your charm, Principal Bubb," the recorded voice in the principal's earring prompted. *"I procured it from Pitch-Black Market. It was confiscated by an enterprising demon guard when zhe uprising in Blimpo was quelled."*

Blimpo, Principal Bubb thought, smoldering silently as she gazed at Marlo's mocking portrait. *I'd love to put that big mess behind me. Fat chance, though.*

"Here we are, Principal," the demon driver said, swatting the flank of its Night Mare with a little red riding crop. "The Provincial Court of Res Judicata."

"I suppose I need all of the charm I can get," Bea "Elsa" Bubb sighed, clasping the chain around the bulging folds of flesh that served as her neck. Instantly, a roguish glint flashed in her eyes and blue, threadlike highlights streaked her coarse clumps of fur.

The principal's stagecoach pulled up to the marble steps of the courthouse. The deafening roar of small engines rumbled outside. A team of six demons with gasoline-powered backpacks swept the area with high-pressure nozzles.

"What's with them?" Principal Bubb asked her demon driver as it briskly hopped off the driver's box and opened the door for her.

"Belief Blowers, Principal, ma'am," the creature said, whistling through its curved orange incisors. "They neutralize bias and muzzle rabid dogma with a powerful flow of specially ionized air. Crucial for a trial of this importance."

Principal Bubb scaled the flight of white marble stairs.

Not that it matters, she thought as she passed a gauntlet of photographers. *Even if you clean the sawdust, a circus is still a circus. And that's just what Judge Judas, the most famous television judge in sin-dication, will turn this into: a circus.*

Principal Bubb crossed into the central portico beneath the courthouse's onion-shaped dome and through a metal detector manned by stocky demon guards with badges pinned straight into their decomposing flesh.

She popped a Super-Minty-Fresh-Ballistic-Free-from-

Halitosis pill into her mouth as she approached the double doors leading to the courtroom. The mint exploded, fumigating the principal's mouth with a twinkling green cloud.

Principal Bubb pushed the doors open, releasing a riot of incomprehensible noise. The only way that there could have been more pandemonium in the courtroom was if there had been actual pandas present.

A hawk-nosed man with a beard that coiled like a hairy snail shell banged his massive gavel on the bench. The hammer sent a cylinder flying up a pole, passing MISTRIAL, DISMISSAL, APPEAL, ACQUITTAL, and CONVICTION, and hitting a bell just above the word JUSTICE. The judge turned to a nearby camera and winked.

"Justice is served," the man said, much to the rowdy delight of his primarily demon audience. "I'm Judge Judas and we'll be right back with the Trial of the Millennium and our first affidavits *affi* these messages!"

Harsh light flooded the coliseum. The game version of Principal Bubb had disappeared. At the far end of the arena, caught in the uncompromising brilliance of the light, was a great, glistening glob.

Slorp! Glump!

The Nyarlathorp, Milton thought with a primal shudder of revulsion. It was a name that didn't exactly fall off the tongue, which was pretty funny in a decidedly unfunny way, as the creature resembled—through Milton's blurry vision—a swollen tongue the size of a small whale.

"Of all the words to describe that thing, I think the best would be 'yuck,'" Sam said, his words smeared with an impending fear-induced narcoleptic episode.

"What does it look like? I can barely see it. I only hear this gross foamy gurgle," Milton said.

"What?" Sara said. "I can barely hear anything."

"I said, what does it look like?"

"It's like a glistening pink monster slug," she replied with a sharp note of disgust. "Studded with thousands of tiny buds. Other than that, I can't really get a good—"

For reasons unclear, Howler Monkey dropped to the ground and proceeded to lick the creature's slime trail. The remaining Terawatts—the ones *not* lapping up monster sludge—stared at their friend, eyes wide with quiet shock.

"It oozes along on this kind of fluttering fringe," Howler Monkey said, smacking his lips. "And kind of tastes like Pepto-Bismol and sushi. The only thing really separating one end of the Nyarlathorp from the other is a ridge of bone wrapped across it like a spiked bonnet."

"What are you doing?" Caterwaul asked, gagging a bit in between her words.

"I can just sort of, like, see it with my tongue," Howler Monkey replied. "Get a picture of it in my mouth, all the different flavors like colors and textures. I can taste this weird, fishy flap of flesh covering some sort of blowhole. Maybe that's where its stomach shot out when it ate—"

"I'm good with what it looks like," Milton said with a cold shiver. "Or *tastes* like."

"Hey," Sara said, pointing to the ceiling at the far end of the rectangular arena. "There's our way out. A portal marked 'Up.' It's painted blue with white fluffy clouds."

Milton saw a word behind the blobby, shapeless shape of the Nyarlathorp.

"And over there?" he asked, pointing down.

"*Down*," Sara said grimly. "And it's painted black with flames."

"I'm guessing that's where we go if we lose," the Sunshine Sneezer said as he wiped his runny nose with the back of his hand.

"Get out of here!" a girl screamed from behind the creeping slug beast. Caught in the Nyarlathorp's shimmering trail was another fallen Zetawatt.

"Tasha!" Sara said. "She's stuck in the monster's slime trail!"

"It's a trap!" Tasha yelled, barely conscious, her voice hoarse from screaming. "There's no way . . . no way to . . . ," she murmured before passing out.

31 · LOOK BEFORE
YOU WEEP

SCHWAA!

A stone portal slid open several yards away from Milton. Out shot five new weapons: twin white gel sacks—like squishy, semideflated volleyballs—joined together by a black bungee cord. The weapons rolled for a few yards down the incline of the stone seesaw floor before coming to a stop. Words sizzled above.

WEAPON: BOLA-CLING
HEALTH: 3 . . . NO, WAIT, 2 . . .

Milton touched one of the Bola-Cling's gel sacks. "Sticky," he said, wiping off his hand before grasping a small leather handhold in the middle of the rope.

Floom . . . Splork!

A wet explosion filled the arena. The Nyarlathorp's dripping stomach spurted out of its blowhole, attached by a long sinewy ligament. It landed with a wet plop a few feet away from Tasha. The stomach opened with a thick nest of wet pink bristles squirming inside. It wriggled toward Tasha.

Milton instinctively swung the weapon over his head and flung it at the sack's stem. The globby end of the weapon wrapped around twice before sticking fast. The Nyarlathorp yanked its outboard belly back into its blowhole, sending Milton tumbling toward it. Howler Monkey gave the ground another lap with his tongue.

"Oaky with fruity undercurrents and . . . ," he mumbled before shrieking, "Milton! Get out of there! The Nyarlathorp is about to attack!"

The horrific, faceless creature reared up, howling with a flutelike whine.

Whooowl!

It charged.

Bumbada-bumbada.

As the Nyarlathorp rushed forward, it tipped the floor of the colossal arena until it was level. Its attack sounded like the muffled, maddening beating of drums.

"Here!" Sara shrieked, tossing Milton a new Bola-Cling. He spun the weapon quickly, then, without thinking, cast one end hurtling toward a stalactite above. The bungee's spring sent Milton up to the ceiling, just as the Nyarlathorp scurried beneath him with freakish speed.

Florpadda-florpadda.

I suppose we could just hang from the ceiling like this until—Milton thought just as the end of his rope began to lose its adhesive power—*we fall to our doom.*

From his unfortunate proximity, Milton could see the countless pink buds coating the creature's slimy, detestable body.

Like taste buds, Milton thought as he gripped the gradually slipping bungee weapon.

Caterwaul wept loudly below.

"He's starting to slip!" she bawled.

Howler Monkey, on all fours beside her, tasted the floor.

"It's just about to launch its— Stop your sobbing, Caterwaul! I can taste how sad and miserable you are!" he said before dissolving into tears himself.

Sam/Sara charged at the creature, twirling their weapon above their heads.

"Get *me*, Slug Bug!" Sara yelled, leading the creature a few slobbering steps away.

Slorp! Glump!

The sticky end of Milton's rope finally gave out, and he plummeted to the ground, landing in a trail of fresh slime. Milton struggled in the Nyarlathorp's syrupy wake as the absurdly disgusting tongue monster shuffled to face him—though it was hard to tell one end of the creature from the other.

Howler Monkey swished the creature's slime trail in his mouth before bolting upright.

"Tears!" he yelled. "It really doesn't like them!"

Tears? Milton thought, his mind fragmented with fear.

Florpadda-florpadda-whooowl!

"Caterwaul!" Howler Monkey yelled. "Pull yourself up to the ceiling, right over the Nyarlathorp!"

"What?!" the long-faced girl replied, flabbergasted, as if Howler Monkey had just asked her to smear bacon grease on her face and kiss a pit bull.

"Yes!" Milton interjected, his frantic mind latching on to Howler Monkey's plan. "Pull yourself up to the ceiling!"

Floom . . . Splork!

The Nyarlathorp shot its stomach out six feet away from Milton.

"Now!" Howler Monkey yelled.

Caterwaul, her cheeks shiny with tears, flung the sticky end of her Bola-Cling toward the ceiling. It curled snugly around a stalactite and pitched her into the air above the Nyarlathorp.

Glorsh!

"Caterwaul!" Milton screamed as the creature's stomach opened. "This is hopeless. There's no way out of here. We're going to lose and be digested by this disgusting slug—one by one."

Caterwaul, bobbing in the air, wept anew.

"Why are you doing this?!" she sobbed as tears gushed out of her wide, trembling eyes.

"Tesla's going to win!" Milton continued.

Glorp! Glorp!

The Nyarlathorp's stomach twitched and wriggled, inch by slippery inch, toward Milton.

"We can't beat the slug thing!" Howler Monkey yelled. "More kids will, like, replace us, be ripped apart by his terrible monsters, and every gamer up on the Surface will have their souls, um . . . drained straight from their bodies!"

Caterwaul's tears splashed along the Nyarlathorp's sleek, taste-bud-studded back. Sam/Sara and the Sunshine Sneezer—stricken with Caterwaul's contagious sobbing—wept into their hands as Caterwaul drenched the creature beneath her. Milton fought against the gooey strands of slime pasting him to the floor. The Nyarlathorp's stomach flopped next to him, its bright pink bristles trembling with hunger.

Florch!

Suddenly, the monster's slavering bulk sagged. Its rosy-pink color drained until the Nyarlathorp was a gently foaming slab of shiny gray sludge.

Glorfle! Glorfle!

It shuffled back a few dozen feet. The stone floor slanted slightly toward it.

Milton tore himself free of the creature's slime trail. Howler Monkey gave the ground a few quick laps before rising to his feet.

"It's, like, really bummed out," Howler Monkey said as he picked a piece of gravel from his tender tongue. "And the salt in Caterwaul's tears isn't doing it any flavors . . . um . . . *favors.*"

Caterwaul squirmed as she fought to hang on to the bungee cord.

"What do I do now?" she cried out.

"Scale the ceiling to the Up portal," Milton called out. "We'll be right behind you. By the way," Milton added with a grin, "nice work."

Caterwaul, despite her hangdog face, laughed.

"My eyes are like sprinkler systems!" she said as she lobbed the other end of her Bola-Cling at a nearby stalactite. "They can rain on any parade!"

The Terawatts traveled across the coliseum's ceiling like apprentice Spider-Men, flinging their sticky-ended bungees like slung webs, swinging from one stalactite to the next.

"Oh no," Caterwaul whimpered as she arrived at the exit portal. "Tasha was right."

"What do you mean?" Milton asked as he swung up next to her.

"It's just painted on," Sara said as she joined them at

the far end of the arena. "It's not a doorway at all. It's—"

"*A design flaw, it pains me to say,*" Tesla's voice boomed from the Sense-o-Rama's embedded speakers.

Milton's face flushed red with anger.

"What do you mean?!" he shouted as he knotted the bungee around his forearm. "We won this level! How do we get out?!"

Tesla laughed a string of sharp, explosive gasps.

"*Beats me,*" he replied. "*To your credit, I never expected you to make it this far. But to my credit, no one needs to. Look up at zhe players on zhe Surface.*"

Milton observed the constellation of eyes sprinkled about the arena. They were like the eyes of a school of dead fish, floating at the top of a gigantic goldfish bowl.

"*Their souls are ripe for zhe taking!*" Tesla exclaimed. "*Which is fortuitous timing, as I need to feed zhe fire. First Fire. Stoke it with fuel plucked straight from zhe soul mine! Zhe Sense-o-Rama and Poe's Shadow Box are more of a drain than I initially calculated. But I learn as I innovate: using real-world findings to push my inventions to zhe next level— something zhat will be much easier to supervise once I'm back up on zhe Surface and zhe whole world is my laboratory!*"

"The Surface!" Milton gasped. "You're returning to the Surface?!"

Tesla brayed into his headset. "*Mr. Fauster, zhe goal of every great gamer is extra lives. And zhat's exactly what I and Mr. Poe intend to achieve: extra lives. As many as we need to shape zhe world to our liking.*"

"You can't be serious," Milton spat back.

"Dead *serious!*" Tesla bellowed. "*Though I won't be dead for long. And I'll be something even more than merely alive. I'll be immortal.*"

"But that's against the rules," Milton said. "And, like you said, every game needs rules."

"*Ah, yes! But every game also has, programmed within, secret worlds ready to be discovered! Hidden levels zhat change everything! So, if you excuse me, while you hang there at zhe end of your ropes—at zhe end of your game—I have a world to enslave. Good day and . . . good game!*"

Caterwaul managed to draw a new reserve of salty tears. Milton looked down at the Nyarlathorp as the tears dried up on its galumphing hump of a back. The creature's bumpy flesh slowly regained its pink hue.

Extra lives, Milton mused. *Hidden levels.*

"We need to swing above the Nyarlathorp," he said.

Caterwaul wiped her snotty nose with her forearm. "So I can cry on it again?"

"No," Milton said as he flung the other end of his Bola-Cling across the ceiling. "I think I've found a cheat code. We're going to make the Nyarlathorp's *mood* swing into *over*action."

He shot across the ceiling, suspended over the slobbering pink slug-whale. Milton dug through the slit in his armor and pulled out his canteen of Hypool-Active Overstimu Lake water.

His friends joined him, hanging from the ceiling. The

Sunshine Sneezer stared at Milton's canteen as if it were an atomic bomb.

"That stuff will drive it crazy," he muttered with a nervous lick of his lips.

"Crazy like a big, slimy, dangerously deranged fox," Milton replied. "Are you with me?"

The Terawatts nodded gravely.

"Of course," Sara muttered, even managing a smile.

Her smile made him feel like every window in the world had been thrown open at once.

"Then it's time to beat this game once and for all," he replied. "One . . . two . . ."

The six Terawatts held their canteens above the Nyarlathorp. Bright red liquid, like blood, trickled out of the flasks. To Milton, it seemed that he and this group of new friends had embarked upon something of a blood ritual: a dangerous ceremony, their lives mingling together, becoming closer to one another than they ever thought possible.

"THREE!"

32 · ON THE VERGE OF
A NERVOUS BREAKUP

FRAGOPOLIS FLASHED AND flickered in that lurid try-way-too-hard-but-it-works-anyway-perhaps-because-it-tries-way-too-hard way that arcades do. Despite its convulsive neon desperation, it was the only place Marlo could think of to go. She had no idea how long her tenure as part of the Decease Corps had lasted so far. All she knew was that if she wanted to stay and not become the birdie-num-num of some swooping hawk spirit, she needed to ground herself in grief. And that meant stoking the sorrow of Hans Jovonovic, who was hanging out inside this glittering Geeks 'R' Us for his awkward double date with Marlo and her BFBC (Best Friend Before Ceasing-to-be) Aubrey Fitzmallow. She looked over the bump of darkness that was her shoulder. Why was that bird spirit trying to eat her? She had been called a thieving magpie by a store security guard once, but apart from that, she had done nothing to ruffle the feathers of the creepy bird community.

The arcade was clogged with dazed kids shuffling around in a stupor outside of the *Heck: Where the Bad Kids Go* game. They gazed expectantly at the large, peculiar booth.

"Best . . . game . . . ever," muttered an Asian kid with a blend of reverence and dull hunger.

Screepy, Marlo thought as she skittered along spots of track lighting. *Has to be some weird coincidence. Though I guess the whole idea of an h-e-double-hockey-sticks for children is so obvious it was only a matter of time before someone up here landed on it.*

Marlo skipped along the shadows of kids waiting in line to play *Heck,* looking for her pseudo-date.

There, toward the back, hovering over a *Scarface*-themed Al Pachinko pinball machine like a question mark on fire, was Hans.

Hey, Hot Stuff. Didya miss me? Marlo thought-texted to Hans's InfoSwank belt buckle. Of course you did. I'm dead and that's really, really sad.

She hoped she wasn't laying it on too thick, but Marlo was desperate.

Hans wiped a tear away from his blue-green eye.

Awesome, Marlo thought and—unfortunately—texted.

The boy cocked his rust-colored eyebrow.

Awesome that we are . . . together. Despite our differences. You know, you being a nerd, me being a Goth . . . oh, and the whole living-and-dead thing, too. The long-distance thing will be hard, but I'm sure we can make it work.

Hans smiled and started jerking around to the techno music blaring out of a nearby *Cattlezone* game, where virtual vegans traversed a roving herd of delicious char-broiled cows.

Is that supposed to be dancing? Marlo thought-texted.

Hans stopped self-consciously.

"I was just . . . making shapes to the music," he muttered, straightening his misbuttoned button-down shirt.

Thanks for helping me out with my mom and dad. I think they might stick it out—despite me messing up everything by getting myself killed. To think, I'd still be here—*really* here—if I had just left that vintage dress of mine behind. The one stuck to the marshmallow bear. Though it *was* one of a kind.

Just then, Aubrey walked through the doors of Fragopolis, wearing the same black vintage Victorian mourning dress Marlo had been wearing at the moment of her untimely passing.

Make that two of a kind, Marlo thought-texted.

"Yeah, yeah . . . *Lenore*," Aubrey called out over her shoulder. "Out here in an hour. Just in time for one of your yummy, macro-moronic meals . . ."

The girl looked cautiously around her before leaning closer to the car.

"Thanks."

Hans's pale face blanched. His freckles came out like dark stars at reverse-night.

"I'm . . . I'm going to break up with her," he mumbled to his belt.

Good. Being me is weird enough when I'm being it.

"No one could be *you*," Hans said as Aubrey approached.

Marlo noted tiny burnt marshmallow stains on the sleeves of her dress.

Ugh, really? Secondhand is one thing, but wearing your dead friend's thrift-store finds is another.

The spitting image of Marlo blew her blue hair from her face.

"Hey, Hot Stuff. Didya miss me?" she asked, cornering Hans. The redheaded boy was shaking harder than a Chihuahua in Alaska.

"Um, hi, Aubrey," Hans managed. "You look . . . nice."

Marlo hated to admit it, but Aubrey did. *Look nice.* And not just because she looked like Marlo, though that helped. How could it not? Underneath all the white pancake makeup and eyeliner, Aubrey was really quite pretty, with a spooky sort of "peaches-and-scream" complexion. And she could tell by the twinkle in her eyes—a constellation of unabashed affection—that she really, truly liked Hans.

"Of course I do," Aubrey said with feigned bravado. "And I just got my license."

"You, um, did?"

"Yeah—to drive you crazy!" she replied with a charming snort.

Marlo glanced down at the carpet. With Hans's poor posture and Aubrey leaning in to him, their shadows looked sort of like a heart, with Marlo's shadow awkward and fuzzy next to them.

It was then that Marlo realized what she had to do. As the old saying goes, if you pretend to love something, then you've got to pretend to set it free.

"Right," Hans replied nervously. "Look, I don't think we should—"

I can't go through with this, Marlo thought-texted.

Hans looked down at the upside-down readout of his belt buckle.

"Huh?"

This whole thing. It was just an elaborate joke.

Hans swallowed, but the lump wouldn't quite travel down his skinny neck.

"But . . ."

Gotcha!

Marlo could feel a tear slicing down her cheek. Being casually cruel used to be so much easier, back when she was sentimentally challenged. Now she felt like she was releasing some animal back into the forest, and it kept coming back so she had to shout at it.

Um . . . wait until the other kids at school find out!

Hans sniffed back a tear. His chest caved in like a

jack-o'-lantern on the day after Halloween. Aubrey grabbed his hand.

"Are you okay?"

Marlo grew suddenly faint.

I can't compete with that. Nothing can distract a boy like the touch of a living girl's hand. I've got many things, but a pulse ain't one of them.

Hans looked up at Aubrey as if he were noticing her for the first time.

Well, I guess if I can't be me, at least Aubrey can.

Hans quickly glanced down at his belt buckle.

Shoot, Marlo thought as she slid her vague shadow away from Hans. *I thought-texted all of that. Gotta seal the deal here . . .*

Ask her if she's an interior decorator, she thought-texted, flinging what was left of her shadow at the boy.

"What?" Hans mumbled.

Ask her if she's an interior decorator.

"Um, are you an interior decorator?"

"Uh . . . *no,*" Aubrey replied. "Why?"

When I saw you here, the whole place became beautiful.

"When I saw you here, the whole place became beautiful."

Aubrey blushed around the edges of her white pancake makeup and smiled. Not Marlo's crooked smirk, but her own, genuine dimpled grin.

If you were the new burger at McDonald's, you would be the McGorgeous.

"If you were the new burger at McDonald's, you would be the McGorgeous."

Aubrey busted up.

"That is so dumb," she said, coiling her white arm around his. "I don't even eat meat. There's so much about me you have to learn."

Dizzy and unmoored by Hans's sudden surge of happiness, Marlo's weak energetic shadow bounced around Fragopolis like a flat, smudgy pinball.

There goes the third point in my cry-angle.

Just then, a sharp, bird-shaped silhouette darted beneath the arcade entrance.

"Oh no," Marlo muttered blearily. *It senses helpless prey.* Me.

A haggard, near-comatose boy summoned the force of will to nudge open the door of a *Heck: Where the Bad Kids Go* booth.

"Dude," he croaked through the crack. "You've been in there . . . forever . . . We're all . . . waiting . . ."

Marlo's vaporous soul projection was tugged across the carpet.

What's going—?

She was pulled into the dark, humming game chamber, with the door pneumatically shutting behind her.

In?

The booth had six walls, each with a sort of mirror, only the mirrors seemed to look out—into another world. The stench of sulfur inside was overwhelming.

Ugh, it's like eating an egg salad sandwich with your nose, Marlo thought.

The boy inside the gaming booth had a sort of metal starfish clamped to his face and a weird, chain-mail smock draped over his twitching torso. His eyes, as blank as a blackboard during summer break, bulged out around the arms of the face mask clutching his head. A tube coiled from the mask, just between the boy's eyes, leading to a glowing yellow box beneath his seat. She felt strangely drawn, physically, to the mask—like that eerie, self-destructive urge to jump when standing on the edge of a cliff. Marlo clung to the shadows on the wall to resist its pull.

She unfocused her eyes, like you do with those weird posters that suddenly turn 3-D if you look at them the right way, and gazed at the vivid images cast all around her.

Graackk! Scree!

A gigantic dark purple tongue the size of a killer whale thrashed about on some kind of massive stone teeter-totter in a cavernous dungeon. The creature was going berserk, roaring and slamming its glistening bulk into the walls. It was as if Marlo were clinging to the dungeon's ceiling, watching the tongue lash at her from below.

It's like an episode of When Disgusting Monster Slugs Attack! Marlo thought, an odd, angry, pepperish taste forming in her mouth. *It's like I'm* inside *the game, only it doesn't seem like a game at all!*

The tongue oozed toward the center of the unbalanced floor.

Florpadda-florpadda.

Something shot out of its body, up toward Marlo.

Floom! Thomph!

Please have that not be a stomach, she thought as the disgorged digestive organ snapped at her face, revealing rows of bright pink bristles.

"Watch out, Dork Knight!" a boy to Marlo's right yelled. "The Nyarlathorp is trying to pick us off the ceiling!"

HEALTH: 0

"Do you *think*?!" another boy shouted with high-volume sarcasm.

"That stuff in our canteens has it in a frenzy!" a girl shrieked. "A full-on Cujo!"

The XXL-sized tongue lapped and lashed at everything around it.

Whooowl!

The creature howled, an unnerving shriek that sounded like a murderous blend of flutes and military drums. Marlo clapped her ears.

"Caterwaul!" a familiar voice yelled as a long-faced girl fell from the ceiling.

It's that crybaby from Snivel.

Another kid, wearing some kind of shredded armor, fell from the ceiling. Wait . . . *two* kids.

And the twins!

Sara, writhing on the ground, attached to her sleeping brother, looked up at Marlo as the monster tongue slammed itself against the wall like a spit-soaked battering ram.

"Milton!" she cried. "Do something!"

Oh no, Marlo thought as she was pulled closer and closer to the twitching boy in the gaming chamber. *Either I'm my brother—again—or that zombie boy playing the game is.*

Milton tumbled from the ceiling. He sprang toward Caterwaul, who was nearest the roaring Nyarlathorp, and dragged her from a sticky trail of rainbow slime.

As Marlo watched the horrific scene in mute shock, she was slowly tugged up a ladder of crisscrossing shadows, traveling across the boy's electrified, chain-mail poncho.

"Throw your canteens at that far wall!" Milton yelled, pitching his flask over the Nyarlathorp's quivering, taste-bud-studded back. Six canteens clanged against the dank stone wall.

Whooowl!

The creature stiffened the front of its body into a quivering point, swiping its appendage over the heads of the terrified Terawatts.

Whoosh! Whoosh!

"What's it doing?!" Caterwaul yelled.

"I think it's tasting the air!" Howler Monkey replied, edging back from the creature.

Back in Fragopolis, the bird shadow forced its way underneath the *Heck: Where the Bad Kids Go* game door. Getting closer and closer to the starfish-shaped mask clutching the boy's head, Marlo entered another plane of reality, ferried by a sort of full-sensory trance. The Litsowo pecked at the dark spots on the floor before settling on Marlo's silhouette cast across the boy's face. The bird spirit darted across the gaming chamber just as Marlo was pulled headfirst through the mirror and into the game, the hungry spirit on her projected soul's heels. The game's announcer bellowed into the Sense-o-Round arena:

"Marlo Fauster has now entered the game."

33 · TAKING LEAVE
WITH THEIR SENSES

"MARLO FAUSTER HAS *what*?!" Milton yelled over the roar of the deranged Nyarlathorp.

Whooooowl! Slosh!

"It's working!" Sara exclaimed as the monster tongue lapped itself against the far wall like an ocean of pink-red muscle. "It wants more Hypool-Active Overstimu Lake water!"

The arena rumbled. Bits of stone rained down upon the Terawatts.

Glorm! Scree! Crashathud!

Milton shut his eyes as Gustator: Sense-o-Round Five crumbled around him.

Florpadda-florpadda . . . bumbada-bumbada . . .

After a moment of silence, Milton opened his eyes.

Howler Monkey was on his hands and knees several feet away, giving the ground a quick lick.

"I think I, like, taste victory," he said as he and the other children stirred from the cold, slanted stone floor. "Kind of gingery with mint flourishes."

"Did anyone else hear my sister's name?" Milton asked.

"I didn't hear anything but that big tongue doing laps all over everything," Howler Monkey replied.

Words written in digital fire burned above.

+ 100 EXPERIENCE POINTS
CONTINUE?

"Continue?" the Sunshine Sneezer said as he rose from the ground. "Continue *where?*"

"Maybe out that massive hole in the wall," Sam replied sarcastically.

At the end of the partially demolished arena was a hole the size of a small garage door. The edges were worn smooth, like those of an old, unfinished lollipop.

"I'm . . . so . . . sleepy," Caterwaul complained from the floor.

Milton pulled her up off the ground. "We can't fall asleep," he said as he walked her down the sloping floor of the arena. "That's what happened to the Zetawatts.

They gave up and the Sense-o-Rama sucked the will right out of them until they were practically senseless."

The children stepped through the hole in the stone wall and into a narrow yet startlingly tall passageway crowded with sputtering electronics equipment, fiber-optic cables, and malfunctioning mechanical boxes. A large, glowing yellow button on the wall just outside the arena blinked SAVE. Milton slapped it with his hand.

"So any kids playing on the Surface will go straight to the end of the game," he explained as he walked into the passageway.

The corridor widened into a large, round chamber so tall that it seemed to have no visible ceiling. In the center of the room was a towering spindle, a throbbing vine of light and mirrors, sending thick globs of honey-orange radiance cascading downward. A coiling helix of glass wrapped around the spindle, a smooth translucent ramp that glimmered as fantastically and improbably as Cinderella's slipper. Blankets of shimmering steam hissed from tangled knots of piping girdling the walls, clouding Milton's vision. The whole thing was like a surreal game of Mouse Trap.

"The light," Milton said as his faltering eyes tried to make sense of the chamber. "It must be First Fire. And it's reflecting down toward Snivel. This is the way out."

A riot of raw sound clopped Milton's tender ears: growls, screams, gasps, gurgles, panting. It reminded him of gym class.

"Watch out!" Sara yelled as she shoved Milton and Caterwaul out of the way of something the others couldn't see.

"Yuck," Howler Monkey complained with a sour face. "It tastes like . . . danger."

Lucky hissed from inside his kerchief pouch, some objectionable odor offending the ferret's phenomenal nose.

"I think we've unlocked a sixth level," Milton said. "Unfortunately. Full of unheard, unseen, untasted, unsmelled, and unfelt sensations."

"A sixth level?" whined Caterwaul.

"Yeah . . . the level leading back to Snivel."

The key, as with all of the Sense-o-Rama levels they had survived, was to work as one. But how? Milton thought.

Working as one.

Milton had an idea.

"Help me collect the hover-boards and sticky bungees," he asked his friends.

"What?" Howler Monkey asked.

"Help me collect the hover-boards and sticky bungees," he repeated, louder, for his comrades' faulty ears. "Together, we're going to knock some sense into this place. *Five* senses."

Within minutes, the Terawatts had bundled the hover-boards together with bungee cords to create a large, levitating raft. They placed the fallen Zetawatts—Tasha,

Joey, Libby, Wyatt, and Ariel—in a writing, muttering heap at the center. Sam/Sara stood up in front of the heap, acting as the vessel's eyes. Sara cradled Lucky in her arms— a small miracle, as the ferret was very particular as to who, if *anyone*, cradled him—where he acted as the group's nose. Howler Monkey lay on his stomach up front, jaw slack, serving as the vessel's sense of taste, with Caterwaul along- side him, flailing hands outstretched, as the craft's sense of touch. Lastly, Milton and the Sunshine Sneezer stood on either side of Sam/Sara as ears. They kicked off and trav- eled, slowly, up the eerie glass ramp amidst a chaotic vor- tex of sensations: swooping hordes of shocking sights, sinister smells, spine-chilling sounds, frightening feelings, and terrible tastes peppered with assault.

Damian Ruffino stood, blocky and blotchy, staring down the camera with a dark, slitted glare. He tried his best to widen his eyes into something approaching innocence but made a wrong turn somewhere along the way, arriving just outside Intensely Unnerving. Necia, dressed in her red-and-white candy-striper jumper and nurse's hat, stood next to him, fussing with Damian's baggy suit that, while making him look like a pallbearer at a hobo's funeral, was perfectly tailored for his nefarious purposes.

"Hello . . . my name is Damian Ruffino . . . at least I think it is. . . ."

Necia quickly patted Damian stiffly on the shoulder with her little rat hands.

"There, there," she cooed. "Here," Necia said as she shoved a pile of Choco-full of Oinkrageous Flavor-Brand Fudge-Dipped Pork Rinds underneath Damian's beaky snout. The boy pecked at her palm until it was clean. Audible gasps could be heard off camera. Damian tried to wipe the bits of chocolate-coated pork from his mouth, but due to Necia's generous slathering of an off-brand Taiwanese pore minimizer and concealer (Derminator X) to cover his chronic acne flare-up, the crumbs and dust were stuck fast to his face.

"Gaming is one of the leading causes of death in America's video arcades," Damian continued, "second only to fire, earthquakes, lightning, flash floods, food allergies, high cholesterol, poor posture, and falling meteorites. But there is one game, *a terrible game*, that made me the way I am today."

Damian forced his eyes to roll back in his head for effect.

"And that game is *Heck: Where the Bad Kids Go*. I only played it for five minutes. And look at me: I'm a hollow shell of a human being, with fewer motor skills than an all-squirrel drag race."

Necia took the microphone.

"It's time for your nap now, Damian," she said as Damian feigned a mild seizure, punctuated by a trickle of drool. Necia trained her dark, spooky, furnace-in-the-basement-of-an-abandoned-house eyes at the camera. "Are you a kid, under eighteen, who likes video games and is currently watching television? If you answered yes to any of these questions, protect yourself and those you care about from the effects of *Heck: Where the Bad Kids Go*."

Dale E. Basye held his head in his hands, whimpering, as the television droned on in the background. The situation was getting more complicated by the moment.

The image of Damian—zombielike, staring into the camera—shrank until it became the backdrop of a television news show. The image switched out to that of a sour-faced old woman whose smug smile looked like it had been stretched across her face with Saran Wrap.

"AGHAST leader Agnes Derleth scored a major coup with the emergence of Damian Ruffino," said the female news anchor, "taking her cause to the next level. Get it: the next level. Just like in a video game."

Her male counterpart shook his head.

"I don't know, Varga," the man tutted. "A video game that renders the player apathetic, monosyllabic, and sullen—sounds like the game turns players into that most loathsome of creatures: a typical teenager." The male news anchor chuckled. "In any case, former writer-turned-video-game mogul Dale E. Basye has a lot of 'splaining to do tomorrow morning at his press conference. Now, in other Las Vegas news, the Sometimes Zoo

Win, Sometimes Zulus casino just got a new blackjack dealer: Jo-Jo the Orangutan."

Dale switched off his ninety-nine-inch wide-screen television and gazed out the window to the small bandstand he had built for tomorrow's event.

Agnes Derleth and AGHAST were bad enough, Dale thought. *Now they've got their new poster boy, Damian Ruffino. What's the boy's angle? He could have just sued for plagiarism. He must not have any evidence. Maybe he's out for . . .*

He drew in a deep breath to calm his nerves.

Money, Dale brooded. *The boy's here for the same reason everybody else comes to Las Vegas.* To win. *If he won't listen to reason, he'll listen to an unreasonably gracious bribe. See, for a winner, Las Vegas is the coolest town on earth. But for a loser . . .*

Dale caught a reflection of his haggard self in the dark television screen.

It's the cruelest.

Is Tesla insanely brilliant or just insanely insane? Milton thought as he and his friends edged slowly up the spiraling glass ramp. The ramp coiled like a transparent corkscrew through clouds of highly charged steam alive with "sense" fragments: a gush of exaggerated sights, sounds, smells, tastes, and sensations intent on disorienting and distracting Milton and his friends. *Has he really found a way of returning to the Surface? And if so, could he actually hold the future of mankind hostage by enslaving a workforce of zombie teens to bring his mad, bad inventions to terrible life?*

Milton heard the sound of wet, massive disembodied jaws opening to his left. He quickly urged the Terawatts' mobile "extrasensory perceptor head" to the opposite direction. Howler Monkey, Sam/Sara, Caterwaul, the Sunshine Sneezer—even Lucky—did likewise, none of them letting on as to what terrible terror they had just averted.

A violent tremor shook the spiral ramp.

"What's happening?" Caterwaul asked from the front of their roving platform. "I've got hold of some bad vibrations."

Milton could hear the sounds of splintering glass as the ramp beneath their feet trembled and quaked.

"We've got to hurry," Milton urged as he kicked hard beneath their hover-raft.

Suddenly, with a great split and shatter, the ramp collapsed. The Terawatts tumbled *up* a dozen feet before hitting the ceiling, which was now somehow the floor.

"A door," Sara murmured through the tingling, electric fog. "I can see it!"

She kicked open a trapdoor with a grunt.

"Um . . . you guys won't believe this," Sara said.

Virtually blind, Milton crawled down through the door and emerged up into Snivel.

Almost immediately, Milton's senses began to return,

one by one. The magnetic locks on his Unity-Tard fell open, as did those on the muscle armor of his friends. They were all just outside of Vice Principal Poe's tent at the heart of the camp compound. Searing blue lightning bolts shot out of the roiling waters of Lake Rymose. Students and faculty rushed by.

"What's going on?" Milton asked one of the demon sloth guards as it ambled, wide-eyed with terror, across the campgrounds toward the forest. The creature stopped and briefly considered Milton with its blankly frightened bloodshot stare. It jabbed one of its curved claws up above its head.

"The sky is falling," the mangy creature murmured through its broken fence of sharp yellow teeth before trotting away, joining the other fleeing students and faculty.

"The sky is falling?" Sara repeated, looking up at the mountains of festering garbage overhead. "But that's impossible. We're suspended upside down over the Dumps."

Milton, his vision returning, gazed up. Millions of miserable tons of toxic trash loomed above. And the Dumps—this piled "blech" yonder of garbage—was tumbling closer.

"If the sky isn't falling, that means that *we're* falling. All of us. And fast."

34 · CREEPSHOW FROM THE BLACK LAGOON

SHAFTS OF BLINDING First Fire stabbed through the grim waters of Lake Rymose. Bolts of raw, angry electricity clawed their way out of the turbulent waters roiling around the wobbling Dukkha Wheel and scratched at the shore. A pack of shaggy black dogs ran wild with their tails tucked tight between their hind legs.

"Looks like something is wrong with Tesla's plan," Howler Monkey said as he stared, gaping, at the chaos around him.

"Yeah, like the fact that—*achoo!*—it was stark, raving banana crackers," the Sunshine Sneezer replied.

"We . . . gotta . . . get out of here," Sam said before his eyes rolled back in his head and he fell into a narcoleptic slumber.

"That must be a pain," Milton said as Sam snored in Sara's ear.

She shrugged one of her shoulders.

"It's not so bad. It's just like half of your body going to sleep ten times a day. At least I get some peace and quiet."

Milton and Sara stared at each other until they forgot they weren't alone.

"Um, this is cute and all," Caterwaul said, her shiny wet eyes staring at assorted children, adults, and creatures running past Lake Rymose, "but we've got to get out of here!"

Milton shook his head clear, though one nagging image held on tight.

Marlo.

He scanned the clumps of people rushing by.

"I'm not leaving without my sister," Milton said. "You guys go on ahead."

Howler Monkey shook his head. "No, like, way. We're a team."

"That's r-r-right," the Sunshine Sneezer said, trying desperately to stifle a sneeze. "We came here together, and w-we're going to leave that way, too."

Milton sifted through the bedlam before him but came up short-sheeted.

"I have no idea where to start looking," he said miserably. "The only person who knows where she is, is . . ."

He turned toward Vice Principal Poe's tent.

"Poe!"

"Be gone, be gone, be gone."

That creep-tastic, tell-tale heart of Poe's, Milton thought as he crept into the vice principal's quarters.

He raced across the room and grabbed the heart. Milton shoved it into his shorts, not wanting Poe to gain the upper hand—or bean-spilling circulatory organ—when confronted.

"Guards!" Poe shouted from the dim gloom.

Too late, Milton thought as a snail demon slithered into the doorway, waggling its stalk eyes. The vice principal glared defiantly from his fainting couch as Caterwaul snuffled back tears.

"Caterwaul!" Milton yelled. "Think of something sad. *Really* sad!"

The long-faced girl blubbered until a shallow pool of salt water blocked the doorway. The snail demon shrugged its slimy shoulders.

"Sorry, Vice Principal," it rasped as it turned to leave. "I'm hyperallergic to salt water. Makes me break out in foam. *All over.*"

The demon fled—as fast as a snail can flee—while Vice Principal Poe shook his head at the guard's glistening wake.

"Where is my sister?" Milton yelled at Poe, quaking with fear and rage.

Vice Principal Poe, dark eyes sunken into his cadaverous face like collapsed coal mines, smirked.

"What could possibly pry such privileged information from my lips?" he said, smoothing a loose strand of greasy black hair to his box-shaped head.

Milton scooped the throbbing heart from his Arcadia shorts and held it, pounding, in his hands.

"It's time we had another heart-to-heart talk," Milton said. He gave the heart a squeeze.

Poe self-consciously clutched his hollow chest as he glared back at Milton.

"Careful!" he gasped. "You'll break my heart!"

The Sunshine Sneezer turned to Milton. "Man, I wish I could unsee that. How did you know?"

"You can see his shirt sort of pucker in," Milton replied, looking at the heart in his hand, which was gasping like a fish on the shore. "It wants to warn us about the rest of him. It's like his conscience or something."

"To be thoroughly conversant with a man's heart is to take our final lesson from the iron-clasped volume of despair," Vice Principal Poe said. He tightened the red cravat around his neck. "It muddled my reasoning with painful memories and pointless mawkishness."

"Then why, like, keep it?" Howler Monkey asked.

The vice principal shrugged.

"Sentimental reasons, I suppose," he replied with a weary sigh. Poe sulked toward the doorway.

"I was just going to visit your sister, anyway," the vice principal said, reaching out for his heart. Milton stuffed it back into his shorts. "Lucky for me I'm not the type of person accustomed to following their heart," Vice Principal Poe mumbled as he brushed past the children to his iron door. "As, in this case, it would only lead to dirty underwear."

They walked out across the sodden ground of Camp Snivel toward the forest.

Milton noticed a pair of shadows streaking past him on the mud. They rushed across the ground, speeding toward the forest: to the exact point Vice Principal Poe was leading Milton and his friends. Moments after the shadows disappeared into the woods ahead, they returned, darting away from the portal leading back to the Sense-o-Rama to—again—make a mad dash for the forest.

Milton looked up at the sky, but it was empty: the same bleak quilt of toxic garbage.

The shadows streaked past Milton for a third time, cycling faster and faster with each pass. One of them looked like a large predator bird pursuing what appeared to be a girl.

"Marlo!" Milton shouted, knowing in his heart of hearts—the one residing either in his chest or in his shorts, he couldn't be sure—that the silhouette in peril was his sister. Marlo had a knack for attracting trouble, even as a disembodied shadow, apparently, Milton thought as he ran through the dark fringe of forest and up the mud-slick ridge.

The shadows darted across a sheet of rain-fog to a dilapidated shack choked with unruly tangles of stinging nettle bushes.

It's like something out of a horror movie, Milton thought as he approached the shack. He tried the door, but it wouldn't budge. There was a keypad panel to the right. Four of the numbers were worn: 3, 5, 6, and 7.

Usually security codes are names, so it's probably someone close to Poe. A name made from the keypad letters: DEF, JKL, MNO, PQR. But who would be important to a loner like Poe?

"You'll never guess the code, Mr. Fauster," Vice Principal Poe said from behind, panting, as he and the others joined Milton outside the shack.

Loner, Milton mused before a grin spread across his face. He wiped the rain from his glasses and jabbed specific numbers on the keypad: 5-3-6-6-7-3 . . . *LENORE.* The door unbolted and opened.

The vice principal's thin-lipped mouth hung open as Milton and his friends stepped inside the shack. Sam tugged Poe inside just as the door whooshed closed behind him.

"Hey, Incredible *Sulk,*" Sam said with a sneer. "We're not through with you yet."

Caterwaul knelt down before the shabby doll in the corner.

"Hey, look," she said with a soft smile as she moved to scoop up the doll. "A dolly. Just like Misty Eyes, my doll back—"

"Mama," the doll cried as the elevator dropped down to the subterranean Shadow Box. Dazed, Milton rose from the floor and noticed another keypad. He looked back at the crumpled figure of Poe, staring back with his unnerving gaze.

"Let me guess," Milton said as he punched the code. "You seem like the brooding, obsessive type . . ."

"Lenore," Poe said miserably as the lead doors slid open. "The death of a beautiful woman is, unquestionably, the most poetical topic in the world."

"What is this place?" Sara asked, wincing as they entered the dazzling chamber radiating honey-orange light. She stared at the three tiered rows of rectangular panels mounted to the walls. "Are those *children?*" Sara murmured with horror as she watched the Unhappy Campers twitching in their tanks. Brilliant beams of golden light streamed from the braided stalk of fiber-optic cables and satellite dishes.

The shadows of Marlo and the swooping Litsowo spirit traveled along the floor and up to a tank on the top tier.

"Marlo!" Milton gasped as he bolted up the flights of stairs. He followed the pair of shadows, locked tight in a shady death grip, to the middle tank, where his sister jerked and struggled in some kind of goo. Out from the shadows stepped the Grin Reaper, cinching its charcoal-gray hoodie tight around its neck.

"Let her go!" Milton cried out as his sister's shadow dove into her tank. It was cast back out behind her tank on a screen before dripping down a duct. The bird shadow followed, milliseconds behind, closing the gap between its beak and Marlo's feet.

"If you go near that tank, Mr. Reaper," Vice Principal Poe said from behind, "our deal is null and void, and you shall never have the last—*or any*—laugh."

Just then, Lucky wriggled out of the kerchief pouch hooked to Milton's belt, his jaws clamped down on van Gogh's severed ear. The Grin Reaper stared at the ferret with its sad, rainwater eyes; then, a few awkward seconds later, the half-frowny, half-smiley face on his chest began to heave and quiver. The creature's body rattled like an oil well about to blow. A geyser of laughter suddenly gushed from his mouth. The Grin Reaper's eyes darted frantically to and fro as he watched his laughter take wing around him.

"*Is absurd,*" he said, his glittering eyes resting on Lucky. "*Weasel with human ear. Is funny. Is hilarious.*"

A radiant burst of light traveled up the Wastrel Projector, shaking apart the Shadow Box as it pulsed to the ceiling. The lights in the chamber went dark for a split second.

Vice Principal Poe bolted away in the commotion.

He ran across the scaffolding and picked up a glowing yellow phone.

"Nikola!" he exclaimed. "Are you there? Our plan is—"

"Perfect," Tesla replied, dripping wet, as he stepped into the Shadow Box. "I am still quite on schedule, ready to push human progress beyond mankind's ability to utilize it with compassion—zhe head gaining final dominion over zhe heart!"

The heart, Milton thought as he grabbed Poe's ticker from his shorts. *Looks like we need a little heart attack.*

"Vice Principal!" Milton shouted as he held the circulatory pump in his palm, over his shoulder like a shot put. "Have a little heart!"

He pitched Poe's heart across the scaffolding and straight into the startled vice principal's chest cavity. Poe clutched his chest, the color returning to his corpselike face, then fell to his knees, weeping.

"What have I done?!" he sobbed. "All I wanted was to be an artist again, to reproduce what my senses perceived in nature through the veil of my soul. But all this . . . all this misery I've unleashed! I turned my morbid imagination into a weapon—a *gloom*sday device meant to lead mankind by the nose to its ruin. My love turned to pain, my pain turned to anger, my anger to unquenchable revenge."

Provost Marshal Tesla marched up the steps as the lights in the Shadow Box flickered. His purple neon necktie cast a sinister glow as he ascended the stairs to the third tier. Tesla looked down at the blubbering Poe with disgust.

"You are having a sentimental breakdown, you wretched mess of a man," he said, his mustache flapping above his sneering mouth. "You said it yourself, Edgar: 'Zhe true genius shudders at incompleteness . . . and prefers silence to saying something which is not everything it should be. . . .'"

Tesla spread open his waistcoat, revealing a pair of satellite dishes attached to his hips. With a swift one-two swivel of hips, he shot twin bolts of electricity at Vice Principal Poe. The miserable man collapsed onto the catwalk.

"So silence you—and we all—shall have," Tesla said. He gave a quick turn, showing off his new weapon with a smile of lunatic pride.

"Do you like them? They're my latest creation, my Hip-Hip-Array: a weapon zhat harnesses and amplifies static electricity. It's powered by sudden body movement and, of course, deadly intent."

"Your plan, it's going down in flames," Milton said, slowly backing away from Tesla to Marlo's tank. "And with Poe out of the picture, you're through."

Tesla passed Poe, giving his unconscious form a kick with his wet boot.

"Ironically, with this machine zhat Poe helped to create, he has made himself obsolete," Tesla said breathlessly. "When First Fire is stoked with souls, it will have enough energy to project me to zhe Surface—not as a weak shadow but as a fully functional energetic clone—and to also simultaneously project my essence *here*, in zhe underworld. I can continue Poe's work to fill zhe Surface with debilitating depression, leading children to seek zhe stimulatory relief of zhe Sense-o-Rama! Zhe last word in multitasking! This outbreak of melancholy will create more fixed points of grief for this machine, zhe Wastrel Projector, so I can send most anyone back to zhe Surface."

Tesla cackled maniacally.

"And there are plenty of bad, bad people here at zhe bottom of zhe afterlife who'd *love* to make a killing back up on zhe Surface!"

35 · DiE LAUGHiNG

THE LIGHTS FLICKERED off and on. In the brief moment of darkness, Milton moved to rush Tesla. The mad inventor sent a savage bolt of electricity into Milton's leg.

"Don't trifle with me, boy," Tesla growled. "I once melted zhe hand of an assistant with X-rays just for fun. Not very scientific, but still pretty cool, huh?"

The pain was both excruciating and lingering. The electricity coiled around Milton's nerve endings.

"Your First Fire . . . something is wrong . . . right?" Milton murmured as he backed away from Tesla.

"Yes," Tesla replied as he examined the tanks, each housing a child imprisoned in bad memory foam. "We seem to have Highly Disruptive Infinite Feedback Loop Disorder, or HDIFLD. Something, *or someone,* got sucked into zhe Sense-o-Rama and is being sent back out to zhe Surface, where zhe whole troublesome cycle starts anew. I'm here to unclog zhe ghost from zhe machine."

Marlo Fauster has entered the game, Milton thought, his nervous glance over his shoulder betraying his thoughts.

A lipless grin split Tesla's frenetic face. "Your sister! Of course . . . *zhat's* why you're here! Sorry to cut reunion short, but I must unplug your sister: *forever.*"

The lights went out again. Milton had to think quick.

"Too bad with all your genius, you can't even keep the lights on," Milton taunted in the dark. "What we could *really* use is a good, dependable lightbulb."

Tesla roared as he charged forward in the darkness. Milton backed into Marlo's tank, felt around for the latch, and released the door.

A livid flare of light surged up the Wastrel Projector. Tesla, blinded by his science, clutched his eyes while Marlo's tank tilted upward. Its glass door flung open, sending Provost Marshal Tesla flying up and over the railing and into the torrent of reckless energy blazing through the Shadow Box. Instantly, the diabolical, off-his-rocker super-giga-genius was vaporized into dust with an angry crackle.

The Grin Reaper peered down from the rail.

"Someone who worked that hard was bound to burn out sooner or later," he said, cracking himself up, then gazing in wonder at his own laughter.

Milton gaped at Marlo, squirming in her prison of goo.

"Is she okay?" Sara asked.

Milton shook his head. "I don't know. I have a feeling if I just stop the machine, her soul won't make it back to her body. I'd be pulling the plug, just like Tesla said."

The shadows of Marlo and the Litsowo darted out from beneath the Shadow Box door.

"I've got to get it *just* right," Milton said as the shadows flew up the stairs toward the tank, "before I—"

Marlo's energetic shadow spilled into her body, with the bird spirit close behind.

"Turn it off!" he yelped, shutting down the machine, the bad memory foam melting out onto the floor. Marlo fell to her knees, coughing. The Litsowo, missing Marlo's shadow as it reintegrated with her body, swooped inadvertently into the machine. The Shadow Box trembled violently as chaotic snarls of First Fire roared up the Wastrel Projector and into the chamber.

"Did I miss anything?" Marlo gasped. She stared at her brother's Arcadia uniform and smirked.

"Nice shorts," she said as Milton helped her off the floor and, in a rare public display of affection, hugged his sister tight.

Marlo beamed her crooked grin. "Please, you'll make me blush . . . and you know how much I hate what that does to my complexion."

"We must get out of here," the Grin Reaper said, looking down at the smoldering Wastrel Projector and adding with a giggle, *"especially now that we just added* fool *to the fire! Get it?"*

Marlo scanned the quaking insides of the Shadow Box and the tanks filled with trapped children.

"We've got to save the others," she said, stumbling to Ferd the Emo boy's tank next to hers, her legs still shaky.

"There isn't time," Sam said. "You can die again if you want, but I'm out of here." He struggled with his sister for control of their legs.

"I'll save them," Vice Principal Poe said, rising to his feet.

The children swung around, startled.

"Sound and fury was Tesla's game," Poe said as he gazed down upon the inventor's ashes. "Sheer contempt for any portrait, just merciless dedication to the frame. Now I see the value of a conscience, despite the pain it brings. It's our soul's critic, fanning the poet's fire, teaching the soul—with reason—to admire."

The Sunshine Sneezer glanced over at Milton, twirling his finger by the side of his head.

"The author of 'The Raven' goes cuckoo," he muttered.

Poe jogged down the stairs to the base of the Wastrel Projector's fiber-optic vines. He flicked two switches in tandem, and the doors of the thirteen tanks sprang open. Children fell onto the floor, two of whom—a girl in pigtails and Ferd—were lifeless and inert.

Marlo knelt next to the Emo boy.

"What's wrong with him?" she asked, her dark eyes wide. "He isn't moving. Is he . . . ?"

Vice Principal Poe climbed the stairs, a look of sadness etched deep in his face.

"Two could not be saved. They have . . . moved on."

"Moved on?!" Marlo spat back. "Where?!"

The Shadow Box shuddered in savage spasms. Sparks showered from the Wastrel Projector's surging vines. Milton put his arm around Marlo.

"We've got to go, Mar," Milton said, hoping his sister's intense dislike of the name "Mar" would snap her out of her shock. "We've done all that we can here. Snivel is falling and we have to help get everybody out of here, or else we'll all be down in the Dumps. *Permanently.*"

Marlo brushed Ferd's hair from his face, the same hair she had made merciless fun of only a few days ago.

"Well, Ferd . . . *AWTY* . . . I guess you made it," she whispered, her soft voice catching in her throat. "You're finally 'there'—hopefully they're playing that awful, whiny music you like so much."

She got back to her feet and joined the other children spilling down the stairs.

As the Grin Reaper led the group away, Vice Principal Poe walked tentatively up to Marlo's tank, twisted a small knob on the side, and stepped inside. The door closed, sealing with a burp, and bad memory foam began to gush inside.

Milton turned as he and the children entered the elevator.

"Where does that box go to?" he asked.

Tears wore tracks through the bad memory foam caked to her face.

"Home . . . sort of."

"Who would Edgar Allan Poe know in Generica, Kansas?"

As the vice principal's shadow was cast upon the screen behind him, a brief flicker of a smile danced upon his face.

"Lenore," he murmured happily, heartfelt and complete, as a devastating surge of First Fire filled the Shadow Box for the last time.

Milton, Marlo, the Grin Reaper, and an assortment of Terawatts and Unhappy Campers ran to the edge of the platform outside the broken, tear-rusted Gates of Snivel.

Mr. Orpheus stepped onto the SighTram and slammed the door.

"Wait for us!" screamed Caterwaul.

The music teacher shut the door behind him and the SighTram chugged away fitfully on its one strained, bowed cable. The tram was packed tight with students and faculty.

"Thorry!" Friar Miles, behind the controls, yelled out to those left behind. "I can't hold any more, and we'll be lucky to thurvive the Thea of Thighs as it is. . . . If I can come back I . . . !"

The friar's voice was lost against the roar of wind.

A group of sopping wet Arcadians, led by Hazelle, joined Milton at the edge of the marble platform.

"Wait!" Hazelle yelled. "Come back!"

The SighTram disappeared in a murk of upturned trash dancing murderously on the wind. Hazelle, normally so composed, dissolved in a torrent of tears. Milton clutched her by the shoulder.

"I don't understand," she sobbed against Milton's chest. "I lived my life by the rules—even my *after*life by the rules. And *all this* happens! It's not fair!! It wasn't supposed to be like this!"

The girl's long, dark hair broke free of its restraining bun and fell down over her face in sodden strands. It was like even her *hair* had given up.

"Their rules only serve them," Milton said, looking back through the dismal Gates of Snivel at the coiling sidewalk, the sounds of the camp's destruction echoing down the corridor. "We have to make up our own rules as we go along."

Lucky poked his head out of Milton's kerchief, tucked into his Arcadia belt. He held van Gogh's ear in his jaws.

The Grin Reaper guffawed, a hearty belly laugh, like a giddy genie being released from a bottle of nitrous oxide.

"What's so funny?" Hazelle yelled before shedding fresh tears.

The Grin Reaper pulled out his humming electric jar and scrunched it up with his eye as if it were a monocle.

"Nothing. Everything," he murmured.

Milton stared at the Grin Reaper, who was gazing in wonder at the butterflies of mirth fluttering around him.

"I have an idea," he said, standing on the tips of his toes and whispering into the Grin Reaper's ear.

The gangly creature nodded and unraveled a stray thread from his hoodie. He tied the end into a little loop, then—carefully following the invisible-to-everyone-else laughter flitting above him—lassoed his guffaw and held it by the string. He tied it to Hazelle's wrist and went about lassoing another.

"What are you doing?" Hazelle sniffed as the Grin Reaper tied a second laugh to her other wrist.

"Nothing lifts spirit like laughter," he said, roping two more fluttering chuckles. *"There,"* the Grin Reaper said as he tied them to Hazelle's ankles. *"Might be enough to make you laugh away. Far away."*

Hazelle, her gray-blue eyes staring at her limbs in disbelief, floated gradually off the platform. A smile, streaming pure and unabashed like the sun peeking through the clouds after the rain, stretched across her pale, oval face.

"I'm flying!" she shrieked with delight as she spread her arms out to her sides like a bird. "I'm free! Whoo-hoo! A kite without a string!"

The Grin Reaper gave Hazelle a delicate shove. Milton grinned as she took flight across the Sea of Sighs, like Wendy off to Neverland.

"*Knock knock,*" the Grin Reaper said.

"Who's there?" Wyatt, his senses fully returned, replied.

"*Interrupting starfish.*"

"Interrupting star—"

The Grin Reaper grabbed Wyatt's face, wiggling his fingers like tiny tentacles.

"That's so dumb," Petula said, crossing her arms like a sulky Transformer before she and the rescued Arcadians laughed. The Grin Reaper rounded up all of their hilarity like comedic cattle in a rib-tickling rodeo. The children took to the air, flapping their arms as they shared their infectious Peter Pandemic of buoyant, incurable joy.

The Grin Reaper had now completely unraveled his hoodie, revealing his face. With his wide, twinkling eyes, mischievous smile, and gray-cast complexion, the Grin Reaper resembled a thousand-year-old boy. After a few more jokes, it was clear that the remaining Terawatts had lost their senses of humor back in the Sense-o-Rama.

"You go," Milton told the Grin Reaper. "We'll get out on our own. We'll use the weapons we brought with us from Arcadia."

"I'll go grab 'em," the Sunshine Sneezer said, bounding away.

The Grin Reaper nodded. *"I will crack myself up then. And, since I have lots of laugh bottled up inside, I can take passenger."*

He turned to Caterwaul. *"You know what meanest animal alive is?"*

"Um . . . no," she replied.

"Is Hippogator. Animal with alligator head on one end and hippopotamus head on other. You know how it go to bathroom?"

"Yuck, *no.*"

"It doesn't. That why so mean."

The Grin Reaper burst out in uproarious howls, struggling to yank threads from his threadbare hoodie and harvest every chuckle, chortle, and titter.

"I don't get it," Caterwaul replied.

The Grin Reaper lifted instantly off the ground. He grabbed Caterwaul and held her in his long, spindly arms.

"But I got you! Get it?"

They soared into the sky, buoyed by gales of liberated laughter.

The Sunshine Sneezer trotted back through the creaking Gates of Snivel, bungee cords slung to his back.

"I assumed that you—*achoo!*—meant these so that we could all—"

"Yep," Milton replied as he took a handful of bungees and handed them to his friends. "Zip-line our way down."

Marlo held the bungee in her hands and examined

the trembling SighTram cable with a disbelieving smirk.

"You never struck me as a daredevil, little *bother*," she said to Milton as she slung her bungee over the quivering cable. "Not even one of the lesser dare demons. But you're different now. I kind of like it."

Her bungee looped around the cable, Marlo approached the lip of the platform.

"But don't worry," she said, blowing blue hair out of her face. "I'll find something new to pick at. After all, you can't outgrow a big sister."

Marlo leapt off the ledge and zoomed down the line across the chasm.

"See you on the other side!" she shrieked against the wind.

One by one, they jumped off the platform and sped down the cable, leaving just Milton and Sam/Sara behind.

"You go," Sara said with a nervous smile. "I'm traveling for two." She tilted her head down to her sleeping brother. "I'll bring up the rear."

Milton blushed briefly before blushing again after realizing he blushed. His embarrassment at being alone with Sara made it easier for him to loop his bungee around the cable and—eyes scrunched closed—leap off the edge of the platform, leaving both his stomach and his awkwardness behind.

The sour wind combed through Milton's matted hair as he careened through swirls of foam packing peanuts, candy wrappers, and medical waste. It was freeing. It was thrilling. It was . . .

Milton felt the bolt mooring the cable to Snivel give way.

. . . *too good to be true.*

He looked back over his shoulder at Sam/Sara, speeding a dozen yards behind him.

"The cable is going to snap!!" Milton bellowed against the howl of wind. "Hold on!"

Ahead of him, Milton saw the SighTram dock at the Moanastery, the passengers swarming out in a panic. The other Arcadians—little blurry dots amidst the tempest of trash—were just behind.

Only a hundred feet or so away, Milton thought as the humid, sickening wind slapped his face. *If it'll just hold for a bit—*

Just then, Milton could feel the wire cord give way. He gripped the cable tightly. The friction seared the palms of his hands as he squeezed himself to a stop.

Like a preteen Tarzan swinging on a metal vine, Milton curved through the air, his feet sticking out in front to brace himself as he rushed toward the cliff beneath the Moanastery.

He screamed before slamming against the rock face, knocking the wind out of him. Seconds later, he felt Sam/Sara crash into the cliff below him. He looked down at the conjoined twins, hanging below by a coiled metal thread.

"Just take your time!" he shouted. "The worst is over—"

Suddenly, a great explosion rent the air. Snivel, dropping from the clouds like a gigantic glass tear, shattered. The Dukkha Wheel spun wildly out of the camp's fractured hull and into the Dumps below. Spinning behind it was something else: a long blade.

Poe's pendulum, Milton thought as he swallowed the pit of dread in his throat. *And it's heading this way.*

The pendulum twisted in deadly arcs, ever closer, until . . .

"Sara!" Milton screamed as the savage pendulum struck the twins gripping the cable below him.

All Milton could see was blood. *Everywhere.* Up and down his arms, spattered on his face.

"Sara!" he screamed again as Snivel and Arcadia, like a pair of conjoined twins themselves, fell, relentless and unstoppable, from the thick cloak of clouds overhead.

36 · THE LAST RESORT

ALGERNON COLE—CLAD in khaki shorts, Birkenstocks, and a macramé tie cinched around his neck—shuffled through a sheaf of papers on the counsel's table. He pulled out a scribbled memo written on a HOLY SPIRITS cocktail napkin.

"Request permission to approach the bench," Algernon croaked as every eye in the courtroom fixed upon him. He coughed. "Sorry, my throat is still swollen from those crazy stinging jelly beans I had, back before I fell asleep and started dreaming this crazy—"

"You may approach the bench," Judge Judas said, winking at the camera. "But do so without your feet touching the floor!"

The decomposing demon hordes crowding the stands hooted and hollered. Algernon eyed them with dismay.

I had no idea my imagination was so vivid, he mused,

sighing. *If I want to find my way out of this awful dream, I better play along.*

He hopped onto his hands and, with the acrobatic ease that only comes when you are doing something you don't think you can do but are doing anyway, Algernon crossed the bar and wobbled his way to the judge's bench. His progress was accompanied by jaunty music and comedic recorded sound effects.

"If I may, Your Honor," he panted after flipping back to his feet.

Judge Judas slammed his jumbo-sized gavel on his raised desk, sending the shot put to TOTALLY OUT OF ORDER with a piercing clang.

"Your *Dis*honor," Algernon said with a dramatic bow of contrition. "Here is my list of proposed witnesses."

Judge Judas stared down his coiled nose at the cocktail napkin.

"Are you serious?" the man said, glaring up at Algernon. "Well, looks like we're all in for one heck of a ride. Bailiff, bring in the first witness."

Judge Judas passed the napkin to a festering, pinched-face demon with a crew cut and a badge. The creature squinted at the shred of paper, gave a shrug, then lumbered down the aisle toward the courtroom doors.

"The court would like to call the first witness," Algernon Cole said, leaning in to the microphone on his desk. "Louie Cipher . . . um, *Lucifer,* take the stand. You're the next contestant on *Holding Court with Judge Judas!*"

Abbot Costello and two other wretched monks tugged Milton and Sam/Sara up to the Moanastery balcony jutting over the Dumps. The refugees from Snivel and Arcadia crowded around them. Their doughy faces flushed with exertion, Abbot Costello and the monks gave one last forceful heave, and Milton came up onto the balcony's lip, pulling himself over in a state of panic. Marlo rushed over to him, shocked to see her brother spattered with blood.

"Milton! Are you—"

Milton grabbed the cable and peered down into the chasm.

"Sara's hurt!" he yelped frantically. "She—*they*—were hit by Poe's pendulum!"

Abbot Costello gripped the balcony floor with his sandaled feet as he gave one final pull.

"Yes," the sullen man wheezed. "We saw. It was awful."

"I can see them," Milton said. "I've got their arms."

Milton tugged the mangled twins up to the balcony, their bodies streaking the marble floor with blood.

The abbot gasped with horror.

"They are *severed*," he whispered as he knelt beside them in his steel-wool robe. "Fetch Friar Bungay," the abbot instructed a fellow monk before returning his rheumy gaze to Milton. "He is our order's physician. If anyone can help them, it is he."

Sam and Sara, Milton could see despite the thick, gurgling pool of blood coating them, were connected by just a few gnarled strands of flesh and muscle. The connection they once shared was now just a raw, open wound.

A thin, pasty man with long ears fringed by his bowl haircut flapped his sandals onto the balcony. He held his frail hand to his mouth, gaping at the twins with round eyes.

"Will they survive, Friar Bungay?" Abbot Costello asked as he flagellated himself with his leather lash.

Friar Bungay examined the oozing gash between the twins.

"I don't know," he said in a reedy voice. "It's a clean cut, though. Poe must sharpen his pendulum regularly. For conjoined twins, their connection seems mostly superficial. No vital organs shared. If I can control the blood loss, they may have a chance. Help me with them, my brothers. To my chambers."

The three monks carefully lifted Sam and Sara from the floor and back into the crumbling, dimly lit abbey. Milton followed, yet Abbot Costello blocked his way.

"It would be best, son, if you let Friar Bungay tend to them in private."

The balcony was suddenly bathed in brilliant, uncompromising light.

"Look!" Petula shouted. "There's a tiny sun on top of Snivel!"

The monks manning their giant bugles—filling the crater with peals of moans and sighs—stopped their bellowing to join the children on the balcony.

For the first time, Milton could see Arcadia from afar: connected to Snivel like the top bulb of a massive hourglass, a timepiece whose time was running out. Tesla's tower showered Arcadia with raging bolts of blue-white lightning before toppling into the Pac-Man building.

"Game over," Milton whispered.

At the bottom of the tapered midsection connecting the upper and lower hemispheres was Lake Rymose, and at the top was the Hypool-Active Overstimu Lake. The conjoined realms dropped slowly from the grim mantel of clouds above. The frenzied blaze of First Fire pierced the billowing fog. The industrious ball of sputtering, sizzling flame sank gently into the lake. Suddenly, great blasts of evaporated water filled the insides of the glass-shelled dominions, with steam hissing from the hull's fissures and fractures.

Mr. Orpheus joined Milton at the rough-hewn stone railing. He sniffed the air with his perfect nose.

"Evaporated sadness . . . dampened mania," the man said in his distant, melancholy voice. "A precarious blend not unlike nepenthe: the potion purported in Homer's *Odyssey* to bring a welcomed forgetfulness to a troubled person's mind, an opiate of sorts, making one heady with hope."

"Hopium," Milton muttered as he gazed at the

explosions of electrified vapor splitting the pendulous glass barrier. He turned to face Mr. Orpheus. "Thanks, by the way, for leaving us behind in Snivel," he sneered, his face patchy with Sam/Sara's dried blood.

"If there is one thing I've learned from my time in the underworld," the smug man said with a dismissive shake of his lustrous curls, "it's to never look back."

"Snivel and Arcadia!" Caterwaul gasped. "They're dying!"

The two realms collapsed in on themselves, from pole to pole, and plummeted into the Dumps. Due to the distance, it took a few seconds for the shock waves to hit the Moanastery. A sharp, crashing boom clopped Milton's ears, followed shortly by a wet blast of tingling steam. Sight and sound disorientingly out of sync, Snivel—followed swiftly by Arcadia—shattered as it struck the mountains of garbage, displacing rubbish while upturning vile clouds of trash. The globe of First Fire flared one last time before snuffing itself out completely with a moist explosion of glittering vapor.

"Something's happening to the Dumps," Howler Monkey said as he gaped over the edge. "It's, like, changing."

The smoldering embers of First Fire mingled with a surging blanket of sparkling mist that tilled the millions of tons of rubbish below. The coiling tendrils sifted through the Dumps with an almost tender curiosity, cascading along rippling waves that transformed the dreary acres of reeking, noxious garbage into a verdant valley of luminous green moss. The mist dissipated into a haze of dancing motes that twinkled in a hypnotic way, like a happy, half-remembered memory. Bits of flaming wreckage rained down, first from Snivel— smoldering cabins and stone from Poe's Conversation Pit that formed oddly playful structures—then from Arcadia. Twisted metal shrapnel from the broken video-game arenas were forged by the flaming death throes of First Fire into bizarre approximations of jungle gyms, slides, and teeter-totters. A lofty section of fuselage from Tesla's tower pierced the heart of the emerald playground, with the charred Dukkha Wheel landing on top with a splintering crack, spinning and smoking like a postapocalyptic Ferris wheel.

"It's almost beautiful," Marlo said softly as she joined Milton by the railing, covering his shoulders with a rough blanket.

Suddenly, the sluglike Nyarlathorp, the tentacled Tactagon, and a wounded Oscithraud landed atop the pillowy carpets of moss, strewn about one of the grassy knolls.

Marlo grimaced. "Ugh . . . make that a monster-sized *almost.*"

A sudden shower of molten metal cast the heinous beasts as freakishly permanent art installations. The smoldering torso of the Donkey Koncourse dropped down at the center of the cast-iron zoo with a clangorous thud.

Wisps of fragrant "hopium," smelling like gardenias and roses growing in a soil of ground-up Pop-Tarts and clove, spilled out the walls of the crater. The smell tickled Milton's nose and, despite the blotches of dried blood on his face, he summoned a weary smile. He put his arm around Marlo.

"Maybe we got to Neverland after all," he murmured.

Marlo shook off Milton's embrace, folded her arms together, and scowled at the sprawling playground below with suspicion.

"Hmm . . . something tells me we're not off the Captain Hook just yet."

37 · THE DEVIL GETS HIS DUE PROCESS

"IF I COULD play devil's advocate here," Algernon Cole said as he approached the witness stand. "You look fabulous."

"Of course I do," the Lord of Darkness said, carefully smoothing his bright black-and-yellow poison-dart frog-skin suit and gleaming razor-blade tie. "I'm dressed to kill!"

In the stands, Bea "Elsa" Bubb noted the devil's lustrous black locks.

"Is Satan wearing a rug?" she asked Ivan the Terrible seated next to her.

"It's his Hell Toupee, ma'am," the wild-eyed man with the unruly beard replied politely. "All the stress of causing distress has been murder on his hairline."

Bea "Elsa" Bubb glared at Lilith Couture, sitting pretty across the courtroom in a black satin minidress and pearls. The elegantly emaciated woman even had an extra-flattering rose-tinted bulb placed directly above her. Lilith rippled her bony, manicured fingers in hello. Involuntarily, Principal Bubb waved her claw in kind, only to discover that Lilith had been waving to her running mate, Mary, Queen of Scots, behind the principal. Bea "Elsa" Bubb pretended to, instead, pat down her hair in order to save hideous face. She stole a look at herself in the reflected shine of Holy Roman Emperor Charles the Bald's head, who was sitting in front of her.

Not bad, she thought. *Despite the bluish hair and crooked smile of that awful Fauster girl, I look centuries younger!*

"You'll do great, Bea," the principal's earring whispered in her pointy ear. *"Your testimony will be broadcast across zhe underworld. Just be sure to support previous administration—Satan—while* not *supporting zhe previous administration."*

Satan's polished cloven hooves fidgeted, their leather tassels trembling, not so much from nerves as from self-contained restless energy. The Epitome of All Evil should be out undermining all that is good, bringing about ruin and corruption. Not sitting on his tail, cross-examined in some stuffy courtroom by bitter magistrates who didn't bother to read the fine print in their contracts.

The bailiff demon lumbered to Satan's side, brandishing a Bible.

"Do you promise to tell the truth, the whole truth, and nothing but the truth, so help you the Big Guy Upstairs?"

Satan recoiled with disgust. Algernon Cole handed Satan an oven mitt. The devil sighed as he slipped it onto his claw.

"I promise to . . . do what you said," Satan grumbled as he set his claw on the Bible, the Good Book smoldering under his touch despite the padded glove, "as much as the Father of Lies can, that is."

The demon bailiff shuffled away as Algernon Cole peered down through his lenseless glasses at his hastily scribbled notes. With a flourish, he wadded up his notes and tossed them over his shoulder.

"Rather than give you the third degree, Mr. Satan," he said slyly, "I'll just have you tell *your* story in *your* words. Totally off-the-cuff, as we've been practicing."

Satan scratched around the nub of his horns.

"Well, in the beginning . . ."

The courtroom sighed as one weary one.

"Fine, I'll skip a bit. The thing is, for centuries, I've been treated as the Big Guy Upstairs's nemesis. As an angry angel consumed by pride and cast out of Heaven to oversee his own dastardly domain. Which is"— the word wriggled fitfully on the devil's forked tongue—"*true*. But lisping gangstas and I share one thing in common. A bad rap. I'm just doing my job: testing the virtue of all humanity and flunking out those who fail. That hardly makes me the de facto mastermind of all malevolence!"

The courtroom was packed with more snickers than a candy machine.

"Humanity has laid all accountability on me for what they've clearly caused themselves. You can blame it on denial, you can blame it on mass psychosis, you can even blame it on the bossa nova, but you *can't* blame it all on me. I'm nothing but a scapegoat. I mean, look at the hooves."

The assorted demons and decomposing historical figures in the court murmured their grudging assent. The prosecuting attorney, Johnny Cockroach, skittered up to the bench.

"If I may cross-examine, Your Dishonor," the beetle-like lawyer said, flipping his long antennae back behind his sloping shoulders.

Judge Judas nodded.

"Mr. Satan," Johnny Cockroach said, his four arms tucked thoughtfully behind his back as he paced in front of the witness stand. "Did you or did you not attempt to hasten the Apocalypse by broadcasting inflammatory religious-themed television shows up to the Surface?"

"Yes and no," Satan answered after stroking his prominent chin. "But mostly yes. Brilliant, huh? There *were* some unauthorized rewrites, but I can't deny those ratings! Simply *boffo!*"

"And did you or did you not attempt to sell the Earth and transport humanity to a deadly dull planet across the galaxy in the"—Johnny Cockroach adjusted his reading glasses as he referred to his notes—"Sirius Lelayme system?"

"No!" Satan said emphatically, much to the relief of Algernon Cole, who was back at the defense table blotting his sweaty forehead with a handkerchief. "But it *is* exactly the sort of thing I would have devised. Uncanny, actually. Whoever hatched *that* beauty was really wearing their thinking horns."

Johnny Cockroach smirked.

"So, Mr. Satan, what you are saying is that you approve of the devious plot and admit to helping it along?"

"Well—"

"You don't deny it?"

"Deny what?"

"Helping it along?"

"Of course not. I mean, I did . . . *a bit.*"

The prosecutor laughed. "Actually, it's rather ridiculous to think that even *you* could have devised something so nearly perfect. It must have been the brainchild of a *true* mastermind—"

"I object, Your Dishonor!" Algernon Cole interjected.

"You object?" Judge Judas replied. "On what grounds?"

"Um . . . hallowed?"

"Overruled!"

Satan bolted up in the stand, sparks shooting out of his flared nostrils.

"I most certainly *could* have engineered the selling of the world and the simulated extinction of all humanity!" he shouted, turning an even deeper shade of crimson. "In fact, I . . . I very well might have!"

Johnny Cockroach straightened his feelers with smug satisfaction.

"I have no further questions," he said as he scuttled back to his desk.

Judge Judas banged his gavel on his table, hitting the bell marked DISORDER IN THE COURT.

As the courtroom descended into chaos, the judge spoke to the camera.

"Well, I've heard of pride before the fall, but *that* was ridiculous!" the pointy-faced man said. "This fallen angel has fallen and he can't get up! It would take a miracle for Satan to survive his testimony, and—as he knows all too well—miracles are in short supply down here. We'll be back with our next witness after these messages."

Satan, flustered and irate, was escorted from the stands by two burly guards.

"*Barring any unpleasant surprises,*" the recorded voice in Principal Bubb's earring said, "*your testimony could double as your acceptance speech!*"

Principal Bubb sneered wickedly to herself as she absentmindedly fingered Marlo's charm, filled to the brimstone with self-confidence.

Looks like I have more than a snowball's chance after all . . .

The monks of the Moanastery celebrated on the balcony, arms hooked, robes twirling as they danced merry jigs. The smiling children clapped in time, laughing as the fragrant, spicy wind of hopium drifted across the crater. The Sea of Sighs still and quiet, the monks could hear whoops and hollers from across the crater.

Abbot Costello leaned over the stone balustrade and peered across the emerald-green valley.

"Well, well," the ruddy-faced man said. "It's true."

"What's that?" Milton asked as Marlo wiped Sam/ Sara's blood from his face with a damp cloth.

"The Hystery," Abbot Costello chuckled, nodding toward a garishly painted structure inset on the opposite side of the crater. "The mythic home of an order of manic monks. Evidently not so mythic after all. We could never see them, what with Snivel and— apparently—Arcadia blocking the way."

The hammering clack of hooves marching across marble echoed throughout the Moanastery. A team of beastly demon guards—a herd of leathery, bat-faced goats—passed through a pair of fallen arches and onto the balcony. The leader reared up on his hind legs, standing at least eight feet tall.

"Milton and Marlo Fauster?" the guard bleated.

Milton shared a wary gaze with his sister.

"This party was just *aching* to be crashed," Marlo muttered.

Milton sighed and stepped forward, hoping—like yanking off a Band-Aid—that getting whatever bad thing was about to happen over with would hurt less if it was done quickly.

"Y-yes?" He gulped.

The demon goat-bat clacked in front of Milton, looming over him as he whipped a rolled-up parchment from his holster. Milton took the paper and unfurled it. After skimming its contents, he looked up at the guard's scrunched-up scowl.

"I don't understand. What is this?"

"It's a subpoena," the creature said, his teeth laced with thick strands of saliva. "For you and your sister to testify at the Trial of the Millennium: the State vs. Satan . . . *now.*"

38 · BEAR WiTNESS

THE SELF-CONSCIOUSLY TALL demon bailiff stooped over into the microphone, stiff and uncertain, though he had been fulfilling this role for centuries. He reread the name on the slip of paper, shook his head, and trudged down the aisle to the courtroom doors.

"The court would like to call the next witness," Algernon Cole said, swallowing hard into the microphone. "The Big Guy Upstairs. You're the next contestant on *Holding Court with Judge Judas.*"

The hundreds of rotting demons, condemned malefactors, and crooked magistrates eyed the double doors with understandable unease.

Just as the festering demon bailiff reached the back of the courtroom, the gleaming oak doors were pushed open. In swept the seven archangels: Michael, Gabriel, Rafael, Uriel, Zadkiel, Raguel, and Sariel.

Gliding into the courtroom with the effortless grace of professional dancers, the seven divine messengers were simply breathtaking. Clad in immaculate white vestments, their movements were perfectly synchronized and, puzzlingly, rendered in a sort of fluid slow motion, like classical Greek statues come to life, performing a water ballet on dry land. The middle angel, Michael, was—unaccountably—cradling a teddy bear in his luminous, alabaster arms.

"Greetings and felicitations," Michael said, greeting the judge. "Long timeth no decree."

Judge Judas fidgeted in his seat like a talk show host upstaged by his guest.

"You're in *my* court now," the judge fumed through the feigned warmth of his tense smile.

Michael's clear blue eyes spread the interior of the courtroom with a thin coat of condescension.

"So I am," he muttered between his permanently pursed lips.

Judge Judas craned his neck over his bench.

"Aren't we a little old for teddy bears?" the judge said, winking at the camera, igniting an audio explosion of prerecorded hoots and hollers.

Michael's majestic wings stiffened. "You might not wanteth to be so glib around the Big Guy Upstairs."

The judge's dark, treacherous eyes widened in shock. "*This* is the creator of the universe and source of all moral authority?"

"No, thiseth be a Teddy Ruxpin doll," Michael clarified in his marbleized tone of perpetual patronization. "*He* couldn't be here today."

"I thought *He* was everywhere?"

"Well, not today," Michael said. "Not in the 'actively intervening' sense. He's like cell phone coverage: mostly everywhere, but some places geteth better reception than others."

The arrogant archangel set the teddy bear on the judge's bench.

"So, as divine messengers, we are here to delivereth His divine message . . . or *He* is, actually."

Michael slipped an audiocassette into the toy's back. The Teddy Ruxpin doll came to creepy, animatronic life.

"I am honored to testify on behalf of my troubled fallen star—a rogue by any other name, but to me an angel who will always be Lucifer—yet I sadly cannot disrupt the proceedings with my Presence," the bear said, its merry eyes rolling around in its head like cartwheeling beetles, its voice soothing, cheerful, and hollow. "But I *will* leave with this anecdote from the last time I saw Lucifer, when he was the gleaming son of Dawn, so full of promise, always ready to pierce me with a well-aimed grin plucked from his arsenal of mercurial smiles."

The robotic bear continued with a grand gesture of its faux-furred arms. "When I created him and his angelic brethren, I commanded them to pay worship to no one but me," Teddy Ruxpin relayed with a languid blink of its eyes. "But then, after creating mankind, I told them to bow in reverence to my most noble of works. Lucifer—to put it kindly—refused. I had always attributed this to pride. But as the years stretch to eons, I've grown to think that perhaps he refused to do so because of his intense adoration for me, and he could not bring himself to bow before anyone else."

Satan quickly wiped away a tear of blood.

"We all make mistakes . . . well, *you* all do," the robotic bear continued, his mechanized head rotating to survey the courtroom. "And Lucifer is no exception. In fact, he has spent his time . . . *down there* . . . perfecting the art of error."

Satan crossed his haunches and sighed. "Damned once all those years ago, now damned again by faint praise."

"So, despite Lucifer's purported actions, show him the love and mercy that I show all of you: the inexplicable glue of serendipity that will always hold you close to me," Teddy Ruxpin declared in his singsong voice.

The spectators packing the courtroom stifled the pitiable wails that ached to be released from their wretched, trembling throats.

"That is all," Teddy Ruxpin said, his tiny metal muzzle opening and closing. "This divine message will self-destruct in ten seconds."

The crowd gasped.

"Just kidding," the robotic bear continued. "Or am I?"

The bear smoldered on Judge Judas's bench before breaking apart in a soft shower of sparks and flame.

The judge cleared away the smoke with his gavel.

"Thank you *so* much, archangels," he said, coughing. "For whatever *that* was. Bailiff, if you please . . ."

Bea "Elsa" Bubb unscrewed the cap from her thermos.

"That should put the fur of God into us all," she muttered.

The bailiff snatched a piece of paper from one of Johnny Cockroach's feelers and walked down the aisle.

"The court would like to call the next witnesses," Johnny Cockroach said, leaning toward his microphone. "Milton and Marlo Fauster, take the stand. You're the next contestants on *Holding Court with Judge Judas!*"

Principal Bubb spat out her scalding HostiliTea on the back of Charles the Bald's dome of a head.

"What?!" she screamed as every head turned toward the door.

39 · FAILING THE PROTEST

"WE'RE MAD AT *Heck and we won't play it anymore!! We're mad at Heck and we won't play it anymore!!"*

The AGHAST protesters chanted outside of Dale E. Basye's mansion, pacing in pious circles in the cul-de-sac like holier-than-thou water swirling around a drain.

"He made a game that makes kids spacey,
Let's pull the plug on Dale E. Basye!"

The crowd was a mixture of priggish adults, dazed children forced into suits and formal dresses, local officials feigning importance, and various sponsors huddled around the snack carts. *KBET: The Only Sure "Bet" in Las Vegas* was on the scene with anchorwoman Biddy Malone shoving her microphone in every sour face like it was a Dirt Devil sucking up the same prepared state-ment served up in slightly different ways. KBET was an affiliate station, so their coverage was sure to be picked up nationally.

"Sacrilegious, sick, and crass
Heck is wrong, so says AGHAST!"

That isn't even a proper rhyme, thought Dale Basye, miserably, from his bedroom window in the south tur-ret. A squeal of feedback, like that from a frightened, radioactive pig, tore through the strictly enforced placid-ity of the United Estates of Nevada.

"Good day, good people of Nevada," Agnes Derleth proclaimed in her prissy, toothless-old-woman-gumming-oatmeal voice. "And it will indeed be a good day—for the righteous, not so much for the wicked." She smirked, her beady eyes tossing daggers at Dale's window. "Thanks to the tireless efforts of AGHAST!"

"From righteousness our group is cast,
We're virtue's watchdogs, so bark AGHAST!"

The crowd barked, howled, and—in one peculiar instance—meowed.

"This protest wouldn't be possible without the gen-erous support of the local, easily outraged community of devouts, including Pastor Prime and her flock at WorshipMart, Nevada's largest megachurch and piety supply store."

The dried-up old woman gave a self-satisfied nod to the side of the grandstand.

"But most of all, we'd like to thank the over-the-top financial and administrative support from the Better Foundation: A *Better* Foundation . . . Get It? Because of the Name."

"Phelps Better," Dale grumbled between gritted teeth. *His little stunt is going to cost me everything.*

Dale rubbed his weary eyes, then put on his pants just like everyone else did: two legs at a time in one frantic jump. He walked over to his elevator and jabbed the button.

"Everybody," Agnes said, freeing her pearl choker from the deep grooves of her neck. "I'd like for you to meet my new *special* friend."

Necia led Damian, face bumpy with acne and slick with Derminator pore-minimizer and concealer, to the grandstand.

"Damian Ruffino," Agnes said as she wrapped her age-spotted arms—which complemented her cheetah-skin cap—around Damian's slumped shoulders.

The crowd cheered as Necia wiped Damian's lips and pressed him to the microphone.

"Thank you, Mrs. Derleth," Damian said thickly, as if his tongue were a slab of corned beef. "I, like many children my age with access to quarters, have played the game *Heck: Where the Bad Kids Go*. And I'm here to tell you, I am not the same happy, conscientious boy who entered the arcade."

Conscientious my foot, Dale fumed to himself as he opened the first of his front doors.

"Even once-beloved activities such as visiting my grandmother and singing in my church youth choir, the Gang Glee Adolescents, have lost their luster," Damian continued. "And hey, you kids out there, have you ever popped a few quarters in a video game? Chances are, you had fun. Maybe you got lucky that time. But what if you played a game that seemed to suck the life right out of you, full of un-Nintendoed side effects that left you forlorn and for-Sega-d? More than twenty kids will play *Heck* by the time I finish talking to you today."

"That's almost twenty-five!" Necia interjected.

"And sixty-two percent of those almost twenty-five kids," Damian continued, "may be ten times more likely to have a sixteen percent chance of being at risk of complications such as brain damage, even death!"

Necia patted Damian on the back as he pretended to cry.

"There, there," she said as she stealthily fed Damian another motivating fudge-dipped pork rind.

Dale took a deep breath and walked past his hedgerow to the grandstand.

"It's him!" Agnes declared with a sneer.

"That awful man!" Necia gasped dramatically into the microphone.

Damian slowly leveled his gaze upon Dale as if it were a weapon. He smiled with smoldering hatred—his eyes a pair of burning match heads—accidentally popping a pimple near his mouth in the process.

Biddy Malone bounded across the cul-de-sac like a panther in a pencil skirt.

"Mr. Basye . . . what do you have to . . . say about what your . . . dangerous game has . . . done to this . . . poor boy?!" she panted as her cameraman rushed to keep up with her.

The crowd went from simmer to boil, just one misinterpreted gesture away from foaming over.

Dale backed into his overwrought-iron security gate, its cold metal touch providing him no security whatsoever.

This is it, he thought as he fought back the Mardi Gras of terror parading in his chest. *Time to face the music.*

Biddy Malone, navigating the sidewalk in her spiked heels, pressed her microphone into Dale's face, like the leader of a firing squad offering its victim one last, huge cigarette.

"Mr. Basye, do you have anything to say about the deleterious effects of your awful game?"

Dale looked up at the sky with his bulging blue-green eyes.

I promise, whoever's up there, if you get me out of this one,

I'll never steal book and video-game ideas from children that end up hurting children again.

A spout of glittering, honey-colored steam shot out from the hedgerowed horizon by the Las Vegas Strip.

The cameraman whipped his gear around and zoomed in close.

Phew, Dale thought with relief. *At least I don't have to keep that promise!*

"It's coming from that new Catholic video arcade: Our Lady of Perpetual Ammo," the cameraman said as he squinted through the viewfinder.

The crowd gawked at Dale.

Right, like this could be my fault, too, he thought.

"Police chatter says that it's some malfunction from one of the games," the bearded cameraman relayed as voices squawked into his earpiece. "That *Heck* game."

Agnes Derleth etched her permanent scowl deeper into her yesterday's-prune-Danish of a face.

"So that immoral *game* has claimed more victims," she said, the question posed as a statement.

The cameraman shook his head.

"No, no casualties. In fact," he added with a confused furrow of his brow, "the police dispatcher says that the children are laughing and lively."

"At a video arcade?" Agnes asked, suitably aghast.

"Yes," the cameraman said with a nod. "Some of the teens are even talking *face to face,* making eye contact, too."

The crowd gasped. A cloud of the golden, sparkling

gas, like vaporized champagne, drifted overhead. Some of the children sniffed the air and smiled.

"It smells like flowers and Pop-Tarts," said a dark-skinned boy with a wide grin. "I should text my friends about this."

He looked down at his phone.

"It doesn't work," he muttered as an Asian girl in a pink dress sidled up next to him.

"Neither does mine," she said with a shrug. "I don't feel like staring at a little screen, anyway. It's such a beautiful day. Hey, what's your name?"

"I'm Mohajit, but my friends call me Mo," the boy replied. "My status is that I'm at an AGHAST protest because my parents made me and— Hey, this is like In-Your-Facebook only real! Will you friend me?"

"Totally!" the girl laughed. "My name is Huong. It supposedly means 'perfume' or something. I'm here because . . ."

Dale, never one to turn up his nose at an opportunity (or turn a blind eye toward a cliché), carefully untangled himself from the distracted, suddenly carefree crowd.

"That's gr-great!" Dale croaked as he crept toward one of the omnipresent golf carts. "See? Much ado about nothing! Sounds like the kids are having the time of their lives . . . their *after*lives! Get it? Because, in the game, they're all dead! Anyway, I'm doing a coffee run. Anyone want anything? No? Okay, I'll be right back!"

Dale sped away, if you define "sped" at "under five miles an hour."

"Oh no, you don't," Damian mumbled as he leapt off the grandstand in pursuit, scarfing one last heaping handful of Choco-full of Oinkrageous Flavor-Brand Fudge-Dipped Pork Rinds.

Dale buzzed along the serpentine pathway bisecting the Avalawns golf course like a slow electric mosquito.

"Good morning, Mrs. Fitzgerald," Dale chirped, as—even while evading a potential lynch mob—he still wanted to stay on the persnickety woman's good side. Mrs. Fitzgerald and her golfing companions grimaced, teed off that their tee-off was interrupted.

"Mr. Basye," Damian said, jogging alongside Dale's golf cart. "Not the best getaway vehicle. Pull over. We need to talk."

Dale looked over his shoulder for a way out, but the path was blocked by decorative boulders on one side and a chain restricting access to the maintenance shed. He sighed. He was trapped between a rock and a barred place.

"What do you want from me?" he said before studying Damian's bumpy face. "And what is wrong with your face?"

"Hormones," Damian spat back, scratching at the sides of his orange-smeared neck. "Man, it's like I have a pulse *everywhere*. But if you think *I* look bad, just wait until the coroner gets a load of *you*—that is, unless you sign this."

Damian handed the middle-aged man a sheaf of papers.

"What are these?" Dale asked.

"Contracts, Blindstein. Forget your contacts?"

Dale set the papers down on his lap.

"You want me to sign away ninety-nine percent of all *Heck*-related monies?"

"I'm nothing if not generous."

"*And* leave you as my heir?"

"In case I find myself needing some extra mad money," Damian said, scratching at his bumpy arms. "You'll be my ATM. I'll just drop by unannounced and make a *permanent* withdrawal."

Dale gulped.

"Why all of this?" he said, nodding back at the grand-stand. "Why didn't you just come forward and unmask me as the shameless, talentless fraud I am?"

"To get your attention," Damian said, wincing with pain as he scratched his pimply head. "And to amass sup-port. Look, no one is going to believe a rotten kid like me. AGHAST was my way of gaining credibility, *plus* an insurance policy."

"How do you mean?"

"If you didn't want to play Let's Make a Deal, then I could have got some serious buckage by hauling your butt to court—though, by the looks of it, I'd have to take two trips. Hitting the buffets *hard,* huh?"

Damian's skin seemed to visibly crawl. His eyes scrunched in agony.

"Are you okay?"

"There they are!" Biddy Malone shouted from the thirteenth hole.

Damian fell to his knees, his body rippling like a cactus preparing to birth a cyclone of baby scorpions.

"I see . . . a black light," he murmured. "Oh no . . . not again . . . not like this. If only I had watched more television and traveled less . . ."

With that, Damian—his chronic, fudge-dipped-pork-rind-aggravated acne looking for some way out of his skin, only to be blocked by Necia's off-brand Taiwanese pore-minimizer and concealer—popped like an enormous, 250-pound zit.

Pus and assorted bully bits spurted everywhere, much of Damian spattering Mrs. Fitzgerald and her companions. Damian Ruffino had indeed died a second time and returned to Heck: for good, for bad, forever.

Dale felt like his sanity was a sinking ship, and the more he tried to plug the holes, the faster it sank.

"Did you get that?!" Biddy Malone shouted to her cameraman.

"I think so," the man replied. "It seems to be working again. Must have been one of those electromagnetic pulse thingies that knock out all electronics within a certain radius."

Oh no, Dale thought. *There are some people in this world who might view footage of a boy who I apparently irreparably harmed with my dangerous video game suddenly exploding right next to me as somewhat incriminating.*

But it's not game over, not yet, Dale thought as he bounded across the golf course to the United Estates of Nevada's retaining wall. *There's always a secret level. It's just a matter of finding it.*

And, as he fell to the other side of the fence, Dale E. Basye became a fugitive from his own life.

40 · COURTiNG DiSASTER

MILTON AND MARLO were shoved down the aisle by the herd of demon goat-bats. A wave of shock and exasperation spread across the courtroom, like someone rubbing a giant cat the wrong way. Principal Bubb's eyes blazed as the Fauster siblings shuffled past. Marlo, her thieving magpie eyes always looking out for shiny baubles, noticed something familiar dangling from the principal's nonexistent neck. She elbowed one of the demon guards in the chest and leaned into the stands.

"I believe that's *mine*," Marlo said as she grabbed the charm necklace, "thank you very much."

With a tug, she reclaimed her charm as the one-sided shoving match resumed down the aisle.

Principal Bubb bolted upright.

"You're not even Marlo—you're *Milton!*" she

shrieked, solidifying her "raving lunatic" status in the jaundiced eyes of many of the demon spectators.

Marlo smirked as she tied the charm around her neck. The heart-shaped pillow of platinum with Marlo's picture in the middle softened into a pool of tingling liquid, absorbing into the hollow of Marlo's throat. Marlo straightened, tall and poised, as if inflated with esteem. Her split ends and a nagging pimple on her chin disappeared, leaving behind just a chalky dab of acne cream. The principal's jaw fell open.

"Why, you two-timing little brats!" she spat, her blue-streaked hair falling out in clumps. "You lied to me back in Fibble!"

"That's rather the *point* of Fibble," Lilith Couture commented loudly. "Or at least it was before it sank—*blub blub blub*—down into truth. Or should I say, *Bubb Bubb Bubb?*"

Laughter spread like a runny nose in a day care as the Fausters were led up to the bench.

"Algernon Cole?" Milton said, completely baffled.

The ponytailed lawyer grinned and held out his hand.

"Milton! So nice to see you again—alive and well—even if all of this is just a crazy, crazy dream! I must be taking shreds of memories and making some kind of subconscious collage!"

"Um, Mr. Cole," Milton replied tentatively. "I don't know how to tell you this, but—"

"Let's get on with it already!" Judge Judas exclaimed, banging his gavel and sending the shot-put bell to COURT IS IN SESSION! "Do you two youngsters need juice boxes and a nap, or can we proceed?"

Algernon Cole held open the tiny door to the witness stand. The Fausters, after a brief butt struggle, finally settled next to each other.

"Do you promise to tell the truth, the whole truth, and nothing but the truth, so help you the Big Guy Upstairs?" the bailiff asked as Milton and Marlo put their hands on the Bible, nodding their consent.

Algernon Cole flipped through a file, then sat down on the defendant's desk.

"So, it says here, Miss Fauster, that you worked for Satan as a . . . production assistant for the Televised Hereafter Evangelistic Entertainment Network Division, otherwise known as T.H.E.E.N.D.?"

Milton fidgeted on the witness stand.

"Actually, that was me," he replied, glancing warily across the collection of creatures crowding the court-room: from Satan to archangels and everything in between. "See, Annubis—the dog god—switched my soul with my sister's back in h-e-double-hockey-sticks."

"So you aren't your sister?" Algernon puzzled.

"No, not anymore."

"Yeah," Marlo interjected, leaning over Milton into the microphone, "*he* got to ride around with dead movie stars while *I* was coated in little white lice and had to battle demon shrimp all while squatting in his gross twerp of a body!"

"But Annubis switched us back after Fibble was flooded with liquid truth," Milton added nervously.

"I see," the lawyer lied, fiddling with his earring as he simply gave in to what he assumed was "dream logic." "So then *you*, Mr. Fauster, served as Satan's PA, as they say in the biz."

Milton nodded.

"Did you ever talk with the defendant?" Algernon Cole said.

"I didn't really ever talk with . . . *him*. Satan. It was mostly through Mr. Welles."

"Who has seemed to have pulled the disappearing act of his afterlife," Judge Judas said. "I guess he proved himself as a magician after all. Continue, witness."

"Well, as a production assistant for T.H.E.E.N.D., it was one of my jobs to review submissions to the network. One show I reviewed was called *The Man Who Soldeth the World*. It was weird. Seemed totally farfetched—about someone, you know, selling the Earth to aliens and evicting all of humanity—but it also seemed so *real*. Shaky, handheld camera. Like a reality TV show."

A collective groan sounded through the courtroom.

"Only *interesting*."

"Do you happen to have a copy of this show?" Judge Judas hissed.

Milton shook his head. "The only copy was in my backpack, back in Snivel."

"Perhaps we can send someone to retrieve it," Algernon Cole added.

"Not likely," Marlo said. "Snivel is now strictly past tense. It went out with both a whimper *and* a bang."

Principal Bubb jumped to her hooves.

"What did you do to my circle?!" she shrieked.

Judge Judas slammed his gavel on his desk. "Order in the court! Let the little dweeb continue."

"Um, thanks," Milton murmured. "Well, as I was saying, the first show—*The Man Who Soldeth the World*—aired, apparently, but basically no one watched it. I think I was the only one to even *see* the next couple of episodes. The 'man' or whatever kept talking about being nearly perfect—"

"Sounds like the defendant," Johnny Cockroach whispered, intentionally by mistake, into his microphone.

"And when I saw the man in Fibble, talking to Vice Principal Barnum—"

"Ah, the pioneer of mass-media sensationalism," Judge Judas said sadly, briefly doffing his powdered wig. "Barnum was the preacher and hollow spectacle was his church. He will be missed."

"He mentioned trying on Barnum's Humbugger mask, which amplified and projected the image of whoever wore it."

"Right," Marlo interjected breathlessly, reliving the

situation. "When Milton and I stormed the Boiler Room, where it was kept, we noticed that the machine was set to Exaggerated Negative."

"Objection!" shouted Johnny Cockroach, wiping his hands fastidiously in that filthy-clean way flies do. "Where is all of this leading?"

"Your Dishonor," Algernon Cole replied. "I assure you that this is all leading *somewhere*." He glanced hopefully at Milton. "Right?"

Judge Judas sighed, fluttering his coiling beard.

"This is Dullsville," he complained. "*Blandeur* extreme. Give me something with a pulse. *A little verve.* Kick it up, kid."

"Okay, okay," Milton replied, exasperated. "The point is, this machine was projecting a huge, scary demon. Not quite the devil, but close—"

"Ah, so the witness is saying that someone resembling the defendant—Satan—was at the scene of the crime!" Johnny Cockroach said, his feelers wobbling with excitement.

"You don't get it," Milton replied. "The machine was programmed to magnify and project the *opposite* of whoever wore the mask. So if Satan had worn it, the projection would have looked like an angel. But since the projection looked like a big demon—not quite Satan, the personification of pure evil—then whoever wore it was not quite perfect but about as close as you can get . . . *an angel.*"

If stunned silence were an Olympic event, every creature in the courtroom would have been given a gold medal.

"*And,*" Marlo continued, breaking the thick hush, "the man mentioned, back in the circle formerly known as Fibble, something about fulfilling the divine Revelation."

"Yeah!" Milton interjected. "And I saw a napkin on his desk in one of the episodes. It had 'Revelation 12:7' written on it, which mentions a war in Heaven, led by . . ."

Milton glared at the archangel Michael in the stands. He sat up, pointing at the divine messenger.

"*Him!*"

The courtroom gasped like a school of fish at a Water-Breathers Anonymous meeting.

"Oooh," Judge Judas said, rubbing his hands together with wolfish hunger, "just when I thought our ratings had flatlined, here comes someone with paddles, shouting, 'Clear!'"

41 · JUSTICE IS
SERVED COLD

"THE DEFENSE WOULD like to call the archangel Michael to the stand!"

Milton and Marlo left the witness stand. Milton stopped briefly to whisper into Algernon's ear.

The archangels rustled their wings with confusion, mostly at being confused, not a state these flawless beings were accustomed to. Michael rose, stately and tall, and extended his magnificent wings slightly farther than any other creature could.

"It would be my honor, Your Dishonor," he said in his smooth, cold marble voice as he glided to the witness stand.

Algernon Cole shook the angel's hand. "It's a pleasure to interrogate you, sir," he said before giving the air a dainty sniff. "Mmmmm . . . ambrosia!"

"Objection, Your Dishonor!" Johnny Cockroach shouted with an aggravated waggle of his feeler. "On the basis of excessive fawning."

"Sustained," Judge Judas replied.

"Fine, then," Algernon continued. "Isn't it true, Mr. Michael, that you are oft referred to as He Who Is Like God?"

"He Who Is *As* God, actually," Michael corrected. "Meaning my similarity is not in likeness but in intent."

"So you presume to know the mind of God?"

Michael shrugged his majestic white wings.

"I *am* ranked as the greatest of all angels," he replied.

His fellow archangels scowled in their divinely beautiful way.

"Not one to thusly blow my own bugle, but I'm also Chief of Archangels; Angel of Repentance, Righteousness, and Sanctification; and the ruler of Fourth Heaven—a charming little place that I've hadeth *totally* renovated while maintaining its original rustic charm. I also wrote Psalm Eighty-five—a marked improvement upon Psalm Eighty-four—what ingratiating drivel *that* was! And I was the fire in the burning bush that spake to Moses. My halo lit up like a flaming hoop! I half expected circus animals to jumpeth through it!"

"It also says that you are the purported conqueror of Satan?"

"How did *that* work out for you, Mickey?" Satan taunted from behind the defendant's table.

Milton scribbled something onto a sheet of paper from the defense's desk, balled it up, and tossed it at Algernon Cole's head.

"Don't make me put you in time-out, young man!" Judge Judas warned.

Algernon smoothed out the paper, considered it with a raised eyebrow, then tucked it into his khaki shorts.

"Mr. Michael, is it true you can only tell the truth?"

"It is true, verily, that I cannot telleth a lie," Michael said snootily, as if talking to a human were as tiresome and absurd as talking to an especially clever Chia Pet. "But the question must be to the point. Only a bull's-eye will—"

"Did you try to sell the world to extraterrestrials and banish all humanity to another planet, making it look like mankind was bringing about the Apocalypse so that you could be some kind of franchised God?" Milton blurted out, unable to restrain himself.

After a moment as tense as a small nun at a penguin shoot, Michael leaned into his microphone.

"Another plane*toid,* actually," he said dryly, with a trace of irritation at his angelic nature. "But, yes, I did all that."

"Objection!" Johnny Cockroach exclaimed. "Why would an archangel become the archenemy of all mankind?"

"Beats me," Algernon Cole replied, smiling a

mouthful of overly whitened teeth. "Let us ask the witness . . . or is it defendant?" he added with a wink.

Feathers ruffled, the six archangels in the stands exchanged looks of shock, resembling a line of pigeons roosting on a live electric cable.

Michael sighed, even his resignation carrying a note of arrogance.

"Well, as we've seeneth with this gross miscarriage of justice, the Big Guy Upstairs is no longer interested in the day-to-day operations of the afterlife. Most audaciously, He keeps putting off established measures such as the Apocalypse, so smitten is He with His little bald monkeys," he said with smooth disdain as he glared at the human personages in the courtroom. "So I decided to take matters into my own, divine hands. Speeding up the inevitable. And if I made a little coin offeth it, so be it."

The angel stretched his wings, their glorious, downy tips tickling the judge's severe, bearded hatchet of a face.

"And my plan was so nearethly perfect that I couldn't bear to let it unfold undocumented. *The Man Who Soldeth the World* served many purposes. To keep my unsuspecting dupes in line"—Michael cast his pristine gaze upon Satan—"as a sort of blackmail device if they backed out. And if found out, to show all of creation that the Almighty has indeedeth fallen, allowing such a scheme to transpire right beneath His 'perfect' nose."

The cameraman signaled to Judge Judas that they were running long.

"That said, Michael," the judge declared, speaking directly to the camera. "It's a pity we don't have any of this supposed footage. Maybe at your appeal. But, justice must be served—before the next commercial break—so I will deliver my ruling."

The lights dimmed, the judge bathed in a spotlight. Syrupy violins poured out of the court's speaker system.

"I've given my verdict a lot of thought in the last few seconds, and I have decided to rule with extreme irony. Michael, though an esteemed archangel who has put in an eternity—not including overtime—serving the Galactic Order Department with honor, has definitely tarnished his halo with this one. And while Satan is unrepentantly despicable—"

"Thank you, Your Dishonor," Satan murmured from the dark.

"—he cannot bear the brunt of this heinous crime on his beastly shoulders. Though his role in Michael's plan, whether unwitting or . . . *witting,* was instrumental to its near success. So . . ."

The camera zoomed into the judge's face.

"I hereby decree that Satan be removed from his post—"

Both Principal Bubb and Lilith Couture let out girlish squeals of delight.

"—and serve, instead, at the holy side of the Big Guy Upstairs."

"What?!" exclaimed Satan. "It is better to—"

"I know, I know," Judge Judas said, "it is better to rule down here than to serve up there. Read the transcripts: I said this would be an *ironic* ruling. That leaves a gaping hole in the gaping hole that is down here. So I can think of no better oddly poetic punishment than to have Michael rule in your stead."

"What?!" yelped every member of the courtroom in thunderstruck unison.

Judge Judas slammed his gavel, the shot put cleaving the bell in two.

"The hand that rocks the gavel rules the underworld!" he shouted before regaining his composure and smiling for the camera. "Justice is served!"

The lights came on as the pompous Judge Judas theme song—heavy on the timpani—filled the courtroom.

Michael's keenly chiseled mouth fell open. Gabriel whispered in his near-perfect ear.

"Whoa, even as near-omniscient beings, we certainly didn't see *that* one coming, did we . . . *Mickey*," the distinguished angel said with his whiff of a British accent as hulking demon guards rushed in where angels dared to tread. Michael's wings whipped out at his sides like feathered switchblades.

"Now, now, Michael," Judge Judas said as he lit up a

cigar. "Don't cause a scene. The cameras aren't even on, so what's the point?"

Michael and Satan were both dragged out into the hallway.

"We will appeal!" they bellowed, the first time the two creatures had agreed on anything since zoning the streets of Heaven to be paved with gold.

Various demons, prominent figures from the underworld, and even a few angels turned to glare at the Fausters. It was as if Milton and Marlo were the Ebola virus in convenient child form.

Principal Bubb clacked with fury toward them.

"How *dare* you waltz in here and upset *everything!*" she seethed, her moist snout flaring. "I was so close to having Satan's job that I could practically taste it!"

"And she hardly has any taste whatsoever!" Lilith said, firing off one last parting shot before she left the courtroom.

Marlo stifled a giggle, but after a short struggle, the snicker emerged, triumphant.

"You think you can change all of the rules to suit yourself?" Bea "Elsa" Bubb roared. "Like the afterlife is your own personal *playlist*? But you've really done it this time. *Really*. Look over there at the angels."

A gaggle of heavenly messengers, not quite "arch" status but definitely holier-than-thou, walked past them, glowering, plucking their harps in a vaguely threatening manner.

"See?" the principal said, claws akimbo. "Even the divine and benevolent want to play Yahtzee with your eyeballs. The upper echelons of the Galactic Order Department were perfectly content with the status quo that granted them preferential status since before time itself. But you messed that up with your prying. Your incessant meddling. You, Fausters, are *far* too big for your britches."

"Britches?" Marlo mumbled. "What are—"

"Which is why I'm sending you insufferably preco-cious brats to—"

"Precocia!" Judge Judas ruled with a bang of his gavel.

"Precocia?" the principal replied with a start. "But—"

The judge leaned over his bench, his gnarled gray beard uncoiling like a tongue that had licked an ashtray clean.

"I have ruled, Principal Bubb. Do you think I *liked* having to play *Freaky Friday* with the Prince of Darkness and an archangel? Do you have any idea how messed up things are going to be?"

"Well, I can imagine that—" Milton began.

"It was a rhetorical question, Nosy Parker. But, while I rule the Provincial Court of Res Judicata, I am ruled by *ratings*. And this was the only knee-jerk, half-baked decision that made sense—and, more importantly, made a sensation. And while you two bite-sized buttinskies may have guaranteed me boffo share, you need to be punished. And since you legally can't be tried as adults, you can try out *being* an adult, which"—the man rubbed his throbbing temples as he set down his gavel—"isn't all it's cracked up to be. Case dismissed . . . though I've dismissed you all long ago."

Principal Bubb motioned for her demon sentries.

"Guards, seize them," she ordered. *"Roughly."*

The goat-bats reared up on their haunches and grabbed the Fausters by their wrists, jostling them down the aisle. Principal Bubb turned to leave, stopping short to review the empty room with wistful resignation.

"Oh well, *que sera, sera,*" she sighed. "I've been neglecting Heck for all of this *business*. It's gone flabby around the middle. And I'm back to cinch the belt. Tight. Sometimes getting exactly what you want is the biggest punishment of all—a punishment I may never know but the Fausters will soon learn firsthand . . ."

The bug-shaped earring dangling from the principal's ear vibrated.

"This Extraordinary Anticipatory Recorded Wearable Incitement Gadget (EARWIG)—another groundbreaking innovation from Nikola Tesla—will now self-destruct so as to conceal zhe identity of its ingenious creator."

Milton and Marlo were shoved down a staggered stairway and into the intimidating marble-floored lobby walled with greenish glass and steel. A small explosion erupted behind them from the courtroom, followed by Principal Bubb's anguished howl of pain. Slumped over by a sulfur water fountain was Algernon Cole.

"I want to see my lawyer!" Milton shouted as the demon guard gripped him by his wrists.

"Go ahead," the goat-bat hissed. "*See* him. See? He's right over there."

"You know what I mean," Milton grumbled. "Mr. Cole! Mr. Cole!"

Algernon, his face wet with sulfur water and tears, walked sluggishly alongside Milton.

"I'm not waking up, am I?" he posed, his red-rimmed eyes strangely hollow, like Siberian snow globes. "This is all real, isn't it? I thought that, after I won the case, the dream would stop. But it hasn't."

Milton nodded with a sympathetic half-smile.

"Sorry, Mr. Cole. But if it's any consolation, even though you're dead, you totally *killed* out there in the courtroom!"

"Thank you," the lawyer said with a wobble of his graying ponytail. "It felt good. Probably because I didn't think any of it was really happening. It's interesting, this place. With my research, it seems that everything here is governed with rules, more so than in the land of the living. It's like they actually, *physically* hold it all together. Which reminded me of your case, and a little loophole I believe I found that could—"

A team of security demons grabbed Algernon Cole by the shoulders as he neared the exit.

"Oh no, you don't," the head demon roared. "You have to be debriefed."

"But I'm not wearing briefs," Algernon joked as he was dragged away.

"Yeah, we get it," the security demon rumbled. "And so will you. *Big-time.*"

The Fausters were shoved through the double doors, greeted by a thousand popped flashbulbs.

A loophole, Milton thought with a grin as he stumbled down the marble stairs. Maybe justice—*real* justice—can actually be served down here after all.

"What are you grinning like an idiot about?" Principal Bubb said, clacking beside them as they headed toward her stagecoach.

"You want to know what?" Milton replied.

"Yes, *what?*"

"Chicken butt," he said before dissolving into exhausted laughter.

Just before he was thrown into the carriage, Milton saw Gabriel outside the courthouse, standing next to a shaft of light.

Gray-blue eyes wide and unnerved, mouth hanging slightly open in incomprehension, and downy white wings spread unevenly, cautiously, out to his sides, the archangel Gabriel stepped back from the beam of uncompromising, almost brazenly pure light. He turned his face away briefly, as if from the crude ambiguity of the future to the comfort of the past, but forced himself back into the light. A tear sliced down his cheek like a tiny jeweled dagger. The debonair angel's face twitched with internal struggle, as if he held the power to avert a cataclysm but was bound by fealty not to. A sharp, castigating gust of wind blew across the marble steps of the courthouse with a roar that overpowered even the incessant flurries of the six Belief Blowers. The wind caught Gabriel's wings with such sudden violence that he could no longer close them.

It was as if a storm were blowing all the way from Paradise, Milton thought as he was led away by a squad of demon guards. Little did Milton know that he was the myopic eye of this unstoppable tempest, an unbidden storm that no creature—divine or demonic—saw coming, and even if they had, it wouldn't have mattered, anyway.

BACKWORD

We (and by "we," I mean you) often view happiness as the ultimate goal of life (though, physically, the ultimate goal of life would be death, with the bulk of our death spent being gravely disappointed that we realized the first goal). But is happiness a fixed destination, or is it an unattainable yet vexingly visible point perpetually on our psychological horizon?

Much of our existence, it could be said, is a teeter-totter ride between happiness and sadness. If we're too light, we can get stuck up in the air, legs dangling, the soles of our feet soon craving stable ground. If we're too heavy, we just sit there like a leaden lump, adhering faithfully and forlornly to the law of gravity. What makes the experience any fun at all is the promise of movement: the motion of emotion.

Happiness and sadness need each other. They're like an old bickering couple at the diner that you see holding hands, slyly, under the table. If we were always happy, we would never truly be happy. It would be like living in Disneyland, the self-appointed Happiest Place on Earth. After a few days, we'd have third-degree sunburns and be completely sick of all the rides. Even six out of seven dwarves aren't Happy living there. But if we just stop trying to be happy, we're doomed to reside in Disneyland's polar opposite—Dismayland—a place where Mickey is caught squealing in a trap, Donald is served à l'orange, and Goofy is . . . well, pretty much the same.

The truth is that happiness is found in its pursuit, not its possession.

There is a virulently infectious song for children with the maddening refrain, "If you're happy and you know it, clap your hands." This is not only reckless advice—especially if one finds oneself unexpectedly "happy" while driving a truck carrying flammable chemicals in an avalanche zone—but it is also misleading. True happiness is something impossible to identify, much less celebrate with the unwarranted striking of one's palms. "Clap on" the glaring light of awareness and you can pretty much "clap off" any shot at happiness.

As any rare insect knows, once something is caught and labeled, it's usually only a matter of time before it *gets a pin through its thorax. So can you really blame happiness for being so fleeting?*

Likewise, even in the upper reaches of the afterlife, happiness is playing one heck of a game of hide-and-seek. And the rules have changed: so much so that no one—from the demonic to the divine—is even quite sure what game is being played. The only thing that anyone knows with any certainty is that the stakes are higher (and lower) than anyone, alive or dead, ever thought possible.

ACKNOWLEDGMENTS

THE BOOK YOU are now holding—printed on the latest in teardrop-resistant paper, able to withstand a salinity of roughly 5.12 percent—was the result of tens of thousands of words painstakingly arranged in such a way that they formed a semicoherent story, in many ways, *this* semicoherent story.

I'd like to acknowledge the countless friends and colleagues who helped with the creation of this book, generously mulling over ideas and scrutinizing various drafts as the manuscript grew and gradually took form . . . but, in all honesty, I can't. Sure, there are exceptions . . . my editor, Diane Landolf, springs to mind, as she so often does, pouncing like a bespectacled Ivy League tiger, savaging self-indulgent prose until it is worthy of public consumption. . . . But, in general, writing is a solitary pursuit, like rugby, only without all the other players, spectators, referees, and that weird oval ball. Plus I seldom write on a field that's one hundred meters long and seventy meters wide with H-shaped goal posts on each goal line and crunch together in a scrum with fifteen other players in a brutal battle of might.

Hmm . . . perhaps writing isn't as much like rugby as I had previously thought.

Anyway, I'd also like to acknowledge Heck's rabid fan base and pray that they seek the medical attention they so desperately require. If it weren't for the constant barrage of encouraging letters and emails . . . well, I'd probably get a lot more work done. But writing these books wouldn't be nearly as rewarding. Seriously. Your freakish absurdity and devotion are my fuel. Keep it surreal, demon hordes.

ABOUT THE AUTHOR

DALE E. BASYE is a writer of staggering humility—voted Most Modest Author five times running in *This Isn't a Real Magazine* magazine. He has made a decent living for himself writing reviews, stories, advertising campaigns, and his parents for money.

Here's what Dale E. Basye has to say about his fifth book:

"There is a time when most everything seems to rub you the wrong way. As if life itself, clad in white socks, had walked across a mile-long shag carpet to give you an annoying shock of static electricity, or to maliciously stroke you on the back with an irritating squeak. (I forgot to mention that you are a balloon.) During this time, you feel as sensitive as a freshly shaved Chihuahua at its first spring formal, and the only course of action is to complain bitterly until you are blue in the face and feeling twice as blue inside. Heck is like that. And, no matter what anyone tells you, Heck is real. This story is real. Or as real as anything like this can be."

Dale E. Basye lives in Portland, Oregon, where he spends his days whittling large pieces of wood into slightly smaller pieces of wood and working alongside the world's greatest scientific minds in hopes of developing the perfect pancake.

PRECOCIA

THE SIXTH CIRCLE OF HECK

AVAILABLE FEBRUARY 2013

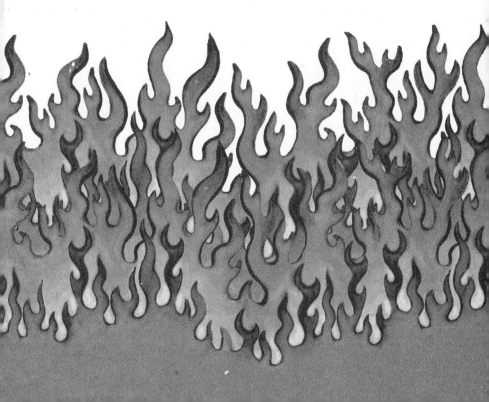